UNFAMILIAR MAGIC

UNFAMILIAR MAGIC

R.C. ALEXANDER

RANDOM HOUSE 🏠 NEW YORK

Text copyright © 2010 by R. C. Alexander
Jacket art copyright © 2010 by Marcos Chin

Visit us on the Web! www.randomhouse.com/kids

Educators and librarians, for a variety of teaching tools, visit us at
www.randomhouse.com/teachers

Library of Congress Cataloging-in-Publication Data
Alexander, R. C. (Robert C.)
Unfamiliar magic / R. C. Alexander. — 1st ed.
p. cm.
Summary: Twelve-year-old witch Desi secretly uses her mother's spellbook with unexpected results, including meeting her warlock father for the first time and becoming like sisters with Cat, who was once her mother's familiar.
ISBN 978-0-375-85854-3 (trade) — ISBN 978-0-375-95854-0 (lib. bdg.) —
ISBN 978-0-375-89308-7 (e-book)
[1. Witches—Fiction.   2. Magic—Fiction.   3. Cats—Fiction.
4. Mothers and daughters—Fiction.   5. Fathers and daughters—Fiction.
6. Demonology—Fiction.]   I. Title.
PZ7.A37788Unf 2010
[Fic]—dc22
2009004856

Printed in the United States of America
10 9 8 7 6 5 4 3 2 1
First Edition

Random House Children's Books supports
the First Amendment and celebrates the right to read.

For Tara and Ryan.
Wherever they are, I am home.

✦ ✦ ✦ ✦ ✦

UNFAMILIAR MAGIC

Prologue

London, twelve years before . . .

THE DOUBLE DOORS to the corridor burst open. A young man charged through them, tall and good-looking in a dangerous way in leather jacket and boots, his expression as dark as his eyes. The nurses checked him out as he strode past, but he did not return their looks; intent on his mission, he zeroed in on his path. When he had gone, the clatter of his boot heels echoed his haste.

✦ ✦ ✦

In another part of the hospital, a woman lay in bed, panting, strands of her long hair pasted to her face. Her features contracted with pain. Her sister, hovering at her side, squeezed her hand. "You're almost there, Cally, just a little more. Keep focusing on the light; concentrate on the light."

At the bottom of the bed, a stout midwife crouched, calm and reassuring, her strong arms ready. "Any time now, dearie. No need to push, just keep breathing—in, out."

The mother-to-be, Callida, arched her back as another labor pain struck. "Too much, Lissa. It's taking too long. I'm scared. Val's not here yet?"

Lissa wrapped both her hands around her sister's. "Can't we do something?" she pleaded with the midwife. "She's been like this for twelve hours."

·✦·1·✦·

The wrinkled veteran of many births shook her head. "Not now. It's too late. The magic of birth is too delicate to risk with any of our spells. It'll happen in its own good time. Come on now, dearie, just breathe. Let your body do the rest."

Callida's face twisted on the pillow, and she let out a groan. Lissa squeezed her hand helplessly.

"Any time now, dear," soothed the midwife.

Lissa bit her lip and dabbed at her sister's forehead with a damp cloth.

⋅⁺⁎⁺⋆⁺

The young man in black turned a corner and swept down an empty corridor. He approached the double doors at the end. With an impatient gesture, he flung them open—while he was still ten feet away.

⋅⁺⁎⁺⋆⁺

Callida panted faster and faster and heaved about as the pains got more intense. Her sister fretted, still dabbing helplessly at her forehead for want of anything better to do. The midwife peered beneath the sheets. "It's time, dear. Push now—give it all you've got," she said confidently. Callida let out another groan.

⋅⁺⁎⁺⋆⁺

The man reached another set of doors at an intersection, spotted a sign—NATURAL CHILDBIRTH–MIDWIFERY—and cried out, causing the doors ahead to fly open with a bang.

⋅⁺⁎⁺⋆⁺

From her bed, Callida echoed his cry. Her eyes rolled up into her head. Her sister looked down and gasped.

"That's done it!" said the midwife, holding a sopping-wet package.

⋅⋅⁺2⋅⋅⁺

"Oh, Cally, you did it!" cheered her sister. "Is it a . . . ?"

"Congratulations," said the midwife, deftly wiping down the newborn. "It's a witch."

·₊·*·₊·*

The night-duty nurse in the midwifery corridor looked up sharply when the doors flew open, and an intense young man bore down upon her.

"Where is she?" he demanded, glowering over the counter.

"Just a minute, please," she said, marking her place in her romance novel.

"WHERE IS SHE?"

The nurse adopted a pleasant but stern look, as if to say she dealt with anxious young fathers every day and was not impressed. "Calm down, please. Exactly who is it you want?"

"Callida."

"And your name?"

"Valerian."

"I don't see you on my list. Only the immediate family is permitted at the birth."

He leaned over the desk to waggle a single finger in front of her eyes. "Tell me now."

The answer escaped her before she could stop it. "Number nine."

He left.

·₊·*·₊·*

The midwife finished wiping the baby girl down, then placed her gently in the mother's arms. "There now, all's well. Safe with your mommy."

·₊·3·₊·

Callida enfolded her child in her love. "My little Desi," she whispered.

"Desdemona," cooed her sister, "you are a perfect, beautiful little darling!"

The midwife said, "Hold still while I cut the cord now."

"Will it hurt her?" Callida asked.

"Not a bit. Won't feel a thing," said the midwife, neatly snipping the cord. Three feet away, sister Lissa doubled over with a sharp pain in her belly.

"Won't hurt mother and child, I meant," chuckled the midwife.

·⁺★⁺★⁺★

Valerian raced down the hallway, checking numbers, frustration mounting until he found himself blocked once again by doors. As he raised his arms, a voice came from below and to the side. "Allow me," said a woman in a wheelchair. She pressed the handicapped button, causing the double doors to spring open.

Valerian scowled at her and ran through the opening.

"You're welcome," said the woman to his back.

Number nine was first on the left. He put one hand to the door and paused, composing himself. Then, with a quick gesture, he slammed the door open against the wall.

·⁺★⁺★⁺★

Callida clasped her baby to her bosom, facing the doorway defiantly.

·⁺★⁺★⁺★

Valerian leaped into the room and whirled about. It was empty. No bed, just a nightstand, scattered vases with flowers, assorted medical equipment, and a bassinet. No Callida. And no baby.

·⁺★4⁺·

The duty nurse closed in on him from behind. "Sir, you can't just charge in here without permission."

He turned on her. "You said she was in number nine," he snarled.

The nurse looked around the room in consternation. "But she is. I saw her just a few minutes ago. She can't have checked out," she said, confused.

As she spoke, her hand clutched the night table where a vase of flowers concealed a fat, round bottle of green glass with a slender, tapered neck. Neither of them looked down, but if they had, they might have seen, inside the bottle, barely visible through the opaque glass, three very tiny, very still figures, one holding an even tinier figure in her arms.

Valerian's face darkened. He made a sudden breaking motion with his hands, and a vase of flowers exploded on a shelf across the room. Struggling to contain his anger, he turned on the nurse. "Where did she go?"

"I . . . I don't know."

He stopped, sniffing the air like a hound. "She was here, all right. I can sense her. Where are you, Callida? Where are you, my love?" He put his hands to his temples and squeezed his head. Another vase exploded.

·⋆·⋆·⋆·

Inside the bottle, three tiny figures held their breath. The fourth figure, the tiniest, was sleeping.

·⋆·⋆·⋆·

"You can't hide from your destiny!" Valerian exclaimed. "I won't let you ruin everything we've worked for." He shook his fist at the fluorescent lights in the ceiling, which glared back unmoved. "It's my child, too, Callida! Mine!" The nurse seized her chance and ran out. "I swear I'll find you," Valerian cried. "I'll never rest till I have my own back!" He rushed from the room, knocking over a table and sending glass crashing to the floor.

⋆_⋆⋆_⋆⋆

The green bottle on the table rocked from side to side, then settled still. Safe inside, Callida stroked her baby while new aunt Lissa huddled as close as she could. The midwife cleaned up the bloody sheets, unconcerned.

A few minutes later, number nine held three full-sized adults and one perfect, beautiful baby girl. "I'll fetch Doctor, then, shall I?" said the midwife, arms full of dirty linens. "She'll want to have a look at the dear little thing."

"Is he gone? Is he really gone away?" murmured Callida, so exhausted she could barely hold her head up.

"He's far away," said her sister. "No trace of his aura for miles. Lord, he can move fast."

The midwife sniffed. "Warlocks," she said gruffly. "They're all the same. Can't live with 'em, can't kill 'em."

Safe in her mother's arms, Baby Desi gave a little squeak.

1

"MOM, COME HERE!" Desi shouted. "I think I broke Dad."

Desdemona stared down into the cardboard crate she had just opened. Inside lay what looked like a middle-aged man in a flowered shirt, motionless, half-buried in crumpled newspaper.

She heard a muffled "Who?" from the kitchen. The next moment, her mother's head poked in, looking harried. "'Dad'? What dad? Where?" Callida asked cautiously, surveying the mess scattered around the living room.

"See, it won't start up," Desi said, shaking the edge of the crate with both hands.

"Oh, you're talking about the golem." Callida smiled and brushed the hair out of her eyes.

"What else would I be talking about?" Desi rattled the box. "Come on, dummy, move."

"Don't do that," her mother said. "It's not broken. It needs the potion to animate it."

That was the word Desi had been waiting to hear. "Right, the potion. I can make it."

"Maybe," her mother said guardedly. "We'll see."

Desi knew what *that* meant. "Why do we need a fake dad, anyway?" she asked, nodding at the thing in the box. "We didn't use it in Paris or before in Hong Kong. . . ."

"Our apartments were way too small. I like it. People leave you alone if they think there's a man around the house," Callida said. "Here in the suburbs, it'll help us fit in. Plus, it does mow the lawn." She tucked a strand of her long black hair under her scarf in a losing battle to keep it under control. Grabbing a box labeled KITCHEN, she said, "Come and help me put the dishes away."

They made their way down the hall to the back of the house, weaving through cardboard boxes and scattered furniture. Desi got there first; she was energized now that they had arrived at their new home. "So, what exactly makes the golem go?" she asked.

"You should know—we've made that potion many times."

Desi shook her head. "That was years ago. And you never let *me* make it. You never let me do any spells."

"You did a spell." Callida looked indignant. "For your birthday last year. I taught you the balloon one, remember?"

"*Hobblebobblebowlameni.* By the time I say it, I could blow up a balloon the regular way. And that's a kid's spell. I'm talking about real magic."

"It's all in the textbooks I gave you. If you would pay more attention to your studies—"

"I've practically got those books memorized," Desi said, exasperated. "*History of Magic, Principles of Magic, History of Principles of Theory of Magic*—I know everything about magic except how to *do* anything. When are you going to show me how to make things fly around the room or transform stuff into other stuff?"

Her mother began unloading the contents of the boxes into the cupboards. "I told you, when you're older."

"That's what you said three years ago." Desi put her hands on her hips. "I *am* older, in case you hadn't noticed."

Callida struck the same pose, mimicking her. "Please don't be in such a hurry to grow up. It's not as great as you think it is." She sighed. "Maybe if you show how responsible you are by helping out more?"

"All right, all right, I'm helping." Desi knew it was time to back off—for now. She reached into an open carton and shrieked.

A black tornado whipped out of the crate, scratching and snarling. Taken by surprise, Desi tumbled backward into a pile of newspaper. "Aargh! Bad cat!" She grabbed her arm. "Watch it, will you?" she snapped at her cat, who had disappeared under the kitchen table. "Your claws are sharp."

"Are you okay?" her mother asked. "Be careful—you frightened her."

Desi checked her arms for scratches. "What were you doing in there, anyway?" she said to the small figure crouched in the shadows.

"Hiding," Callida answered for her Familiar. "She hates change; you know that. Moving is hard for her."

"Welcome to the club. You still shouldn't use your claws," Desi griped with her head under the table. Two big yellow eyes glared back at her resentfully from the shadows, making her feel guilty. "Sorry about the yelling. I'm a little freaked out, too, you know," she confided to her cat. "Did you check out your sandbox? I set it up in the garage first thing."

"Could we get back to work, please?" Callida bent down to open another box. "I'm tired of eating fast food. I want my kitchen back."

Desi surveyed the crates, reaching into the nearest for a jar that caught her eye. "What are 'granulated lizards' wings' for? I didn't even know lizards had wings."

"I'll take that, thank you. You put away the dishes."

Desi dug in, unpacking the heavy handmade plates and bowls and stacking them in the cabinets. She found the cookbooks and arranged them on a shelf: *Chicken Soup for the Wizard's Soul. Potion-Brewing for the Compleat Idiote. Zen and the Art of Broom Maintenance.*

Even with the books and dishes, the cupboards seemed pitifully bare—years of constant moving had taught them to pare down to the basics. Desi looked around at the flat white walls of the kitchen/breakfast room/family room. "This house is too big and too empty," she said. "It's like we don't fit."

"I could get used to this real fast." Callida straightened up, stretching her back. "It's ten times the size of our last apartment, and we finally have a spare room for an office. You don't like having a real room instead of that glorified closet you had in Paris? And don't forget, there's a huge backyard."

Desi *had* forgotten the yard. Peering out the back window, she saw a mass of green topping the back fence. "Hey, check it out. There's a forest out there."

Making a dash for the door, she had barely got her hand on the doorknob when her mother cried, "Desdemona! Do not go outside, please."

"Mom. Chill. It's just a backyard."

"Not tonight. I haven't unpacked the watch-gnomes yet, and it's almost dark."

"So I'll set out the gnomes. I know where they are." Desi made it halfway down the hall before her mother's voice stopped her.

"We'll set out the gnomes in the morning, but right now we need to stay inside and unpack," Callida said firmly. "Besides, I want Devil to take a look around first."

Giving up on getting out—for now—Desi knelt down to peer into the darkness under the table. "Devalandnefariel! Come on. Here, Devalandnefariel, please come out. We need you."

Two yellow eyes lit up in the darkness, hooded, suspicious. "Oh, don't sulk." A shadow slowly emerged, taking the shape of a sleek black cat streaked with silver markings. "She's mad," Desi said, sitting down on the floor to scratch her best friend behind the ears.

"Yes, I know. You hate moving. I don't blame you," Callida said softly. "But I need you to take a look around."

Devil the cat glared at her family warily.

"Lucky girl, you get to go outside," Desi said. "Check it out. See if there're any werewolves in the woods."

"It's just a park, Desi," her mother said, shaking her head. "There are no werewolves."

"So then why can't I go in my own backyard?" She decided to push her mother a little more. "What are you so afraid of?"

The cat jumped into Desi's lap, put her paws up on her chest, and hissed—a cat hiss, jaws wide in a silent scream.

The cat's sharp eyes burned into hers. An image seared Desi's brain—danger, a shadowed figure, dark and menacing.

"What is it, Devil? Mom, what is she hunting for?"

"Nothing," Callida said. She picked the cat up from her daughter's lap, careful to avoid her claws, and dropped her by the back door. "I'm just being sensible. We've only been here a few hours." Callida had that old look again—tight-lipped, nervous. She opened the door. "Go for a prowl," she said to the cat, lowering her voice dramatically. "You know what to do. Check out the woods, the yards on both sides. If anything smells wrong, let me know." Devil stuck her head out the doorway, going still, listening, while Callida waited. "And leave the poor dogs alone." She shut the door, forcing the cat outside.

Desi pressed her nose to the glass and saw a dainty shadow flicker, swallowed up by the darkness. "Will she be all right, alone out there?"

"Devil? Don't be silly. That's her job." Callida pointed with a wooden spoon. "The silverware goes in the top drawer by the sink; the pots go under the stove. Leave the newts' eyes and ground dung beetles to me." Callida opened another crate. "And let me know if you find the blender."

2

DEEP, DANK EARTH. Sweet grass and moldy leaves. Buzzing insect wings, the clicking of tiny feet. Mouse and mole, squirrel and vole. Scents of possum and raccoon. No sign of werewolves; the little one had been wrong. But dog, strong and rank, not far off. Remember that, for later.

Devil slunk deeper under the cover of the bush while her eyes adjusted. Her eyes were good in the dark, but not as good as an owl's, and owls' wings gave no warning. The whirl and bustle of the woods at night surrounded her, and she took her time sorting it out, letting scents and sounds sink in as she crouched in the cool earth.

No danger yet.

A high wooden fence enclosed the yard. A trap? No, she could claw up it in a flash, leaving heavier beasts behind. Too bad for the dogs. Her pupils expanded, widened, pulling in tiny fragments of light. An oak tree took shape on the other side of the fence, reaching its gnarled arms over her yard. Better and better. A leap to the top of the fence, another to the branch—she would have the whole tree to climb. The world below would be hers to command.

Devil pulled her hind feet underneath her, ready to move. Her tail twitched in anticipation. A last check around—nothing moving bigger than a bug. Then: a flash, a bolt of power, and she was up the fence into the branches of the oak. She froze, listening, her whole body a radar screen. A rustle of leaves when the air stirred. No sounds from the squirrels; they were there, of course, but were smart enough to stay quiet. No scent of magic. Holes gave off an acrid, burning stench, but the night air was clear and clean. Nothing set off her inner alarms.

A little farther up in the tree, on the other side of the trunk, an enormous wooden box clung to the branches. What was a box that big doing in a tree? It was obviously human-made.

Humans! Was there no place they didn't intrude? Fortunately, they were slow and couldn't smell dog droppings if they stepped in it. She crept closer to investigate.

All of a sudden the wind shifted, and she smelled it. How could she have been so blind? Something was here, close, maybe within striking distance. Escape? Leap into space? No, freeze; maybe it didn't see her. It reeked like nothing she knew—animal, human, demon? She couldn't tell, and that alone set her fur prickling like a porcupine's quills. The scent came from that box. *Show yourself, tree-box thing. I'm waiting.*

Time passed, and no time. All was calm, quiet, dark. Devil drew the cool night air through her nostrils. The strange new thing stayed deadly still and quiet, a very un-human sign. Not good. She had to get closer for a look. Pushing back her instinctive fear, she crept along the oak branch, slowly, determined to be as silent as the thing she was stalking.

Her path ended at the trunk of the tree. Leaping to the

branch above her, she scrambled around the trunk to creep up on the wooden box, where the strange thing lay hiding. She paused, nose in the air, while a fresh breeze brought her news from below: an old dog, garbage cans, and chemicals. The yard stank from the poisons humans spread on their grass, and dwellings, and lives.

It was the stink that betrayed her.

Rounding the trunk, she placed her two front paws in the opening of the box . . . precisely between the claws of a snarling, shadowy thing. The thing shrieked, tiny fangs gleaming white in the moonlight, and leaped into the air. Taken by surprise, Devil leaped, too, flinging herself away from the box. She tumbled through the dark, twisting madly to get her feet underneath her just in time to land safely on all fours—right on the back of a huge gray dog.

The dog howled in fright, springing to its feet. Devil sprang straight up into the air, claws out, teeth bared, leaping blindly into the night, ready to fight whatever she touched— which happened to be a bunch of garbage cans. She slipped and slid over the lids, struggling for a claw hold. The dog was tight behind her so she pushed off, knocking the can into its face: paper, cardboard, and damp plastic flew everywhere.

Devil used the diversion to sprint across the yard toward the back fence. Overhead, she spotted the strange creature, which was bounding through the oak branches in the direction of the woods. Whatever it was, it practically flew; with one great leap, it cleared the back fence and landed in a pine tree on the other side. Then, with a rustle and a squeal, it disappeared into the forest.

Devil was hot on its trail, but before she could claw up the fence to reach the woods, a gate opened in her face, startling her. A strange human appeared, charging right at her. Instinctively she doubled back, only to be jolted again when the door to the house opened, and another, larger human emerged, shouting, framed in light. Blinded, outnumbered, desperate, she zigzagged to trick dog and man into a front-end crash; then, as her pursuers collided, she clawed the fence, sailed up and over, hit the soft deep grass of her own yard, and sprang for cover—right into Desi's arms.

3

THE SNARLS, BARKS, screeches, whines, and crashes had drawn Desi out of the kitchen just in time to see her precious kitty streak across the yard and catapult into her arms.

"Are you all right, girl?" she asked, trying to cradle Devil while avoiding her needle-sharp claws.

"Desi, get in here right now and shut the door!" Callida ordered from inside.

"But, Mom, something scared Devil." Desi felt a rush of excitement. The fresh night air stirred her blood. "Somebody's out there."

Callida charged out on the deck next to Desi, arms outstretched for battle. "Who's there? I command you to show yourself."

Excited voices came from behind the fence bordering their yard. Desi heard a call of "Hang on!" and to her surprise, a boy about her own age emerged from the foliage of the oak tree, tightrope-walking the limb that overhung her fence. "Did ya see it?" he asked eagerly. "Some kind of wild animal! I tried to catch it, but it escaped into the woods."

The gate to Desi's yard swung open to reveal an older teenage boy, tall, hulking, and sheepish. "It was only a big squirrel," he protested. "Sorry. Is your cat all right? I saw her take off when the trash cans went flying." He pointed at

Devil. "Don't be scared, cat. Our old dog Max is big, but he wouldn't hurt a fly."

Desi stepped forward on the deck to face him. "My cat isn't afraid of dogs."

Callida took a long, deep breath, visibly unclenching. She peered past both boys, searching the darkness. "I'm sorry if Dev—if our cat upset your trash cans," she said absently. "She's new here and a little nervous. I can help you clean up in the morning."

"I hope Devil didn't hurt your dog," Desi said. "Sometimes she likes to show them who's boss."

"Your cat's named Devil? Cool." The boy in the tree swung his legs over the oak limb and dropped to the ground. "I'm Jarrett. That's Bob. We live next door." Jarrett was a lot shorter than his brother, but as he stepped forward into the light of the porch, Desi realized he was taller than she was.

"What were you doing up in that tree?" Desi asked, stroking Devil's cheek to calm her.

Jarrett gave her a friendly grin. "I was checking to see if any more weird animals were hiding in our tree house."

"You have a tree house?" Desi asked, intrigued.

"Since we were little kids," replied Bob. He set his jaw stubbornly. "But there's no weird animals."

"Except you?" Jarrett needled him.

The big teenager joined Jarrett at the edge of the porch. Wrinkling his nose, he sniffed at him suspiciously. "You were out in the woods again tonight, weren't you? Do you have a death wish?"

Jarrett ignored him. "Just moved here?" he asked Desi.

Callida interrupted. "I'm glad to meet you both, but it's dark and we have a lot of unpacking to do. Sorry again about the mess."

"No problem," Jarrett said. "Cleaning up the yard is Bob's job."

"It's okay." Bob shrugged. "But you might want to keep your cat in your yard."

Desi couldn't let that slide. "You got something against cats?" She hugged Devil closer, making the cat squirm.

Bob ducked his head. "Nah, they're okay." He stepped up onto the deck to pet Devil, but she was still miffed and swiped a claw at him. He backed off. "All right, girl, I won't touch you without your permission. You're pretty, though," he admitted.

Jarrett hopped up on the deck to join them. "Don't worry about ol' Bob, Devil-Cat. He's big, but he wouldn't hurt a fly." Amazingly, the cat offered her cheek for him to scratch. "You can come over to my yard anytime."

Devil yawned to show what she thought about being invited to a place she already considered her property.

Desi felt awkward, holding her cat in her arms while this boy petted her. This close, she noticed his tawny hair, down to his shoulders, and his deep summer tan. He kept stroking her cat under the chin, smoothly and gently. "So where did you move from?" he asked Desi.

Callida cut between them. "Good night, boys. Come inside, please," she said to Desi. "We've got a lot to do." Despite her resistance, Desi found herself being herded inside.

Once in the kitchen, Callida shut the door and then,

chanting softly, drew a symbol across it with her finger. The dead bolt clicked into place by itself.

Peering out the window, Desi could see the two brothers climb up onto the oak branch to go home. Though they were still bickering, each gave a hand to help the other when he needed it. She envied them. "Why'd we have to go inside?" she asked. "We were just getting to know our neighbors."

"At night, in an unfamiliar neighborhood? Are you kidding?" Her mother sounded defensive. "You can talk to those boys some other time."

Desi saw her chance and grabbed it. "All right, then we can make the potion for the golem now."

Callida surrendered. "Why not? We're going to need it. I noticed the grass was really high."

And she scores again. The boys were forgotten—this was magic! "I'll get the big cauldron," she offered eagerly.

Desi began to tear open boxes. Normally this was the only good part about a move: uncovering treasures buried weeks ago when they had packed, getting reacquainted with her old stuff. Tossing aside crumpled newspaper from inside a big crate, she exposed a musty-smelling monstrosity: an old clock carved with vines and weird, contorted faces—half-animal, half-human, all chipped and worn.

"This ugly old thing." Desi grimaced as she hauled it out. "Why do we keep hauling it around?"

Callida rushed over to take it from her. "It's an antique. It was given to me when you were born. It's very valuable."

"It's grotesque is what it.is." Desi checked the clock's hands, carved to look like bird's claws; they pointed to two-thirty. "It doesn't even tell time."

Her mother placed the clock on the mantel over the fireplace with great care. "It's fine. Did you find the cauldron yet?"

Desi kept digging around until she turned up the old copper kettle. It was so heavy it took two hands to lift it onto the stovetop. "Now what?"

Callida held out a jar. "Could you please measure out one gram of granulated lizards' wings? Use the scale—it has to be precise."

"What if we make a mistake?" Desi asked, meticulously weighing out the powder, grain by grain, onto a digital scale.

"You can never tell," Callida said. She stopped taking jars and bottles off the shelf and turned to Desi with a serious look. "Magic is difficult at best. Sometimes it just doesn't work; sometimes strange things happen you never thought of."

"Like what?" Desi asked. "Like it would grow hair on its face and howl like a werewolf?"

Her mother laughed so hard she almost dropped the blender.

Desi was relieved. She made it her job to lighten the mood whenever her mother got too serious. Lately, that seemed to be more and more often.

Callida pulled herself together. "Let's not find out, shall we? How about measuring out exactly one ounce of scarab beetle juice?"

Desi got started and then remembered something. "Aren't we going to use the big book?" She looked around the kitchen for the massive old volume of spells and potions she had never been allowed to touch.

"Don't need it. I've done this so often I've got it memorized." Callida dripped an oily black liquid into the blender.

"Almost out of zombie's blood. Good luck getting any more around here. Remind me to add it to the list for your aunt Lissa to send us."

Desi wrinkled her nose at the foul smell. "Slow down. I'm supposed to be learning this. What's next?"

"Add the lizards' wings and the beetle juice to the blender, push purée, and don't forget to hold the top down tight."

"Yes, Master, I hear and obey," Desi said, smirking. Her mother laughed again.

After the mess was thoroughly blended, Desi poured it into the cauldron, careful not to spill. Devil was either curious or hungry, because she appeared suddenly, jumping up on the counter to sniff the contents of the pot. She sneezed, shaking her head in disgust.

"That's not for you, greedy thing," Desi said. "It would probably turn you into a toad or something." The cat turned her back disdainfully and jumped down onto the floor to vanish down the hall.

Callida pulled out a cutting board. "Looks great. I'll chop the cattail root, and we're done."

Thirsty, Desi fished a can of soda out of the fridge. "Why do we want to be left alone?" she said between slurps.

"What?"

"You said this dad thing—"

"A golem, technically."

"—this golem dad would make people leave us alone. Why?"

Callida chose her words carefully. "In some places, women alone can be very vulnerable."

"So now we'll have a man in the house, even if it's fake," Desi mused. "So we can relax. Be ourselves, right?"

Callida sighed. "We still have to be careful, keep a low profile. Not everybody can manipulate the subtle forces of the spirit world. People are frightened when you have abilities that they can't have."

Desi considered. "Why is it that we can do magic and other people can't?"

"I thought you said you studied your textbooks?" Callida smiled. "What is magic?"

Desi rolled her eyes and recited, "'The living world of elemental spirits that lies in and around our world, and the power to control those spirits.'"

"And you know that our world is drifting farther apart from the realm of elemental spirits. With each passing year, it becomes more and more difficult to touch that other world and more dangerous when we do."

"Which is why we have Familiars, like Devil. I know all that. That's not my question. Why is it we can do magic and other people can't?"

"Talent. Some people can run faster than others; some are smarter at academics. We witches can still control the unseen world of spirit. But even most witches aren't very good at it anymore. It takes special talent as well as training to—"

"Do I have talent?" Desi asked, feeling a rush of pride.

"Absolutely. It runs in the family." Callida began methodically cutting the roots into thin slices.

"So we're different from everybody else, but having a father around makes us look normal?"

"It helps."

Desi finished her soda and crumpled the can between her palms. "Where is my real father?" she asked as casually as she could.

"Ow!" Callida stuck her finger in her mouth.

"What's wrong?" Desi had known something would happen. Something always seemed to go wrong when she asked about her father.

"Nothing, just nicked myself," Callida said hurriedly, looking upset. "I hope I didn't get any blood on these roots. I'd have to start from scratch."

"Why don't you ever talk about him?" Desi asked quietly.

"Who?"

"My real dad—remember him?"

Her mother didn't answer for several seconds, bearing down on the knife as if the roots were unusually tough.

Desi threw her can into the recycling bin, where it hit with a crash. "I bet I don't even *have* a father."

"That would *really* be magic," Callida said. "Everyone has a father. Don't they teach you these things in school?" She made a face.

Desi made a face back at her. "Duh," she said sarcastically. "Prove it. Show me a picture of him."

Callida hesitated. "I don't have any." She stopped chopping. A hint of pain flashed behind her mother's eyes as she admitted, "Just before you were born, a fire destroyed everything—all our pictures, everything."

Despite knowing it might cause her mother more pain, still Desi had to ask, "So why did you two break up? Couldn't you have, like, fixed it with magic? You know, whatever was wrong?"

Her mother looked tense and sad. "Magic couldn't solve the problem with your father and me. Magic *was* the problem."

Desi was confused, but before she could sort out the million questions in her head, her mother changed the subject, as she always did. "I thought you wanted to learn this potion?" Callida asked. "You have to pay attention." She dumped the cattail roots into the cauldron. "See, it almost boiled over." She hurried to turn down the heat. "Magic is very tricky—it can backfire on you when you least expect it."

It was the second time her mother had said that. Desi watched her carefully. Callida was keeping her eyes on the cauldron, as if she saw something in the bubbling potion that Desi couldn't see. It bothered Desi that her mom wouldn't look at her, but she couldn't quite bring herself to interrupt.

After several minutes, her mother broke the silence. "It's ready," she said quietly. "I'll pour it into a pitcher so it's easier to handle."

Desi led the way back to the front room, carrying the potion in a pitcher, Callida close behind. They halted in front of the giant crate with the body. The slick, shiny face made Desi's stomach screw up.

"Now we stick the funnel in its mouth and pour the potion in," Callida said.

"Oh, gross."

"I thought you wanted to do this. Here, let me. You pour." Callida was all business again. She pried open the dummy's stiff lips and shoved the funnel inside. "Don't be so squeamish. It was never alive. It's just a golem."

"What did you make it out of, anyway?" Desi asked.

"Crushed beer cans. And the sports sections from newspapers."

"You made my father out of beer cans and old newspapers?"

Callida looked exasperated. "You were getting on my case about recycling, remember?"

Desi made a face. "No wonder it turned out so disgusting. You know, I used to tell my friends I was adopted."

Just as she had hoped, Callida burst out laughing. The cloud that had gathered over her mother's head vanished. "Would you just pour?" Callida said through her giggles.

Desi tipped the contents of the pitcher into the golem, watching the liquid gurgle slowly down its throat.

"That should do it," Callida said. "Now you can kick it."

Desi booted the side of the cardboard box, hard. "Hey, dummy, wake up. Get to work."

The pasty face took on color; its eyes shot open. "Herro. How'reya? Have'nicedary," it mumbled.

"Help me lift it out of the box," Callida said. She took one arm, and Desi grabbed the other, heaving the golem upright. It was big, even for a man, with a massive potbelly under a wrinkled Hawaiian shirt and Bermuda shorts.

"Nice day?" it whimpered.

"It'll take a while for the potion to really kick in. Let's get it into its chair," Callida said. They wrestled the golem dad into a vinyl recliner in front of the TV. It slumped and began to slide to the floor.

Desi pulled the lever on the recliner to lift its feet. "Did you have to give it hairy knees?" she said, disgusted. Devil apparently agreed. She had come over to check out the fuss, but now she showed her disdain by turning her back to saunter away, nose in the air.

Callida wrapped the golem's thick fingers around the TV remote. They stood back to admire their work. "There. Real magic. Satisfied?"

The golem's face lolled to one side, eyes gaping, its tongue hanging out.

"Enchanting," Desi said.

"I'm tired," said her mother. "Time for bed."

Desi yawned. "I didn't know magic was so much work. Good night, *Dad*," she said sarcastically.

"Havanice sday," mumbled the golem.

4

DESI WOKE TO the morning light. She had a moment's panic when she first opened her eyes: Whose room was this? It was no place she knew! She cast about from the flat white ceiling to the bare white walls. *Where am I?*

A familiar furry face popped into view and Desi relaxed. She felt Devil's breath on her cheek as the little cat snuggled up in the hollow of her neck. Devil usually slept curled up on her feet, but now her soft warm fur cuddled Desi's cheek, as if saying, *Everything is new and strange, but we are together.*

Now that Desi was awake, it all came back in a rush. *We moved again.* Minneapolis, Minnesota, USA. Houses all the same, wide paved streets that went in circles, with almost no trees.

There's a forest behind the backyard.

Where did that thought come from? Devil was awake now, too, filling her world with a black nose and huge yellow eyes. "Did you say that? Sometimes I can't tell if it's you in my head or my imagination," Desi said. "I wish you could just talk like people." The cat stretched and hopped lightly to the floor, clearly ready to start the day. "Just give me a minute," Desi said sleepily. "Some of us have to put on clothes, you know."

She scrambled out of her sleeping bag and into her jeans

and sneakers, pulling on a T-shirt from the pile spilling out of her suitcase on the floor. After a brief trip to the bathroom, she stumbled past the cardboard boxes in the hall—boxes she was going to have to help unpack later, she knew—and down to the kitchen.

Her mom was already up and busy, carefully winding the old clock that she had placed on the mantelpiece the night before. "Good morning," she said cheerily. "Coffee's on. Did you sleep well?"

"Yeah, I guess. New place and all," Desi said. She poured a mug of coffee from the antique brass press. "How about you?"

"Oh, fine." But her mother didn't look fine. Her eyes were shadowed with fatigue.

Devil was poised impatiently at the back door, so Desi let her out. The morning air was brisk and inviting. She leaned against the door frame, warming herself with her bitter, smooth drink while she adjusted to the chill.

"I know you miss our old place and your friends," her mother said. "I do, too. But this place will be good, too." She put on an air of cheerfulness. "It feels safe here. Full of possibilities."

The new day beckoned to Desi, but as she headed for the open air, her mother caught her. "Don't forget," Callida said, "the watch-gnomes need to be set up before anything else. I can help if they're too heavy."

"I can do it." Desi walked out onto the back deck, savoring the new day. Her backyard seemed cool and damp and fresh and wonderful. The woods behind the tall back fence were a lot smaller than she had imagined last night—young pines and oaks, hardly grown up, thin trunks packed close together. Still, anything wild appealed to her. She stepped down onto the wet grass.

"Gnomes first, please," her mother reminded her from the kitchen door.

Desi set her mug on the deck and climbed back up to examine the four large crates set there. They hadn't gotten any smaller over the last few weeks, coming up almost to her chest.

"Hi." The boy from last night, Jarrett, called out to her. He was balanced on the big oak branch that reached over the fence into her yard. "What's up?"

"Nothing." Ignoring him, she opened the flaps of the nearest box and pulled on the stone head inside. *Oof.* They hadn't gotten any lighter, either.

Jarrett dropped lightly to the ground and crossed the yard. "Looks heavy. Need help?"

"No, thanks," she huffed, a little flustered by his sudden appearance. She strained to lift the big concrete figure. "I can do it myself."

"Okay." He shrugged but didn't leave. Couldn't he take a hint? She hefted the statue—a stout little man in a pointed hat and beard—and, hugging it to her chest, staggered across the lawn to the back fence, barely making it before her load slid out of her arms. Infuriatingly, Jarrett tagged along.

Feeling edgy and somehow caught in the act (the watch-gnomes definitely belonged in the category of none-of-the-neighbors'-business), she crossed back to the boxes and tugged the next gnome free, pointedly ignoring Jarrett, who seemed mildly amused. That redoubled her determination to do it herself.

The statues seemed to be getting heavier; on the second load, she almost tripped and fell on the way to the side fence. After she dumped the gnome against the fence, she had to pause for a moment, red-faced, hands on knees, to regain her strength.

While she was catching her breath, Jarrett examined the statue. The gnome had chubby cheeks, a bow mouth carved in a perpetual smile, and fat little hands clasped across a round belly. "Most people put them all together in their front yards," he said casually.

"We're not most people." She turned the gnome around so that its nose was almost touching the wooden slats.

"Looks like he's standing guard," Jarrett said.

This one sees the truth. Startled by the thought, Desi looked up to see Devil sprawled on the branch over her head.

You're right, she thought back to her cat, and mentally kicked herself. *I have to be more careful.* To cover up, she answered Jarrett with her mother's catchall lie. "It's traditional— they do it like this overseas."

The little cat walked daintily out to the end of the oak branch to offer her cheek to Jarrett. He took the hint, stroking her with one finger. "What else can I do?" He spoke seriously to the cat. "I tried to help. You talk to her." The cat purred contentedly.

Desi felt a bit jealous; normally Devil never took to strange men. *Strange boys,* she corrected herself quickly. Flustered, she shot out, "Don't you have something to do?"

Jarrett nodded seriously as he continued to caress her cat's cheek. "Yeah, and I'm doing it." Devil had her eyes closed; her blissful expression made it clear that she agreed with him.

Desi decided to ignore them both and went for the next gnome. This time it was all she could do to get it out of the box before she had to drop it on the deck.

Jarrett followed her, cradling Devil in his arms. "That's the biggest one I've ever seen," he confided to the cat.

"You've never seen one like this before." Desi felt prickly all over. The boy was too close to the gnomes, not to mention her cat. And her.

"Sure, they're all over," he said. "And concrete fairies and stone frogs—"

"Oh, no, these are different," Desi interrupted.

"Really? How?"

Desi felt an overwhelming urge to tell him, just to see what he would say, but she clamped her mouth shut, determined not to utter another word. Instead, she grabbed the gnome's head with both hands. When Jarrett put Devil down and took hold of its feet, she didn't object. Together they carried the gnome to the other side fence and put it in place.

As she was turning it around nose-to-fence, she saw Devil streak across the yard, onto the deck, and through the kitchen door. Something was up to make her cat move that fast, and it wasn't breakfast. But between the gnomes and Jarrett, she was too distracted to wonder about it further.

By the fourth gnome, she was grateful to have help. This one she posted in the front yard facing the street; then she remembered she hadn't turned the first gnome around nose-to-fence, so they returned to the backyard. As she passed through the gate, she was taken aback; the golem was staggering down the back steps toward the shed, clomping like Frankenstein's monster from the movies. She felt Jarrett halt behind her.

The oversized golem wrenched open the shed door, almost pulling it off its hinges, and then fell forward to collapse on top of the riding mower parked inside. As they watched, it wormed around until it was sitting upright, then turned the key. The mower roared to life, lurched forward into the shed wall, choked, and went silent. The golem slumped forward, staring at the wall with a stupid expression.

"Is he all right?" asked Jarrett.

"He's always like this," Desi said in disgust.

"So's my uncle Ed," Jarrett sympathized. "Especially on weekends."

The figure in the shed bolted erect and turned the key again. Mower and rider jerked, shifted, and backed out of the shed. As Desi and Jarrett circled the yard to get out of the mower's path, the golem waved its beer can at them, shouting, "Have a nice day!"

Jarrett waved back. "Yeah, you betcha!"

"Desi? Desi?" It was her mother calling.

"I gotta go," she explained to Jarrett. "We're still unpacking." She was grateful for an excuse to get away—the "Dad" thing was mortifying. "Uh, thanks for your help."

"No problem."

The riding mower ground up against the wooden fence, making a horrible noise and scraping off splinters. Desi cringed.

"Yeah, just like Uncle Ed," Jarrett said. "See ya . . . Desi?"

He left through the gate. At that moment it dawned on her: She had never told him her name—he had learned it from her mother calling her. Not sure if she was pleased or irritated, she went inside.

When she came through the kitchen door, she was surprised to see her mother dressed in a business suit. "I have to run in to the office for a meeting," Callida said.

"But you said you didn't have to start work until next week."

"I know, but apparently the author is being stubborn about making the cuts I suggested." She smiled wanly. "She keeps insisting that the spells in her book are real magic."

"And are they?" Desi asked.

"Yes," her mother said, putting on her suit coat. "That's why they have to be cut."

"But if people can't *do* the spells, what's the harm in reading about them?"

"If you had lived through the witch hunts, you wouldn't ask that question. Study your history." Callida opened the door that led from the kitchen to the garage. "I won't be long. The watch-gnomes look great. Stay in the house or the yard until I get back."

"We were going to paint my room," Desi said, disappointed.

"You know, if you want to get started on your own, there's paint and rollers in the basement. You can paint it off-white like ordinary people do."

"You said I could paint it any way I wanted, with magic. What good is having powers if I never get to use them?"

"We already have all the power we need right here,"

Callida said cryptically, placing one hand on Desi's heart and the other on her own. Noticing Desi's frustration, she met her gaze earnestly. "Look, I understand. I really do. I'd rather be here with you, fixing up our new place and helping you practice your spells." She sighed. "I promise we'll do it as soon as I get back. We want to make our new house our home." She straightened up, glancing at the ugly old clock over the fireplace, which was still stuck at two-thirty. "You'll be fine. Devalandnefariel," she addressed the cat, who had been listening from atop the kitchen counter, "I'm going out. Stay alert. Eyes and ears open. No catnaps." She shouldered her briefcase. "Cell phone charged, Desi? Good. Bye, hon. I love you. See you in a couple of hours." Callida bustled out the door to the garage. In a second, Desi heard the roar of the old Porsche they had brought over from France.

She put her elbows on the counter with her face inches from her cat's. "It's started again. Now she'll be too busy to help me with magic even when I can talk her into it." Devil gazed at her sympathetically. "Like, I'm supposed to paint my room with paint? I'm a witch. What happened to waving my hands and *Poof!* Chartreuse?"

Devil's eyes narrowed; evidently she wasn't fond of chartreuse.

"I wish you could talk," Desi went on. "You're a Familiar— you can go off to magical places anytime you want." Desi tried to persuade her. "You could guide me somewhere magical—someplace, I don't know, where I could be myself and practice magic all the time. You must know someplace like that."

Devil backed up, hissing. The message was clear: *Danger!*

"Not you, too," Desi said, exasperated. "I get enough of 'dangerous magic' from my mom. I'm a very talented witch; there are plenty of spells I can do right now."

For a moment, the cat rolled her big yellow eyes to the ceiling; then she dropped lightly to the floor, padding across to nose at the broom closet.

"What's in there? A door to another world?" When she opened the door, only the broom fell out, almost hitting her on the head. "There's nothing in here but the broom. . . . Oh! Right, broom/witch, witch/broom. Are you going to show me how to fly on it?"

Devil meowed petulantly, a clear negative.

"So what good is it?"

The cat sat up straight and raised her eyes at the kitchen ceiling again. A vague image came into Desi's head—something about the broom and the ceiling. She held up the broom, but she couldn't quite reach, so she dragged a chair from the kitchen table. Balanced on the chair, she asked, "What am I supposed to do?" She got no answer but could sense Devil's frustration. This was just too complex for the cat to communicate to her. She had to figure it out on her own. Was there some sort of secret in the ceiling? Grasping the broom by the straw, she tapped the handle against the ceiling in several places, trying different spots. On the third knock, a crack appeared in the plaster overhead.

The rapid spread of the crack startled her so much she jumped down off the chair. Just in time—a secret hatchway swung open, releasing a huge book that fell, hitting the counter with a loud crash that sent the cat scampering for cover under the table.

The book lay there for a moment while she stared at it. There it was, her mother's most precious possession, the answer to all the magical questions she had ever wanted to ask: the *Book of Secrets*.

"Fan-freaking-tastic!" Her hands trembled a bit as she unfastened the latch on the worn cover. She reverently turned pages crusty and stained with use. "Let's see . . . *fat reduction, fillet of souls, finding spell, flatulence*." A feast of magic lay spread out before her eyes. What to do first? Something not too tricky.

A Spell for Colourisation. Yes! She'd paint her room—her way. What could possibly be dangerous about painting a room?

Bundling the big book in her arms, she knelt down under the table to thank Devil. "You're the greatest," she said. "This means everything."

Desi lugged her treasure upstairs, Devil padding along smugly behind her.

5

ONCE IN HER room, Desi locked the door and lowered the blinds. She definitely needed privacy for this. Sprawling on her bed, she opened the *Book of Secrets,* turning its pages gingerly with the tips of her fingers. Devil nosed at it warily. "Okay, the Word of Power for colourisation is *Tintoturner.* No problem." She practiced saying it several times. "And the hand Sign is like waving a brush." She imitated the diagram in the book. "Okay, got it. Now all together." She raised both arms in the air, pointing at the bare white walls. On the bed, Devil cringed expectantly, crouching as low as she could. *"Tintoturner chartreuse!"* Desi exclaimed.

Dense green smoke swirled through the room, blinding her temporarily, choking her until she broke out coughing. When the smoke cleared, she saw that everything had turned light green. Everything: walls, ceiling, carpet, her clothes, the dresser, and all the boxes of stuff—absolutely everything save the *Book of Secrets* itself.

She was ecstatic. "I did it!"

Chartreuse Devil wailed at her from the chartreuse bed. Desi examined her chartreuse hand. "Whoops, I'm green. Now I really am a wicked witch," she laughed. She whirled about the room. "I am a great and powerful sorcerer!"

Giddy with success, she bumped into the bed and fell on her back.

Devil complained. Desi sat up. "All right, I agree, it wasn't a complete success. Too much yellow in the green." She laughed again. Devil looked sullen.

"Okay, okay," Desi said. "You want to be black again, black it is." She raised her hands. *"Tintoturner black!"*

This time when the smoke cleared, she could barely see; the room was so black, it reflected almost no light. "Now *that's* a black cat," she joked to Devil, who had almost disappeared against the bedcovers. "But it's too dark in here. *Tintoturner aquamarine!"* She waved her hands. "Way too blue. *Tintoturner polka dots!"* Polka-dotted smoke was something to see. Polka-dotted Devil clawed at the door to get out. "Oh, where's your sense of humor? All right, time for something completely different. *Tintoturner persimmon!"* Orange smoke filled the room; everything in it turned the same dusky orange color.

"I like it," she said, "and when I get tired of it, I can change it anytime I feel like it. Now, all I have to do is change us back to normal, hang up my stuff on the walls, and I'm really home again."

Devil wailed. Desi replied, "Whatsamatter, you didn't think I would do this without reading how to fix it, did you?" She placed both hands on the bed. *"Restorio!"* The quilt regained its many colors, and the bedsheets were faded white again. *"Restorio!"* A touch, and the carpet was blue once more. *"Restorio!"* Her dresser regained its mahogany sheen.

She reached out to lay hands on Devil. "Now, hold still." Devil dashed underneath the bed. "Okay, see if I care. Stay orange for a while." The cardboard boxes returned to brown; one by one, she restored each of her possessions to its original color. Everything except for her computer; she liked it persimmon.

Finally she knelt to peek under the bed. "You ready to get fixed yet? Sorry, poor choice of words. Come on out." Yellow eyes glared at her resentfully from an orange face. "Okay, whenever you're ready." Desi had plenty else to do. She got busy arranging her most treasured possessions on her shelves, hanging pictures on the walls, and putting away her clothes.

Finally, when she had her space just the way she wanted it, she got on her knees again to call her cat out from under the bed. That's when she heard the garage door opening. "Mom's back already? Get out here, will you?" Devil drew back to the other side of the bed. "Hurry up! Do you want Mom to see you like this?" That's when it struck her—she glanced down at her persimmon arms. Quickly she sat up and placed both hands on her chest. *"Restorio!"*

Her clothes changed instantly, but to her dismay, her arms stayed persimmon. So did the rest of her body. She looked in the mirror; her freakish persimmon face stared back at her. Clasping her hands to her face, she shouted, *"Restorio!"* Nothing happened.

Now she started to panic. "Just stay calm," she warned Devil as her own stomach began to churn. Frantically scanning the book, she heard the car door slam. "I need more time." She threw open her bedroom door. Persimmon Devil darted out between her legs. Desi scrambled down the stairs, slowed by the cumbersome book. In the kitchen, she caught up with her cat, who was scratching at the door. "Quick— into the backyard."

Once outside, Desi frantically flipped pages; she had to locate the spell again. "If Mom finds out I took her book, she'll ground me for life. By the time I learn magic, I'll be too old to use it." She saw movement through the kitchen window. "Into the woods!" Devil clawed up and over the back fence while Desi slipped through the gate. Just in time— as she closed the gate behind her, she heard her mother's call.

Desi fled down the forest trail past a tangle of foliage. When she had gone far enough that she was sure she would not be seen, she knelt with the book on her persimmon- colored knee. Breathing hard, she paged through it until she found the colourisation spell again. "'Cast only in a well- ventilated space,'" she read. "'Avoid contact with skin or hair.'

"What?" she exclaimed. "'Spell cannot be removed from maker but will wear off in less than one hour.' Oh, thank you, thank you, thank you," she sighed. She just had to avoid Mom for a while. . . .

That left Devil. "Hey, you, come back." The little persim- mon cat was hard to see—lots of the leaves were orange— but Desi saw her tail twitch. "Come here. I have to turn you back." She reached out, but her cat was too quick. Devil darted into the woods and disappeared.

Desi had to set the heavy book down in the leaves so she could follow her, abandoning the trail to push through the brush. "Don't be stupid," she shouted. "Aw, come on, let me unspell you." Brambles tugged at her feet; branches whipped at her face. A hidden tree root caught her foot, and she fell into the brittle leaves.

"Uh, hi!" Someone was coming toward her through the woods. She quickly scrambled to her feet.

It was Jarrett. He had a funny look on his face. Panicked, she checked her hands. Hallelujah, her skin was back to normal!

A bitter burning smell wafted by, making her scrunch up her nose.

"I'm not smoking," he said defensively. "Everybody says I'm out here smoking something, but I'm not."

"It's none of my business," Desi said quickly, just relieved not to be Persimmon Girl anymore.

"I come out here so I can do what I want and nobody will bother me," he explained.

Desi knew how that was; in fact, she had her own secrets to hide. "Sorry. I won't bother you," she said quickly. She turned away, scanning the trees for her cat.

"No, wait." Jarrett pointed to a cardboard box that held brightly labeled fireworks. "I take them apart to see how they're made; then I put them back together different to see what happens."

"I won't tell anybody," she said. She almost asked if he had seen a persimmon cat but caught herself in time.

"You want to see something special?" he said, his expression lighting up. "I was about to set a Singapore Sunburst off over the marsh."

"Maybe later," she said, distracted. Her cell phone rang. She sighed; she had forgotten she had it on. "Just a sec. Hello?"

"Desi?" Her mother sounded tense. "Where are you? I need you back here right away. Now, please, hurry."

"Mom, I'm just out in the woods—" But there was no point arguing; her mother was truly upset. Okay, yes, she understood; she'd be right home.

Devil would have to stay persimmon a while longer, she thought. It was a pretty sure bet her cat wouldn't show herself to Callida looking like a furry orange fruit. "I gotta go," she told Jarrett.

There was an awkward pause. She knew she had to answer her mother's call, but the abandoned *Book of Secrets* nagged at her from the back of her mind. She also wanted to retrieve her kitty from out there in the woods, but some new, unfamiliar part of her wanted to stay here. How come every time she started talking to Jarrett, her mother called her into the house?

First things first. Devil and the book would have to wait; she could only hope it wouldn't rain. Clearing her head, she scanned the woods for the trail home and realized she had gotten turned around. "Uh, which way are the houses, again?"

He came up to her side before pointing into the trees. "The trail is right over there. Just keep going uphill. Um, say," he said before she could start off, "if you ever want to hang out at the mall sometime? All the guys you'll meet when school starts hang out there, or you can just, you know, whatever." He was looking right into her eyes. "Or, like, come by my house sometime. If you want."

"Sure." It was all she could think of to say—her head was whirling too fast from everything that had happened in the last few minutes. "I gotta go." He nodded.

Desi started for home, feeling uneasy about turning her back on Jarrett, and the book, and her cat.

6

AS SHE ENTERED the kitchen, Desi saw her mother shaking her head in dismay at the weird old clock on the mantel.

"It can't be," Callida fretted. "Not this soon." Then she saw Desi. "Where were you?" she demanded, visibly upset. "I called and called."

"I told you—in the woods." Desi felt guilty about taking her mother's book, but her mom was acting overprotective again. Defiant, she said, "What's the big deal? I already did my room, and it's not dinnertime."

Her mother glanced at the old clock again. Why was her mother so obsessed with a clock that didn't tell time? Desi checked it herself; the hands now pointed to a quarter past eleven, six hours slow. Callida was muttering, "We've still got time."

Odors from the cauldron bubbling away on the stovetop caught Desi's attention. Judging from the smell, it was the same stinky mess they had made to wake up the golem dad. "You made more potion without me? You said you were going to let me do it." Her mother didn't seem to hear her. "Is everything okay? How was your new job?" Still no response. Her mother stared at the clock, seemingly lost in thought.

"You know," Desi added, "it's perfectly safe out there in

the woods—just a park, like you said. You should come out there sometime."

As she spoke, the old clock sounded once: a deep, sonorous *BONG*. Callida jerked upright as if woken from sleep. "No time for that. Listen. This is very important. Start packing your things. Not just clothes—pack up the boxes in your room and take what you can out to the car; it's in the driveway. The golem will get the rest. I made more of the potion to keep it working at full speed." She took off, dodging around the counters to the hall.

"What do you mean, pack?" Confused, Desi chased her mother up the stairs into the master bedroom. Callida began running between the closet and the bed, where an old beat-up carpetbag was propped open. She dumped clothes and shoes into it haphazardly. "What's going on?" Desi asked.

"Honey, Desi, please do what I say." Callida looked pinched and worried, but she didn't slow down.

"You're packing up to *leave*?" Desi said, aghast. "Why? We just got here!"

Callida paused just long enough to say, in a strained voice, "We have to hurry. I can't explain. You have to trust me. I need you to start packing."

"Two days? We've been here two days and we're moving already?" Desi sat on the bed. Her head was reeling. Had her mother found out about her doing magic already? "Is it because of my room?"

"You'll get another room, just as nice. I promise. Now, please, get ready."

"But I just set my room up the way I want it," Desi protested. "I'm making friends. I have plans. We can't move."

"I don't like this any more than you do, but I have no choice. We'll talk about it in the car." Callida closed her bag with a snap, looking resolute. "If you're not going to pack your things, then I'll do it."

"I'm not going anywhere." Desi folded her arms. This was all happening too fast. The abandoned *Book of Secrets* haunted her, and what about her kitty? "We can't go. Devil's not here."

Callida looked startled. "Of course she's here. She'll show up when we call her."

But would she, dyed orange? Desi felt herself panicking. "I won't leave without her."

Callida looked like she was at the end of her rope. "Desi, please—"

"No!" Desi jumped up off the bed, desperate to do something. Callida tried to grab her arm, but she pulled free. "I'm not leaving!" she cried. "You don't love me or you wouldn't do this." She ran out into the hall and down the stairs.

"Desi, come back!" Her mother tried to chase after her but tripped over the boxes on the stairs. Feeling guilty, Desi almost did turn back, but her anger and resentment won out, so she ran out the back door, slamming it shut behind her. Briefly she considered heading back into the woods, but the uneven ground would only slow her down. Instead, she grabbed her racing bike from the shed. As she tore off down the street, choking back tears, the last thing she heard was her mother shouting her true name to the world.

"Desdemona!"

7

HEART-POUNDING FEAR. Claws gripping wood. Hide, safety in shadows. Quiet at last.

Devalandnefariel was confused—and she didn't like it. Thinking was for witches and humans and the smarter demons; she ran on instinct. Just now, her instinct had told her to run up a tree, so here she was hidden in the tree house in the yard next to hers.

She had felt Desi's yearning to learn magic, so she had shown her the big old dusty book, and what happened? Her beautiful fur ruined; she looked like some clownish calico. The magic book was still out there, half covered in leaves. Wrong—she felt it. Now her family was fighting—the waves of energy struck her head. She quivered, tense and irritated. She had to act, kill something or run away, but she didn't know which. She heard Desi ride off on her bike and Callida shouting. Her family's discord clamped onto her heart. She squeezed her eyes shut, hunching down on the floorboards of the tree house.

BONG! She heard the sour old clock sound, even out here. That meant something, but she couldn't think what. At the same time, from the opposite direction, she sensed something hot, big, stinky: a Hole to the other World had opened up. Far away—but it could never be far enough. It reeked of Chaos. Bad thing.

Humiliating orange fur or not, she couldn't ignore this. With a pang of guilt, she remembered the strange creature of the night before. She had never warned her family.

Danger is near!

Running along the branch and into her yard, she met Callida hurrying out from the kitchen. *"Devil?"* Callida exclaimed at seeing her mortifying new color. "What in the Two Worlds have you been into? Never mind. Find Desi. Now!"

Devil rolled her yellow-green eyes up in frustration. *I am no slobbering hound to go trotting down the street,* she thought. *Pay attention: a Hole to the other World has opened up, and a strange creature is near.*

Callida was too upset to listen. "What do you mean, you're not a dog?" was all she said. "If you can't even find Desi, what good are you? Stop talking and listen to me."

Devalandnefariel glared back.

BONG! BONG! The annoying old clock struck twice.

"Oh, never mind. I'll use a Summoning Spell." Callida ran back into the house.

Devalandnefariel followed. *Will you stop running around like a chicken and listen?* she tried to say. But the witch paid her no mind.

In the kitchen, Callida snatched the broom from the closet, grasped the handle above the straw, and, raising it into the air, tapped the ceiling three times. A crack appeared, taking the shape of a door, which swung open and down from the ceiling.

Callida gaped at the empty space. "My book!" she gasped. "It's gone!"

BONG! BONG! BONG! The old clock sounded three notes of warning.

Callida checked its hands and her shoulders sagged. "There's no time, anyway," she whispered. "Look at the Alarming Clock. Quarter to twelve! It's never been this late before."

Devalandnefariel could only stare at her, willing her to understand. "You feel it, too?" Callida said. "Yes, danger is coming closer. He's tracking me." She laughed bitterly. "Maybe *he* has a dog."

Devalandnefariel cried out contemptuously to show what she thought of that.

"What can I do?" Callida cried back. "I've got to save my precious girl. Desi's alone out there somewhere. If I go looking for her, I'm leading danger right to her. If I stay here to fight, I may never see her again. I can't stay and I can't go, and I can't leave her alone," she said, her face red with desperation.

Devalandnefariel pounced up on the counter. She arched her back, eyes blazing, snarling her defiance.

Callida scoffed. "Great, so you'll protect her. What are you going to do, dial nine-one-one with your paws?" Then she hesitated, her comment apparently giving her an idea. "Of course!" The witch slammed her hand on the counter, making the already jumpy cat jump. "It's practically the same potion. They're both cattail-based. Just needs catnip, for a cat." She rummaged in a cabinet, throwing bags and jars on the counter. "Got it." She carried two jars over to the cauldron, which had been bubbling away all this time. Dumping the catnip inside, she stirred vigorously and then added a pinch of lizards' wings.

"I'm sorry," she assured Devalandnefariel, who had wisely decided to retreat to the edge of the island counter. "But I have no choice. I have to do this for Desi's sake. Look, lots of catnip. Yum." Callida raised the spoon to her nose and took a deep whiff. "Ugh."

She ladled the black goo into a bowl and set it down on the counter, blowing on it to cool. "Here you go. Dig in." Devalandnefariel crouched lower on the edge of the counter. *Is that supposed to be for me? Desi is in danger and you're making lunch?* She stretched her neck forward an inch, sniffed, and then pulled back sharply. *Yuck. Throw it to the dogs.* She leaped to the floor to get away.

"What's the matter?" Callida complained as Devalandnefariel retreated under the kitchen table. Callida shot a glance at the Alarming Clock and shivered. "This is the only way. You have to eat this. Please?"

Devalandnefariel crouched lower, glaring at her. *You like it so much,* you *eat it.*

Callida cursed, then muttered, "Familiar or not, a cat's a cat." She searched the pantry, found a can, and carried it to the electric can opener. "Have it your way. I don't know what this will do to the potion, and I don't care." She inserted the lip and pushed the button.

The sound triggered a reaction deep inside the cat. She poked her nose out; the smell of tuna tantalized her, making her mouth water. Impatiently, she waited for the can to go around. At last, Callida scraped the tuna fish over the goo and set the bowl on the floor. "Here, kitty, kitty."

Devalandnefariel was mesmerized. The lure of the tuna was irresistible. She crept up to the bowl, stretched her neck out cautiously, and tested it with her tongue. Delicious. Instinct took over and she began to devour the tuna, swallowing it in great gulps.

She glanced up to see Callida looking down at her in satisfaction. When she went back to eating, out of one corner of her eye, she saw the witch check the old clock, cringe at what it told her, and run upstairs.

Devalandnefariel licked the last of the tuna from her mouth. She knew that her greed had overcome her good sense, but she never could resist when she caught a whiff of fish. She felt stuffed full.

Too full. Something was wrong, horribly wrong. Her stomach twisted. She got ready to retch it all back up, but her throat spasmed and nothing came out. Lights burst inside her eyes. Snakes crawled under her skin. She tried to run, but her legs buckled under her, and she could only twitch helplessly on the kitchen floor. Weak as a kitten, she raised her head to mew for help and saw Callida towering over her holding a robe, looking revolted. Devalandnefariel had never felt such fear. She called out, piteously, to the only mother she had ever known. What was happening to her?

Her body swelled up like a balloon, great patches of bare skin appearing beneath her fur. Her head bulged, then flattened, like a ball of clay molded by some unseen hand. Over and over she blacked out, but flashes of light brought her back. At one point she felt a pile of cloth thrown over her, burying her. Was she dying?

The cloth shrank, tightening around her body. Her head poked out through a hole, aching terribly. Her whole body throbbed. Gradually, she felt the strength flow back into her legs. She rose on her front paws. They felt cold and hot at the same time. Her back legs wouldn't work right—she got a glimpse of misshapen, clammy feet poking out from under the robe.

Her vision cleared. She saw her own agony mirrored by the shock in Callida's face. Where was her nose? She couldn't see her own nose. She opened her mouth to wail, but her jaws felt strange.

Callida gasped. "You're only a girl!"

Her paws poked through the arms of the robe, settling it down over her shoulders. Hairless, human paws. The truth hit her, and she exploded with fury. "What did you do to me, you old witch?" she screeched. "My fur, my tail!" She felt her face. "My whiskers, gone! I'm horrible!"

"I'm sorry." Callida looked grim. "I had no choice."

"My paws and claws!" she shrieked, staring at her bony, naked arms. "I have monkey hands. You turned me into a hairless monkey!" She tried to reach out to claw Callida.

"Quit whining," Callida said. "Nobody hurt you." She grasped the girl's hands, checking both sides. "You're not a monkey; you're human. You're perfectly normal as far as I can see." She let go, and Devalandnefariel shrank away.

"How could you do this to me?" she said. She huddled on the floor, trying to crouch on all fours, but her legs wouldn't work right.

"You're still a cat. This is just temporary. Now, listen to me carefully," Callida said sharply. "I have to leave. You need to stay and take care of Desi. There's no one else to watch over her and no time to explain things." Callida grabbed her front paws, pulling her up; amazingly, her head rose as high as the witch's, though her back feet were still on the floor. "I thought you would be older," Callida said, "but I can't help that now. I gave you a human shape so you can think and talk. Stay alert and watch over Desi. And that means at night, too. No catting about. Do you hear me?"

"In this body?" The girl shuddered. "I'm ashamed to have anyone see me. Ugh!"

Callida gave a mirthless laugh. "You'll survive. You can wear my clothes and sleep in my room. I'll be back in a day or two."

"And you'll make me myself again?"

"Absolutely." Callida fixed her attention with a stare. "You just focus on Desi while I'm gone. It's her we have to worry about."

They glared at each other, eye to eye. Neither blinked. Then a sudden noise made them both jump.

BONG! BONG! BONG! BONG!

The hands on the Alarming Clock clicked straight up, pointing to twelve o'clock. As they watched, a little door on its face swung open to reveal a tiny winged gargoyle. The intricately carved monster slid forward until it was clear of the door; then it spread its wings and opened its mouth.

It stuck out its tongue.

"Too late," Callida said in a hush. "No, wait. He'll be

locked onto my aura. I can lead him away." She grabbed her carpetbag and ran for the front door.

"Who?" the girl cried. "What is it?"

Callida halted in the open front door. "Tell Desi I love her. Be wise. Take care of my sweet girl." She ran out the door.

The girl tried to drop to all fours to run but tripped, rolling over in a tangle of arms and legs. For a moment she lay on the floor, gasping for breath; then, drawing her hind legs under her body, she straightened up, precariously balanced in the air like a performing dog. She staggered down the hall, one foot ahead of the other, arms out for balance.

By the time she reached the front door to look for Callida, the witch's car was already fading out of sight down the street. The girl clung to the doorway for support, the whirl and confusion of her new senses making the world spin.

Cautiously, exposing only her eyes, she peeked out the doorway. As she watched, a rider on a motorcycle appeared from the opposite direction, cruising slowly. Face concealed by a dark visor, his black helmet turned from one side to the other as he crept up the street. When the rider came level with her house, he slowed even more. She pulled back to hide, then peeked out again with the corner of one eye. The dark mirror of his visor was facing her. Instinct made her jerk back, but her curiosity forced her to risk another glance.

The faceless rider lowered his gaze to something hidden inside his leather jacket. Something underneath the jacket wriggled. The rider paused, head down, until it ceased its movement, and then looked up again. He did not stop. He rode on at the same creeping pace, checking the street on both sides, moving in the same direction Callida's car had taken, until he was out of sight.

Too much, the girl thought, shivering. It was all too much. Through all the confusing sensations and strange feelings, sights, and sounds, one message came clear: when in doubt, hide.

8

LESS THAN AN hour later, Desi dropped her bike on the side-walk in front of her house. Her first impulse had been to get away, so she rode, heading nowhere in particular. For a long time she had pedaled off her anger until she got there: nowhere in particular. It was at the end of a cul-de-sac with houses identical to hers that she realized there was no place she could go, and there wasn't anyplace she wanted to go without her mother, anyway. So, tired out more from her anger than her ride, she headed home. At least, home for a while. There was always the hope that she could talk her mother into changing her mind.

As she started up the front walk, she got a shock. The front door was wide open—a thing she had never seen before, ever. It was like a giant sign proclaiming the crime she had committed: Desdemona Ran Away. Her mother must be ter-ribly angry to forget her own rules like that. Desi gulped back the knot in her throat and went inside.

"Hello?" The bare walls rang hollowly; her voice echoed back from the kitchen. She shut the front door behind her. "Mom?" Maybe her mother was still in her bedroom, pack-ing. She went upstairs and peeked in the door. "Mom?"

Except for the mess, the room was empty. Then an invis-ible hand squeezed Desi's heart. Her mother's carpetbag was missing. It wasn't in her own room, either, or anywhere else upstairs. She raced downstairs and through the hall to the kitchen. No sign of it anywhere.

Growing more anxious, Desi opened the garage door and flipped on the light. Her heart began to pound. The old Porsche wasn't here—there was nothing but cardboard boxes and oil stains on the concrete floor—but it hadn't been out front in the driveway, either. It didn't make sense; if her mother was driving around looking for her, why had she taken her carpetbag but nothing else? Desi closed the door and paced the kitchen, trying to think. Her mother's cell—of course. But when she called the number, a ring from the kitchen counter made her heart skip a beat. Her mother had taken the car but had left her cell phone behind.

Desi stood very still. She tried to listen past the blood pounding in her ears for any little sound—Devil, anything.

Then she heard it: something heavy moving in the house.

"Mom?" She ran, relieved and desperate to make up with her mother, but when she got to the front room, all she saw was the golem dad in its chair in front of a blank TV. Desi was so disappointed, she lost it—and did something she never would have dreamed of doing normally. She asked the golem, "Do you know where Mom is?"

It turned its head to look at her. "Hi. How are you? Have a nice day." Then it turned back to the TV.

Stifling a scream, she ran out the front door and into the street.

Outside it was still light and mostly quiet. Down the street, a few little kids were playing, ignoring their mothers' calls to come inside. Through the next-door window, she could see Jarrett talking to his parents, laughing in their own house, snug and cozy, one big happy family. She felt sick in the pit of her stomach.

She stood there for long minutes, feeling lost, until the neighbor's front door opened and Jarrett appeared with a bag of garbage in his hand. "Hey, Desi." He looked at her curiously. "Anything wrong?"

The words popped out of her mouth before she could think. "My mom's gone." It seemed an easy thing to say, but, in fact, she didn't remember it ever happening before in her whole life.

"Oh." He stuffed the garbage into the can by the side of the house. On his way back to the front porch, he paused, looked at her closely, and said, "You know, you can hang out for dinner with us, if you want."

She could see his parents bustling around inside, picking up, arguing, laughing. Somehow she found that her feet had taken her across his yard. "Okay."

·₊*₊*₊*

"Of course you can join us for dinner," Mrs. Wilkins, Jarrett's mother, said warmly. "You're more than welcome, Desi. Do you like pasta?" Jarrett's mom bustled about a kitchen identical to the one in Desi's house, but this one was warmer, friendlier, and more lived-in. She and Jarrett's father switched places from the stove to the sink with the ease of years of practice. "If it's all right with your father," Mrs. Wilkins continued.

"My father? Oh, right, him," Desi said. She had felt better

the instant she stepped inside Jarrett's house—the lights on everywhere, the TV blaring away, the sounds and smells of cooking from the kitchen, all the bustle of a family in each other's way. The demons in her mind were beaten back by the forces of domesticity. Plus, after a lifetime of constant moving, she was used to meeting new people in unfamiliar houses. She took a deep breath and began to relax a little. "My dad won't care."

Mrs. Wilkins clucked sympathetically. "I'd still like to give him a call so he won't worry," she insisted.

"ET, phone home," Jarrett quipped, handing Desi their phone.

Not knowing what else to do, she dialed her house phone. Someone picked up—was her mother back? "Hello?"

After a long moment came a deep, hearty voice. "Hi, hello. How are you?"

Now what? She was still in a daze, and, anyway, what was she supposed to say to the golem?

"Do you mind if I take that, dear?" Desi surrendered the phone, resigned to whatever came next.

"Hello? This is Trish Wilkins, Jarrett's mother? Oh, I'm fine, thank you. How are you? Say, we'd love to have Desi join us for dinner." She paused, clearly puzzled. "I'm really just fine," she said carefully. "Well, okay, then, you have a nice day, too." She hung up. "I guess it's all right. Desi, the bathroom's down the hall if you want to wash up. We're eating in five minutes." She shook her head consolingly and went back to cooking.

Reprieved, Desi found the bathroom with no problem—

the layout of the house was identical to hers. Before she closed the door, voices echoed down the hallway.

"She's sweet," Mrs. Wilkins was saying to her husband. "But that father of hers . . . ?"

"No kidding," he replied. "Nice lawn, though."

9

DEVALANDNEFARIEL WOKE UP, not immediately and completely awake as she had always done, but fuzzy, disoriented. What a horrible dream—someone had moved the furniture, her water dish had been put where the food dish should have been, and nothing had smelled right.

She tried to stretch her muscles but was too cramped; she was in a closet—Callida's, by the smell of it. That was not too strange; she had slept in closets before, but something felt wrong about this one. Then it came back to her.

Oh, rats, we moved again. I hate change.

This new house had tiny, cramped closets; at least, it seemed that way, judging by how hard it was to wriggle out. Her muscles ached from her uncomfortable sleeping position—again, strange, for her. Her insides were queasy. Hairball? Maybe eating some grass would make her feel better.

She squeezed through the closet door only to fall flat on her face, nose to the carpet. Something was very wrong. Across the floor, she spied a mirror leaning against the wall, waiting to be hung up. She crept up to it timidly, afraid of what she would see.

A strange human girl stared back at her. Her stomach lurched. It all came flooding back, the terrible thing the witch had done to her. This girl was her reflection, her black hair above white-rimmed eyes set in a too-flat face. This was her puny little nose and pink, flabby lips. Her gleaming white fangs had shrunk to small, even teeth. Her bad dream had become a living nightmare.

But Devalandnefariel the Familiar had faced nightmares before. With an effort, she struggled to her feet, using the bed frame for support. Impossibly high in the air, she towered over the furniture. Everything looked so different from this position. It was like perching in a tree . . . but the tree walked with you. She took a few tentative steps and found that, miraculously, she could walk on two legs.

I really am a human, at least on the outside, she thought. *Inside* she felt mixed up, mostly herself but with new bits and pieces mixed in, too.

The girl tested her new senses. She could smell almost nothing. She strained for the sounds that would tell her who was in the house, but whether she was deaf or the house was quiet, she heard nothing but the blood pounding in her ears. A wave of panic started to sweep over her as she realized how defenseless she had become.

Refusing to give in to fear, she focused on vision. That was better. Her new height gave her a commanding sweep of the room. Objects seemed clearer. She was not only seeing better but also understanding better what she was seeing. The room organized itself; everything had meaning. It was clear from the mess that Callida had left in a hurry. *Leaving me in charge,* she remembered. *Against some unknown danger.* Her old determination came flooding back.

She stretched out her front legs—no, arms. "I still have eyes. I have ears, as pitiful as they are, and though my claws are short, I have a longer reach." She surprised herself by speaking aloud in human speech. "And now I can make myself understood, even to big, stupid humans," she proclaimed to the room.

Her mind was working clearly now; in fact, she was thinking more sharply than ever before. Her first task was to locate Desi. She opened the bedroom door and started to descend the stairs, carefully at first, then faster as she learned to trust her new upright posture. Going downhill was easier on two legs than four.

At the bottom of the steps, a foul scent led her to the front room and the golem. She felt relieved that her new nose could at least smell *that*. Before she could move on in search of Desi, the talking thing rang, and the golem picked it up in his hand.

"Hello?" It was Desi's voice, coming from inside that thing! Then a new voice came, talking about Desi, and Jarrett's mother, and dinner. Devalandnefariel ignored the golem and the strange talking device. The important thing was that Desi was safe for now and close, somewhere near the boy Jarrett—probably in the house next door. With that clever realization, she relaxed enough to feel a second, overwhelming sensation—hunger. She was starving, hungrier than she had ever been in her life. Desi was in charge of the food; she would find Desi and get her dinner. It was very simple.

In the kitchen, she balanced in front of the door for a

moment, wondering how she could get out, until it came to her—*I'm human now.* Clumsily, she grasped the knob, twisting it back and forth before she finally opened the door. Outside, she tottered across the grass to Jarrett's house, her new mouth watering in anticipation.

10

NEXT DOOR, DESI accepted a plate from Jarrett's mother. "Since we have a guest, I thought it would be nice if we all sat at the table together for once," said Mrs. Wilkins pointedly. Jarrett about-faced on his way to the TV and pulled out a chair in the family room. As they were sitting down, a knock came from the front door.

"It's always at dinnertime," Mr. Wilkins grumbled.

"It might be Desi's father," Mrs. Wilkins replied. "I don't know if he really understood she's eating here."

The thought of the golem appearing at the door made Desi cringe. "I'll get it," she said quickly.

"No, no, I'll take care of it." Mr. Wilkins put down his napkin and disappeared down the hall. A moment later, he returned alone, looking exasperated. "Nobody there," he reported.

The knocking came again, followed by a scratching sound.

"Now it's coming from these doors," Jarrett said. He slid out of his chair to yank aside the curtains covering the sliding glass doors.

"No friends over at dinnertime," yelled his father. "Oh, except you, of course," he added to Desi.

Jarrett was standing in front of the door with one hand

on the handle, watching someone scratch long fingernails on the glass.

"Who is it?" Mrs. Wilkins took charge. "Jarrett, where are your manners? Open the door."

Jarrett slid the door open. Immediately a tall young woman brushed past him in a rush to get into the room. She halted just inside, staring with intense green eyes.

"You are here," she said, fixing on Desi. "I am hungry. I need you to get my food."

Desi stared back. The teenage girl wore a long, colorful bathrobe, a petulant expression, and nothing else.

The others turned to Desi expectantly. "What?" she said, bewildered. It was all she could think of to say.

The girl looked upset. "You're supposed to set out my food by now, and my dish is empty."

"I'm sorry, dear, have we met?" asked Mrs. Wilkins pleasantly.

"No," said the girl. "I live next door. I watch over Desi while her mother's gone." The girl turned to Desi. "This is all your fault."

"My fault?" echoed Desi. She looked at the girl intently. There was something familiar about her.

"Do you know each other, dear?" Mrs. Wilkins asked Desi.

"Of course she knows me," the girl answered for her. "I'm her Familiar."

Desi jumped back, knocking over her chair.

"You're her family?" Mr. Wilkins asked, misunderstanding.

"No," Desi said, backing against the wall. "It can't be."

"She's not your family?" asked Mr. Wilkins, puzzled.

"I don't believe it," Desi said. She peered at the girl accusingly. "Devil?"

"Where?" said Jarrett, looking under the table for the cat.

"Don't call me that," said the girl formerly known as Devalandnefariel. "This was all your mother's idea."

"How could she do this to me?" Desi wailed.

"Who did what?" Jarrett asked, looking concerned.

"It's *me* she did it to," said the girl. "I'm the one who should be angry."

Mrs. Wilkins interrupted politely. "Desi, could you introduce your friend?"

Desi was so upset she couldn't get her brain hooked up to her mouth.

"He knows me," said the girl in the robe, nodding at Jarrett. She licked the back of her hand and used it to smooth her shining black hair. "I'm the cat next door."

"Cat, Cat-rina," Desi blurted out. "My cousin Cat, she's here while my mother is gone—"

"Oh, good," Mrs. Wilkins said. "Your father will have some help, then. It makes it easier."

"Hi, Cat," Jarrett said. "Sorry, I didn't know, or I would've asked you to dinner, too."

Cat leaned down to rub her cheek against his. Jarrett grinned.

Mrs. Wilkins's eyebrows shot up, and she got to her feet, taking over. "Nice to meet you, Cat. I'm Mrs. Wilkins, and this is my husband, Mr. Wilkins, and obviously you've met Jarrett." She picked Desi's chair up off the floor. "Sit down, please, dear," she said to Desi. "Dinner is getting cold. You too, Jarrett."

Desi collapsed in her seat, afraid to speak. She couldn't take her eyes off Cat.

Cat looked around the table suspiciously. "I'm hungry," she repeated.

"You're welcome to join us for dinner," Mrs. Wilkins offered with rigid cheerfulness. "There's plenty. I'll just set another place. Jarrett, will you call your brother?" Mrs. Wilkins went out to the kitchen.

"BOB! DINNER'S READY!" Jarrett yelled from his chair. Desi jumped in her seat. Cat cringed as if slapped.

"I could have done that," his mother chided, returning with the extra plate and silverware. "Cat, you can sit here next to me."

From the stairs, a loud clomping signaled the appearance of gigantic white sneakers, muscular legs, disheveled gym shorts, a sweat-stained T-shirt, and a big head topped with rumpled blond hair. Eyes half-closed from sleep, Bob spotted the food and dropped in his seat beside Jarrett.

"Bob?" prompted his mother. "This is Desi's cousin Cat, from next door? She's looking after things while Desi's mother is away." With strained politeness, she indicated Cat, who was wriggling around, trying to get her arms and legs inside her bathrobe so they'd all fit on the seat of her chair.

The big teen looked up from his plate, fork in hand. His eyes grew bigger than his glasses. Cat, now perched on all fours on the narrow wooden seat, turned a complete circle, trying to get comfortable.

"Ahem." Desi stomped her feet on the floor. She pointed to her own legs. Seeing this, Cat unwound and put her feet on the floor, stretching her long legs to brace herself from falling.

A red flush spread across Bob's cheeks and down his neck. "Caff?" he choked. "'Scuse me?" He leaped to his feet and disappeared upstairs.

Jarrett grinned wider, clearly enjoying the scene.

Smiling through clenched teeth, his mother said, "Pasta, Cat?"

Cat put her nose to the offered dish and sniffed carefully. "Paugh!" she snorted. She turned her head away.

"Sorry," Desi said desperately. "Cat's, uh, allergic to pasta. It, uh, makes her break out."

"Oh, I'm so sorry," Mrs. Wilkins said. "How about some salad?"

At the sight of the green stuff, Cat looked outraged.

"No!" Desi cut in before Cat could say anything rude. "She's on a diet. I mean, um . . ." She knew she sounded lame, but she absolutely couldn't let this strange girl let the cat out of the bag.

The pounding resumed on the stairs, and Bob reappeared, minus his glasses, wearing new jeans and a clean T-shirt advertising a rock band tour. His hair was wet and disheveled all in one direction.

"Uh, hi," he said to Cat while staring at his feet. She ignored him. Bob took his seat.

"Looking good, Bob," Jarrett teased. Bob elbowed him in the ribs.

"Are you new here, Cat?" asked Mr. Wilkins. "I don't remember seeing you before."

That was a tricky question. Luckily, it was taking Cat a moment to figure out the precise truth, so Desi cut her off again. "No, I mean, yes, Cat's new; she just got here this morning." Desi glared at Cat, daring her to speak. "It's been a big change for her." Cat looked sullen.

"Speaking of changing, I hope you didn't just run out of the shower looking for Desi?" Mrs. Wilkins asked.

Desi and Cat both looked at her, confused.

"Your bathrobe, I mean," Mrs. Wilkins explained.

Before Desi could think up an excuse, Cat spoke. "Her mother gave me this clothing. I do not have any of my own."

"You don't have any clothes with you?" Mrs. Wilkins asked, surprised.

"FIRE!" Desi shouted the first thing that came into her head. Everyone stared at her. "A fire destroyed everything," she said weakly. "That's why she came to live with us."

"I'm so sorry," Mrs. Wilkins said. "It must have been awful. Was anyone hurt?"

Desi improvised fast. "No, no, just her clothes."

Cat frowned at her. "Is this not right?" she asked Mrs. Wilkins, plucking at her bathrobe. "I am not used to wearing clothes."

Across the table, Bob broke out in a fit of coughing. Mr. Wilkins pounded his back heartily.

Mrs. Wilkins looked at Desi, as if waiting for a good explanation for Cat's remark.

"She's from France?" Desi said helplessly, shrugging her shoulders.

Bob's coughing got worse, so Mr. Wilkins pounded him harder.

·⋆·71·⋆·

Jarrett surveyed the table, looking pleased, like the cat that ate the canary. "This is great," he said, "sitting down together as a family."

"And how old are you, Cat?" Mrs. Wilkins asked, changing the subject. "You look about the same age as Bob."

"I am fully grown. I am now entering my fourth year," Cat said proudly before Desi could stop her.

"Of high school!" Desi butted in. "Cat's just starting her fourth year of high school."

"So you're in Bob's class, then. How nice," Mrs. Wilkins said. "Maybe he can show you around."

Bob looked ecstatic.

"Bob doesn't have a lot of friends," Mrs. Wilkins said.

Bob looked like he wanted to slide under the table.

"Will you be going to school here, if you are staying a while?" Mr. Wilkins asked.

"School?" Cat said, looking confused and mistrustful.

"I know, felt that way myself when I was your age," Mr. Wilkins said, leaning toward her. "Bob can help you get oriented. He's a straight-A student."

Cat turned her suspicious glare on Bob, pinning him like a mouse. Bob squirmed.

"Cat's homeschooled," Desi rushed in.

"Wish I was," Jarrett said, shaking his head appreciatively.

"So you'll be home a lot, then?" Mrs. Wilkins asked. Bob brightened up.

"But really busy all the time," Desi shot back. She was getting in deeper and deeper but didn't know what was the right thing to say. "Cat's always busy learning things."

Cat looked trapped for a moment; then her scowl relaxed.

"Yes. There are things I want to know. Maybe you can show me?" Cat bared her teeth at Bob. To everyone but Desi, it looked like a smile.

"Uh, yuh, buh, enh," Bob replied. He held on to the table to keep from floating up to the ceiling.

Mrs. Wilkins brought the conversation back to dinner. "Can I fix you a sandwich, Cat?" she asked. "What would you like?"

"Fish."

"I can open a can of tuna. White or whole wheat bread?"

Desi had a sudden vision of Cat, crouched on the table, face buried in her plate. "No!" she shouted, jumping up.

"No bread. Just fish," Cat replied, licking her lips. She stood up as well. "I have to go."

"You just got here," Jarrett said, looking disappointed.

"You aren't staying for dinner?" Mrs. Wilkins asked.

"Yes, dinner, but I have to go," Cat stated firmly. "Where is the sandbox?"

"Sandbox?" said Desi with creeping dread.

Jarrett got up from the table. "I had one when I was a little kid. It's probably still there, under the leaves," he said. "What do you need a sandbox for?"

"If there is no sandbox in the house," Cat said, "I will go outside."

Jarrett slid open the back door for her.

If the idea of Cat eating was scary, the image of Cat in the sandbox was a nightmare. "No!" Desi exclaimed. "I mean, yes, we've got to go. Uh, my dad misses me." Desi grabbed Cat's hand, pulling her away from the table and toward the front door. "Thanks for dinner. Goodbye!"

Cat yanked her hand away. "Jarrett is showing me his sandbox," she said, furious.

"You like ours better—I mean, you can go at home." Desi shooed Cat into the front hall. "Just come on, will you? Your food is at our house. Goodbye!" she yelled from the hall.

"Do you have to leave already?" asked Jarrett, starting to go after them, but they were already out the door.

"Buh-bye!" Bob blurted as they left.

11

DESI BANGED OPEN her front door. "Mom?" she called.

"I told you she is not here. She ran away," Cat said.

Desi was too upset to take her cat's word for it, so she combed the house again. There was no sign of her mother. When she got back into the kitchen, there was no sign of Cat, either. Desi was worried that the girl had gone back to Jarrett's house. Then she heard a voice from the garage.

"I can't fit into my sandbox," Cat complained.

"Oh, for . . . ," Desi muttered. "Stop!" she yelled, running into the garage.

She showed Cat how to use the bathroom. In a few minutes, the girl emerged, scowling. "I can't believe you humans waste clean water for that. What if someone drinks it?"

"You're supposed to flush," Desi said, pushing past Cat to flush the toilet.

When she returned, Cat was complaining again. "I'm hungry."

Desi snatched a bag of dry cat food from inside a kitchen cabinet. She shoved it at the girl. "Here."

Cat turned up her nose at the sight. "I get canned food at night."

"Tough," Desi said. She dropped the open bag on top of the island counter and stared at the strange person in her kitchen. This was nobody she knew. Where was her kitty? "I still don't believe any of this. Why would Mom leave without me?"

Cat frowned at the bits of dry food spilled out over the counter. "You ran away, remember?"

"She wouldn't just leave. She'd wait for me or come looking for me or something."

"She ran out. After turning me into this." Cat looked down at herself and shuddered.

"But why?"

"So I can take care of you."

"No, why would she leave without me?" Desi's heart sank at her own words.

"She did not explain." Cat tossed her head. "Who cares? The important thing is she took away my beautiful fur and turned me into a naked ape." She bent her head down to try to lap up some of the scattered bits of food. It was not easy.

"Will you stop?" Desi said. "My mother wouldn't just take off without leaving some sort of message; I know it. Concentrate—did she say when she's coming back?"

Cat put her new, larger brain to use recalling what had been said. "Yes, she said she would return in one day or two. Maybe two whole days until I get my real body back."

Desi was so relieved she almost cried. "Only one or two days? That's not so bad. What else did she say?"

Cat squinted in concentration. "She said, 'Tell Desi I love her. Be wise.' Hmm, and she also said, 'Take care of my sweet girl.' But you do not seem very sweet to me."

"What do you expect?" Desi exclaimed. "You just show

up, in *their* house, looking like . . . like that." She waved her hands at Cat in frustration.

Cat stuck her nose in the air, looking offended. "This new body was not *my* idea. If you're going to be rude, I am leaving. Jarrett's mother promised me tuna fish."

"No, don't go back there—"

"I don't have to listen to what you say. I am dominant here; your mother said so." She tried to lick the food pieces up off the counter, but they just slid over the edge. Giving up in frustration, she said, "I'm so hungry. This is worse for me than it is for you. At least you are still you. Look at me."

"I *am* looking, but I don't recognize you. Devil, is that really you?"

"Don't call me that. My name is Devalandnefariel." She paused thoughtfully. "You know, I never was able to say my name before. It sounds beautiful when I say it."

Desi collapsed in a chair. "You have to say your name is Cat. You can't let anyone know you were—you are—you." It sounded so weird, saying that.

"No." Cat shrugged. "Why pretend I'm a hairless monkey like the rest of you? I am a superior species, and you'll just have to live with it." She gave up on the spilled cat food, trying instead to shove her nose into the bag.

Desi was dumbfounded. "Because if you tell them you're a cat, they won't believe you."

Cat pulled her nose out of the bag. "Then I will tell them the truth—that your mother is a witch and she put a spell on me." She glared at Desi. "And so did you. Orange fur!"

"It was persimmon, and it's not my fault you ran away

before I could change you back." Desi waggled her finger in Cat's face. "Look, people don't believe in witches or spells or cats turning human, and it's lucky for us that they don't. If you don't want trouble, you gotta say you're my cousin Cat and that you're here to help out while Mom's gone. Got it?"

Cat sulked. "All right. I'll act like a people, like you say, but I won't eat pasta. Bleah!" She stretched and yawned. "I'm still waiting for my dinner."

"You've got hands," Desi said. "Get it yourself." She couldn't help herself; the hurt made her want to lash out. She missed her mother, and she missed her dear little kitty.

Cat's eyes lit up. "I forgot. I have hands." She reached gingerly into the bag to pull out a handful. "My favorite, liver-flavored Kitty-Bits—crunchy and not too oily," she said, tossing back the food and chewing noisily.

"That's so gross," Desi said. Her whole body ached. She felt like she couldn't take any more. "I'm going up to my room."

When she got upstairs, she tried to read for a while but couldn't concentrate. The fight with her mother haunted her, and her cozy persimmon walls nagged her; she had left the precious *Book of Secrets* in the woods, and it was too dark to go looking for it. She decided to try to sleep and get up early to find the book.

Alone in the house after all that had happened, she felt too vulnerable getting undressed, so she unrolled her sleeping bag on top of her covers and crawled in as she was. As worn out as she felt, sleep wouldn't come. Finally she got out of her sleeping bag and went down the hall to check her mother's room. It was dark and empty, but her mother's things all around made her feel safer, so she got her bag from her room and spread it out on her mother's big bed. She was just fading out when a figure appeared, silhouetted against the doorway. "Mom?" she asked hopefully.

"Your mother is still gone," said the tall girl in the doorway. "I am tired. I have watched long enough."

"Watched for what?" Desi asked skeptically.

Cat opened her mouth to speak, looked troubled, and shut down, half closing her eyes. "For nothing," she said with a secretive, impenetrable look. "That is why I am stopping." She began to lie down on the bed at Desi's feet.

"What are you doing?" Desi said, shifting uncomfortably.

"Going to sleep," said Cat.

"There's no room," Desi complained. "You're too big." She still couldn't accept that this strange girl was her beloved cat. "Can't you sleep somewhere else?"

"Too alone," the girl said. She crawled up to the other side of the bed. Desi lay there for a minute, wide awake, thinking hard. *Mom, why did you leave? Was it something I did?*

Everything is so new and strange, but at least we are together. Startled by the thought in her head, Desi turned over and saw the girl, curled up on the bed with her back to her, hugging herself for warmth. Desi pulled the blanket from the foot of the bed and threw it over her cat.

In the middle of the night, she woke to the familiar feel of a warm body curled around her toes.

12

"*DEVALANDNEFARIEL . . .*"

Cat opened her eyes at the sound of her name, instantly alert. Her first impulse was to make sure that her Desi was within reach; here she was, safely wrapped in her sleeping bag, lost in her dreams. Sprawled across Callida's big bed, the girl seemed so much smaller and more helpless than Cat remembered.

Outside, a harsh wind howled at the window, but here in Callida's bedroom, everything was still. Except Cat. Every nerve in her new body tingled with the electric sizzle of magic—powerful magic, and close. *In my territory,* she realized, indignant.

Cat tried to slip out of bed without waking Desi, but the girl was stretched out on her robe, so Cat slipped out of that instead. At the bedroom door, she paused, listening to make sure that Desi was still asleep before she went out. The storm's fury intensified, battering at the walls, demanding to be let in. Cat shivered, doubly naked without her sleek fur coat. *I hate thunderstorms,* she thought. A desperate urge seized her to run and hide under the bed. But the threat of magic was too strong; she tiptoed out, closing the door behind her. Where she was going, Desi must not follow.

Once down in the kitchen, the hair on the back of her

neck stood up. Looking around, she saw slick gray tendrils of fog creeping out from under the door to the basement, like grotesque arms grasping for prey, and her heart began to race. *A Hole,* she thought with disgust. Wrinkling her nose, she stepped gingerly through the fog. Throwing the door open, she steeled herself to face the strange gray mist inside. The Hole, or Portal, as the witches called it, was a gateway to other worlds. She had to know who—or what—had opened it. It might be some monstrous otherworldly creature, or it might be Desi's aunt Lissa paying a visit.

There was only one way to find out. She plunged in.

Immediately she was bathed in gray—gray above, gray below, gray on all sides as far as she could see. The instant the fog surrounded her, a nagging doubt hit: Had she lost her powers as a Familiar along with her tail? She might never get out again, and Desi would be left alone, unprotected. Then she heard her name: "Devalandnefariel . . ."

It was Callida's voice, faint and far away. The witch sounded desperate. Cat slipped quickly through the fog.

"Devalandnefariel . . ."

Now the voice seemed louder, coming from just behind her. "Devalandnefariel, thank the gods," Callida whispered, barely getting the words out. The witch appeared out of the dismal fog, deathly pale. "I've been calling you for . . . I don't know how long." Callida staggered, trembling. "I'm cold."

"Foolish witch," Cat said. "Why do you travel the Mists without me?"

"I called you with a Summoning Spell, but you didn't come." Callida's body seemed thinner, stretched. "I need to know if my daughter is safe."

"Desi is safe—safer than *you*. I am watching over her."
Cat took hold of the woman's wrist. It was a rag, with little
weight or substance. "I did hear my name called, once, but I
did not feel any Summons. I came only because I sensed the
Hole opening up."

Something gnawed at Cat's new brain. Callida's spells
were not usually the kind that could be ignored. What storm
howled so loud it could drown out her Summons?

"We should go home to Desi now. You have been here
too long. You are fading."

"No!" Callida had no strength to pull away, so she dangled helplessly, almost on her knees. "Take me back the way
I came. To London—Lissa's house. I don't dare go home."

Cat was seething with curiosity but was used to co-
operating, at least some of the time; so, keeping a firm hold
on Callida's wrist, she led her through the fog cautiously, one
foot ahead of the other, letting her instincts lead her.
Abruptly, there it was: the Hole. She couldn't say why, but
she knew it was the right one. "Here. This is where you came
in. Jump."

It was almost too late. Callida wavered, far away, so Cat
dragged her to the edge, shoved her between the shoulder
blades, and leaped in after her.

At the bottom, she hit something hard and something
soft. The something hard was Callida, as cold and stiff as the
hood of the car on a winter morning. The something soft was
Desi's aunt Lissa.

"Oof!" the plump woman exclaimed while chafing her
sister's arms to get the blood flowing again. "Who are you?"

she asked Cat as she helped Callida to the other end of the sofa while Cat untangled her new monkey arms and legs. "Have we met?"

"Yes. I am Devalandnefariel the Familiar," Cat said.

"Oh, the cute little kitty. I never would have known you." Aunt Lissa eyed her, hands on hips. "Cally always could do the most marvelous things. You're younger than I would have thought."

Cat shivered. The Mists were unpleasant but not cold for a Familiar; here she was freezing.

Aunt Lissa clucked. "Why don't I get you something to put on, dear? My flat is always so chilly, even this time of year." As she hurried down the hall, her assorted bracelets, anklets, and necklaces jingling, her voice rose to a sugary pitch. "Pompy, sweets, look who's here! Your best friend!"

An ancient feline ball of fluff came plodding around the corner, its fur a motley of orange and white tipped with gray. The moment the animal saw Cat's new body, its hair bristled out as if its tail had been plugged into a light socket. Hissing madly, Pompy about-faced and waddled out as fast as her fat little legs could carry her.

Feeling naked for the first time, Cat tried to cover herself with her long, bare arms.

Aunt Lissa soon returned, tsking, "What's got under her fur?" She was carrying a pile of blankets to throw on her sister and a bright neon paisley muumuu for Cat. "There," Aunt Lissa said proudly, draping the dress over Cat's head and stepping back. "Classic. Looks good on you. A little roomy." The muumuu billowed around Cat like a tent. A shrill whistle startled her. "Oh, the tea," Aunt Lissa said, jangling into the kitchen.

Still rankling from the old cat's reaction to her, Cat turned sourly to Callida. "Why didn't you get Pompagloriana to guide you through the Mists?" she griped.

"Pompy? She's been Lissa's Familiar since we were teenagers. She's practically senile. I trust *you*." Callida threw off her blankets. "Tell me how my daughter is," she insisted.

"Desi is sleeping in your bed," Cat said. She curled up on the other end of the sofa. "She wants to know why you left us. I want to know, too."

Callida looked her straight in the eyes. "Devalandnefariel, if I tell you what the danger is, would you tell Desi?"

Cat met her gaze. "Of course," she said honestly.

Callida slumped. "Then I can't tell you."

"Then tell *her*," Cat said, feeling resentful. "I will bring her here."

"No!" Callida said. "It's far too risky."

"Without me to guide her, yes. You are only a witch; I am a Walker-Through-Worlds. I will bring her through safely." As she said it, Cat realized it was true; she had just done it, and she could do it again. Despite all the changes her body had gone through, she was still her Familiar self with her talents intact.

With a clanking of cups and jewelry, Aunt Lissa bustled in, carrying a tray. "Here we are, nice hot tea," she said soothingly. She handed a cup to Callida. "This is what you need. You too, missy." She held the tea tray out to Cat. "Do you take cream?"

The delicious aroma hit Cat's nostrils. "Yes," she said quickly. Ignoring the tea, she bent her head to lap greedily at the pitcher of cream. To Cat's dismay, Aunt Lissa let out a shriek of surprise and snatched the tray away.

Setting it down out of Cat's reach, she glared mildly at Callida. "I can't believe the chance you took," Aunt Lissa scolded her sister. "Thank the stars Devil showed up. Otherwise you might have been trapped in the middle of nowhere—like that time I tried to take a Portal to Hong Kong and ended up in Kansas, but worse! Really, what were you thinking?"

"I had to know that Desi was all right," Callida said, unyielding.

"How could she be, all alone in that northern wilderness? She should be here. I'm dying to see her again. It's been forever."

"We've discussed that. She's safer there. Besides, she's not alone; Devil is with her."

"But, Cally, her sitter is a kitty-cat." Cat bristled at the implication. "No offense, Devil."

"I know, I know, don't rub it in," Callida said, eyeing Cat critically. "What can I do? It will be all right. Desi is very responsible."

"Of course she is," Lissa went on brightly. "They both are, but we all know how that goes." She looked away dreamily. "The distractions of youth, you know: boys, heavy metal, piña coladas—"

"Don't be silly," Callida protested. "Desi is just a child."

"—nose rings, string bikinis, panty-line tattoos—"

Callida looked startled. She scowled suspiciously at Cat.

"—wild parties, chugging contests, all-night poker games—"

"Lissa!" Callida pleaded. "Stop!"

Her sister sighed, reliving past glories. "They'll be fine. You're only young once."

Callida shook her finger at Cat. "Your only job is to take care of Desi, understand? Don't leave her alone for a second unless she's safely in the house. No straying. No distractions. No visitors, especially male. Got it?"

Cat was feeling slighted. "If you do not trust me, why do I not bring her here with you?"

"I can't," Callida said grimly. "First of all, traveling by Portal is very risky. That's why I summoned you instead of her." Cat did not care for that, but she let it pass for Desi's sake. "Secondly," Callida said, "she can't be here. She can't be anyplace anyone knows her." At that, Aunt Lissa looked glum. "Look out the window," Callida prompted.

Cat put her nose close to the glass overlooking the street. "I cannot see anything," she said, exasperated.

"Look with your inner eyes."

Cat closed her eyes. Immediately she sensed it. "Something is watching us." She didn't know what it was, but she felt its relentless scrutiny.

"Every place Desi has ever lived is being watched," Callida warned her gravely. "Everyone she has ever known is a link to her."

Cat felt the hairs on the back of her neck rise. "Why my Desi? She has never done anything to deserve this."

Aunt Lissa said, "It's not what our Desi has done; it's what she might do if—"

"Lissa, be quiet!" Callida commanded.

"You know how I feel, Cally," her sister said. "I don't see what harm it could do to tell her—"

"I'll decide what's best for my daughter." Callida bristled with anger, but Cat sensed the fear underneath. When she spoke again, it was with tight-lipped control, squeezing out every word. "Some . . . *people* . . . might want to use her, make her do things she wouldn't—and shouldn't."

Cat was still confused. Callida was afraid of what her little Desi might do?

Callida continued, forcing herself to speak calmly. "I know you both want to help, and I appreciate it." She turned to her sister. "But the best thing you can do is what I asked you. Both of you."

Aunt Lissa clucked and got up stiffly, leaving the room without a word. Callida addressed Cat. "Go back and take care of Desi. She is perfectly safe; now that I'm here, no one can find her there. But we just moved to the States, and . . . there are ordinary dangers everywhere. She's still so young."

"For how long?" Cat said. "How long do I have to be like this?" She thrust her legs out from under the muumuu, scowling at her toes.

"Until I come back." Seeing the crestfallen look on Cat's face, Callida softened her tone. "It won't be long; I promise. I've set a trap, with me as the bait. The hunter will finally become the hunted. When the trap is sprung, I'll settle this business once and for all." Callida looked grim.

"And if it isn't?" Cat knew all about lying in wait. It was too often in vain.

"Then I'll come back, restore you to your proper form, and take us all away someplace where we can be safe together."

Cat was skeptical. "Is there such a place?"

Instead of answering, Callida turned away.

Aunt Lissa reentered the room, bearing a strange object. Callida took it and held it out to Cat. "Have you ever seen one of these before?" she asked softly. "Go ahead, you can touch it."

Cat sniffed it and then turned it around in her hands: a golden cat's head on a short, intricately carved shaft, its two enormous ruby eyes glowing bright. It tingled in her hands. "What is it?" she asked suspiciously.

"A device that lets me keep an eye on Desi," she said. "With this, I can see her anytime I wish."

Cat was puzzled. "If you have this, why did you risk traveling by Portal without me?"

"I needed to see you first," Callida said cryptically. She took the magical scepter back from her and stood up. "Time to go back." She waved her hands at the framed picture on the wall, a mountain landscape. The frame began to glow. From behind the hills, a gentle mist appeared, drifting slowly into the painted valley. Soon the painting disappeared, hidden by the Mists. "You know the way. Remember," Callida warned her, swallowing hard, "don't come here again, whether by plane or Portal. You might spoil my plans. And no matter what Desi says, keep her far away from here. She's much safer where she is." Cat could see the effort it took for Desi's mother to say those words.

Cat climbed up on the sofa, peering into the fog seeping from the open Portal. "What if she goes down a Hole without telling me, like you just did?"

"There's no way Desi can open a Portal on her own, thank the stars. Most witches can't do it at all, and even I couldn't until I was seventeen."

Lissa giggled. "But then you did it every night to sneak out to see Val—"

"Please, Lissa." Callida looked pained. "Don't worry," she continued to Cat. "Portals are difficult, especially without training, and I've been careful to avoid the whole subject of—"

"Black magic," Lissa whispered portentously.

"—risking using the world of elemental spirits for our own purposes." With a glance at the seeping gray mist, Callida seemed to realize that she was doing just that, for she abruptly changed the subject. "Devalandnefariel. Thank you for coming to help me. I need you. Don't leave Desi alone again. Please?"

Cat recognized the cry of a mother for her lost kitten. Her stomach felt like she had been drinking sour milk, but her role in her family was clear.

"Wait!" Aunt Lissa was waving a piece of plastic at Callida. "It's your credit card. What if they want to go to a movie or something?"

Callida took the card and slid it inside the muumuu's paisley pocket. "Devalandnefariel, I'm counting on you," she pleaded.

Cat leaped.

⋅₊⁺⋆⁺₊⋆

The trip back through the Land of Mists was normal, if anything to do with the world of spirits could be considered normal. Cat knew the way without thinking. That's what it meant to be a Familiar: to walk with confidence where even witches faltered and humans could not go at all.

Dropping down the Hole-That-Felt-Like-Home, she landed in her kitchen. It was just as she had left it, reassuringly dark and silent, safe from the howl of the storm outside. Cat yawned. In a few seconds, she would be snuggled at Desi's feet, where she always slept. No matter how new or strange the place they moved to, sleeping at Desi's feet made it home.

She reminded herself that Desi was not in her own room but had moved to her mother's big empty bed. *Poor little kitten. This is almost as hard on her as it is on me,* she thought.

"Let me go!" Desi's cry echoed down the hallway. *Her kitten was in trouble!*

Cat raced down the hallway from the kitchen to the front door as swiftly as she could on two legs. As she reached the entryway, she was shocked to see her Desi, out of bed, beating at a much larger figure. Her panic quieted when she got close enough to recognize that brainless, smiling face—it was only the golem, standing with its back to the front door. Desi hammered on its protruding belly, yelling, "Get out of my way! They're waiting for me!"

The golem took no notice. It stared blankly past her head, casually scratching under its armpit with the TV remote.

Cat hurried to take hold of her charge. "Why are you out of bed? You must not go out of the house without me," she said sternly. But Desi couldn't hear her. Cat realized Desi's eyes were closed—she was asleep.

From the other side of the front door, the wind howled. Still asleep, Desi struggled against Cat's grip. "Let me go. My friends are calling for me. They're waiting for me."

Cat held Desi tight as the wind beat fiercely at the door. After a few seconds, receiving no answer, the storm at last fell silent.

Desi shivered in Cat's arms.

"Come, little one," Cat said, leading her gently up the stairs to her room. "Whoever was calling, I know one thing— they were not your friends."

13

CAT WAS STARVING, tired, and out of sorts. Though the noise of the storm had passed, her fear that Desi might try to run off again kept her pacing the halls all night.

She didn't dare nap. In her old body, Cat could often sleep with her eyes open. Now when she slept, her senses shut down, leaving her defenseless. Humans were a puzzle. Was it normal for Desi to walk in her sleep? Or was there some strange witchery afoot? Cat couldn't tell; Callida's magic had muddied the tracks.

Toward daylight, Cat curled up in her favorite stuffed chair, tired out from too much thinking. Normally she was not one to chase imaginary rabbits, and the dawning light made her worries seem smaller.

She had hardly closed her eyes when Desi's footsteps on the stairs woke her. Desi seemed her usual self, as much as Cat could tell. Neither spoke much, which suited them both. After a breakfast of a quart of milk and a handful of Kitty-Bits, she joined Desi for a sunbath on the back deck. Cat sat as she was used to, tucking her long hind legs underneath her body. The crisp air nipped at her new toes.

Desi spoke. "What a night. I was so busy in my dreams I woke up exhausted." She sighed deeply. "As soon as the sun is bright enough, I've got to get Mom's book back. I hope it was all right, out in the woods overnight in that storm."

Cat remembered all the way back to yesterday, ages ago. Callida's secret book. For all she cared, the squirrels could bury it.

"It was wrong for Mom to run off like that, right after our fight. She didn't leave a note or anything. You sure she said she'd be back in a day or two?"

"She said that," Cat answered truthfully. At the touch of the sun, dew steamed from the grass. The rising vapor reminded Cat of the Mists. She shivered and hugged herself against the chill.

"Fall comes early here," Desi said aloud. "Hope you brought your winter coat."

Cat held out her hairless arm forlornly. "I don't have my coat anymore."

"I was joking," Desi said, examining her muumuu curiously. "Just a suggestion? You should put on a different robe. That looks like something Aunt Lissa would wear." She got to her feet. "I'd better find that book."

Cat winced as the gate banged shut. She closed her eyes against the rising sun. She desperately needed a nap.

Instead, she got up and trailed Desi around the woods, careful not to be seen. Desi was easy to hear, thrashing through the brush. After a long wait, she followed Desi's noises back to the house and watched her go inside—without the book. Relieved, Cat gratefully plodded upstairs for a nap.

When she woke, a glance at the sun through the window told her the day was half over. Remembering Desi's advice about clothes, she changed back into Callida's robe before going downstairs to the kitchen for some food. Desi must have heard her, because she came down a few seconds later to peer into the refrigerator.

"You know," Desi said carefully, as if she had planned out what to say, "I was in the woods looking for the spell book, while you were napping. I searched everywhere, but I can't find it."

Cat tried to avoid the subject by eating. She selected a promising can with a picture of a chicken on it. But though she pried at it with her claws, it wouldn't cooperate.

"So, anyway," Desi continued, "I was thinking, if you could help me find the book, I could use a spell to contact Mom."

Frustrated, Cat turned the can upside down, looking for a way in. Her stomach was growling at her. "That does not sound like a good idea," she said, recalling her persimmon fur. "I do not trust your spells."

"I tried to change you back," Desi protested. "You ran away. Anyway, I need to see Mom. Something's really wrong, or she wouldn't have just disappeared like that. I need to talk to her."

Cat instinctively knew that if Callida had thought it safe to talk to Desi, she would have, but it did not seem smart to say that aloud. But Desi's yearning struck her like a blow. She couldn't face it, so she turned her back on the girl.

Desi didn't take the hint. "Are you going to help me find the book or not?"

Wasn't her body language plain enough? Humans and their words. "No."

"Fine." Desi slammed the refrigerator door shut. She did

not sound fine. She sounded hurt. Cat almost gave in—she could easily sniff out the book—but she had a creeping feeling she had made a mistake showing Desi where it was hidden in the first place. Sometimes helping was no help.

They shared the kitchen in silence for several minutes while Cat struggled with her can of cat food. Finally, she gave up and handed it to Desi, who only scowled.

"Why should I help you?"

"I'm hungry."

Desi tossed the can on the counter. "You're human now—act like it," she snapped. "People don't eat that stuff."

"People?" Cat stopped chasing the can in surprise. "That's right. I am a people now. Forget this 'stuff'—I can get fresh fish at the market. I can eat a whole chicken if I want."

"Not without money you can't," Desi taunted her, leaning back against the counter. "They don't give you anything at the market unless you give them money first."

"Do you have money?"

"Not hardly any," Desi admitted.

"Is there anything *here* good to eat?" Cat asked hopefully.

"Mom has the fridge spelled to fill itself," Desi said. "Mostly healthy stuff—vegetables, spaghetti, casseroles." She stuck her nose in the fridge and pulled out a bag of carrot sticks.

"Bleahh," said Cat, sticking out her tongue at them.

"Besides," Desi said, crunching a carrot, "if I did have money, you'd just buy something gross, like raw fish. And I hate sushi."

"What's sushi?" Cat's curiosity was aroused. "Do cats like it?"

"I told you, raw fish, but it's mostly in restaurants, and we don't have the money for going out to eat." Desi grabbed a frozen dinner and stuck it in the microwave.

Cat sniffed it but turned up her nose when she saw the picture of vegetables on the box. "But some humans do go out to eat?" she asked. "Who? I need to learn these things."

Desi sat down at the kitchen table. She seemed to get over being mad now that she had a chance to teach Cat. "Well, lots of people go out to eat. Parents and kids, teenagers on dates. Kids mostly go out for hamburgers and things."

"I like hamburgers, I know; I've smelled them. Does Jarrett go out for hamburgers?" Cat licked her lips.

"Sure, I guess. Hey! Wait a minute. Forget it. No way Jarrett's taking you out to eat."

"Why not?" Cat smirked. "He likes hamburgers. I like hamburgers."

"He just can't is why," Desi said. "Girls like you have to go out with older boys—you know, like on a date."

Cat considered for a moment. "Bob looks older. Does he have money?"

"How should I know?" Desi jumped to her feet. "Oh, no. You"—she pointed a finger at Cat—"are *not* going out on a date with Bob."

"Why not?" Cat ticked off the list. "He is an older boy; he has money; he knows about sushi."

"Why not?" Desi waggled her hands in the air, as if groping for a reason. "Because," she finally declared, "you can't ask a boy out unless *you've* got money to pay for it, and you don't. So there." The microwave beeped. Desi retrieved her dinner and took it to the table.

Cat paced back and forth, toying with her plan. "Bob is a tom; I'm pretty sure," she said. "Yes, he definitely acted male. So, no problem getting him to do what I want." She thrust out her arms, arching her back in a long, luxurious stretch. "The real question is, sushi? Or hamburgers? Or maybe a whole, freshly killed chicken, with the heart and liver still attached." Cat licked her lips and started to purr. "Choices, choices, choices . . ."

She snatched a handful of Kitty-Bits and started to munch. Looking revolted, Desi turned her back to finish her meal.

Since Desi was safely busy inside the house, Cat took the opportunity to go outside. Crossing the yard, she sprang lightly onto the overhanging branch of the oak tree.

Desi stuck her head out the kitchen door. "Where are *you* going?" she asked, sounding suspicious.

Balanced on the branch, Cat recited, "I am going to find the older boy Bob and tell him to take me out where the sushi fish is and pay money for it." That was a lot of talking for Cat, so even though Desi shouted at her to stop, she tightrope-walked the branch, crossing the fence and leaping down onto the grass on the other side. Her ears picked up the sound of Desi opening first the gate to her yard and then the gate to this yard, so she didn't worry—she knew her kitten was staying close.

Jarrett was there, feeding the old dog, which took one look at her and slunk away, tail between its legs. "Cat," Jarrett said brightly. "Nice to see ya. Hey, storm keep you up last night? We had a tornado watch."

"I want Bob," she said. When Jarrett looked puzzled, she

continued. "I want him to take me where the sushi fish is so I can eat it. Does Bob have money?"

Jarrett grinned. "Bob? He's loaded. Delivers pizzas; he's rolling in dough. Is this like a date? Or is Desi going, too?"

Cat heard a grunt of surprise. She wheeled just in time to see her Desi, red-faced, vanish behind the open gate. "Yes," Cat said, loud enough for Desi to hear, "she cannot stay home alone." From behind the gate came Desi's yelp of protest.

Jarrett said, "So, if it's not a date, how about we all go?"

Cat considered. "It will be good. But I need Bob; Desi says so."

"Got it. He's the car and the cash. He's in the basement, practicing karate." Jarrett led her around the other side of the house to a low door set into the hillside. He opened it and hollered, "Hey, Bob, someone to see you!"

Bob's head popped out, and then the rest of him appeared, dressed in a white outfit with a brown belt. "You know better than to interrupt me in the middle of my katas."

Jarrett just grinned at him. Bob stared back. "What's so funny?"

"Oh, right." Jarrett motioned to Cat. "You'll have to come closer. He's blind without his glasses."

Cat moved in close, really close, until her face was inches from Bob's. "I want you to take me out to pay money for the sushi fish, and I will eat it. Okay?"

Bob's eyes grew round. "What!"

Cat frowned at him. "Did you not hear? Are your ears blind, too?"

Bob gulped. "You mean, go out, like, on a date?"

Cat considered. "Date" was a lot shorter, and they all seemed to use the word. "Yes. Date."

"Wha . . . when?" Bob stuttered.

"I am hungry now," Cat said.

"I think she means tonight," Jarrett said.

"Okay." Cat was very hungry, but she was used to waiting to be fed. "I will date tonight." Since there was nothing more to say, she walked away. But before she could swing up onto the branch that led over the fence, a commotion made her turn back.

"I've got to take a shower!" Bob was shouting. "What time exactly?" Jarrett shrugged. "Where's my glasses?" Bob struggled with the door handle. He yanked it open and tripped over the threshold. "I need my glasses!"

Jarrett was peering through the basement window, so, curious, Cat turned back to join him. Inside, Bob was flailing around the basement, throwing things in the air in a frantic search for his glasses.

"You won't catch me getting that crazy about a date," Jarrett said, shaking his head.

"He is just being male," Cat replied. "They get very excited about their food." She headed back to the tree. "When he has calmed down, bring him to my house. I am going to take a nap."

14

DESI STEELED HERSELF for a confrontation, biding her time in her own yard until Cat dropped from the oak branch onto the grass. "I'm *not* going out for sushi," she said in a loud whisper in case anyone next door was listening. "I hate fish, raw or cooked. And what do you mean telling *him*"—she didn't dare say Jarrett's name out loud—"that I can't stay home by myself?" She was so humiliated, her ears were burning.

"I am hungry," Cat replied calmly, without breaking stride. "You cannot stay here alone, so you must go with me to eat." Desi had to chase her into the house.

Once in the privacy of the kitchen, Desi folded her arms. "So you think you can ask Jarrett and not even ask me first? Well, you can forget it. I'm not going."

"Yes," Cat said with maddening calm. "We are not going now. We are going tonight."

"You can't tell me what to do. You are not my mother," said Desi, furious.

"No, I am not your mother. What a strange idea," Cat replied. "Your mother left us. Do you remember?" She straddled a seat facing the window.

"Only yesterday, and only for a day or two." Desi collapsed in a chair. She had never felt so alone in her life. She had to struggle to keep back the tears.

"What are you doing?" said Cat, who evidently could see out of the corner of her eyes. "Are you crying?"

"No, I'm not," Desi sniffed.

Cat sniffed back in reply. "I am the one who should be sad. Look at this body. I did not ask for this. It is all your mother's fault. She told me it is my job to take care of you, and that is what I am doing." Cat stood up. "I am going to nap on the big bed. You must not leave the house."

Desi's resentment boiled over. "I don't have to do what you say," she lashed out.

"I do not care what you do, as long as you do it inside the house." Cat turned her back and went upstairs.

Desi sat in the empty kitchen, terribly alone. She wasn't used to being alone. Her whole life, she and her mother had traveled around the world together, taking care of each other, and never, ever, had she not known where her mother was or when she was coming back.

"Mom, where are you?" she cried in frustration. Hearing the question spoken out loud gave her an idea.

She crept upstairs as quietly as she could. There was no peep from Cat in her mother's room. From a box marked OFFICE in the spare bedroom, Desi dug out a large plastic-rimmed hand mirror. Holding it out in front of her, she chanted, "Mirror, mirror, in my hand, answer true what I command." As she said the words, they struck her as childish; she wondered if she had been taught a kid's rhyme just as a joke. Would the mirror answer to anything? But those were not the questions she wanted to ask.

"Tell me where my mother is," she commanded the mirror.

The surface of the mirror wavered, rippling like water until words floated to the surface and firmed:

```
<Error H41Q9-212746, object or person
not found.>
```

"I know that—that's what I'm asking you. Where's my mother?" She missed the old mirror, which had answered aloud when she talked to it. It had gone silent last year after many years of service.

A long string of words appeared on the surface of the mirror:

```
<Error H41Q9-212746, object or person
not found. Rephrase search.>
```

This new model was not as wizard-friendly. "Why don't you tell me where my mother is?" Desi asked, frustrated.

```
<Error H41Q9-51212G, object or person
out of range. Search range of handheld
mirror limited to local household use
only.>
```

So her mother was too far away for this stupid mirror. She had asked her mother many times for a full-length mirror of her own, but of course Callida had said they were too expensive, and to wait until she was older. Now she had to think craftily. "Tell me how I can find out where my mother is."

The answer came quickly.

<Use a Finding Spell.>

Desi wanted to shake the mirror but was afraid it might break. "I don't *know* any Finding Spells." Then she realized this could be her big chance. In as deep and commanding a voice as she could manage, she ordered, "Tell me the Finding Spell."

<Error PDQ-6018, access restricted by Spell-Nanny. Password required. Please chant password.>

"Stupid mirror," she said. Her mother must have figured that she would try to use the mirror someday for more than just biology homework. But there had to be a way around it. She thought quickly. "Tell me where I can *find* the Finding Spell."

<The Book of Secrets.>

Her mother's book—of course! The mirror would show her where it was. Why didn't she think of that before? Running downstairs, she dashed through the kitchen but stopped with the back door half open. Cat had warned her to stay in the house.

Ha! She slipped out the door, across the yard, and through the back gate without one ounce of guilt.

At the entrance to the woods, she questioned the mirror in her hand. "Where do I find the *Book of Secrets*?"

<Under the fallen leaves.>

Patience, she told herself. *It's just a stupid mirror. You can make it do what you want.* "Tell me exactly where I go to find the *Book of Secrets.*"

In reply, an image appeared in the mirror—of tiny trees and a tiny Desi seen from overhead. A red blinking arrow pointed off the trail. "Gotcha!" Desi set off through the woods in the direction of the arrow. She had to dodge around some trees and other obstacles, but finally, in the mirror, she could see tiny Desi standing on the tiny red X. She kicked at the leaves near her feet. Worn brown leather appeared, intricately patterned. Desi breathed a sigh of relief, stuck the mirror in her back pocket, and rescued her treasure. She carefully brushed it off to look for damage, but it seemed unhurt. Then she retraced her path.

Back inside the house, she went straight up to her room, locked her door, and plopped down on her bed to study the book in private. "Finding Spell, come to Mama," she muttered, flipping the pages.

Fortunately, the book was alphabetical. Unfortunately, the spell covered the whole page and the next. It had never occurred to her that a spell could be so complicated. Her room-painting spell had been just one word and one gesture; this had fancy hand waving, weird poetry, and even potions. *This will take all day,* she fretted. *And I don't even know if I can pronounce some of these words.*

She consulted the magic mirror again, but it only kept asking for the password. Frustrated, she was just starting to dig deeper into the book when the doorbell rang.

Who could it be? Her mom wouldn't ring the doorbell. Then it hit her. The date. Bob. Jarrett. She ignored the bell, hoping whoever it was would go away, but the doorbell kept ringing. Reluctantly, Desi put down the book and went to her mother's room, where she found Cat stretched out on the big bed in the paisley muumuu.

"Your date's here," Desi said with her hands on her hips. "But I'm not leaving, and neither should you. You don't know how to act like a human girl."

Cat lifted her head from the bed. "But *you* do, so you must come, too."

Desi couldn't think of a good answer for that one.

The doorbell rang again. Cat sprang to her feet.

"Wait, let me get it," Desi said, holding up her hands to stop her. "A word to the wise? If it *is* Bob, don't come downstairs until you get dressed. People don't go on dates in a bathrobe—especially not in that awful neon tent you're wearing." Desi turned and bolted down the stairs to answer the door.

It was Bob, looking squeaky-clean in khakis and a button-down shirt. This time his hair was under control.

"Uh, oh, hi, uh, is your cousin, I mean, is, uh, you know, Cat?"

Desi gulped nervously. *Bob and Jarrett and me and . . . my cat?* She tried to think, but her brain was so overloaded all she could do was put on a big, phony smile and yell, "Cat! Bob's here!"

There was no answer. Not knowing what else to do, Desi invited him in. Bob crossed the threshold, stumbling over it in the process. They waited, Bob shuffling his feet, hands in his pockets, until something he saw made him come to attention. Desi turned around, expecting Cat, but instead she followed his eyes to the loud Hawaiian shirt in the recliner in the front room. *Oh, no,* Desi thought, *why didn't I make him wait outside?*

Bob looked curiously at the man inside the shirt, who was staring blankly at a blank TV screen. Desi hurried into the room. "This is, um, my dad."

To cover while she hunted for the TV remote, she gave the golem's foot a kick. It waved a meaty hand in Bob's direction. "Hi, how are you?" it asked in a gruff and hearty tone.

"Hi, uh, h-hello, Mr.—" Bob stammered.

"Have a nice day," said the golem, rotating back to the TV. There was no other word from the golem. It ignored Bob completely.

Bob seemed relieved to be ignored.

Desi finally found the remote. When the TV came on, two cuddly cartoon bears were singing. She hurriedly switched channels until she found a football game.

She had been standing guard over Bob because of her mother's rule never to let anyone past the entryway, but Bob seemed too shy to move, so after a long, awkward wait, Desi said, "I guess I'll check on Cat." Upstairs, she found Cat still in her mother's bedroom. The girl was locked in a death struggle with a baggy black wool sweater, and the sweater seemed to be winning. Eventually Cat's head popped out of the neck hole. Desi announced, "Bob's waiting."

Cat waggled her hips until the long sweater settled over her ankle-length flowered gypsy skirt. "Good. I am very hungry. We will go now."

The thought of Cat running wild at the sushi bar forced

her to follow, dreading every step, until she caught up with Cat in the entry.

When Cat saw Bob, she got straight to the point. "Good, now you will buy me sushi?" It wasn't really a question.

Bob stared at his feet and stammered, "Uh, yeah, uh, umm, sushi? Um . . ."

That was good enough for Cat. "I am very hungry." She pushed past him and out the door. When he scrambled to catch up, he bumped into her.

"Ow!" she cried, holding her bare foot in one hand. "Horrible monkey feet."

"Sorry," said Bob, staring at her legs. "Umm, you probably have to wear shoes in the restaurant."

"Shoes!" Cat said. "Horses need shoes." She closed her eyes. "First a monkey, now a horse. Paugh!"

Bob looked confused. "Are you hurt? Do you want me to get them for you?"

"No. Stay." Bob did as he was told. Cat slipped past Desi and disappeared into the house. She was gone so long Desi wondered if she had changed her mind; but at last Cat appeared, stepping gingerly down the porch steps in fuzzy pink slippers. "Shoes," she said, gliding past.

When she got to the street, Cat halted stiffly in front of the car, staring at it with an enigmatic expression. Bob, who had already gone around to the driver's side, waited for a moment, looking confused, and then rushed around to open the passenger door for her. But instead of getting in, she pulled back, tense and hesitant.

Desi wondered what Cat's problem was. The car was

compact but clean. Bob held the car door open, clearly puzzled as well.

After an eternity, Cat asked, "You want me to go in the car?" in a tone that sounded like she was asking, *You want me to jump off the cliff?*

"Uh, sure, yes, if that's all right?" Bob murmured. "Is something wrong?"

Desi felt sorry for him. He was starting to get that he was in way over his head.

Cat bent down and sniffed the car. She pulled back quickly and straightened up. "You will buy me sushi, all I can eat?"

"Uh, yeah," Bob stammered. "Sure, I . . ."

Cat jumped into the front passenger seat and sat very still. Before Desi could get in, Jarrett came charging up, opened the back door, and slid into the seat, panting. "Made it. Sorry, guys, I just got out of the shower. Someone was hogging the bathroom again." He shot a look at Bob, who blushed. Then Jarrett switched to his sunny grin. "Hey, Desi. Hey, Cat."

Desi, seeing no other choice, climbed into the backseat. Immediately, Cat hopped out of the front and slid in beside her, shoving her against Jarrett. "What are you doing?" Desi complained.

Cat huddled at her side without answering. Bob looked like he wanted to say something but didn't; head down, he shut the door and went back to the driver's side.

Desi was petrified. The backseat was tiny and cramped; practically her whole body was touching Jarrrett's. Jarrett just grinned apologetically and squirmed around to buckle up. She couldn't look at him. When she tried to push Cat over to get some room, Cat pushed back—and she was way stronger than she looked. Desi ended up practically sitting in Jarrett's lap. She was so close she could smell the soap from his shower. His long, wet hair was touching her neck.

Jarrett stayed silent the whole way, hands in his lap. She did, too. She didn't dare budge; she hoped her face wasn't as red as it felt. Cat sat hunched over, looking miserable.

An endless ten minutes later, they reached the mall parking lot and found a spot. Thankfully, the second the car came to a stop, Cat leaped out, letting Desi escape from the backseat. Cat stayed close on her heels as they went into the restaurant.

Samurai Sushi turned out to be just a counter and a row of booths with the usual paper lanterns, a hole-in-the-mall clinging to the outskirts of the main shopping area. Desi led the way, bracing herself for Cat's next move.

15

CAT COULDN'T RELAX until she was inside the sushi place. She had always hated riding in cars—it meant change, and change was bad. She tried not to think of moving or trips to the vet and concentrated instead on the smells.

It smelled delicious in here—what she could smell. She felt frustrated with her little nose and focused hard on her sense of scents. It took an effort, but she could make out fish; cooking oil; humans, of course; useless vegetables; acrid smoke—Desi had said the fish was raw. Were they going to ruin it with their fires again?

She followed a female human into the comfortable darkness at the back of the room and noticed that they were being led away from the windows, even though the room was almost empty. Did she want to sit in the window, where she had a better field of vision? She decided not. Too much newness— better to hide somewhere protected. The female led them to a high-backed box with a table between two short couches. Cat slipped quickly into a corner, making sure that Desi stayed next to her for mutual protection. The males tumbled in opposite her.

The female put things on the table in front of them, bared her teeth, said, "Enjoy your meal," and immediately left. A minute later, another female appeared, mumbling something

Cat didn't understand. Everyone was staring at Cat, so she decided to stare back at Bob, boldly.

Bob gulped. "Uh, I guess nothing to drink; just water for me, please, thank you."

Desi said, "Cat wants water, too, don't you, Cat?"

Water, Cat understood. "Water, and fish. Do not burn it first. Okay?" She bared her teeth politely like she had seen the humans do.

"Of course. We have the ahi—that's the tuna—and mahimahi, and the special today is swordfish. . . ."

"Yes." Cat was satisfied. It was there; she could smell it. Her tiny new jaws were salivating.

"The sampler, then," said the female, after a pause. The others spoke in turn, and she left.

Cat caught Bob looking at her again, so she stared him down; he quickly lowered his gaze to the table, turning red. Just as she thought: big as he was, he would offer no challenge when the food came. But when she tried to assert herself with Jarrett, he met her stare with a bold, curious look. *Like a playful young cat,* she realized, relaxing. She noticed he was darting glances at Desi, who was ignoring him by looking at the ceiling. *Bad strategy,* she thought. Young or not, males needed to be shown who's boss right from the beginning.

The female returned, bringing food. Cat cautiously drew in the delicious aromas from the dish set on the table before her. They had buried the fish in leaves and things, but it was there, just like she had imagined, and it smelled wonderful. She was sure that she could pick it out from its trappings. Now she understood the reasons for tables—humans in their awkward upright posture could easily bend their necks to reach their food. She put her nose against the meat and savored its sweetness, then gave a careful lick. Perfection. She scooped a tiny bite up with her tongue but lost most of it. This would take some practice. She opened her mouth, lapping out with her absurdly short, smooth human tongue, lost the piece of fish again, and sat up straight, frustrated but determined.

Without warning, Desi poked her with an elbow, making her jump. When she looked around warily to see what was wrong, she got a surprise: They were all using their paws to eat. Bob's head was bent, and his eyes were buried in the plate, so he did not see her watching him. He was using a tool in his paws, his "hands," to pick up his food. How bizarre! Cat could do that, too; she had her own hands and fingers, so she grasped her own tool and poked her food. It was difficult at first; she had to try several times. But finally she managed to get a portion of the fish off the dish and into her jaws. Amazing! How clever, these humans. She hadn't given them credit. Obviously they used this tool to separate out the real food from the mess of green stuff that cluttered up their plates. She neatly pried another mouthful of succulent flesh from the foul-smelling seaweed and bland rice. It tasted so good she almost chewed it before swallowing. She was in heaven.

Hurriedly Cat gobbled up all the meat before anyone else could snatch it from her, glancing up occasionally to make sure they were undisturbed. No one was near, but she got another surprise—Jarrett had picked up his water bowl and was pouring the contents down his throat. She thought he was going to choke or gag, but he just put the bowl down gently.

Cat knew then she was in a whole new world. She decided that if she had to look like a monkey, she would act like one, too. Grasping her own water bowl in her paws, she tentatively poured a little into her mouth. Immediately she burst out in a fit of coughing and choking. Desi tried to cuff her on the back like she had done something bad, but she fought her off.

"Are you okay?" Bob asked. He seemed worried.

Cat caught her breath. "Yes. Okay." She was determined to get this. If a mere human could do it, she could, too. She poured tiny drops of water into her mouth, just like lapping it with her tongue. Much better.

As she ate her good fish, Cat checked on the others from the corner of her eye. The two males were eating rapidly, each with one eye on their food and the other on her and Desi. That made sense: one careless moment and—*Phwppt!*—your dinner was in someone else's stomach. They didn't seem to be guarding against each other, though. Bob finished his food first but made no move to steal Jarrett's portion away from him, though as the stronger male he easily could. Was he sick? Cat waited to see if he regurgitated his meal, but he sat there unconcerned, looking at her with his round monkey eyes. This puzzled her until she realized they were family, just like she was with Desi. Family she understood. They might tussle with one another, but when it came to the important things like food and safety, they were one against the world.

Desi had hardly touched her food—understandable, with

all the changes they had been through. Cat chided herself to be more kind. She had been so young when she was taken away from her own mother that she hardly remembered her, but the pain of losing her was still strong inside her gut. To show her sympathy, she shared some of the fish out of her own mouth, dropping it onto Desi's plate when no one was looking.

···*·*·*·*

Desi swallowed hard as she watched Cat bat a piece of tuna around with her fork, playing with it before she went in for the kill. *She's still a cat inside,* Desi thought. *I'm on my first date, and I'm double-dating with my cat.* She took a deep breath. *Chill out. It's not really a date. Jarrett's just here for the sushi.* She risked a glance at Jarrett, and quickly looked away. He was smiling at her.

"Anyone up for hanging out at the mall?" he offered. "Might as well—we're already here. You can check it out before school starts."

The tempura chicken in Desi's stomach began to dance around. Between worrying about her mother and keeping Cat out of trouble, she was too nervous to enjoy herself. Queasy, she pushed her plate away.

Seeing that Desi had finished eating, Cat declared, "I am not hungry anymore. We can go now."

Bob looked up, surprised. "Uh, now? Cat, uh, do you . . . ?"

Cat met his gaze with her piercing green eyes. "The food was good. Good Bob."

Bob deflated like a punctured tire, but he didn't give up. "Uh, do you want to, you know, like, a video or something?"

"No, I have eaten enough," she replied.

"Thank you, oh, thank you," Desi muttered under her breath. Jarrett looked at her earnestly. He seemed disappointed.

Suddenly Desi felt a little disappointed, too.

"We are going now," Cat said, practically pushing Desi out of the booth.

"Just a sec," Bob said, pulling out his wallet. "I have to pay the check."

Back at the car, Desi realized she couldn't possibly go through another trip like the first one, no matter how nicely Jarrett acted. She stood her ground. "It's too crowded in the back for three," she declared. Cat looked sullen.

Jarrett broke the stalemate. "I'll ride up front with Bob," he said with an exaggerated air of martyrdom. "I'm used to it. Besides, when I get my learner's permit, he'll be the one riding next to me."

He slid into the front seat, and Desi breathed a sigh of relief. But on the way home with Cat beside her, watching the back of Jarrett's head while he went on about the mall, she couldn't help thinking that the wrong person had changed seats.

16

WHEN THEY PULLED up in front of the house, Cat was the first one out again, leaping to the sidewalk before the car came to a complete stop. Bob scrambled around the front of the car to stop her before she could get inside the house. "Um, Cat, you know, maybe we could, you know . . ." He clearly still had hopes for this evening, but as Cat watched him impassively, he petered out. "If you liked it, we can go back anytime," he finally blurted.

"Tomorrow. I will eat again tomorrow," she said.

Bob brightened. "So, then, you know, like, tomorrow night?"

"Wait a minute." Desi wasn't sure she could handle another night like this so soon. "You'd have to ride in the car again," she warned Cat.

"The car." Cat looked upset, as if she hadn't thought about that, but then she gave in. "Okay, in the car."

"Well, without me this time," Desi said. "No more Japanese for me."

"There's plenty of other kinds of food at the mall," Jarrett cut in. "Anything you want."

Desi felt torn. It had been her first dinner date; she had enjoyed it when she wasn't too nervous. Amazingly, Cat hadn't ruined everything. So far the boys seemed to like her no matter how weird she acted. But it was too risky—she might go catty at any moment, and with her mother gone, Desi was responsible. "Sorry," she replied. "Count me out."

"You cannot stay home alone," Cat countered. "Your mother said I must watch out for you, remember?"

Desi couldn't believe she said that, right in front of the boys. She felt her face go red. She opened her mouth to protest, but nothing came out. It couldn't get any more embarrassing.

Yes, it could. Cat said, "Now Desi and I must go into the house to sleep."

Desi stared at her, mortified. "It's not even seven yet."

"Your bedtime is seven p.m.?" Jarrett asked Desi, looking shocked.

She felt her cheeks burn. "Of course not," she declared. "But I have a whole list of things to take care of. So much to do, you know, with Mom gone and all."

"Okay, then, catch you tomorrow?" Jarrett asked cheerfully. He looked so relaxed and inviting at the same time. He made it all seem easy, all of them going out together, just when she had decided it was too risky.

"Absolutely," she said. "Tomorrow. The mall. You can count on it."

Jarrett's face lit up.

Bob still looked dejected. "If I went to bed this early, I'd be up all night," he pleaded to Cat.

"Yes," Cat said. "Up all night." She moved in close to Bob. "There are more important things to do in the dark than sleep." Her cheek grazed his. "Happy hunting, Bobcat," she purred.

Jarrett raised his eyebrows. Desi led Cat into the house before she could do anything else embarrassing.

"Bobcat," repeated Bob, in a daze, as Desi closed the door.

⋅₊⁺₊⁺

Desi sat on the edge of her bed, waiting impatiently for Cat to go to sleep on her mother's bed in the next room. In her mind, she could still see Jarrett, with his laughing blue eyes and sympathetic grin. Even when Cat treated her like a baby, he had acted like she was important.

She wished she could tell her mother about tonight. She wished her cat was little again. She had to get her life back to normal. Desi missed her mother so badly she ached.

What was she waiting for? She had the *Book of Secrets*, didn't she? Slipping the book out from where she had hidden it under her mattress, she flipped through its pages, ignoring the absurdly complicated finding spell. She was searching for inspiration and found it under *S: A Spell for Summoning*. Desi didn't just want to find her mother; she wanted her to come back. This was much better: short and sweet, just two words of power to learn and no lizards' gizzards required. It needed a picture drawn on the floor, but she was good at art.

Since she couldn't draw on the carpet and wanted more privacy from Cat, anyway, she gathered up the book and the magic mirror and tiptoed down into the kitchen. Once she found a Magic Marker, she tossed aside the braided rug in the middle of the kitchen floor and began to copy from the book.

Excited as she was, halfway through, she had second thoughts about marking up the floor. Luckily it was a washable marker; she tested with a finger and it wiped right off.

She finished her careful copy and checked the book. It seemed simple enough—a five-pointed star with strange insignia at each point. The book called the star a Portal. Perfect.

Next: *It is recommended to place a piece of the person in the center.* It didn't make sense—if her mother was here to give her something, Desi wouldn't need to summon her in the first place. She decided to skip that part.

The gesture was easy, just curling a finger, but she practiced the tongue twister, *Conjurgalus Visitatem,* several times. Then she skimmed over the small print at the end:

Warning: Misapplication or other misuse of this spell voids all warranties and can lead to disaster.

It was less scary than the warning on her toothpaste tube, so she ignored it.

Kneeling on the floor just outside the Portal, she took a deep breath, shivering with excitement. Then she let the breath out slowly, the words coming with it: *"Conjurgalus Visitatem Callida."* She crooked her finger.

Inside the Portal, a tiny flame appeared, flickering like the tip of a candle. Smoke rose around it, a swirling haze that seeped out toward the edges of the drawing. Desi tensed up, thrilled. She had done it. This was no simple colorizing spell—this was magic only a powerful witch could do.

The smoke reached the outlines of the Portal and stopped, filling the area inside. It thickened within its boundaries into an ugly stew; then it began to boil, erupting and folding in on itself. Slowly, the dark, roiling mass coalesced, taking form. The shape was crude at first, wavering at its edges, but after a few minutes, Desi could make out a smoky face, a head and shoulders, and a body—a girl or woman sitting on the ground, cross-legged, in the center of the star. The smoke solidified; the gray mass blossomed into colors. Now Desi could see the face clearly—not her mother's. It was the face of a girl.

"Hello," said the girl. She looked oddly familiar. She could have been in Desi's class at school; she seemed to be the same age and size, with the same brown hair as Desi. She was smiling. "Who are you?"

"Awesome," Desi said. She had summoned this girl with magic! It took her a moment to collect herself. "Um, hi, my name is Desi. Do you know where my mother is?"

"No, I'm all alone here; in fact, I'm lonely," the girl said. She reached her fingers tentatively to the edge of the Portal, then pulled back. "I don't have anyone to talk to where I am."

"Where is that?" Desi asked. She had done something marvelous, but she wasn't sure what.

"I like your house," said the magic girl, looking around the kitchen. She brushed her bangs out of her eyes. She looked so much like Desi that they could have been sisters, except for her eyes—they were glowing embers. "Would you like to have some fun together?"

"Sure, I guess. I thought I was summoning my mother. Do you know her? Her name's Callida."

The girl shook her head sympathetically. Then she brightened. "Do you like magic?" she asked.

Desi couldn't help bragging. "Yes, I'm a witch. I performed this spell."

"Awesome. You're really good." Her expression lit up. "Hey! We can do magic together! All you have to do is let me out."

"How?" Desi was puzzled.

"With your finger. Just wipe out any line of the Portal. It'll be great!"

It sounded great to Desi. Many times, when she was younger, she had dreamed of hanging out with another witch her own age, someone to share secrets with. She had always had friends, but . . .

"Okay, just like this?" Desi put her finger on the line and started to wipe it away, then stopped.

"Go on," said the girl.

Desi thought hard. She was supposed to be finding her mother. And when she did, what would her mother say? Desi doubted she would like the idea of bringing a magical girl in the house while she was gone. What if Desi got grounded, magically speaking? "I sort of don't have time right now," she said to the girl, who seemed eager to get out. "I have to find my mom."

"I know lots of ways to find people," the girl said. "Let me out and I'll help you."

"If you tell me your name, I can call you when Mom gets back," Desi said, starting to get worried. Her first impression had been mistaken—the girl was plainly older than she was, and her frown made her look gaunt and severe.

"Don't you want to find your mother? You'll never do it without me," the girl said sternly. Her face reddened with anger.

"Whoa," Desi said, startled. "I didn't exactly invite you here, you know." Or maybe she had, by accident. She decided she just wanted to finish this. "Or if I did, I'm sorry," she said, trying to be polite. "You have to go now so I can use this spell again. Sorry."

"You don't know what *sorry* is," snarled the girl. "Yet." She was definitely older than Desi had first thought, and bigger. Wisps of her hair began turning to smoke, swirling around her like a miniature tornado. A gray tendril reached the place where Desi had smudged the line with her finger, probing the boundary. The finger of smoke inserted itself in the tiny crack, trying to wriggle through.

Desi looked up in horror to see the girl's face melting. It sagged like gray mud. Her grotesque features pulsed, her nose and cheeks erupting in spouts of black smoke.

Desi knelt on the floor, spellbound, as the creature dissolved into smoke, growing into a black cloud that filled the Portal to its borders. When she felt something hot on her knee, she looked down to see that a tendril of smoke had wormed its way through the tiny gap. Her skin burned where it touched her. And more greasy black smoke was wriggling through.

Desi jumped to her feet. "Go away!" she shouted, but the thing had no ears to hear her.

Searching around for help, she spotted the magic mirror on the table and snatched it up. "What do I do?" she demanded.

The mirror answered with a long string of numbers. Before she could ask it a better question, the smoke rose, encircling her outstretched hand. As it touched the mirror, the glass clouded, turning black. Frightened, Desi batted the mirror at the smoke, trying to fan it away, but the dark mirror began to glow bright red, burning her hand. With a cry of pain, she flung it to the floor, where it shattered with a crash.

The smoke was still forcing its way through the crack, billowing upward to form a new cloud outside the Portal.

Desi seized the braided kitchen rug and began to beat at the smoke. "Go. Away. And. Don't. Come. Back," she said, banging the thick rug down as hard as she could. At the last stroke, she flung the rug down over the Portal, covering it. It lay flat, with only a few last stinking strands of smoke in the air.

Desi waited, not daring to breathe, but there was no movement from the rug. After a few long seconds, she took a deep breath and broke out coughing. "Oh, man, oh, man," she said, clearing her throat with a drink from the kitchen faucet.

A strong whiff of something burning made her turn back to look at the rug. It still lay flat on the floor, but this time smoke rose, not from the edges, but from the center. The innermost braided circles glowed red-hot; as she watched, the fabric charred black and crumbled into ash. Flames erupted from the steadily growing hole in the middle, actual fire, dancing and spreading in a small circle.

From within the circle, as if from under the floor, a head emerged. Just a head—a melted, twisted skull with flaming hair and glowing eyes. It turned about, searching, until the eyes—coal-black with burning centers—found Desi. The mouth gaped as if to speak, revealing fangs of fire; the only sound that came out was the hissing of flames.

Desi watched, hypnotized, as slowly the head rose into the air on a pedestal of fire. The flames spread until they burned higher than she was. The intense heat stung her face. The flames took on a vaguely human shape—a slim body; flickering arms and legs; and, above all, that awful face, mouth gaping as if trying to scream. Desi was too stunned to move.

The creature extended fiery arms toward her, at first tentatively, then, finding no resistance, thrusting at her with claws of fire. Desi tried to get away but backed up against the sink, trapped.

Suddenly a screaming black blur swiped at the flame. Long black hair blocked Desi's view; a bright flowing robe blocked the heat. Cat hissed and snarled, pouncing at the flame, then leaping back.

"Get water!" she yelled. "That thing that spits water behind you!"

She snarled again and the flame thing retreated a little, only to roar back with searing heat.

Desi was shocked but not too much to act. It took her only a moment to get what Cat was talking about. She cast about behind her for the kitchen faucet and pulled out the sprayer. Flipping on the water, she aimed a jet past Cat at the fire.

It was only a fine spray, but as it struck the flames, the creature acted as if it was in pain, writhing and shrinking away. The monster held up arms of fire, but it had no protection, and it screamed soundlessly with a burning tongue. Desi trained the spray on the creature like a firefighter with a hose, following the flames down to the ground. Soon it was formless and shrinking fast. Now the only hissing came from the water on the flames.

Cat hovered silently, eyes blazing with fury. The fire shrank, wavered, and went out.

"Nasty things," Cat said. "They hate wet more than I do. It burns them like fire."

"What *was* it?" Desi asked, holding the spray steady to soak the steaming rug.

"A fire thing. A demon." Cat hunched over, shuddering. "They smell bad."

"Is it dead?"

"Was it living?" Cat sniffed at the soggy ashes. "I don't think so. It's tricky."

"Can it come back?"

"Not if you get rid of the Hole," Cat said.

"The what?" Desi asked, confused. She was shaking so hard she could barely stand.

Gingerly, Cat pushed the scorched, sodden carpet aside with her foot. Only half of the Portal drawing was still intact beneath the mess; the rest had been wiped away by the beating of the rug. "The Hole, the gateway to the demon's world. Your mother calls it a Portal. Clean this away. All of it. Then it cannot come back."

"How do you know so much about these things?" Desi asked.

"Your mother sends me to them with messages sometimes," Cat said. "A foul place. And nothing smells right." Parts of her hands were singed red and raw. She licked them tenderly.

"I . . . thanks," Desi said. "I just wanted to . . ."

Cat didn't look at her. She was shivering all over, and not from cold. With one motion, she pulled the sodden muumuu over her head and threw it on the floor, disgusted. "You made me wet." She pointed her nose at the pile of charred rug, muddy soot, and broken glass. "You did the mess—clean up the litter." She headed for the stairs, stepping carefully around the wet spot on the floor. "Witches," she hissed to herself.

Desi resented being ordered around, but she was still in shock and a little ashamed. How could her spell have gone so wrong? Wasn't she a real witch? She had never heard of a girl who turned into flames before. Why hadn't her mother told her about Portals and demons? Was she ever going to be able to do real magic?

Desi didn't know what to think, but she did feel grateful to Cat for coming to her rescue, so she gulped back her resentment and picked up the broom. As she swept the shards of mirror into the trashcan, a broken, angry face glared back at her from each jagged piece—the flame-girl's face.

Shocked, Desi dropped the broom and trash can. Sharp glass spilled onto the floor. Cautiously, she peered into the pieces of mirror again. It took her a long moment to accept the truth. It was her own face reflected in the glass. The girl in the Portal had looked exactly like her.

17

LATE INTO THE night and all through the next morning, Desi lay on her bed with the image of the fire-demon burning in her head, pouring over the *Book of Secrets,* trying to figure out what went wrong. The trouble was, the spell book was written like a recipe book—it told you what to do but didn't explain how or why.

Even more confusing, the book's introduction mentioned *The Four Paths to Power, Ascending in Potency,* and she had no idea what those were. Her other texts mentioned only two kinds of magic: spells, which were based on the power of words and ideas to create reality, and potions, which were based on the magical properties inherent in material things. But she found it suspicious that none of the other magical texts spread out around her mentioned any drawings on the floor or flaming girl-demons wearing her face. Something told her this wasn't a coincidence; this had something to do with the kind of magic her mother never talked about— "dark magic." And was there a fourth, even more potent, kind of magic?

She knew the Web wouldn't be any help. People like her mother were busily scouring any real info about magic off the Net as soon as it appeared. She had looked up "witches" and "magic" many times when she was younger, only to find offers for psychic readings and astrological fortunes.

Frustrated but determined, she decided to consult the only person around who knew anything about this stuff. Cradling the *Book of Secrets* in her arms, she went next door to her mother's room.

As she entered, Cat, dressed in the same outfit she had worn to the restaurant the night before, instantly raised her head from the bed where she had been napping. Sitting down at the other end of the bed, Desi offered her the book. "Can you explain some of these spells?"

"No," Cat said without looking.

"Why not?"

"I do things, but I cannot explain them. I do not know witches' tricks. I simply do what I do."

"So you can *do* magic, but you don't *know* magic?" Desi tried to hide her frustration. It was plain Cat wasn't a witch. In fact, from the way she was licking the back of her hand, it was clear she wasn't even really human. "Great, so now you can talk, but you can't explain anything. What's the point of being human, then?"

"I don't know," Cat said seriously. "Can you tell me?" She got to her feet, stretched, and examined her body with a sour look. "When I was myself, I ruled my territory; my food was waiting for me; I didn't need clothes with my beautiful fur coat; my senses were sharper; I ran faster on four legs; and whenever I wanted to cuddle, I just crawled into your lap."

For once, Desi understood exactly how this strange girl felt. "Well, it's hard on me, too. I'm more alone this way than if Mom hadn't changed you. Where'd my little kitty go?"

Cat got on all fours and crawled toward her. "I am still here." She tried to climb into Desi's lap.

"What are you doing?" Startled, Desi tried to push the girl off, but she was way too heavy. "You're too big. You're hurting me. Get off." A panicky feeling swept over her. She finally twisted out from underneath and stood up. "You're not my little kitty anymore. I wish you were. I miss her."

Cat curled up on herself, looking forlorn. "I miss me, too," she said quietly.

Desi gulped. As hard a time as she was having accepting this, she knew it had to be harder on Cat. Picking up her book, she said, "Don't worry, Mom will be back any day now, and everything will be fine again." Cat shut her eyes, blocking out the world. To cheer her up, Desi added, "You hungry? Bob will be here soon to take us to the mall. You'll like that." Cat opened her eyes, looking skeptical.

Leaving Cat to her nap, Desi returned to her room to study her witchcraft. If Mom didn't show up soon, she was determined to dig through the book of spells until she found a way to get her mother back herself.

⋆⁺⋆⁺⋆

On a sunny stretch of asphalt a little after one o'clock that afternoon, Bob eased the car into a parking space outside the mall. "Okay, here's the plan," he said to Cat. "While the kids pick up Jarrett's soccer cleats, we run in and get a bite at the sushi bar, and then we'll meet them later at the food court." It was a long speech for Bob; clearly he had been practicing.

Before Desi could object to being called a kid, or object to being paired up with Jarrett, Cat said, "Desi must stay with me, and I stay with Desi."

··⋆129··⋆

Desi didn't like that much, either, but Bob spoke first. "But if we just pop in for a bite . . . ?"

"One bite will not be enough," Cat replied. "I am very hungry."

"Okay." Bob threw his hands up, surrendering. "So we all go to the shoe store, then we all go to the sushi bar."

Desi sighed inwardly, but Cat deserved a break. And, really, how bad could it be?

"It is decided," Cat said. "First shoes, then raw fish. It will be good."

·₊*·₊*

Under a high roof dotted with skylights, Desi stopped in the mall's entrance to take it all in. She hadn't been in a mall for years, and never one as big as this. Trees under glass, miles of shops, acres of shoppers roaming the tile amid flashes of light and color; she was impressed. But not as much as Cat.

Cat had frozen just inside the doors as if hypnotized, bombarded by the play of light from the skylights, the echoes of the voices of a thousand shoppers, and the music from the loudspeakers. Everywhere there was motion competing for her attention. She couldn't fix on any one thing; she turned her head from side to side trying to catch it all at once. Cat was dazzled.

Her nose twitched at the enticing odors of food in the air. "Why didn't you tell me?" she asked reverently, looking as if the sky had opened up to reveal paradise.

"What?" asked Desi.

"This. I never knew. All this time, it was just past those doors."

Jarrett came up. "You should take a look around. It's really great—especially the food court," he said eagerly. "I can get my own cleats," he told Bob. "You show Cat around. Desi and I'll meet you by Chicken Lickin'."

"Chicken Lickin'?" said Cat in awe. She flicked her tongue across her lips.

"Great," Jarrett said, taking that for a yes. "See you guys there. You want to, Desi?"

Did she *have* to babysit Cat to make sure she didn't get into trouble? Or could she get out on her own for once? She sneaked a glance at Jarrett. He had an excited glint in his eye. Her spirits soared, but she was careful not to appear too eager.

"Sure." She shrugged. "Why not?"

Five minutes later, a quarter-mile from where they'd started, Cat was ricocheting down the main mall drag. She moved fast, darting from one display to the next, reaching out a hand only to pull it back, enticed and afraid. The stalls in the center of the aisle attracted her the most. She stopped, mesmerized, as a flying saucer hovered in the air inches from her nose. "As seen on TV," a nearby salesman exclaimed.

She quivered, shivered, tensed. Before Bob could say anything, she exploded, batting the UFO to the ground. She poised above it, daring it to fly again.

"Hey!" yelled the salesman.

"Well, you shouldn't fly those things in people's faces," Bob said, squeezing in between the salesman and Cat, but Cat, who had lost interest now that the saucer was dead, quickly moved on. She dashed from window to door, dodging and darting between slower shoppers. Bob followed, apologizing continuously as he bumped into a steady stream of traffic.

Next, Cat's eye was caught by several cute little animals waddling and somersaulting on a table behind a large glass window. Cat froze, mere inches away from the glass. Inside, a little girl playing with the animals looked up and smiled, holding out a tiny bird with yellow feathers for Cat's approval. Cat flashed her teeth and looked around for a door in the wall of glass. Spotting it, she slipped inside.

The little girl set the bird back on the table. It fluttered around, hopping and squeaking. Cat couldn't take her eyes off it. She snuck up carefully, gently, so as not to frighten it. Closer, a few feet, she was within striking distance now: she pounced, sweeping the bird into her mouth with one lightning move.

The little girl jumped back and began to cry. Cat, her mouth full, retreated through the door with her prey. She almost clawed Bob as he caught up to her in front of the shop.

"What's the matter?" he said, looking worried, seeing her bulging cheeks. "Why were you in that toy store?"

Something was very wrong. The bird was still moving, but it tasted terrible. "Paugh!" She spat it out onto the floor, coughing to get the taste out of her mouth.

Bob looked revolted. Cat turned stiffly and walked away. "Jarrett was wrong," she said, still trying to spit out the plastic feathers. "Not all food here is good."

Desi was surprised at how quickly Jarrett got his shoes. He didn't even try them on, just pointed, asked for his size, and handed over his money. Another difference between girls and boys.

They set off together down the main hall, a high, wide, double-decker promenade filled with shoppers. There was no sign of Cat or Bob; they had already vanished into the crowd.

She was just thinking how odd it was to be walking with him—no Mom or Aunt Lissa or teachers, just the two of them alone together—when he surprised her by saying, "This is great. I never get to do this."

"You must come here all the time; you live right nearby."

"Yeah, but never alone—I mean, you know." He grinned at her. When he smiled, his whole face lit up, making his blue eyes sparkle.

"School starts next week," he mock-groaned. "What grade are you going to be in?"

She had to think. "I'm not sure. The schools are always so different."

"I bet you're in eighth, like me. That's the only good thing about this year—we'll finally be the oldest." They were passing all sorts of shops, but he paid them no attention. "So, France, huh? Cool. What was that like?"

Pressure was building up inside her, a strange feeling. She almost started to tell him about what it was like being a witch and traveling all over the world, and how she wanted to learn magic and have her own life but how worried she was with her mother gone—maybe even tell him about being afraid of being alone but feeling okay here, walking beside him.

But inside, she heard her mother's warning: *Be careful; they don't like it if you're too different.* She picked her words carefully before she spoke. "You know, school, my mom's job. Paris was fantastic." She caught herself. "I mean, if you like big cities. You had to speak French."

It got her off the hook. Jarrett started talking about his recent trip to Quebec and went on from there. But the pressure in Desi's chest wouldn't go away.

₊₊*₊*

Drunk with the wonder of the world, Cat danced down the aisles, drawn by one shining, twirling thing after another—whirling, spinning, jaws wide-open, senses reeling.

Bob chased her, looking nervous.

From inside a brightly lit store window, a menacing figure glared at her, a life-sized photo of a human girl in black, brandishing cat claws, head masked by a hood with cat ears. Cat approached the thing like she would a mirror. It was like her, but not. She saw the tight shorts, the cropped top, the bare belly. It challenged her—sleek, muscular, feline.

She swung around to scan the passing crowd. For the first time, she really paid attention to the young females and how they dressed. They weren't all the same or all different. Some had pants, some skirts, but none of them, none at all, wore clothes like hers—they wore far less. She scrutinized her own baggy black sweater and full-length flowered skirt. Now their clothes made sense. So much easier to move, so much more freedom.

She stalked through the crowd, wriggling out of her skirt, never breaking her stride as it dropped around her ankles. *Humans are like so many kinds of animals,* she thought.

Today she was a snake, shedding her skin. Stepping gracefully over the skirt, she continued on, unburdened and free, wearing only her long black sweater.

Out of the corner of her eye, she caught Bobcat staring at her legs, his face beet red. Or was it her skirt he wanted? The big male was hovering near the skirt as if to pick it up. If he liked it so much, *he* could wear it. Cat kept moving. She couldn't care less.

From somewhere nearby, delicious scents tickled her senses. Catching their trail in the air, she began to step carefully, head up, legs raised high, sniffing deeply. Entranced, she paced in slow motion through the crowds, tracking the smells to a long row of shops with a dazzling array of foods. To her delight, she spotted chicken, beef, pork, even tuna. She glided to the nearest display, where the aroma of fresh meat sang to her.

"Can I get you something?" Bob asked, running to join her.

"No need," Cat replied. "I can get it myself." She waited until the female behind the counter had turned her head, then, leaning over the glass, she flicked one paw into the tuna salad, quickly popping a handful into her mouth. It was perfect—fresh and delicious. She was even getting to like the stuff they mixed in with it.

Bob looked shocked. "Don't do that!" He glanced around crazily to see if anyone had noticed, but Cat had already spotted the fried chicken at the next stall and dashed away. This time she chose speed over stealth. As she rushed past, her arm snaked out to snatch a chicken leg. Clutching her prize, she streaked through the tables and darted down the steps nearby. Spotting a big tree in a box, she quickly slipped out of sight between the concrete planter and the wall.

Bob poked his head over the edge.

"It's mine," Cat snarled, overcome with hunger. She bared her teeth around the chicken leg. "Get your own."

Bob raised his hands submissively. "Okay," he said. "I'll get a table?"

In seconds, Cat had cleaned off the leg bone. She licked her lips and peered around the planter. Bob was seated at a table a few feet away with a tray of food. He looked lonely. Cat felt a pang of guilt—Bobcat would never try to steal from her. Bobcat had fed her sushi. She slunk over to the table and sat down on the floor beside him. To make up, she rubbed her cheek and shoulder up against his leg. Bob stiffened.

"Don't! I mean, get up!" He pulled her to her feet, looking around anxiously. "Sit down!"

Cat sat on his lap. She rubbed her cheek against his hair. It smelled sweet, like flowers. Bob didn't move. The aroma of honey-glazed chicken aroused her appetite, so she delicately plucked a piece of it off his tray and popped it into her mouth.

"Delicious," she purred, licking her fingers. "This place is better than catnip."

Safe and warm on Bobcat's lap, she turned her attention to the many humans sharing the room with her. She had never paid close attention to them as individuals before— without their cars, they weren't a threat—but now she used her new brain to sort them out. It wasn't easy. Crowded together, with their dangling limbs and flat faces, they blended into one alien mass. They were so unfamiliar to her that they all looked alike.

She concentrated. Some were standing, the rest sitting; some ate hungrily, while many were chattering away. She realized that they were all gathered here to feed. Of course! A feeding grounds! Now she could tell the humans apart. Over there, a herd of plump cows grazed placidly at their table. Nearby, a pack of young wolves greedily tore into their meat. Farther on, two waterbirds with legs like stilts pecked at their meals, keeping sharp lookout at the same time.

Behind her, a flock of birds with brightly colored feathers and sharp beaks screeched noisily, but not as loud as the bull at the next table, bellowing to his mate for "More ketchup!" The young ones darted around everywhere underfoot, returning to their mothers only to feed.

Another part of Cat's new, more complicated world fell into place. Feeling smug, she snuggled into Bobcat's lap to get comfortable.

"Hey there. How's it going, Bob?" Three humans stood over the table, holding trays of food, staring.

Cat wondered if they were a threat. If so, she could easily fight them off. The male was smaller than Bobcat, and the females looked soft.

"Huh," said Bob, who looked both pleased and embarrassed to be caught with Cat in his lap. He quickly slid Cat to the chair next to his.

The taller female, as slender and poised as a deer, spoke to Cat first. "Hi there. I'm Amy."

It wasn't a question, so Cat didn't answer. After a moment, Bobcat said, "Uh, yes, uh, Cat, uh, her name's Cat. This is, uh . . ."

"Like I said, I'm Amy. Nice to meet you." Cat noticed that Amy wore even less than she did, leaving her long brown middle and slender brown legs bare.

"I'm Nicole," said the shorter girl. She flipped her hair, tied back in a bushy tail like a fox's, and pointed her nose at the boy whose head had been shaved poodle style. "This is Patrick."

Patrick the Poodle stared at Cat. Nicole the Fox inched closer to him possessively.

"So, like, what's up, Cat?" said Amy the Doe. Apparently she was the leader of this pack.

Cat was stuck trying to figure out what might be up. Bobcat finally ventured, "Cat's just got here. She's my next-door neighbor."

"New, huh?" Amy set her tray down on the table, folding herself gracefully onto a chair. Cat noticed she kept her head up, her huge eyes wide and alert, sweeping the room for signs of danger. Smart girl.

"Where did you live before?" Nicole the Fox inquired. She wore a strange collar around her neck, a gold chain with a sparkling stone dangling from it. Very impractical, but foxes were notoriously vain.

"Before I came here, I lived in Paris," Cat answered, relieved that there was something she understood.

"Whoa, France. Polley-vous fransay?" asked Patrick the Poodle. He plopped down next to Cat. Nicole the Fox quickly trotted around to place her chair between them.

"Yes," Cat replied, "I do, but while I am here, it is better if I speak like you."

"You do great," said Amy. "I can hardly hear an accent."

Cat's stomach was growling; the odors from their trays assaulted her. "I am still hungry."

"Want some French fries?" The poodle offered his eagerly. Cat leaned over a little and smelled them. Her face wrinkled up.

"She doesn't want French fries," the fox chided. Nicole was darting sly glances at Cat, then at Patrick. "Did you try the garden salad?"

Cat looked at the greens and was puzzled. "I don't need to throw up now," she said politely.

"I'll get you something. What do you want?" Patrick was groveling like a typical dog, his tongue practically hanging out.

Nicole looked like she wanted to give Patrick a nip. Cat realized that the fox regarded the poodle as her mate. Cat quickly compared Patrick the Poodle with Bobcat. Bobcat was bigger, stronger, and didn't slobber all over her. No contest.

She surveyed the table. "That, that, and another one of those," Cat said, pointing. "But, please, do not bother. Bobcat will get it for me." Patrick was clearly willing to fetch, but she didn't trust anyone else with her food.

Bobcat was already scrambling up from the table. "Uh, fried chicken, tuna salad, and a hamburger," he said, looking relieved to have something to do. "Got it." He quickly escaped.

"Are you on that all-meat diet?" Amy asked, placidly munching her greens.

Cat, as she always did when she didn't understand, remained silent and looked wise.

"You call him 'Bobcat'?" asked Nicole pointedly. "Are you *with* Bob?"

"Bobcat is not here now, so how can I be with him?" Cat said, puzzled.

This drew a laugh from the girls. "But you're, like, hanging out together?" Amy asked.

Cat gave up and shrugged. "Yes."

Patrick slumped, his posture signaling disappointment. No matter how loudly they barked, dogs' body language always gave them away.

"You and Bob! That's great," Nicole said, perking up.

"I'm kind of . . . surprised, you know," said Amy hesitantly. "I haven't, like, seen Bob with a lot of girls."

"Why?" Cat asked, detecting a challenge. "Bobcat is not bad, as males go. He is big, strong, healthy, well behaved—"

That drew a titter from the girls.

"There are very few males that I trust," Cat finished.

"Tell me about it," said Nicole.

"Hey!" Patrick yipped.

"I suppose it's really difficult, with, you know, a really shy boy, 'cause you have to start the conversation all the time," said Amy, blinking her soft brown eyes.

"When we are together, we do not waste time talking," said Cat. That drew more titters.

"I wish all girls were like you," said Patrick. "Man, do I."

"You know what I hate?" said Nicole sharply. "Guys who say they like you but then pay attention to other people."

Turning away from Patrick, she flipped her bushy tail in his face.

"I think I'll go see what's keeping 'Bobcat,'" Patrick said, slinking away with his tail between his legs.

With the last male gone, Cat felt a big change sweep the table. While the boys were around, the girls had barely touched their food, but now they dug in. After a few bites, Amy pulled her chair in closer to Cat. Nicole visibly relaxed and took some clothing out of a bag, holding it up for the others to see. "You probably won't like this, but it was on super sale."

As far as Cat could tell, it was only more clothes, but Amy made admiring noises. Cat was surprised at how comfortable she felt among these females.

When Amy displayed her own prizes, Cat noticed the girl's long fingernails, painted violet with sparkles. "Pretty claws," she said, pointing.

"What? Oh, thanks." Amy glowed. "I did them myself."

"I got mine done at the salon in the mall," said Nicole, showing off her own long nails. Hers were painted red and yellow with little stars. "But I don't know; I'm thinking of changing them."

Cat quickly hid her own short, plain nails under the table. "Do all of you have painted claws?"

"'Nails,' we say here," Nicole corrected her. "Not everyone does, but it's a lot of fun."

Cat flexed her claws under the table. *Why aren't mine longer?* she wondered. At that moment, she felt them slide smoothly out from her fingers, just like they had formerly from her paws. She proudly held them up to show the girls. "My . . . *nails* . . . are long enough but are not colored."

"Ooh, nice," exclaimed Nicole.

"And needle sharp," said Amy, pricking her finger on the end of one. "Is that the style where you came from?"

"Yes," said Cat. "This is normal in my old world. But I wish to have mine in colors like yours."

"Clip Art Hair and Nails, the salon here in the mall. They can do anything," said Nicole.

"I will tell Bobcat to show me," Cat said.

"So why do you call him 'Bobcat'?" Nicole asked again.

Cat said, "I call him Bobcat because he acts well trained, but he is really an animal."

After a moment's stunned silence, Cat's new girlfriends broke into a wave of laughter, which turned into giggles when Bob returned with a tray, Patrick at his heels. And even though Cat didn't understand everything, she felt sure something good had happened.

18

AS DESI WANDERED the mall with Jarrett, she kept reminding herself to listen, not talk. That way, she couldn't slip up about magic, or Cat, or anything else that might get her into trouble. Problem was, that strategy left them with long, awkward silences. "Your parents seem nice," she said after one lull that threatened to go on forever. The topic seemed safe enough. Lame, but safe.

"Sure, my parents are nice. Everybody here is nice." Jarrett sighed. "The mall is nice. Our house is nice. My friends are nice, school is . . ." He grimaced. "Okay, school bites, but what else is new."

"What's the problem with nice?" Desi asked. Between her mother's disappearance and Cat's big changes, she could use a little "nice" right now.

"I'm drowning in 'nice,'" Jarrett said. His voice took on an edge she hadn't heard before. "There's more important things than, you know, 'be nice and on time' and 'do your homework' and 'get the grades.' There's gotta be . . ." He tossed his long blond hair in frustration. "Oh, forget it."

"No, what?" Desi stopped walking, and Jarrett turned to face her. "Tell me."

He paused, hesitant. "People say I'm looking for trouble, but I'm not."

"What are you looking for?"

But he wasn't listening; he was staring past her head, frowning at something behind her.

Desi turned to see a small store with a darkened door and windows draped in black curtains. The sign on the door read:

MURDSTONE'S HOUSE OF MAGIC
MYSTERIES REVEALED · ILLUSIONS MADE REAL
AMAZE YOUR FRIENDS, CONFOUND YOUR PEERS,
REVENGE YOURSELF ON YOUR ENEMIES

"Ooh, scary," Desi moaned. She laughed. "Gimme a break."

But Jarrett examined the sign eagerly. "Now, that's my kind of store."

"Tricks for kids," Desi insisted. "Hokey pocus."

He put his head next to hers, almost whispering. "Don't you feel it sometimes? Like it's all around, only you can't quite see it?"

"What?" she asked, confused by the sudden change in him.

"*Magic,*" he whispered.

A shock went through her body. She must have let some of her astonishment show in her face, because he backed off suddenly. "Just kidding," he said. He looked away, but not before she caught a glimpse of his embarrassment.

Jarrett recovered quickly. "Might as well check this place out while we're here. Good for a laugh." Without waiting for her to answer, he pushed through the door and disappeared inside. Desi paused, worried that Jarrett might be disappointed—or was it her own disappointment she feared?

·₊*·₊*

When Cat walked into Clip Art Hair and Nails, a girl no bigger than her with frizzy purple-streaked hair got up from her magazine to greet her. Cat noticed the girl's claws: one-third the length of her fingers, painted red with gold stripes. Cat immediately flexed her hands, extending her own nails to the same length.

"What great nails," said the shopgirl, taking the hand presented to her. "Acrylic? And so, you know, pointed. Ouch!" she said as she pricked herself. "How did you get them so sharp? Like, stiletto chic, you know?"

Cat didn't know but was relieved that the girl's questions didn't seem to need an answer. "Paint my nails," said Cat.

"Fantastic! Let me show you what I've got," she said, pulling Cat over to a display of samples.

Bob, who was cowering in the doorway, said, "Uh, maybe I'd better go find the kids?" Neither girl answered him, and he slunk out.

"I like black," Cat said to the shopgirl.

"Nasty," she replied.

Ten minutes later, Cat sat with her hands stretched out on the table, admiring their transformation. Her nails were long and razor sharp, painted silver with black stripes. She had never, ever imagined claws as beautiful as this.

"So, like, you're dry. Like 'em?" the shopgirl asked from behind the counter after the only other customer had left.

Cat jumped lightly out of the chair and stretched. "They're purr-fect," she said, smiling. She got a kick out of baring her teeth at people.

"Stellar," the girl gushed. She was trying to pick up some coins off the counter, but her long nails made it impossible, so she slid the coins clumsily off the edge into her other hand.

"Why do you leave your nails out?" Cat asked curiously.

"Huh?"

"Your beautiful claws, why don't you retract them?" Cat held out her own long claws and concentrated; the nails slid back into her fingers.

The shopgirl's eyes bugged out. "How did you—? Where did you get those?"

Cat had learned the right answer. "France," she said simply, heading for the door.

"Hey! Wait a minute!" the shopgirl yelled, dashing around the counter. "You're, like, nineteen-seventeen, with tax."

Cat ignored her. She was done here; now she had to find Desi. She darted down the hall, leaving behind the shopgirl with her peculiar cry: "Nineteen-seventeen with tax!"

19

WHATEVER IT WAS Desi expected inside Murdstone's House of Magic, the reality stopped her cold. It was darker inside the shop than outside, with a faint musty odor. It felt vaguely familiar, like places she had visited growing up.

At one side of the long, narrow room, in front of the counter, a tall dark-haired man was performing for a small crowd of children and their mothers. Desi and Jarrett watched from a distance as the man, handsome in black from his leather jacket to his shining snakeskin boots, held the group spellbound with a stream of cards and coins and colored scarves that appeared from thin air. He chattered constantly in a voice too low to be understood, while his black-gloved fingers wove invisible tapestries in the air.

"What are you saying?" asked one boy.

"Ancient words, from the deepest places of the Earth," he answered. His voice charmed them—low, lulling, teasing. The movement of his fingers was hypnotic.

"Why are you doing that with your hands?" asked a girl a little older than Desi.

"I am shaping the forces of the supernatural, like you mold figures in clay," he said. He enfolded her with his smile, then released her.

Intrigued, Desi turned to Jarrett. "Do you see what he's

doing?" But to her disappointment he had left her, and was pushing through a mass of kids at the opposite end of the room, crowding around a monkey in a little hat and coat. Perched on the steps of a precisely carved model cathedral, the monkey looked like a comical gargoyle come to life. As the little creature danced, the kids cheered, captivated.

The mothers were already captives, their defenses disarmed by the magician's charms. Pierced by his coal-fired eyes, their blushes betrayed them. "Watch carefully, now," he dared as he pulled an apple out of a preschooler's ear and then made it vanish in midair. Desi watched, fascinated, as he transformed a handkerchief into a live dove, wrapped the dove in his hands, and then unfolded his hands to reveal a single red rose. He handed the rose gallantly to the nearest woman, who was clutching a toddler. "A thing of beauty," he said. Her cheeks blushed as red as the rose.

Standing in the doorway, watching the show, Desi lost all sense of time. The magician bent to each child in turn, performing for them individually. He took his time with each one and seemed to pay special attention to anyone Desi's age. He worked methodically through the crowd, patiently, never neglecting the mothers for too long.

Abruptly he was done.

"*Abar'ashel!*" he shouted. The magician raised his hands above his head, a fountain of sparkling lights erupting from his fingertips. Blue smoke swirled over the heads of the crowd.

The truth struck Desi like an electric shock. *These aren't tricks,* she said to herself. *He's doing real magic.*

Desi edged against the wall of the magic store, alive with

anticipation. Spotting her, the magician pushed through the slowly dispersing crowd to greet her. "Welcome to the exciting world of magic," he said with a flourish. This close, though still handsome, his face showed deep lines of concentration. "Come, join us," he said warmly. "There is nothing here to be afraid of, merely harmless illusions."

"I wasn't afraid," Desi said. "And those weren't tricks." She lowered her voice. "I know what you were doing."

"Really?" His face lit up. "And what was that?"

Desi caught herself in time and dropped her eyes, shaking her head.

The magician raised his arms in a theatrical shrug. "How about some candy?" He stuck out his hand, pulling a chocolate coin from her ear.

Desi frowned, wanting better.

"Ah, too old for that, of course. How about this?" He held out his upturned palm. In the center of his glove lay a tiny piece of crystal, almost too small to see. He murmured gently; it began to grow rapidly in all directions like a living thing. In a moment, a multipointed crystal took shape, like a sparkling city in miniature. Desi leaned closer for a better look. Deep inside the crystal, flames sparkled in red and silver and gold. It was the most beautiful thing she had ever seen.

"For you," he said, extending his hand. "Because you believe in magic."

With a conspiratorial wink to Desi, he swept away to the sales counter, where customers were lining up.

Desi was left alone holding the precious crystal. For long moments, she lost herself in it. Then, realizing she had not thanked the magician, she looked up—to see the monkey staring at her. Or was it just her imagination? When she looked again, the monkey had gone back to showing off for the kids.

The magician was occupied with his customers, so Desi looked around for Jarrett. He had his back to her, so wrapped up in the monkey's antics he had apparently forgotten all about her. Feeling miffed, she decided to ignore him.

She inspected the shelves nearby, where a mummified weasel and a withered hand on a marble stand alternated with beginner's rope tricks and whoopee cushions. She ran her fingers over cracked leather volumes with titles engraved in exotic languages stacked next to a pile of paperback books labeled *101 Magic Tricks You Can Do at Home*. Something about the place whispered secrets to her—secrets just at the edge of her hearing, beckoning to her.

The show over, most people in the store made their purchases or just filtered out. The magician waved each of them to the door with a warm farewell whether they bought anything or not. As Desi hoped, the minute the counter crowd dispersed, he came over to join her.

She had just picked up some antique silver jewelry that had caught her eye. "You have discerning taste," the magician said, nodding in appreciation. "That bracelet can be used to bind its wearer in devotion to you, if they are weak-minded and you are strong."

Desi put it down fast. "That was real magic you were doing," she said.

"Sadly, all life is an illusion." He shrugged. "Nothing here is what it seems."

"No, really," she said. She was determined to get to the truth. Speaking so quietly that he had to bend low to hear her, she whispered, "I know. I can do it, too."

"Really?" he whispered back invitingly. "What can you do?"

Desi hesitated. This was going too far. "I . . . I can't."

"Ah," he said. He began to turn away, dismissing her.

"You don't understand," she protested. He faced her again. Desi felt the warmth of his patient gaze. How could she explain? She had been bound by secrecy all her life. Determined to make him understand what she couldn't say out loud, she returned his gaze boldly, looking him straight in the eyes.

His eyes were like deep black pools. For a moment, in their depths, she thought she saw herself.

They remained this way, sharing an unspoken connection, until Jarrett came barreling up between them. "Did you see what that monkey was doing?" he laughed.

The magician straightened up to his full height, every inch the performer. "Ask Mungus to show you his magic tricks." He winked. "I'll bet you've never seen a monkey pull a rabbit out of a hat before."

Jarrett looked astounded. "The *monkey* does magic?" He dashed to the other end of the room without looking back, shouting to Desi, "Come on! You're missing the best part!"

She wasn't so sure she was. Before she could decide about joining him, the magician bent low again, speaking for her ears alone. "Can I trust you?" He seemed to come to a decision. "There is much about my magic that I am forced to hide from the world. I cannot reveal the true enchantment of this shop to just anybody. Do you understand?"

Desi nodded, her heart beating fast.

"These others"—the magician dismissed everyone else in the room with a toss of his head—"cannot see beyond the confines of their own tiny little world. Miracles happen before their eyes, and they call them 'tricks.' They have to— if they knew the truth, they'd be frightened or envious. But you . . ." He hesitated, then in an earnest tone continued. "You're different. You see the truth, and you're not afraid."

Desi nodded again. The pressure in her chest came flooding back. Finally, someone who saw her as she really was. Someone she could talk to openly about her magic!

"Hey, Desi?" She shook free from her whirling thoughts to see Jarrett at her side, looking puzzled but cheerful. From a shelf above her head, the monkey crooked its neck toward her, its sharp little teeth bared in concentration. They all seemed to be waiting for her to do something, and she had no idea what.

"Desi!" Cat's wail from outside the store was so loud that it penetrated the thick, curtained windows. "DESI!" Her cry sounded desperate.

"I've got to go," she said to the magician. She gave him a quick look, hoping he would understand that she really didn't want to.

A dark cloud seemed to pass across his face and he looked away, but when he met her glance again, his expression showed only respect. "I understand. Please, come back and see me anytime, when you are not so busy. My door is always open to you." He bowed. Feeling self-conscious with Jarrett standing right there, she murmured goodbye.

Desi pushed through the door, ready to tell Cat off for yelling at her like an errant puppy. But her protests died when she saw Cat, minus the bottom half of her outfit, standing in the middle of the aisle with her eyes closed and her shoulders hunched in anguish. Bob was hovering close by, helpless.

"What's wrong?" Desi asked, hurrying over. She had never seen her so distressed.

Cat opened her eyes, big and round with worry. "I lost you. I was following your trail, and it just ended, like you never were!"

"I'm fine. I'm right here," Desi said, trying to calm her down. She felt a pang of guilt and chided herself. Cat was only trying to watch over her like she had been told, and here she had ditched her the first chance she got.

"Sorry. My fault. I completely lost track of time." Desi forced herself to sound cheerful. "Did you have fun checking out the mall?"

"No." Cat wrinkled her nose like she smelled something rotten. "I am not having fun anymore. We are going." Desi didn't mind. She was determined to see the magician again, but another time, when she had more privacy.

Before she could let Cat lead her away, Jarrett emerged from the magic shop, beaming.

"Awesomely awesome place," he exclaimed, showing off his purchases. "See this? It's a gizmo so you can eat fire. And look at this!" He held up a pamphlet with a lurid cover.

"'Secrets of Sawing Your Friends in Half'! They have the greatest stuff in there. Have you seen it?" he asked Cat and Bob. "They've got a monkey running around, too, like at the zoo, but you never see tricks like that at the zoo!"

"A monkey is in there?" Cat asked, eyeing the magic shop suspiciously. "With tricks?"

Bad idea, Desi thought. She followed Cat's gaze to the black curtains hiding the magician and his secrets. "Witches' tricks," Cat had called them. And Cat was even more overprotective than Mom; she hardly let Desi out of her sight. If Cat saw what was in that shop, she wouldn't even let Desi brush her teeth by herself.

Desi clenched her fist and felt the sharp points of her crystal prick her palm. She was glad Jarrett had found *his* kind of magic, but she had to keep Cat from meeting *her* magician. She thought fast.

"Zoo?" she repeated loudly to distract Cat's attention from the shop. From the look on her face, Cat didn't get it. "You have a zoo here, with animals?"

It wasn't working. Her nose aimed at the dark curtains, Cat began to stalk the magic shop, each foot placed precisely in front of the other, a wary hunter sneaking up on her prey. Desi was racking her brain for a way to stop her when, with a sudden cry of *"There you are!"* a girl with frizzy purple hair stormed down on them.

"Nineteen-seventeen with tax!" the purple-haired manicurist proclaimed like a protester shouting a slogan. She cornered Cat. "Like, my money?" she demanded.

Scowling, Cat turned to Desi. "What does she want?"

Desi shrugged. "Money, I guess. Don't look at me."

"Nineteen-seventeen with tax," the manicurist repeated. "Pay up, or I'm calling security."

Hearing that, Bob flinched. "I got it," he said hurriedly, reaching for his wallet.

The manicurist snatched a twenty out of his fingers. "Have a nice day," she said, showing them her back.

"We can go to the zoo tomorrow," Bob quickly offered to Cat as he escorted her down the hall. He seemed anxious to get away.

That suited Desi just fine. She tightened her fist around her precious crystal, guarding her secret.

This day had been full of surprises.

20

THAT NIGHT, DESI lay in her bed, flipping through the pages of the *Book of Secrets* without really seeing them while her thoughts competed furiously in her head for attention. Was the magician really who she hoped he was? She wanted someone she could share her magic with, a teacher who would open the doors that her mother had always kept firmly closed. She needed a friend she could relax around. Jarrett was, well, fascinating and maddening at the same time, but she would always have to be careful around him. And Cat was too weird, too tall, too alien in her new body to confide in; she wasn't the same cuddly creature that Desi had once whispered her secrets to. It was like she and Cat had lost each other. Suddenly Desi wanted her mother so badly she ached.

She sat up with a start. Cat had said that Callida would be back in one or two days, and the two days were up—without even a word! This was too much. She wasn't going to wait any longer.

After quickly dressing, she checked the house to make sure that Cat was out. She was pretty sure that Cat wouldn't approve of what she was up to.

When she was sure she was alone, she slipped into the small office room, where most of the boxes were stored. Quietly, she opened box after box, spreading their contents around the floor. An album fell out. Desi picked it up and carefully opened it. Inside were many photos, mostly of her—Desi in white blouses for tidy school portraits, Desi in front of the castle at Disney World, Desi at five on her first bike, little Desi enthralled by the live fairies dancing on her birthday cake. There were other pictures, too. There was Aunt Lissa in flowing orange and black robes decorated with signs of the zodiac; it was not a Halloween costume—it was how she always dressed. There was even one of Devil as a kitten, looking so cute, suffering the indignities of Desi's hug.

She leafed through the pages. There, finally, was one of her mom. It was Callida's birthday. She had posed for the camera, smiling proudly, holding up a drawing Desi had made for her. That had been a great party: At a park near Mexico City, some of their neighbors had appeared unexpectedly, carrying wonderful food and drinks. A few months later, those same neighbors had helped Desi and her mother move.

Desi slid the photo from the album and looked closer. Her mother's face showed no signs of worry or nervousness; that had been a great day. Callida looked relaxed and glowing, younger than Desi remembered her. She realized with a shock that her mother was growing older, too fast.

She had to see her mother, now.

She carried the photo into the kitchen along with the *Book of Spells*. Whatever had gone wrong before, now she was prepared. Wasn't she a witch? It was in her blood. If her mother could do it, she could. She was careful this time to close the drawing of the five-pointed star completely, leaving no gaps, taking extra care with the figures at each corner.

Finally, checking and rechecking for flaws, she placed the photo of her mother in the center.

At the last minute, she remembered the book's precise instructions: *a piece of the person*. She ran back upstairs, casting about for inspiration. She found it in the bathroom. Gingerly she plucked a few long hairs from her mother's brush.

Back in the kitchen, she put the hairs with the photo at the center of the drawing. Now there could be no mistake about who she was summoning. She cleared her throat and, beckoning with her finger, pronounced loudly and clearly, *"Conjurgalus Visitatem Callida!"*

Smoke began to curl out from the edges of the photo. A brief surge of fear seized her. Nervously she checked the borders of the Portal for cracks. As before, the smoke swirled upward, forming a miniature storm centered on the picture of Callida. This time, however, it did not coalesce. Instead, an image formed inside the smoke, flickering through it, a face, an upper body, hands. It was her mother.

"Mom!" Desi cried. "Mom, can you hear me?"

But it was still only an image of her mother, wavering in the smoke. Callida had her hands out, as if to ward something off. She turned about in a circle, looking worried.

"Mom, it's me! Can't you see me?"

Callida was talking, reciting a string of words unbroken, but Desi couldn't hear anything. It was like a TV with no sound. Then suddenly the smoke cleared. The image solidified, and Desi could hear her mother.

"Who's there? Show yourself, coward!" Callida cried.

"Mom, it's me." Desi reached out to the image, but her hand passed right through it. There was nothing to touch.

Callida cried out to someone beyond Desi's view. "I need your help! This is it! He's here!"

"Mom, no, it's me," Desi cried. "Can you hear me?"

"He's trying to pull me in. He must have known it was a trap." Callida tried to push against the air. "I'm being crushed. It's not a Summons—he's trying to destroy me."

Desi was horrified. "Mom, no! I'm sorry. I just wanted you to see me." Desi was too shocked by what was happening to think or move. She could hardly breathe. "Mom!"

"Help me, Lissa," Callida cried. "Lend me your aid!" Smoke whirled up and around Callida's face. "You're not going to get away with this!" she shouted. Callida folded her arms around herself and bowed her head. Her lips moved, but she spoke too low for Desi to hear. Within the center of the swirling smoke, a bright silver light formed, circling Callida and wrapping her like a cocoon. Soon she was entirely encased in light, a crystalline armor against the smoke. As Desi watched, still too frightened to move, the light grew outward, filling the Portal, pushing against its borders, shining so brightly that Desi had to close her eyes and then shield her face with her arm. The next moment, a flash of light penetrated even her closed eyelids. She staggered, blinded for a moment. All was quiet.

Desi opened her eyes slowly, afraid of what she might see. Her mother was gone. The Portal was intact but empty except for a small pile of ash in the exact center—all that was left of her mother's photo, the precious one of her proud, smiling face. Desi started to reach in for the ashes, then thought better of it and stood up, scuffing out the lines of the Portal with her foot. She was tired and shaking all over. *What if I had actually . . . ?* It was too terrifying to think about. She knew her mother had been strong enough; the silvery light had broken the spell, but still . . .

The thought made her so angry she shoved the *Book of Spells* off the counter, sending it crashing to the floor. So much for magic.

The noise of the book hitting the floor echoed through the empty house. There was no sound of Cat running to see what was the matter, no one to complain. Desi wanted someone around, anyone, even to yell at her. With nowhere else to go, she went back to bed, forlorn.

Restless dreams haunted her sleep. All that night, she heard her mother calling to her, but no matter how fast Desi ran, she could never quite reach her.

21

BY THE TIME Cat came home from her nightly prowl through the woods, the moon had set, bringing full dark. Formerly, the night had been her ally, hiding her from her enemies, helping her sneak up on her prey, but now it was all wrong. Since her transformation, she had lost her connection with the earth and its vibrant messages. Her hearing seemed dull, and her new monkey brain couldn't make sense of the scents around her.

She froze at the crack of a stick breaking underfoot. It was *her* foot. She was wearing Callida's old boots, and they made noise even a dog could hear. So much for stealth.

The problem was this body—too many changes too fast. She still felt the same inside, but outside, it was like she didn't belong in her own skin. No one could see who she really was . . . not even her closest friend.

A distant sound tickled the back of her brain, a call that was more felt than heard. Was the call Callida's? Had she opened a new Hole to come back? Now that she was listening with her inner senses, Cat was picking up a hint of strange magic. Something was not right. Forcing her new big feet to hurry, Cat rushed home.

Once inside the house, she sniffed around. Everything was in its place, but the disturbing scent of magic lingered.

When she checked upstairs, Desi was missing from her bed, and she wasn't in Callida's big bed, either. A warning tingled at the base of Cat's spine. A quick dash through the house confirmed her suspicions—Desi was gone. *Kittens have no fear,* she snarled to herself. *They just run off into the wild world expecting it to be kind.* And it never was.

Remembering Desi's walk in her sleep two nights before, she ran to the front door. Panic was gnawing at her, forcing her to fumble with the latch for endless seconds. When she finally did get it open, a violent gust of wind almost yanked it shut again; it took all her strength to get through.

She darted outside, peering past the light of the street-lamps into the darkness between. The wind raced by her ears, snatching sounds away before they could reach her, leaving only a roar.

Doubling back, she spotted a small figure swaying on the sidewalk at the other end of the street. Relief and alarm flooded over her at the same time—it was Desi, looking frail, the wind whipping her pajamas in the moonlight.

Cat bounded down the sidewalk to seize Desi's arm. "You were to stay home," she snapped. "The house was empty when I came back, because you were not in it."

Desi pulled away. "Let go. My mother is calling me. Don't you hear her?"

Cat listened, but all she could hear was the howl of the gale. "No," Cat said. "You were dreaming again. Come inside the house now."

"No, I have to go!" Desi flailed desperately. The storm wailed, sending garbage cans rolling down the street. Cat seized the girl by the scruff of her neck as a squall struck, almost knocking them off their feet, trying to tear Desi from her grasp.

But Cat's new body was strong. Bending, she picked Desi up in her arms. Ignoring the girl's protests, Cat leaned into the wind, pushing against it. She forced her way down the sidewalk, fighting for every step. The storm tore at her like something alive, threatening to send them both flying, but she bent lower, determined not to give in.

Finally she reached the edge of her yard, her muscles screaming. Desi had stopped struggling and hung limp in her arms as if dead. Cat clutched her tighter. Pushing her fears aside, she aimed for the safety of the house.

Climbing the front steps, Cat wondered how she was going to get the door open—it was hard enough for her at the best of times—when it was flung open in her face. A huge shadow blocked the doorway. "Hi, how are you?" the golem said cheerfully. It quickly stepped out into the gale, making room for Cat to pass. When she and Desi were safely inside, it followed, slamming the door shut behind them, leaving the wind to screech impotently on the other side.

Cat collapsed to her knees in the hall, still clutching her precious bundle in her arms, letting her nerves settle in the welcome silence. The golem plodded blithely by. "Have a nice day," it said, sinking into its recliner.

Cat searched Desi's face for signs of life. She pressed her to her chest. Was that Desi's heart beating or her own? Then she felt Desi's chest rise and fall, and Cat relaxed. Desi was asleep. It was a deep sleep, even for a human.

Was she ever really awake? Cat wondered.

The wind outside still shrieked, jangling her nerves. Who

was calling to Desi? It was definitely not Callida. What was screaming out there in the night besides the wind?

Cat had no answers, so, as usual, she decided to ignore what she did not know and concentrate on staying alert—and alive—in the present. Tenderly she hefted Desi in her arms. *Callida knew what she was doing after all,* Cat thought as she effortlessly carried the unconscious girl up the stairs. *In my old form, I could not have guarded her so well, even with teeth and claws.*

This new body of mine has its good points.

22

DESI WOKE UP in her mother's bed to find Cat at her feet, sprawled on her back, deep in slumber. Desi was surprised; she was sure she had gone to sleep in her own room. But since she also remembered her mother's voice urging her forward through a hurricane in the dead of night, she decided to write it all off as a very weird dream.

Down in the kitchen, she could still see the smudges of last night's drawing on the kitchen floor. That had *not* been a dream—images of Callida, angry and fearful, came flooding back to her. Had she really almost crushed her mother last night? She couldn't believe that her magic could be that powerful. And what had her mother been shouting about? *"He's this"* and *"He's that"*? Who did she mean? Callida had been asking Aunt Lissa for help, so she was probably in London. Why hadn't her mother just taken Desi with her? Why hadn't she called? She had some explaining to do.

Desi still missed her mother desperately, but as she washed her breakfast dishes and put them in the rack, she decided to give up trying to contact her. If Callida couldn't be bothered to pick up the phone, then two could play that game. Desi would simply wait. Then, when Callida returned, Desi would have proven to her that she could make it on her own. She wasn't really alone, anyhow, with Cat and the boys next door and now the magician.

That's what she had to do next: see the magician and find out if he was for real. A glance out the front window showed Bob in his driveway, washing his car. Perfect. Good old Bob was better than a taxi. Now, if she could only think of an excuse to get Cat into the mall but away from the magic shop. Food, clothes, movies, the mall provided anything you could want as long as you gave it what *it* wanted—money.

Going upstairs and entering her mother's room, Desi saw that Cat was awake, so she didn't have to worry about making noise as she dug through a cardboard box.

"What are you hunting for?" Cat asked as she wriggled out of her neon muumuu and into the old knit minidress.

"Cash, checkbooks," Desi said, tossing papers on the floor. "Credit cards. Coupons good for a free drink. We can't keep letting Bob pay for everything."

"Bob invited me," Cat explained patiently. "It was a date."

"Not this time." Desi upended an old jewelry box, showering herself with cheap imitation rings and plastic bracelets. "You need clothes and we need money. I can't even go to a movie if I want."

Cat picked up the muumuu and reached into the pocket to pull out a plastic card. "This is for movies. Your mother gave it to me."

"Mom's credit card?" Desi exploded. "You've had this all along and you didn't tell me?"

"We did not go to a movie," Cat said calmly. She knitted her brows, perplexed. "What is a movie?"

⋅⁺⋅⋆⁺⋆⁺

Cat was fine with going to the mall again, so after microwaving some frozen fried shrimp for Cat's breakfast, Desi took her to see Bob. But when she pitched the idea of a return trip to the mall, she ran into a hitch.

"Do we have to go back there?" Bob complained, vigorously polishing an invisible speck from the hood of the car. "It's just a bunch of stores. We were there yesterday."

Jarrett came out of the garage to join them. "I thought we were going to the zoo?" he piped up. "It's only a few miles south of the mall. We could hit it first and stop for dinner afterward at the food court."

"I'll be glad to take you," Bob quickly offered to Cat.

To Desi, Jarrett's plan was better than nothing. "Does this zoo have a lot of small animals?" she asked, trying to entice Cat.

"It's got a great snow monkey exhibit," Jarrett enthused. "And musk oxen and meerkats—"

"What kind of cats?" Cat asked.

"They're not really cats," Jarrett said. "They're sort of like prairie dogs."

"Cats who are dogs," Cat said disdainfully. "I do not think I would like that."

"Come on. It'll be fun," Desi said. What would reel in a cat's attention? *Aha!* "Are there any fish there, at the zoo?" she asked.

"The aquarium is my favorite part," said Bob.

"There's an aquarium? With *fish*?" Desi repeated, dangling the bait.

Cat arched her neck, stretching to get one ear closer.

"A whole coral reef behind glass, filled with every kind of fish," Jarrett said.

Cat was hooked. "Yes," she said. "I want to see these fish. I will come."

Bob, who all this time had been glancing at her while pretending not to, smiled and said, "Great, I'll get the keys."

⋅₊⁺₊⁺

If Cat had thought the mall was wonderful, once she saw the inside of the zoo, she thought she was in heaven. Hundreds of animals, each with their own delightful smells and sounds, all of them safe behind walls waiting for her to make her choices. Of course, some of the animals were big—too big—but they were safely behind walls as well, as Jarrett quickly explained.

Cat wasn't surprised to see that her presence caused a stir; ducks and other waterbirds scattered as she paced down the lanes, parrots complained, small mammals chattered at her angrily. She ignored them; there was too much to see and do.

They passed the snow monkey exhibit, watching the monkeys swing and leap through the air like weird goldfish in a giant, dry bowl. Dozens of them dashed about their enclosure with no way out. Cat was fascinated, tracking the monkeys' movements with wide eyes. She thought about jumping the railing to have some fun. They knew she was here; that was certain. The biggest ones were sounding the alarms, and the mothers had gathered up the little ones, but so many sounds and smells beckoned to her from the rest of the zoo that she decided to wait. The monkeys weren't going anywhere, and she smelled fish.

Cat pressed her nose against the glass wall of the aquarium. She could feel it—it was solid and strong. But she could see through it just like magic, and there on the other side was a world from her dreams. Fish! Darting fish, swimming fish, diving fish dressed in silver and orange and every other color. Moving fish, hiding fish, little tiny fish, and some so big she had to fight the urge to run.

A small one in rainbow scales drifted right by her. Cat's whole body quivered on alert. She leaned forward, bumping her nose against the glass. So near, and yet untouchable. Cat was torn between fascination and frustration.

A little while later, she crawled eagerly through tunnels alongside some human children to get closer to the prairie dogs, only to find that the glass always stayed between her and her prey. Her disappointment came from more than hunger—she wanted to play with one, to catch it and watch it struggle to get away.

The birdhouse was her favorite. She twitched nervously, but not as nervously as the birds—there was no barrier between her and them. In this room-sized cage, all the birds flew freely. "No one's ever let me inside a birdcage before," she said.

Bob leaned over her shoulder to peek at the sign. "This one's the tooki-tooki bird," he read. Long feathers flowed out from the bird's tail in white and gold. "It's beautiful, and very rare."

"I am very hungry," Cat said, licking her lips. "Is there anything here we're allowed to eat?"

Bob looked at her in surprise. Desi cut in. "Yum, roast parrot," she joked loudly. "Tastes like chicken."

Bob laughed nervously. "I guess we could go for something," he said.

Cat's nose led her straight to the zoo's food court. She was constantly hungry these days. The food she had always eaten at home no longer seemed to satisfy. She had even tried her dry food with milk from the refrigerator; it ought to have been delicious but instead tasted bitter and soggy. She seemed to eat way more than she used to and discovered that she liked a lot more things. Today it was hot dogs.

Bob had bought them all hot dogs and what he called "pop," with milk for Cat. Cat carefully poured a few drops of milk on her tongue and sniffed her food. Not that she minded eating dog, but it really didn't smell anything like any dog she ever knew. It was more like the mixed dead meat and grain that came in her food cans. That was safe enough, so she delicately slid the meat from its bread holder, nibbling a tiny bite off the end. It was good.

Bob was staring at her with an unreadable human expression. Something was wrong. Jarrett was laughing, not unusual for him, but so was the couple at the next table. Desi just looked disgusted and kept her eyes on her own plate. Cat made up her mind to ignore them and finish her food when she noticed that Bob's eyes were as big and round as an owl's. She stopped in midbite, holding the dog in the air, and glared at Bob. "Yes?"

"Uh, nothing," Bob said. He picked up his own dog, still in its roll. So that was the problem. She wasn't supposed to touch the meat with her fingers; she was supposed to use the bread thing. Why hadn't anyone told her? Eat this with the fork thing, that with the spoon thing—now she had to use the bread thing. The witch had given her hands, but she wasn't supposed to touch her dog with them, even though the others were using their fingers to eat their bland, mushy

"French" fries. Which Jarrett explained weren't even French. The eating habits of humans were bizarre.

Cat replaced her hot dog in its roll, waiting for Bob to make the first move. He shrank under her inspection, dribbling mustard on his shirt while nervously nibbling a tiny piece from his dog.

If that's the way you want it, she thought.

Holding the roll firmly, she took a big solid bite out of her own. It took some practice, but she was careful not to get any bread in her mouth. This dog wasn't hot, but it was delicious. *So that's why humans keep dogs around,* she realized with joy. *It turns out dogs are good for something after all.*

23

DESI WAS NOT enjoying the zoo. Her thoughts were miles away at the magic shop, for one thing, and the rest of her was busy chasing after Cat, who was sizzling like a firecracker about to go off. She began to think that coming here had been a mistake.

Jarrett came up to her side. "Want to check out the 'Creatures of the Night'?" he asked. "There's bats and snakes and other nocturnal animals. They keep it lit up all night and dim the lights during the day so the animals that are active in the dark are awake when people can see them."

Jarrett had been paying attention to her the whole time at the zoo; apparently today was turning out a lot better than just "nice" for him. And she was getting used to him dashing off after wildebeest or Siberian tigers or whatever else caught his eye. He made up for it when he came back every time, bubbling over with excitement.

So with a quiet nod to hide her goose bumps, Desi followed him through the double doors into the next corridor. But before they could enter the "Creatures" exhibit, they heard an uproar from down the hallway.

"A monkey is loose!"

A crowd quickly formed in the corridor—kids squealed

and yelled, shouting, pushing and shoving, laughing, and in one case crying. Parents tried to muscle their way through, reaching for their kids, but they didn't stand a chance.

"Come on!" Jarrett said. Without waiting for Desi, he darted after the mob, chasing the monkey that was screaming madly and leaping from wall to wall down the hallway.

It was the second time in two days he had left her for a monkey!

Well, he could have it. Annoyed, she pushed through the heavy doors to the exhibit, determined to enjoy the zoo without him.

Inside, by the dim red glare, she saw a tall man in a well-worn leather jacket, his long hair tied back in a ponytail. He was facing away from her, intent on one of the displays. It couldn't be, could it? Then he turned her way, and she caught her breath.

"Why, hello again." The magician smiled at her warmly.

She smiled back, tongue-tied.

"Are you here with your friends?" he asked politely.

"No, they—he's chasing a monkey," she said, realizing too late how stupid that sounded.

But again he surprised her. "Aha. You're too clever to waste time chasing Mungus like the others." He smirked. "They'll never catch him. Don't worry, he'll come back after he's led them on a merry chase."

"That was *your* monkey?"

"You could say that," he answered cryptically. "Mungus can be quite his own person sometimes. I often bring him here to the zoo in the vain hope that he will see how lucky he is to be with me." He shook his head ruefully. He was just as handsome as she remembered, but the reddish glare from the exhibit cast his face in stark shadows, making him look mysterious. "I hoped we might see each other again, but I never imagined running into you here," he said. "Perhaps it is . . . serendipity."

Desi remembered her magical gift, patting her bag to make sure it was still there. "I never said thank you for the crystal," she said. "It's beautiful."

"It was nothing." He dismissed her thanks with a wave of his hand. "I'm glad it amused you." He retreated into the nocturnal exhibit, his long dark hair and leather jacket blending into the shadows. "These are my favorite," he murmured. She drew closer to hear him. "Creatures that stay hidden from humans but that nevertheless live extraordinary lives, with abilities undreamed of." Desi followed him deeper into the room. "These flying foxes, for example"—he stopped by a wall of dark glass—"hunt at night, often in complete darkness, using only sound and scent."

Desi joined him for a better look. Inside, a huge foxheaded bat spread wide leathery wings and flapped to the other side of the enclosure. The magician moved to the next window, where a coil of fat boa constrictor lazed by the side of a pool. "You aren't afraid of snakes, are you? They do what they must to survive, like the rest of us."

Desi pressed up against the glass to show she wasn't afraid. *What kind of life is that, hiding under cover all the time, scared to go out in your own backyard, knowing people are afraid of you just because you're different?*

"I'm so happy we could meet again." The magician's voice jolted her out of her thoughts. "I was sorry our talk was interrupted. As I remember, we were speaking of the difference between illusion and reality."

"I knew it," Desi said excitedly. "That was real magic you were doing."

The magician smiled and put his finger to his lips. "Our secrets must never be shared with the uninitiated." His eyes twinkled. "I'm impressed. How did you know?"

"You make the Signs and the Words together, right? My mother says you have to do both, or it doesn't work."

"I'd like to meet your mother. Is she here?" The magician peered into the shadows as if he expected to find her, though they were alone.

"No," Desi said as casually as she could. She moved to the next enclosure, where a hairy spider was tiptoeing up a tree branch.

"I have handled those," the magician said. "Surprisingly soft and prickly."

"Aren't they poisonous?" Desi asked, reading the sign over the window.

"Anything can be dangerous if you do not know what you are doing," the magician replied.

Desi sighed. "That's what my mom always says." *But Mom isn't here,* she thought, feeling a twinge of resentment.

"And she's right," he went on smoothly. "But a life without risks isn't worth living. Don't you agree?"

"That's what *I* say, but my mom . . ." Desi shrugged.

"Mothers always try to hold their children back. That's

what mothers do. They want their babies to stay babies forever."

"Right, and they never understand when it's time to do things for yourself."

"I couldn't agree more. I can see that you are ready to create important magic," the magician said. "What spells has she taught you?"

Desi looked down at the floor. "The balloon one, Hobblebobble . . . you know." She didn't want to talk about the other spells she had done—something had always seemed to go wrong.

The magician spread his arms and shrugged. "That's a fine spell for beginners, but for a grown witch like you—"

"You know I'm a witch?" Desi blurted out.

"We special ones always know each other." He paused, considering. "Are you ready for a challenge? A spell that's a bit more . . . demanding?"

"Now?" Desi was taken aback. "But . . ." She trailed off.

"Of course, if you aren't sure . . ."

"No, I'm definitely ready." Desi squared her shoulders. "Try me."

"One moment." The magician went swiftly to the entrance doors, ran his finger across them, and murmured. Desi heard a click as the lock slid into place. "Don't worry," he said, seeing Desi's concern. "You can get out anytime you like—try it." Desi joined him, and the door opened at her touch. "The lock is for *them*," he said, dismissing the outside world with a wave. "What they don't know can't hurt us." As she followed him deeper into the room, Desi was surprised to find that her stomach was doing cartwheels.

"Watch and listen," he said in a low voice. He flicked his thumb out from between his fingers. *"Inferni."*

Instantly his thumb spouted flame, like a candle. The magician opened his hand, showing her that there was no trick or hidden device. The thumb burned brightly. "Go on," he said, "test it." She put her hand out gingerly, waving it over the flame. It was hot. She pulled back quickly.

"For ordinary people, a trick," he said quietly, "but for you, your birthright." He wrapped his thumb in his fingers to put the flame out. "Your turn." He moved closer to Desi. *"Inferni.* Say it."

Desi tucked her thumb in her hand, then flicked it out fast. *"Inferni!"*

Nothing happened.

"No need to shout." He glanced at the doors. "It doesn't matter how loudly you say it. In fact, it's best to keep it to yourself. Again."

"Inferni," she whispered as loudly as she could. Her thumb flicked out. Desi saw a spark flash at its tip. She felt a sudden thrill.

"Concentrate," the magician urged her. "Again!"

"Inferni!" she whispered again, flicking her thumb out.

Her thumb burst into flame. Desi started to panic, but there was no heat from below. She watched her thumb burn painlessly.

"I knew it," he said. His face seemed lit up by the glow. "Blood always tells."

Desi didn't ask what he meant. She was too fascinated by the flame.

Loud, excited voices drew their attention to the other end

of the room, where doors marked EXIT were suddenly thrust open, letting light flood in. Quickly the magician waved his hand over the flame to extinguish it, just in time for an agitated monkey to scamper across the floor and climb onto his back. A swarm of eager children followed close on the monkey's trail, chased in turn by a mob of excited parents. At the back of all the commotion, Desi was surprised to see Cat appear, flanked by Jarrett and Bob.

"Here you are," Cat cried, slipping through the crowd to reach Desi. Pouncing on her, Cat grasped her wrist. "I knew if I looked for the trouble I would find you." The crowd surged past, swarming over the anxious-looking magician and his monkey and sweeping them away.

"Ow!" Desi tried to pull away, but Cat's grip was like iron. "You're hurting me!"

Ignoring her protests, Cat dragged her out through the exit. Desi felt her temper rising. It wasn't enough she had been interrupted in her magic lesson; now Cat was hauling her around like an errant puppy in front of Jarrett and Bob. "Let go of me!"

Cat sniffed suspiciously. "What were you doing in there?"

"Looking at animals," Desi retorted. It was partly true. "It's a zoo, right? That's what we're here for?"

Cat wrinkled her nose. "Something is very not right." She sniffed again. "I cannot tell what—there are too many animals covering its trail. But it smells wrong."

Bob drew in a breath. "Probably the skunks. They're right around the corner."

Desi wondered if Cat could detect the magic she had

performed—she didn't know how far the girl's senses went—so she stalked off down the corridors of the "Minnesota Natives" hall in the opposite direction, leading the others away from the monkey and its owner.

After a few minutes, Cat seemed to relax, but Desi was too furious to calm down. Here, finally, someone was helping her to be the witch she knew she was, and Cat had dragged her away by the hand like a little kid, humiliating her in front of her new friends. Desi's face was burning hotter than her thumb had. It seemed like everyone was conspiring to keep her from learning magic.

They stopped in front of the lair of the northern bobcat, or lynx, as the sign overhead said. Jarrett stood between Desi and Cat, glancing back and forth between them, as if he knew something was amiss. Bob stood quietly on Cat's other side, looking happy, for Bob. The male bobcat sat up as they approached, alert, his sharp pointed ears twitching. Quickly the female took her station between the male and the onlookers, snarling a challenge—right at Cat.

For a moment, Cat and the lady lynx stared each other down, eye to eye. The jealous female raised her hackles, puffing out her fur to look bigger. Cat straightened up to her full height, then turned on her heel dismissively. "Oh, chill out," Cat teased the lynx over her shoulder. "You can have him. He's not my type." She rubbed her shoulder against Bob's. Now Bob looked happy enough for anybody.

"Anybody for the dolphin show?" Jarrett suggested cheerfully. "They've got a new orca. If you sit down front, you're guaranteed a big surprise."

Desi was still fuming about what Cat had done, and

at Jarrett's words, she knew she finally had a chance to teach Cat a lesson. "You mean a show with really big fish?" she taunted.

"They're not fish, you know," Jarrett objected. "They're mammals."

"I like fish," said Cat, flashing a last smirk at the female bobcat.

"This way," Bobcat said.

24

CAT HALTED AT the top of the steps that led down into the concrete auditorium. Far below, past the expectant heads of the audience, an enormous pool glistened blue-white from the reflections of the lights overhead. "Water," Cat said warily.

"That's right, fish live in it—big ones," Desi said, coming up behind her. "Let's get good seats before the place fills up."

Cat stepped gingerly down between the empty rows of concrete benches. The seats were hard but dry and were beginning to fill up with people. Cat was uncomfortable with so many humans packed so close, but she wanted to see the big fish, so she followed Desi.

Desi kept going. "Down here, guys. We want to see the fish close up," she said.

"They're not fish," Jarrett said in exasperation. "They breathe air just like we do." He joined Desi at the bottom row, which was almost empty. Desi picked a dry spot and sat down. Cat sat next to her, with Bob at her side.

"I do not see any fish," Cat said.

"In a minute," Desi answered, "there'll be all the fish you want."

All around them, music came over the loudspeakers. Cat hunkered down to wait.

"Is this okay?" asked Bob.

Cat didn't know what to answer. So much water so close put her nerves on edge. She could see clearly into the water; the pool was just a few feet away, but there were still no signs of activity.

"This is gonna be a blast," said Jarrett. "I can't wait."

A figure appeared on the other side of the pool, a young woman with a bucket. A faint aroma teased Cat from across the water. There were fish in the bucket; she was sure of it. She sat up expectantly. Her head jerked forward. Suddenly, there were the fish! They shot up at the female's feet, begging like dogs, but bigger, much bigger than any fish she had ever seen. Then the girl dropped tasty little fish in their mouths. Cat's mouth began to water. Her stomach growled.

The girl waved her arm and the fish disappeared. Cat was disappointed. Was that all? Then, from the center of the pool, two gray forms shot straight up out of the water high in the air, sleekly shining, flying without wings. Fish that flew! The audience cheered, and Cat felt their joy. How marvelous!

The fish did a flip in the air and disappeared under the water. Cat waited, tense and excited. "Will they come closer?"

"Man, will they," Jarrett said.

Bob looked excited, too, but he was looking at Cat instead of the water. On the other side, Desi was also watching her. "Just wait," she said.

The crowd hushed. The water stilled. The girl with the bucket was talking and waving her arms. "Ladies and gentlemen, and boys and girls, let me present our newest addition, born just over two years ago in captivity but already topping the scales, the world's biggest little orca, Keeru!"

Cat scanned the quiet surface of the pool. *Come out, little fishy,* she thought. *Fly for me. Shake your tail.*

The world exploded. Water pounded her—wet, cold water flying everywhere, sending her senses reeling. In the center of the wave, a cavern opened up, deep and wide, a dark hole rimmed with glistening white stones. Teeth! Rows of jagged, slicing teeth lining gaping red jaws, behind it a slimy tail in black and white.

A nightmare fish. Death beckoned, jaws open to swallow her in a single bite.

Her instincts kicked in. *RUN!* they shouted at her, so she did, scratching and clawing up the concrete mountain past the unfortunate slower victims. She spotted a clear path up the stairs and scrambled over knees and backpacks, ignoring the cries of the herd of humans in her way. *UP!* screamed the voices inside, so she climbed straight up to the mountaintop, feeling the hot wet breath of the giant flying fish on her neck. Reaching the peak, she leaped onto a steel support girder and clambered into its branches.

Cat clung to her perch, thoroughly soaked, chilled, all her senses on alarm. Safe at last, her heartbeat began to slow. The screams inside her quieted. She felt her luck and only then remembered the friends she had left behind. Shivering, Cat turned to look down into the carnage below.

* * *

Just sixty seconds earlier, Desi had tensed up, ready for the deluge.

"Yee-ha!" Jarrett yelled when the wave hit. As it had been trained to do, Keeru the orca slid onto the landing, sending a torrent of water onto the crowd; then it posed, openmouthed, for the cameras. The front row was drenched.

Bob had thrown his arm up to protect Cat, but it was like opening an umbrella under the ocean. Desi hadn't expected a splash this big, but it made her "surprise" even more perfect. She shook the water out of her eyes to see Cat fly up the stands using the crowd as stepping-stones. She had never seen anyone move so quickly. Bob scrambled for the aisle to catch up with her. Desi followed after him more slowly, leaving Jarrett behind hoping for another splash.

At the top, they found Cat, drenched and bedraggled, clinging to the steel beams that held up the roof. Just below them, the audience was laughing and pointing as the show went on. Cat was watching, too. She saw that no one was hurt. She saw a man ride the big orca's back. She saw the trainers put their hands and even their heads in its huge jaws. Cat saw all this and looked forlorn.

Desi felt sick. She had wanted to get back at Cat, but this was too much. Cat, her Cat, was really miserable. Desi wished she could take it all back. She had never expected this.

Then something else happened that she had not expected. Bob was standing underneath Cat. He didn't move away, even though water from her dress was dripping on his head and shirt. He didn't say anything, either, just reached up to Cat with his too-big hands and waited.

Cat was scowling, but instead of ignoring him or driving him away, she took his hands, dropping into his arms. He held her gently; she did not pull away but wrapped her arms around his neck and clung, shivering. Then Bob, big dorky Bob, who could barely even talk when a girl was around, put his other arm under Cat's legs and picked her up as easily as he would a child. Cat didn't struggle; she just clung tighter, her wet wool dress soaking them both. Bob didn't seem to mind.

Cat spoke in a low voice. "I thought it was going to eat me."

Desi stood in her own small puddle in the hot afternoon sun, feeling cold.

25

BAKING IN THE sunny zoo parking lot, they all dried off quickly, except for Cat. Her black wool sweater dress, the same one she had worn every day, was soaked and sagging, and Cat's hiking boots squished as she walked. Desi, feeling even sorrier than Cat looked, resolved to make up for her dirty trick—and maybe see the magician again while she was at it. "We need to get Cat to the mall for a new outfit," she said.

"Sure." Bob nodded. "We'll go straight there." He helped Cat settle into the rear seat. Cat sat stiffly, fists clenched, while he tenderly fastened her seat belt for her. Desi slipped into the hot car beside her, damp and uncomfortable, guilt forming little drops of perspiration on her forehead. "To the mall, James," Jarrett joked, sinking into his accustomed seat next to the driver. "And don't spare the horses."

The minute they entered the mall, Cat took off fast, trying to ignore the wonders appealing to her from all sides. Bobcat was following close on her heels, but Desi lagged behind with Jarrett. Cat slowed just enough to keep her in sight. Instinct led her straight to the row of clothing shops she had seen before. To her delight, just as Bobcat caught up to her, she ran into her new human girlfriends.

"Cat!" Amy batted her big doe eyes. "And Bobcat, too. Great to see you again. Are you looking for a dress for the dance?"

"Is that the same outfit you had on yesterday?" Nicole asked, sharp as a fox, as she inspected Cat's bedraggled wool dress. "I bet you didn't bring that many clothes with you, right? Amy, we've got a wardrobe emergency here!"

"You poor thing. Don't worry, we'll take care of you," Amy declared, taking Cat's arm.

"I know the perfect place—really hot stuff," said Nicole, taking her other arm.

Cat was too confused to speak, but it didn't matter; they didn't wait for an answer. Together they escorted her through the mall like a queen, or a prisoner.

Desi and Jarrett caught up just inside a store decorated with headless silver dolls in sparkly outfits. Bob eyed the racks of girls' clothing uncomfortably. "Uh, I'll just be in Media Mania next door, okay?"

"Great idea," Jarrett said enthusiastically. "Desi, you coming?"

"Yes," Cat replied, "and no. Desi, you must stay here with me. Learn about clothes. Someday you will need them, too."

"Yeah," giggled Nicole. "Someday some boy will ask you out to a dance, and you don't want to go naked."

"Speaking of the dance . . ." Amy appraised Cat's soggy hiking boots. "Shoes, definitely."

"Those are so L.L.Bean," Nicole agreed.

"You can't dance in those." Amy shook her head.

"Who is dancing?" Cat asked.

"We are," Amy said. "It's, like, the first big dance to kick off the school year. Didn't Bob tell you?"

Bob gulped. Cat pinned him with a suspicious look.

"Tomorrow night in the school gym, eight o'clock," Nicole added. "Bob can drive, can't you, Bobcat?"

"Don't let him get out of it," Amy said. "We're all going to be there."

"If Bob doesn't want to go," Nicole put in slyly, "you can go with us. There'll be plenty of other people to dance with once we're there."

"That's the fun of it, dancing with lots of different people," Amy agreed, pointing her toes as if she were dancing.

"I'm taking Cat," Bob said. "She's going with me. Right?" He looked pleadingly at Cat.

"I only ride with Bobcat," she answered firmly.

"That's settled," said Amy. "Now for your party clothes."

Bob escaped out the door. Jarrett signaled Desi with a quick jerk of his head before he, too, vanished, leaving her stranded.

·*·*·*·

Desi grinned like a good sport, hiding her frustration. She figured this was her penalty for the trick she played on Cat, being sentenced to deathly boredom in a boutique when she really wanted to see if the magician had returned to his shop. Finally, after hanging out for what seemed like forever, she got her reprieve. Amy and Nicole had piled clothes and advice on top of Cat, who looked like she was about to bolt.

"I will wear this," said Cat, grabbing the dress on the top of the pile without looking.

"Aren't you going to try it on?" insisted Amy.

"I am already wearing clothes," Cat replied, confused.

"So, like, change. We'll wait." Amy started to pick through blouses.

Cat sighed. She dropped the heap of clothes, grabbed the hem of her dress, and yanked it up toward her hips.

"Whoa, wait a minute!" Nicole cried, grabbing Cat's hands just in time. She glanced around frantically to see if anyone had noticed.

"You, like, can't change here," Amy said, quickly hiding her smile. "You've got to use the dressing room, you know?"

Cat didn't seem to know. The sales clerk came running over at the commotion. "Is anything wrong?"

"Everything's fine." Amy took charge. "Our friend's from France. Different customs. Where's your dressing room?"

Cat was led off to the changing rooms under protest. "Do not put one whisker outside of this store!" she cried to Desi as she was whisked away. Desi was wondering if she should seize this chance when Nicole reappeared. "Good, you haven't magically vanished," she said. "Cat said I had to watch you. How old does she think you are, six?" She rolled her eyes, and Desi laughed nervously. "Don't do anything I wouldn't do," Nicole giggled. Flipping her ponytail, she went off to hunt for more bargains, utterly ignoring her.

Desi was glad to be ignored. "I'll just pop next door for a second," she called out gaily to whoever might be listening. Then she hurried out the door.

Jarrett was just slipping out of a nearby video-game store. "Up for some magic?" he asked, grinning mischievously.

Desi grinned. "You read my mind."

* * *

The magic shop was just as dark and musty and familiar as Desi remembered. It reminded her of her aunt Lissa's house, with all the weird stuff on the walls. Just as she had hoped, the magician was there, talking to a few older kids by the counter.

"Where's the monkey?" Jarrett demanded, charging toward the rear of the shop.

"Resting. He had a hard day," the magician said absently. Jarrett tapped impatiently on the doors of the monkey's miniature cathedral, which were shut tight. "Leave him alone," the magician ordered. "Come back tomorrow."

Looking up, he spotted Desi. For a moment their eyes met; then, with a quick glance at Jarrett, he said, "Or perhaps Mungus has rested enough. Yes, why not? Time for him to do his job." He walked over to the miniature cathedral and bent low, whispering into the doorway. A tiny head poked out, blinking off sleep. The monkey seemed to look straight at Desi, then disappeared, reappearing a moment later wearing its cute little hat and coat.

"Come, everyone, come see the new tricks Mungus has learned." The magician herded the other kids toward the monkey's house at the rear of the shop. Scowling, the monkey began to juggle Ping-Pong balls.

Jarrett waved at Desi to come look, but she deliberately lagged behind, picking things up at random from the shelves until the magician drifted her way.

"I've never been able to make that work," he said, tapping the primitive artifact she was holding, a wooden mask carved and painted like a skull with gaping eye sockets.

"They say that once someone touches it, you can put it on and appear to them in a vision, but"—he took the mask from her gently—"it probably requires a great deal of magic from both sides." He carefully replaced it on the shelf. "I am pleased you're back, after we were so rudely interrupted." He smiled.

Desi felt a rush of anticipation. "I can't wait to practice the spell you showed me. I really appreciate you taking the time—"

"No need to thank me," he demurred. "It's my privilege. I knew from the start you had a special gift."

The compliment made her feel awkward. "I hardly even know how to do anything."

"Because you have not been properly taught!" The magician did not raise his voice, but his intensity shook her. "Do not underestimate your abilities. Even with months of training, many witches cannot master *Inferni,* and you did it as easily as writing your name." He studied her respectfully. "In a world where fewer and fewer can do less and less, you are the exception. You have a responsibility to claim your heritage. Are you up to the challenge?"

Desi was too thrilled to speak, but she nodded.

"Then come with me if you want to learn more," he murmured. "There is something I want to show you." He opened the door to the back room. Jarrett, as usual, was so totally entranced with the monkey's antics that he had forgotten about her. Desi slipped through.

The back room was much less impressive than the shop, containing just shelves and utility panels and ductwork. The magician took a tightly lidded woven basket off a shelf, placing it on the floor in the center of a clear space.

"What I am about to show you is something few witches can do, or warlocks for that matter, but I think it will be no problem for you."

Desi knew a dare when she heard one. "I'm ready. What do I do?"

The magician smiled. "Nothing just yet. Watch, first, while I prepare. It will be your turn later." He began to wave over the basket with intricate motions.

"Later?" she blurted out, disappointed. "I thought *I* was going to do it. See, this is just what my mother does—promise to teach me later. That's why I can't do anything."

The magician glowered for a moment, hands in the air, and then looked thoughtful. "You're right. Why not? Someday you can show her what you've learned." He stood up. "This will require every ounce of your concentration." Desi could barely hold in her excitement. "But first just a little preparation. I'm not doing it *for* you"—he held up one hand to ward off her protest—"only to give you a glimpse of what lies underneath."

He pried off the lid of the basket and took out a short, ordinary-looking rope. Raising both arms above his head, he stretched the rope taut between his fists. He spat out one word—*"Naja!"*—and the rope began to twist and writhe in his grasp. Suddenly he was holding a hooded snake, a cobra, and as he brought it down, level with her head, Desi could see its pitiless eyes darting and its slender tongue fluttering between the cruel fangs.

"Others may see only a rope, but you will know the spirit that lives inside," he commanded.

Defiantly, Desi squared her shoulders and stuck her chin out, showing that she wasn't afraid.

He spat out, *"Naj'nul,"* and cracked the snake through the air like a whip. She flinched but didn't back away. The snake became an ordinary rope again.

"You are ready," the magician said, admiration showing in his face. "I'm sorry I doubted you." He stooped to replace the rope in the basket. "Now, come here. Move your hands exactly as I do." He began waving his hands as if he were cupping steam from a kettle.

She knelt by the basket, copying his gestures.

"Then," he commanded, "once, and only once, say *Ess-scale-ate.*"

Swallowing hard to clear her throat, she repeated the Word of Power: *"Ess-scale-ate."* She waved her hands. The basket wobbled slightly, and she stepped back in surprise.

"Don't stop!" the magician barked.

Blood racing, she spelled the basket to shake. The end of the rope poked out, weaving about like the head of a snake. Slowly it rose into the air, swaying as if hypnotized.

"You've done it. Incredible," the magician said, awe in his voice. "What would your mother say if she saw this?"

"She means well," Desi said, moving her hands in steady, hypnotic waves as the rope snaked its way upward. She was so nervous she couldn't stop herself from talking. "It's just, you know, just the two of us, so she takes everything so seriously." The magician seemed deep in thought and did not answer. "It would have been different, you know, if my father had been with us. He would have helped teach me."

That got his attention. "Your father abandoned you? Is that what she told you?"

"No," Desi said, focusing on the end of the rope wriggling in the air. "She told me she left him. She said . . . she said she was afraid."

"And what about you?" the magician persisted. "Would *you* be afraid of your father?"

"No," Desi answered without thinking. "Why would I? My father is my father."

"Good." He stepped back, raising his gaze to the ceiling. "Done. Perfect. I couldn't have done better myself. Take a look."

Desi looked up and gasped. The rope rose high into the air, reaching up to the ceiling. But now the wires and ductwork were obscured by clouds that seemed to come from nowhere, boiling down like steam from an upside-down pot. The end of the rope disappeared into the mist. "Where does it go?"

"I'll show you," said the magician. "Step in closer to the rope." He backed away to give her room. "I'm curious. Haven't you ever wanted to meet your father?"

"Oh, yes," Desi said, not taking her eyes off the rope. "All my life I wanted to see him. Mom's great, but it's always just the two of us, you know?" She walked around the basket, fascinated, eyes glued to the ceiling. "She's always like a mom—hovering. It would be different with my father. I could do things with him. I could trust him, too; I'm sure of it." She moved up closer to the rope, trying to follow it into the mists overhead. "I haven't told anybody this, but I keep thinking that someday he'll turn up, and everything will be the way it was supposed to be."

Feeling a sudden tug at her leg, she looked down. Somehow the rope had become coiled around her ankle. Startled, she looked to the magician for help and got a shock. He had such a strange look on his face, as if he were ashamed and angry at the same time.

Desi didn't understand—had she done something wrong? The emotion in his face was so intense it frightened her. For a moment, neither of them moved. Then the rope snaked upward and began tugging at her leg, almost pulling her feet out from under her. She felt a moment's panic; then the magician rushed to kneel at her feet.

"Careful," he said. His hands trembled as they untangled the rope. "Get back. It can be dangerous."

Freed, Desi jumped back. "Yeah, that's what Mom says," she joked weakly.

The magician waved and chanted, then clapped his hands once. The rope fell to the floor, slack.

"Aren't you going to show me where it goes?" Desi asked, disappointed.

"Not now," he said. He wouldn't look her in the eye. "This was a mistake."

"You said I did it perfectly," she protested, her pride hurt.

"You did. No one could do better." The magician looked up at her as if he had never seen her before. "Don't worry; I promise you will learn everything you wish to know."

Desi felt energy rushing up through her whole body.

"But I need to think more carefully about . . . how best to teach you." He put on a smile, but behind it, Desi could sense his conflict.

A loud banging from the door interrupted them. "Hey, your monkey is going bananas," Jarrett shouted from the other side. He rattled the knob but apparently couldn't get in.

"I'd better go," the magician said, rising to his feet. "Mungus can get out of hand sometimes." He opened the door, holding it for her as she went through.

Out in the main shop, the boys were jeering at the monkey, which was hopping up and down, screaming back at them in contempt. Frowning at the hullabaloo, the magician clapped his hands together loudly; hearing that, the monkey stopped, looked over at the magician, saw Desi, and then really went crazy, throwing cards, books, tricks, and anything else it could get its little hands on. The magician turned to her apologetically. "You'd better go now. Quickly. When he gets like this, there's no reasoning with him."

Desi hesitated. "Should I come back sometime, or . . . ?"

"Yes, of course. We share a destiny, Desi. I see that now."

"You know my name?"

"Oh, Desdemona, I know you well," he said warmly. "We share the same dreams, you and I. Nothing can keep us from our destinies." A shrunken head flew past their ears, missing him by a few inches. He turned his back to deal with the monkey.

Desi signaled to Jarrett. "We'd better go. Cat will be throwing things herself if she can't find me."

She turned around to find herself face to face with Cat.

"Here you are," Cat said, quivering with indignation. "Always you never obey."

Tall and muscular in new black jeans and a T-shirt, Cat looked ready to kick some butt. Desi bit her lip. She wanted to make up a retort, but Cat had gone completely still, focused on a point behind her head. Desi wheeled around. The monkey had vanished, but the magician had stepped forward to greet this newcomer.

"And who is this?" he asked with a patronizing smile.

Cat's lips pulled back, revealing her teeth. Desi knew it wasn't a smile but a warning. In a flash, Cat leaped to station herself between Desi and the magician.

"Cat, wait!" Desi cried, annoyed. Cat had taken an instant dislike to the magician—that was clear—but why? The magician, a glint in his eye, only continued to glide toward them, as casually as though Cat had asked him to tea. But Desi could feel the tension between them. They were like two magnets closing to the point where no force could hold them apart, when abruptly Cat seized her arm and pulled her away.

"Come now, little one. Playtime is over," Cat snarled. She dragged her through the door and down the hall.

"What do you think I am, a pull toy? Let go!" Desi struggled, but it was no use; Cat had a grip of iron. They were halfway around the corner before Cat's grip loosened enough that she could tug free.

Cat was squinting and hunching her neck with her head touching her shoulders, just like a scared cat. "Never stray from me again, and never go back there."

"Why?" Desi asked resentfully. "You can't tell me what to

do." Passersby were staring, so she lowered her voice. "You're my cat, remember?"

"Warlock," Cat hissed.

"Who?" Desi exclaimed. "You mean the magician?"

"Magician, warlock, wizard—words, words, words," Cat spat. "That shop reeked of dark magic."

"Good," Desi said defiantly. "Just the place I want to be. I'm a . . ." She lowered her voice even more. "I'm a witch. Magic is what I do."

"Not that kind," Cat said. "And not with a strange warlock. I do not trust him. We will not come back to the mall while he is here."

Before Desi could protest, Bob and Jarrett caught up to them. "All finished shopping?" Bob said hopefully.

"Yes," Cat replied curtly. "We are leaving. Now." Bob was jolted by the force of her reply and looked hurt. Cat set such a fast pace down the hall that the others could barely keep up with her.

Desi needed some time to think. She spotted a restroom.

"Wait for me," she said, detouring inside. She was outraged when Cat followed her in. "Do you mind? A little privacy?" Suspicious, Cat even checked the stalls for strangers before leaving her alone.

Desi told herself to calm down and think. She couldn't just leave; she had to let the magician know why she couldn't come back. A quick cell phone call to Information didn't help. No surprise; he probably used a crystal ball or something, anyway. Desi wished for the ten thousandth time that her mother had taught her more about the world of magic.

Cat or no Cat, she was determined to see the magician again. *There's got to be some way to reach him.*

Catching sight of her face in the mirror, her blood began to chill. As she watched, her reflection dissolved, the flesh melting away until only a skull was left, a death mask with dark holes for eyes, grinning mirthlessly back at her. Horrified, she put her hands to her cheeks; with relief, she touched warm skin.

The skull in the mirror faded slightly, becoming a ghost skull through which the face of the magician flickered, intent and serious. Desi realized that he was wearing the skull mask she had picked up in the magic shop.

"Can you see me?" she asked. The skull-face in the mirror nodded but didn't speak. It couldn't—it had no mouth opening, just a wide row of painted white teeth. "I can't come back to your shop, but I want to learn more," she said quickly, pantomiming in big gestures in case he couldn't hear. She thought fast. The high school dance was tomorrow; if Cat was really going . . . "Can you come to see me tomorrow night?" she continued, speaking slowly and clearly, in case he was reading her lips. The skull-face nodded again. "Do you need my address?" It pivoted from side to side. She hoped that meant it could find her. "Great. I don't know what time—after dark, I guess. We can talk then." The image started to fade away. "Wait!" She pressed her hand to the mirror but felt only cold glass. The skull disappeared. She was looking at her own face again.

Desi took a deep breath. She had known she could do it. She could do anything if she wanted it enough. Her hands tingled from the excitement. No, just her right hand. She turned it over with a slowly dawning dread. There, etched on her palm in letters of fire, burned the words AFTER DARK.

She watched, spellbound, as the words faded away, leaving no trace. It was several minutes before she recovered enough to rejoin the others.

26

FAR INTO THE night, Desi lay awake in her bed, squirming around to get comfortable. The day had been too important to let it slip away. She wanted to hold it, examine it before she wrapped it up safe for the night, like her precious crystal tucked away in the drawer of the nightstand beside her.

She finally had a friend who was a witch like her, a warlock. And he had called her "special." Jarrett and her other friends seemed to like her well enough, but they didn't really know who she was—and they might not be so friendly if they did.

With a wave of his hands, the magician had opened a door into a new world. Her mother would never approve, but she didn't care. It gave her a thrill to think about what lay ahead. So much hovered at the edge of her fingertips. It was hers if she could just reach out a little further—she was sure of it. And the magician was going to help her.

Eventually she drifted into sleep. She dreamed that teenage Cat was holding little Devil in her arms and wouldn't let Desi touch her. Her mother flew by on a stick topped with a cat's head with glowing eyes, holding out a book with the secrets of magic in it, but every time she got close enough for Desi to read what was in it, she whisked away, always just out of reach. And she dreamed about the magician; he was calling to her from the middle of a pool of low fog, beckoning to her, holding out his arms for her to join him, if only she had the courage to wade into that misty unknown. . . .

A horrible, shrill shrieking dragged her out of the dream and back into her bed. The sound pierced her brain, sending shivers down her spine. Desi struggled so hard to escape the sound that she got tangled up in her covers and had to roll out of bed onto the floor with a bump before she could wriggle out of them. The shrieking went on, rising and falling, over and over.

Cautiously she stood up to look out the window. Her room was at the back of the house, but she still expected to see the flashing lights of emergency vehicles reflected from the street. Instead, the only light was from the night stars.

The awful noise continued. It seemed to come from all sides but also from below, under her window by the fence. All of a sudden, her intuition told her what it was, though it was a sound she had never heard before.

The watch-gnomes were shrieking their warning.

Desi stumbled down the stairs to the back door, hitting her shin painfully against a kitchen chair in the dark. She was hesitant to turn on a light with something unknown out there, but by the time she reached the door, the incessant wailing ground her nerves so badly that she cared more about stopping the noise than whatever caused the gnomes to give the alarm.

As soon as she yanked open the back door, a blast of chill air hit her. Good thing she was wearing leggings under her sleep shirt. Her bare feet stung in the cold. Out on the back deck, Desi paused to try to make sense of the night. The gnomes' shrieking hammered at her brain, warning her to run away, and it took a lot of effort to ignore it. Against the sky, she could make out the dark mass of the fence, and above it the tangle of sharp black lines that were branches. Clouds blocked the moonlight.

She jumped down off the deck rather than risk tripping on the stairs in the dark, then crossed the yard to the fence. When she got close enough to see the watch-gnome clearly in the dark, she stopped short. It was pointing! One stubby little arm, which used to be carved on its chest, was now stretched out with a fat finger pointing toward the woods. It was carved from stone, so it shouldn't—couldn't—move. But even so, it had changed.

The gnome's lifeless mouth kept up its horrible noise. This close, the shriek of the watch-gnome almost split her skull open. She held her hands to her ears to shut it out but had to let go to boost herself to the top of the fence so she could see over it.

On the other side, farther back in the woods, she saw something move. A frantic shadow was leaping from branch to branch, too big to be a squirrel but too nimble to be anything else. Suddenly a bigger shadow appeared right in front of it, pouncing on its victim. Desi saw a struggle; she heard an inhuman scream. The smaller shadow shot straight up into the highest branches. The larger shadow lagged behind. They both vanished in the dark. Everything went still.

Abruptly the wail of the watch-gnomes died. It was like a weight had been taken off the back of her neck; she felt lighter. Desi took a deep breath. Slowly the normal night sounds of distant cars and rustling leaves returned. Her arms ached from gripping the fence, so she let go and dropped to the grass.

Strong hands grabbed her, jerking Desi around as if she were a rag doll.

"Foolish girl! What are you doing? Get inside!" It was Cat.

"Let me go!" Desi struggled, and Cat let go. Desi braced herself for another assault, but instead Cat bent down to examine the little watch-gnome. Desi joined her to see what she was looking at. Watch-gnome statues all had big noses and bug eyes for no better reason than that they were funny, but this one wasn't cute anymore; the gray stone nose had been broken off and the eyes ripped and slashed, the face scarred beyond repair. The end of the pointing finger was missing, and the stone mouth was frozen open in a now-silent scream. Desi wondered what would bother to attack a watch-gnome and what had the strength to gouge solid rock like that. She shuddered.

"What did this?" she asked.

Cat stood up straight, looking past the fence into the woods. "Bad thing."

"Did you see it? What did it look like? Was it an animal?"

Cat touched the broken stone where the gnome's nose had been. "No raccoon can do this. I could not see it in the dark, but it moved fast, on two legs and four, through the branches as fast as on the ground. It had a tail." She scowled. "It smelled wrong."

Something about that description nagged at the back of Desi's mind, but her head was still ringing from the wail of the watch-gnomes. "It was you I saw chasing it, right? I heard a scream."

"I almost caught it. I got my claws into it." She held up one hand, extending her long, sharp nails. She sighed when she saw how the beautiful new polish was chipped and scraped off. "My pretty claws. How do they do it? How do human girls keep their nails so pretty and still fight? I have to ask Amy."

"Well, it's gone now." Exhausted, Desi looked up at the night sky. The air was cool and quiet. Too quiet. That racket should have woken up the entire neighborhood, but she didn't see any lights on or hear any voices. "The gnomes were so loud. Why isn't anyone else awake?" she asked Cat.

"They are our gnomes," Cat said, "not theirs. Humans cannot hear them. Even their slobbering dogs cannot hear them. Gnomes cry out only for witches and such folk."

"*You* heard them," Desi said.

"I hear everything."

Cat yawned, and for the first time, Desi noticed that she was still wearing her new black jeans and shirt from the mall. "You never went to bed," she said. "You've still got your new clothes on."

Cat looked down at her mud-stained pants. "This will lick off."

"Tomorrow I can show you how to use the washing machine, if you want."

"That would be better." Cat looked Desi over carefully. "You should go back to bed. Your hairless feet will be cold."

Desi looked down at Cat's bare feet, which were

scratched and covered with mud. "Yours are the same as mine."

Cat shook her head sadly. "Yes, the wrong feet. Too big, too slow. I couldn't pounce right, and I couldn't move through the branches. I am too human." She started toward the house. "Come, Desdemona," she said. "Humans sleep at night."

27

HUMAN OR NOT, Cat had no intention of sleeping while the intruder was at large. She sat up the rest of the night, cat-napping in the chair by the back window. At the first light of dawn, she jerked fully awake; she had to prowl her territory to see if all was well.

Outside, she searched the forest carefully, but there was no sign of the intruder—that trail had gone cold. Instead, she was greeted by a symphony of new life: birds and frogs, squirrels and bugs, all feeding and fighting to survive under the cover of dawn's half-light. Cat felt her blood stir—it reminded her of the excitement she had felt with Bobcat and Amy and Nicole, her new friends. Funny, she had never needed friends before—family was enough—but now, crouched still and silent, watching the forest wake up, she wanted someone to share this new world with her.

She couldn't wake Desi; her kitten had been up late and needed her rest. Besides, some instinct was pulling her toward Bobcat's house. And Bobcat was expecting her—he said so. When she had left him yesterday, he had said, "See you in the morning," and now morning was just peeping through the treetops.

Cat always let her instincts guide her actions, so a few minutes later, she found herself in Bobcat's tree house, spying through the oak leaves at the windows of his home a few feet away. She didn't know yet which window was Bobcat's, but she was patient.

Turning her head, she focused her hearing at the nearest window and was rewarded by the sound of running water—as if it was raining indoors—which meant somebody was standing in the shower on purpose. Cat shivered, repulsed by the thought.

She waited. A few minutes later, a light came on in the next window, and Bobcat entered the room, wearing only a short white cloth wrapped around his middle. Cat waved to him to get his attention. He must have seen her—he looked straight at her through the glass—but instead of opening the window, he acted very strangely, raising his arms over his head and tensing his muscles like he was angry. But he didn't look angry; in fact, he was making weird faces through the glass.

Bobcat kept turning from one side to the other, moving his arms around, tensing his muscles and relaxing, always keeping one eye on the window. Cat was puzzled until she remembered: Bobcat was male. He must be making threat postures to scare off another male. Of course—in the gray dawn light, Bobcat took her for a competing tom. Why else would he be acting so ridiculously? She was a little offended that Bobcat could mistake her for a male; she would straighten that out right now.

Cat gathered her feet under her and leaped the gap to the house, landing nimbly on the narrow eave of the roof under his window. With her agile human hands, she gripped the sill while tapping on the window glass sharply with her claws. Bobcat opened the window, wearing an apprehensive frown.

Cat immediately sprang through, surprising Bobcat so much he fell on his backside. "Get up! Get up, Lazy Claws! Time to pounce! Time to prowl!"

"Cat? What? What are you talking about?"

"What am I talking about?" Cat raved. "It's another dawn! Birdies are singing, mousies are creeping, frogs are hopping; there's a whole wide wonderful world out there waiting to be hunted!"

Bob sat up and clutched at his alarm clock. "Jeez, Cat, it's not even seven yet."

Cat reached for his arm to pull him up, but Bobcat scrambled backward across the floor, clutching the cloth around his waist, until he was backed up against his bed.

"This is no time to rest, Bobcat. Get up. You can nap all afternoon."

Bob looked shocked. "How did you get in here?"

"Is this a game you are playing?" Cat said impatiently. "You saw me—I came in through the window."

"What are you doing here?" Bob's face was getting red. "I mean, uh, it's all right you're here, but—wait a minute." Bobcat must have been cold, because he dragged the covers off his bed. He stood up, clutching the bedspread around him, but it got tangled around his feet, so Cat tried to help him. Too late—they both fell backward in the bed, Cat on top.

"What's wrong, Bobcat?" she said suspiciously. She nuzzled his cheek with her nose. "Aren't you glad to see me?"

Bob's whole body turned red. "Yeah, sure," he mumbled, pulling his arms free of the blankets. "I just need a minute, that's all. You kind of surprised me." Cat took this as a welcome, wriggling happily on his chest.

A knock came from the door, and then a voice. "Bob, are you all right?" The doorknob rattled.

"Fine, Mom," he croaked. Wild-eyed, he grabbed Cat's shoulders to shove her away. "Get off!" he whispered to Cat as loudly as he dared.

Cat sat up, complaining loudly. "Hey. No pushing."

"Bob? Who is that?" His mother's sharp tone penetrated the bedroom door. "What's going on? Open the door, please."

Bob scrambled out of the bed, pulling his bedspread with him. "Just a second," he yelled. He grabbed his pants from the floor, and while trying to untangle them under the bedspread, he rasped, "You're not supposed to be in my room at night."

"That is no problem, then," Cat said, sitting on the bed with her arms crossed. "The night is over. It is morning now."

His mother rapped on the door. "Bob, please open this door. Now. Is that girl Cat in there with you?"

"Yes," Cat yelled, even as Bob was desperately shaking his head. He sagged, one leg in his pants, one out.

"Bob, you know the rules." Mrs. Wilkins's voice projected through the door, sounding strained and formal. "No overnight guests without permission, especially in your room. Cat, you have to leave."

Cat leaped to her feet and walked over to the door. Bob threw out a hand to stop her. "Don't open the door!" he whispered madly. "Wait till I get my pants on!"

Cat didn't open the door. Instead, she addressed it loudly. "I am not staying overnight. I have just come here for Bobcat, and I am waiting for him to put his pants on."

Bob tripped over his pant leg and fell on his face. There was no sound from the other side of the door.

Cat stood over him. "Bobcat," she demanded, "do not just lie there. Do you want to come prowling with me or not?"

Bob shook his head.

Bobcat's mother said, "Cat, please open this door." So Cat opened the door. Mrs. Wilkins entered, hands on hips, shaking her head, her jaw clamped tight.

Across the hall, Jarrett appeared in his doorway. "What's up?" he said groggily. "Did somebody say Cat's here?"

"It's too early," his mother replied without taking her eyes off Bob. "Please go back to sleep."

"I can't," Jarrett answered. "Too much yelling. Hi, Cat." He waved.

"No one is yelling," Mrs. Wilkins said firmly. "Go back to bed."

"Way to go, Bob." Jarrett started to close his door but opened it again. "Someone should tell Bob his fly is open."

He smirked at his big brother and then closed the door.

Mrs. Wilkins said, "Cat, I really think it's best if you go home."

Cat sat down on the sill of the open window and swung her leg over. Her eyes narrowed at Bobcat. "The next time you say 'See you in the morning,' I will not believe you." Without waiting for an answer, she swung her other leg over the side and dropped to the ground, landing lightly on all fours. Through the window, she heard Bob's mother sigh.

"Oh, Bob, I'm so disappointed in you."

I was right all these years not to need friends, Cat thought as she headed home to snuggle up to Desi. *Family is enough. At least there is one person I can count on.*

28

CAT'S BEEN STICKING *to me like a burr all morning,* Desi complained to herself as she left her house for Jarrett's backyard. Cat had woken her up way too early by crawling onto the foot of her bed. Worse, she had instantly dropped off to sleep, leaving Desi to toss and turn with the sun in her eyes until she gave up and got dressed. Next, Cat had joined her downstairs, insisting that Desi thaw out frozen fish sticks for breakfast before she had even finished her coffee. As if that wasn't enough, Cat proceeded to plop down at the kitchen table across from her, scratching the oily breading off the fish with her long fingernails before she ate it. Desi was so nauseated she had to dump her cereal in the sink.

For the rest of the morning, Cat had acted like Desi's shadow, trailing her wherever she went. Whether Cat was still suspicious about the magician or just being overprotective, she was cramping Desi's ability to practice her spells. And Desi wanted to be perfectly spell-checked for the magician's visit.

When it came to *Inferni,* Desi felt she was red-hot, having practiced it the night before. Now, with Cat finally tucked in her room for a nap, it was time to master the rope trick— and maybe to see where the end of the rope went when it disappeared.

A brief search of the house turned up several baskets but no rope. Reluctantly she called Jarrett. She *did* want to see him again, but not today, with only hours to practice before the magician arrived. But Jarrett had seemed eager to help.

Passing under the big oak tree on her way to Jarrett's back door, she heard a loud "Hey!" from overhead. When she looked up, there was Jarrett, sprawled lazily in the tree house with a long coil of white rope swinging from his arm.

"Hey, yourself," Desi answered, shading her eyes against the sun. "Thanks. That's a nice rope."

He broke into a big grin. "You betcha. Bob's a genuine Boy Scout."

"Well, thanks again. Just drop it." She held out her arms.

"Come get it." He dangled the rope playfully over her head.

"Why?" she asked, half annoyed, half curious.

"That night, when you moved here? I was climbing this tree when I met you."

"So?"

Lowering his voice like it was a big secret, he said, "You really wanted to climb, too. I could tell."

Impatient as she was, that was too much like a dare to ignore. Desi scrambled up the ladder to the tree house. By the time she got there, Jarrett had clambered out onto a big branch.

"Do you mind?" she said, clinging to the tree-house wall and cautiously stretching out one hand for the rope. "I'm kind of in a hurry."

"Going mountain climbing?" he teased, holding the rope just out of reach.

"No, I'm . . . just—" She made a try for it and almost lost her balance. Quickly he grabbed her arm to keep her from falling.

She knocked his hand away with a dirty look. What kind of game was he playing? "I'm doing an experiment," she lied.

"Need an assistant?" His eyes sparkled sky-blue. "I work cheap."

"Sorry. You're not exactly qualified for this job." She took a breath to get centered and looked down. The ground seemed to be a long way away. "You going to give me the rope or not?"

"Sure." But instead of handing it to her, he dropped it. Before she could bawl him out, he leaped to a lower branch with the ease of a young lion, swung on his stomach, hung briefly by his hands, and dropped to the ground, his long hair flying. "Here ya go," he said, picking up the rope and offering it to her.

"Wait there." He had obviously spent his whole life climbing this tree, but she hadn't, so she played it safe and shimmied down the ladder, aware that he was watching her every move. On the ground, she quickly crossed to where he was waiting and snatched the rope away. From the idiotic grin plastered across his face, Jarrett obviously thought that he was being cute. She almost flashed *Inferni* in his face just to see what he would do, but she controlled herself. Instead, she merely said, "Thanks, gotta run, goodbye," and took off.

"Want to try out my new fireworks?" he appealed to her back as she was leaving.

"Later," she yelled back, already halfway through the

gate. *Him and his silly fireworks,* she thought. Talking to boys made magic look easy.

Back in the house, Desi selected a large bowl-shaped basket, a souvenir of one of her many trips to India, and after checking to see that Cat was still upstairs napping, tiptoed out as quietly as she could.

Once in the woods, she took off down the trail, stopping every so often to make sure she wasn't being followed. Free at last, she penetrated deeper into the forest. Now the trees were taller, blocking the sun. Descending into a gully lined with ferns, the trail then rose slightly to the perfect spot, an isolated clearing of dark grass ringed with large trees—a fairy ring.

This was an enchanting spot for performing spells, much better than that dusty closet the magician had used. Sweeping the ground in the center of the ring with her foot, she carefully put the basket down and coiled the rope inside it. Butterflies began fluttering in her stomach, but she clamped them with iron determination.

Stepping back to give herself waving room, she cupped her hands as the magician had taught her. She took a breath and exhaled, *"Ess-scale-ate."*

Desi waved her hands. A passing cloud shaded the fairy ring. She kept waving. Birds twittered, mocking her. She waved on for more than a minute, with the breeze waving pine branches around her, a copycat mime in green. Still the stupid rope just lay there without so much as a twitch. Something more was needed. What was it the magician had said about seeing the spirit inside?

She picked up one end of the rope and held it at arm's

length. Closing her eyes, she visualized holding a snake. She could see it in her mind's eye, a writhing, hissing serpent. She repeated the magician's spell in her head, and hoping for the best, shouted to the winds, *"Naja!"*

At once the rope in her hand began to wriggle. Quickly she opened her eyes; the rope was still a rope, but it was moving and, more amazingly, changing. Fascinated, she watched the end of the rope split in two, taking the shape of open jaws, with two twisted strands curving down to form fangs. More threads unraveled to spread out like the hood of a cobra. The head of the rope began to struggle violently, but she couldn't let go; it took all her strength to keep those fangs away from her face.

Something struck her knee. A quick glance showed her that the whole length of the rope had slipped out of the basket and was twisting about on the ground. Heavy coils whipped at her legs. Worried she would be tangled up, she gave a fierce cry, hurling the fanged end of the rope away from her as hard as she could while leaping back down the forest path to escape.

When she had reached what she felt was a safe distance, she paused to let her heart stop racing while she figured out what to do next. A few yards away, the rope was still thrashing about madly; to her dismay, it slid into the dense carpet of undergrowth, slipping beneath the leaves until it vanished completely. *Great, now I've got a magical rope on the loose.* The thing was so long and heavy it made a rustling noise as it moved. Desi froze, listening hard. The rustling noise was getting closer.

Stepping slowly so she could hear the rope as it slithered toward her, Desi crept to the base of the nearest tree. The thing seemed to be stalking her. She reached the relative safety of the tree trunk. Now she heard it clearly, just on the other side of those roots—precisely where Jarrett was standing when he stuck his head out from behind the trunk. "Surprise! Hiya, what's up?" Jarrett held up a colorful skyrocket. "Got a match?"

"Quiet!" she commanded. It was bad enough she hadn't heard him coming, but now with him yakking, she couldn't hear the rope. Where was it? He might be practically standing on it. "Don't move!"

He looked excited. "What is it, a snake?"

Yeah, a fifty-foot-long supernatural snake. Then she heard it, a rasping sound right beneath him. "Do as I say," she pleaded. "Walk around the tree to my side, one step at a time. Watch where you put your feet."

"Is it a rattler?" Maddeningly, Jarrett ignored her, peering around like a kid on a treasure hunt. "I don't hear a rattle. Probably just a rat snake."

"Get away from there!" she shouted.

Looking affronted, Jarrett said condescendingly, "Don't panic. Snakes are more afraid of you than you are of them."

Desi saw a flash of white from behind the tree. Desperate, she reached out to rescue him by sheer force, but, wearing his idiotic grin, he countered with a fake lunge and pretended to wrestle.

He stopped with a jerk. "What the . . . ?" he exclaimed, scowling at his feet.

The leaves around his feet erupted. The rope snaked around his legs, tying them together. "Hey!" he cried. Tripping, he went down, then shot feetfirst up into the air as the rope hoisted him into the tree.

Desi frantically threw her arms around his waist, hoping to drag him down, but the rope sent coils snaking around her as well, binding her to Jarrett and hauling her up with him. In a flash, they both were dangling from the tree, Jarrett upside down, Desi head-up, kicking desperately to free herself.

A few feet above the ground, they stopped rising. Desi hoped that meant they were too heavy for the rope, but instead it began to slowly tighten around her chest, squeezing the breath out of her.

No time left—she ransacked her brain for the magician's counterspell. It was hard to imagine this strangling menace as just a rope, but she forced herself to see it in her mind, limp and lifeless. Gasping for air, she cried, *"Naj'nul!"*

The tightening stopped. Desi sucked in precious air. Worried, she twisted her head around to look at Jarrett. To her relief, his eyes were open—and he was laughing!

"That was wild! Let's do it again!" he shouted, as if he was on a thrill ride. Desi couldn't help herself; she broke out laughing, too, out of sheer nervous release. *Another* spell gone haywire?

"Are you and Jarrett playing?" Below her, head level with Desi's waist, a very curious Cat was poking her nose at them. "Because if you are setting a trap, you will not catch anything that way."

Embarrassed, Desi struggled to get loose, but she was tangled up like a kitten in a ball of yarn. "Could you help untie us, please?" Dangling in the air this way, the rope was cutting off her circulation, making her toes tingle. She had to kick her feet to get the blood flowing again.

Cat began to pick at the rope, but it clearly puzzled her. Jarrett, his face beet red from the blood rushing to his head, started squirming around to get free, but between his squirming and Desi's kicking, they were swinging back and forth like a pendulum, making it impossible for Cat to untie them. Worse, Jarrett was wriggling around while tied up to Desi, his head next to her stomach and vice versa. She felt her face going redder than his. If only he didn't look like he was enjoying this so much.

It was ridiculously humiliating—tied up to Jarrett, swinging in the air, Cat batting at them trying to untangle the rope—so naturally Bob showed up. Was everybody in the world taking a walk in the woods today?

"Hey, Cat," Bob called out from a few feet away. "I just want to explain about this morn—" His eyes bugged out. "Cat? What are you doing to them?"

"I am helping Desi and Jarrett play in the trees," Cat said, concentrating as they swung back and forth. "Can you play, too? It is not easy."

Seeing the astounded look on Bob's face, Jarrett laughed so hard he was speechless. Desi was speechless, too, but not from laughter. What kind of a witch was she? Were *any* of her spells ever going to work the way she wanted?

"Here, let me," Bob ordered. He took Cat's place brusquely, forcing her to move out of his way.

Bob was tall enough to grab hold of the rope and quickly sorted out the tangles. Desi got loose first and dropped to her feet. Above her, Jarrett began to squirm free. Seeing Jarrett about to fall headfirst, Cat tried to catch him, but Bob shoved between them, flipping his brother over before he hit the ground.

Cat scowled at Bob, indignant at being brushed aside. "If you do not want to have fun, you can play by yourself."

Jarrett got to his feet, shaking his head admiringly while he brushed himself off. "Yeah, dude, lighten up. We were having a blast."

"Desi wasn't. Look at her." Bob was pointing at her, and she felt herself blushing harder.

"It was Desi's stunt in the first place," Jarrett protested, but he looked concerned for her, too.

They were all staring at her, as if she needed taking care of. They were worse than her mom. *I can do this,* she thought. *All I need is privacy to cast my spells in peace.* It was clear that she could create magic any time she wanted, but if she was going to learn to control it, she needed practice. "I'm going back home," she said, frustrated.

Still grinning from ear to ear, Jarrett pleaded with her. "Can't you show me how this works?" Examining the rope in the tree, he added, laughing, "Only this time don't get caught in your own trap."

Desi bit her lip. Jarrett's curiosity was proving to be a whole other problem. "Maybe later," she said.

Cat looked thoughtful and declared, "Not here. This forest hides too many snakes. Next time, you and Jarrett must tie yourselves up in the yard."

·₊*·₊*

After Desi left, Cat dissected the recent scene in her mind, puzzled. Desi and Jarrett had been perfectly safe and laughing when she found them playing with the string. So why was Bobcat acting like a grouchy hedgehog?

Jarrett picked up a shiny tube from under the leaves, and Bobcat acted even more grumbly. "You know you're not supposed to have that," he growled. "There's a reason they're illegal here, you know."

Jarrett ignored him and walked away, admiring his shiny toy, giving Cat a "bye" and a wave but nothing to his brother.

"You wanna get your face blown off, that's your business, but not around anyone else!" Bob yelled after him. Then he wheeled with a guilty look to confront Cat. "What?"

Cat moved in closer to stare him down. "Why are you behaving like this? If you do not act more playful, we will not have fun at the dance tonight."

That seemed to really get to Bob. His jaw set and he replied, "Well, then maybe we don't have to go."

Cat was confused. "Of course we have to go. Amy and Nicole both said so. You said you will drive." A thought struck her. "Are you grouchy because you are driving your car? I don't like riding in your car either, but don't worry, I will put up with it."

Bobcat swallowed hard. "If you don't like my driving, maybe you should go with somebody else."

"No." Cat was used to riding with Bobcat, and that was that. "You have to take me. Then if you are grouchy, I will dance with other people, like Amy said."

Bobcat turned pale. "Forget the dance. Forget the whole

thing," he said bitterly. "I just remembered I'm busy tonight, anyway."

He stalked off, sulking with his whole body, even from behind. Cat was totally bewildered. Was Bobcat acting this strange because he was human or because he was male? Worried, she trotted after him.

"Bobcat. Stop. Where are you going?"

He kept stomping through the woods. "Home. I got stuff to do."

Cat followed him as far as his gate, but once there, he slammed it in her face. Distraught, she turned her back on him and his house to show she didn't care. She crouched down on all fours, licking her hand. It didn't feel right. Nothing felt right in this new body. She felt sad and lonely. Lonely was an unfamiliar feeling.

29

TO DESI, COUNTING the hours until the magician's visit, the rest of the day seemed to drag on forever. Eventually, finally, the afternoon shadows lengthened into dusk; Desi grew excited, then worried—the dance that would draw Cat away from her post started at eight, but she showed no signs of getting ready.

Desi found Cat upstairs, napping on the big bed. "Want me to help you with your new dress?" she said, sitting down beside her.

"I do not need it. I am staying home tonight," Cat replied.

Catastrophe! Cat would never let the magician anywhere near the house. "How come?" Desi asked desperately. "You'll have fun. You'll see all your new friends."

"I do not have fun with Bobcat." Cat rolled over, turning her face to the wall.

The truth dawned on her. "Did you guys have a fight?" Cat didn't answer. She realized that arguing with Cat was like, well, arguing with a cat. Nobody was more stubborn; she might as well argue with the wall. But she knew someone she could persuade. "I'm going next door. Be right back."

She headed straight for Bob's backyard. When she peeked through the basement window, she spotted him where she hoped he'd be, working out in the basement, alone.

"Hey, Desi," Bob said tiredly when he answered her knock. "Jarrett's upstairs." She noticed the hangdog expression on his face as he let her in. She got right to the point.

"What's with you and Cat not going to the dance? Did you have a fight?"

Bob slumped on the old worn-out sofa. "Nah. I don't know. Not happening."

Desi stood over him, hands on her hips. "What did you do? Did you say something dumb?"

"I don't know." Bob raised his hands to appeal to the ceiling.

"Well, are you at least sorry you said it?"

He nodded. "Yeah, I guess." He sure looked sorry.

"Good." She ran out the door.

Back home, Cat was curled on top of the kitchen table, staring out the window. "I talked to Bobcat," Desi told her. "He said he's sorry for everything. Now are you going to the dance?"

Cat's eyes tracked the squirrels running up and down the trees. "Dancing is for silly human girls. I hunt, I prowl, I guard my territory. I have no time for foolishness."

"But you're human now," Desi persisted, hiding her growing panic. "You love your clothes and new nails. You'll love the dance when you get there."

"I am only human on the outside," Cat said primly. "Inside I am still me. Some people cannot handle that."

"You *did* have a fight with Bob, didn't you?" Desi thought carefully. "I know it's hard when people don't accept you for who you are. But give him a chance. Everything's happening so fast." *Or not fast enough*, she thought desperately.

Cat licked the back of her hand and smoothed her hair, pretending to be unconcerned. "It does not matter. Bobcat said he could not go. Today he said it. He is too busy."

"Too busy for you?" Desi couldn't believe it. "That doesn't sound like the Bobcat I know. Wait here." She dashed out.

This time she didn't wait for Bob to open the basement door but barged right in. He was still where she left him, slumped on the worn-out old sofa. "What's so important you're too busy to go out with Cat?" she demanded.

He shrugged. "I got stuff to do, you know; 'sides, like, Dad's getting picky about the car. . . ." He trailed off. Desi hovered over him, refusing to let him off the hook. "Look, I could handle the mall," he admitted. "Her running around like that? I thought it was crazy fun, you know? And then, like, at the zoo, she . . . but then this morning? Before I could even get dressed? And, then, jeez, later, in the woods? You gotta admit that was weird. . . ." He shook his head morosely. "It's too much. I can't keep up. I never know what she's going to do, you know?"

Desi did know. Sometimes she felt exactly the same way about Cat. Sitting down on the couch beside him, she said, "You're right. Cat's not like other girls. She's always herself, no matter what. That's what's great about her." As the words came out, they surprised her. When Cat was a little kitty, she had taken her independence for granted, but now, as a girl, Cat seemed unique and wonderful.

Bob was staring down at his feet. She waited for him to say something, but he was acting like she wasn't there. "Okay," she said, standing up. "Suit yourself."

But she couldn't leave like that. With her hand on the

doorknob, she about-faced and told him, "Cat's not weird, you know—she's different, and that's all right. If you can't appreciate her, that's your problem. You don't deserve to go out with someone as great as her." Her temper flaring, she yanked open the door.

"Don't you think I know that?" Bob's sorrowful tone stopped her at the last second. He went on. "Who am I kidding? Look at her—she's so cool and beautiful. She does what she wants and doesn't care what anybody thinks." He rubbed his face with his hands. "You know what's gonna happen at the dance? I'll look like an idiot, and she'll laugh at me; then she'll dump me for some jock or something. I know she's way out of my league, and I don't need to go to a dance to get it shoved in my face."

Desi's heart jumped into her throat. She felt for him; Bob hadn't said this many words to her in the whole time she'd known him. She sat down beside him again, collecting her thoughts. "First, Cat doesn't laugh at anybody. Or anything. You should know that. Second, she likes you." Bob started to protest. "She does. She wouldn't waste time with you if she didn't. So, like, what's she going to do? Who knows? I don't even think she knows. Anything could happen. You just have to let Cat be Cat." She thought about the other day, when Cat had tried to crawl into her lap. Her best friend had been right there all along, and she hadn't recognized her. "Just take good care of her, okay? And let her sit in your lap sometimes."

Bob nodded. "You think she still wants to go?"

Desi stood up. "Definitely. I'll tell her you'll come by as soon as you're ready." She checked him over. He seemed more cheerful. "See ya in a few minutes," she said encouragingly. As she was going out the door, she added, "Might want to take a shower first."

She was so intent on her mission that when she opened the gate to go into her own yard, she literally bumped into Jarrett, who was just coming out.

"Oh, sorry!" Taken by surprise, she asked, "Were you at my house?"

"Oh, here you are," he said, acting more jittery than usual. "I was looking for you."

"Sorry, I'm in a hurry. Later." She started to edge past him, impatient to get Cat ready for her date.

"It *is* later," he said, blocking the gate. He had a mischievous twinkle in his eye. "Good news. Mom and Dad had to go to a funeral and won't be back for two days. Bob's going out with Cat, so I thought, if you want, we could, you know, watch TV, light off some fireworks. What do you think?"

"Tonight?" In her mind's eye, she could see herself hanging out with Jarrett, really alone, just the two of them, without anybody looking over her shoulder. Any other time it would be fantastic, but why tonight, with her special visitor due? Her head was spinning.

"Look," Jarrett said, shrugging like it was no big deal. "Come over, we'll make popcorn, whatever. Want to?"

She did want to. She was getting a little chill up her spine just thinking about it. But if she stood up the magician, he might not come back. She sneaked a glance at Jarrett. For all his casual "whatever," he was serious. If she turned him down now, would he ever ask her again? She wished she could explain how important the magician and his magic were to her.

That was the problem. Whether he believed her or not, she couldn't tell him the truth. "Uh, sorry," she said, trying to hide her frustration. "I'm, uh, really, really busy." She thought fast. "My father needs me around, to, you know . . . he wants some time together, just the two of us. Sorry." That was it—blame it on her golem dad; that's what it was for.

"You'd rather spend time with—" He looked at her in disbelief. "Can't you get out of it?"

She started to elaborate, but the lie caught in her throat. She was getting sick of all this sneaking around. Jarrett had his arms crossed, frowning. He looked as frustrated as she felt. Averting her head, she squeezed past him to escape into her house. It was all so unfair.

30

AROUND SUNSET, BOB showed up at the front door, neat and tidy in his white button-down shirt and khaki pants, standing at attention like an overgrown Boy Scout. Desi made him wait outside. Upstairs, she found Cat in the master bedroom, struggling with the buttons on her shiny new dress.

"This is worse than a collar," Cat said. "I don't know why you humans put up with these things."

"Bob's here," Desi said. "He's waiting for you out front."

"Tell him to go away. I should never have thought of leaving you here alone." Her fingers tore at the mismatched buttonholes in desperation.

"Quit ripping at it; you'll tear it," Desi replied. "I'm not alone. I've got the watch-gnomes and dummy dad. It's a full house. We'll have a party."

"What am I doing?" Cat said plaintively. "I don't belong in these clothes. I'm not like the others. What is a dance, anyway? I'm not going." Cat's long fingers curled up into fists. Desi had never seen her so fretful.

"Everybody has trouble with buttons," Desi said. "Here, let me."

She stepped up to straighten out the mess, but Cat jerked away. Desi saw that Cat was close to panic. "I didn't think anything scared you," she said.

"Why not?" Cat said. "I have never been to a dance. New things are strange, and strange things are dangerous."

Desi was taken aback. "But they can also be fun, and exciting. Half the fun is not knowing what will happen."

"Too much is new already."

Desi realized that Cat was afraid. A new place, with new friends and different customs? Desi knew how that was. "It's just a school dance. And all your new girlfriends will be there. Just stick close to them and do what they do."

She gently began to sort the buttons into their proper places. Cat stood up straight, staring into space as if facing a firing squad, or a bath.

"There you go, all done," Desi said, finishing the buttons. She smoothed out the silky fabric. It looked pretty, just the thing for a special night out. She stepped back to look Cat over. "You look great." She really did. Desi felt a stab of jealousy.

Cat looked down at her bare arms and legs and shivered. "You'll need a coat," Desi said. "These nights get chilly. Wait a minute." She dug through the back of her mother's closet until she found it: At the far end, wrapped in plastic, hung Callida's coven cloak, the black satin cape that her mother had worn at special witches' ceremonies before Desi was born. The cloak reminded her that her mother was a witch, too, and wouldn't be here tonight. That gave her a sad kind of pain.

She draped it carefully over Cat's shoulders. "There," Desi said. "Perfect. Bobcat's waiting. You'll have fun."

Cat took a deep breath, exhaling slowly. "Thank you," she said. She walked out the door without looking back.

Desi remained behind for a second, puzzled, until she realized that she had never heard Cat say those words before. An unexpected memory came to her of a day, years before, when she first saw a furry black bundle alone in her basket. The kitten had been tiny, helpless, and afraid, depending on Desi for warmth and safety. Desi had felt a rush of pride, and love, and protectiveness as she cradled the new member of the family in her arms. For some strange reason, she relived that moment as she followed her now-grown-up Cat down the stairs.

When they got downstairs, they saw that Bob was still waiting outside as he had been told, shuffling his feet, looking around for something to look at. At the sound of the girls' approach, his whole face lit up like somebody had hit a switch. Then he saw Cat, in her shiny little dress and sleek, calf-high boots. He sucked in a lot of air real fast.

Cat spotted him at the same time, eyeing him up and down warily. Suddenly she stiffened like someone had struck her and without warning pivoted and ran back up the stairs. As Cat rushed by, Desi saw a wild expression on her face. She was afraid Cat had lost her nerve and was running away to hide, but Cat shouted back to her, "I forgot. Make him stay."

Bob looked desperate, so Desi rushed to reassure him. "She just forgot something. Girls have a lot to think about on dates, you know." From the look on his face, Bob didn't know.

They waited long seconds. Bob couldn't seem to catch his breath—he was starting to turn blue. And Desi was afraid the magician might literally pop up at any moment. She had just decided to check on Cat when she heard her on the stairs.

Bob started breathing again. "Uh, hi, uh, you look—um, I'm here," he said to Cat.

Cat glided straight through the door and down the steps without a word, carrying a large shopping bag with handles. Bob followed, hovering like he wanted to get close but didn't have the nerve.

As Desi watched the couple parade down the sidewalk all dressed up on their way to the dance, she felt a little envious—until she recalled her own plans. "You guys have fun," she called out. "Don't worry about me. You don't have to hurry back."

Cat dashed back to her. "You will not run away again? Promise me you will be here when I get back."

"Don't worry. I'll be here, watching TV with 'Dad.' Just kidding." She decided to cover herself in case Cat came back unexpectedly. "Jarrett asked me to hang out with him for a while. If I'm not in the house when you get back, don't freak out; I'm around."

Bob gallantly opened the door of the little car for Cat. As she got in, she looked angry, which meant she was nervous. Bob just looked nervous, fumbling with the car keys. To Desi it seemed like they took forever, but finally the car pulled away. She ran back inside.

Passing the front room, she noticed the golem, slumped in its customary chair in front of the TV. Now that Cat was safely out of the house, Desi took a break, plopping down in a chair across from the big dummy, which stared vacantly in her direction, slack-jawed.

Without intending it, words came pouring out of her. "There's nobody else to talk to, so I guess you're it, 'Dad.'"

When the golem made no move to stop her, she went on. "I really wish Mom were here. This is practically the biggest night of my life. I mean, I feel a little guilty about inviting the magician over, but he's one of us. He's a real warlock." The golem didn't look impressed.

She sprang out of her chair, pacing back and forth. "I know what you're going to say. 'No strangers in the house.' But if he doesn't come here, I'll never see him again. Cat's so stubborn—yesterday at the mall she practically scratched his eyes out." She sighed in frustration. "Yeah, sure, he's a little . . . intense. But how would you feel if you knew you were different and had to go around pretending to be like everybody else?"

Apparently the golem would feel stupid; it certainly looked stupid.

"The point is, he's my friend, and he's going to teach me some useful, important magic, the way Mom wouldn't, so when she gets back, I can prove to her I know what I'm doing. Who knows when I'll get another chance like this?" She glared at the golem, daring it to contradict her. "If anyone has a problem with that, they can say so. Only, Mom's not here, is she?" She choked back the feelings rising in her throat. "Well? What do you have to say for yourself?"

The whole time she was talking, the golem had not moved a muscle. "Thanks for listening," she said sarcastically. She knew it hadn't heard a word. "Some father you are. You're pathetic, do you know that?" Her resentment surprised her, but she couldn't stop the sudden flood. "I don't need you." She wanted to shake the stupid thing. "You were never around when I did need you!" The golem stared straight ahead, unblinking.

"You stupid lump, why can't you ever do what I want?" she yelled in its face.

It couldn't. It wasn't really her father, just an animated junk pile. Realizing how foolish she sounded, she turned her back on the thing. "Have a nice night," she said scornfully as she stamped down the hall toward the kitchen.

That must have activated some mechanism, because it finally responded. "Hi, hello, how are you?"

"Drop dead," she answered without looking.

Next she hurried out to the backyard to pick up the watch-gnome guarding the back fence. "I don't know what sets you off, but I'm not taking any chances," she said, lugging the gnome into the house. Setting it down in the closet, she contemplated its broken, scarred face. "Sorry, but I can't risk you scaring him away." The broken finger pointed at her accusingly, so she turned it against the wall.

One by one, she dragged the other gnome statues into the closet. "You can have a vacation," she told the group, breathing hard from the exercise.

As she shut the closet door, she thought she heard a noise, so she opened it again to look. The gnomes had changed. Their hands were now pressed to their faces in an expression of alarm. The little stone mouths were open in shock.

"Don't look at me like that," she said, feeling guilty. "You don't understand. Not a sound, got it?" She closed the closet door firmly.

31

THE INSTANT BOBCAT pulled the car to a stop in the school parking lot and untied her from the seat belt, Cat leaped through the door. She didn't go far; stealthily, using the shadows cast by the big overhead lights for cover, she checked out the strange people surrounding her. People dressed up for the dance were talking in groups or streaming toward the gym. "This is good," Cat said after she had checked out the crowd. "I look like the other girls."

Cat stood tall, fierce and vulnerable. When Bobcat got out of the car, she read his body language carefully. He was looking only at her, not the others, and his chest was swelled up with pride. His neck was tensed—good, that showed caution. He came around to her side. "Ready?"

She looked him over from his shoes to his hair. "No. There is a problem. You do not look like the other males."

Bob gulped.

"Here." Cat held out her bag. "Take it."

Bob took the bag, opening it like there might be a skunk inside, though it was just some clothes. Mystified, he took out a new shirt and jacket. "I don't get it."

"So you can look right," Cat said. "Amy warned me—if you do not look right, they will attack you. It doesn't seem to matter how you smell."

"You want me to put this on? Here, in the parking lot?"

"Hurry," Cat said. "I want to find my friends Amy and Nicole. We will be safer in a group."

Bob squeezed back into the little car. It was a tight fit; he squirmed around like a butterfly in a cocoon while Cat stood guard. After a minute he got out, straightening his new jacket.

"Better," Cat said. "Much better."

Bob blushed as she circled behind him. Her next move caught him off guard. Reaching up, she rumpled his hair and took off his glasses.

"But I can't see!" he protested.

She put her face close to his. "Can you see me?"

"Uh-huh."

She rubbed her cheek against his. "That's all you need. We can go now." She strode confidently toward the gym. Bob hurried to catch up with her.

Amy and Nicole were waiting for them at the entrance to the gym, along with Patrick and a few other people Cat didn't know. "Hi, Cat," Amy said. "And Bobcat! You look sharp."

"Does the shirt fit?" Nicole smirked. "I picked it. Fifty percent off."

Amy introduced Cat to the rest of the group. There wasn't time to sort them into types of animals, but at least she could tell male from female: When the females saw Cat sidle distrustfully away from the males, they surrounded her and made her welcome. The males didn't say much; they strutted around as they always did, looking hungry. It seemed human males were not much different from tomcats.

Amy led the way into the dance. Inside, the cavernous room was strung with paper that might be fun to play with later. The lights were low, and the few people present stood in groups, talking. Was this all a dance was—more talking? If so, they could have it.

Eyes began to turn toward them. Cat caught Bob slinking toward a corner, trying to hide. Quickly she blocked him. "Stand tall," she whispered in his ear. "When you're with me, you're the top cat."

"The what?"

"The dominant male."

"This is a joke, right?"

"Status is not a joke. Position is everything."

"I know." He shook his head sadly. "I'm not a football hero; I don't even drive a cool car."

"You are not listening. You're with me. You're my mate—*date* for the evening," she corrected quickly. "That makes you Number One. And they all know it." She indicated the room.

It was not just pride, though she had her share. She was right; almost everyone nearby was staring at her. At him. At them. Facing the room, slowly she rubbed her back against his chest, up and down, like she was scratching an itch. Her hair brushed his cheek. Bob looked down and saw the whole rest of her, then looked up again, fast. With a deep-throated rumbling purr of contentment, Cat reached back to grope for his hand and pulled him farther into the room. So far, so good.

They had made a good show of dominance at first

encounter, and now she felt acceptance, even if there were a few stares. Most of the stares were for her; that was also good. The males were supposed to look, and the females— no, the other girls—were not a threat. Her new girlfriends were showing her around and introducing her to even more friends. Cat felt her defenses relax. She might even enjoy this.

She quickly checked to make sure Bobcat was in his place at her side. That was no problem; he was hovering over her like a mother with a new kitten. No, she reminded herself, like a possessive male. She looked at him again, and he smiled at her shyly. He did look good, even compared with the other males in the room. Bobcat was not the largest but was big enough, and he was strong in a quiet way. Now that he was without his glasses, she could see that his eyes were kind. And with him at her side, the other males kept their distance; she had felt that right away. More than that, though, there was something different about him. Cat dug deep inside herself and knew what it was. She could trust him.

A sudden commotion made Cat tense up again. The crowd became excited, restless. Bright lights chased away the comforting dark, moving and flashing in rhythm to music that Cat felt as well as heard, loud and throbbing in her gut. All around her, people went crazy, wriggling and hopping like bugs did in the death madness before she ate them. Frightened, Cat checked on her friends—Amy was wiggling but was smiling at Cat, which meant she couldn't be mad with fear. Nicole was hopping up and down with Patrick, who had his eyes closed. Even Bobcat, who normally stood straight up, was bending and jerking. He stared at her with eyes glazed over, like he couldn't really see her. What was happening? Cat felt the pounding thrust of the noise inside her. Was she going crazy, too?

As her panic quieted, she heard something inside call to her. The music pulled her in and took her. She watched the others so she could copy them, but they were all too different from one another. Some were jerking around and waving their arms; some were hopping; some were swaying, fixed to one spot. It didn't seem to matter, so Cat let the sound inside move her. This was totally new—before, every noise had a meaning, and loud sounds meant danger, but now she was so swept up by the wave of gyrating people she forgot to be afraid.

Cat let the energy of the crowd soak into her. She had never felt so uncatlike before. No longer alone, she was part of the crowd. Someone touched her, but she didn't freak, just moved aside and kept moving. A thrill shot through her; she had only felt this intensity before when some small animal quivered helplessly before her, awaiting the blow. This time she was the victim, batted about by the thrum of the music. She leaped high, twirling in the air to land spinning. She forgot Bob; she forgot herself, whoever she was supposed to be. She was sheer energy, vibrating to the beat. Her excitement charged the crowd; everyone around her began to jump and spin wildly. Like a never-ending chase, they fed on her and she on them. And through it all, above and below, was the music.

Cat was dancing.

32

DESI SAT HUDDLED on the back deck, her arms wrapped around herself against the evening cold. She had grown tired of waiting inside, so now she hugged her knees and listened for any sound that meant her guest had arrived. Though the afternoon had been warm, the temperature had dropped with the sun. She was sorry she hadn't put on a sweater but didn't want to risk leaving her post. Somehow she knew that her visitor wouldn't come knocking on the front door; he would show up quietly in back, calling her name. So she waited, shivering slightly.

"Hi, Desi?" She jumped to her feet. She had a visitor but not the one she'd expected. Instead, Jarrett dropped onto her lawn from the overhanging oak branch. "Hey," he said eagerly. "You done with your dad? Wanna come over? I've got the whole house to myself."

Desi panicked. The magician could show up at any minute! Or worse, change his mind and run off when he saw Jarrett. "What are you doing here?" she shot at him.

Jarrett looked taken aback. "Sorry, I saw you sitting there, you know, and I figured—"

"You figured wrong." She knew she sounded harsh, but she couldn't help it. What if he had caught her doing magic? If she blew their cover, the magician might never speak to her again—and her mother would haul her to the other side of the world. She had to get rid of him. "I'm really busy now, Jarrett," she said. "Goodbye."

"Well, I thought . . ."

Desi stared at him, her heart pounding so hard her mind had blanked out. She didn't dare tell him the truth, and she didn't want to lie. All she could do was keep staring, hoping he would get it.

Now Jarrett looked angry. "Yeah, well, whatever." He jumped for the oak branch, banged his knee hard, and scrambled over to his yard without another word. Edgy and ashamed, Desi listened until she heard him slam the door to his house.

"Finally. I thought he would never leave."

Desi gasped as the magician's voice came from right behind her. She whirled to look up into his face, half shadowed in the dusk. He continued. "I was watching him skulk in the bushes. Is he a problem?"

"Uh, no, just a friend, you know." She caught her breath.

"Be wary. His kind spy out of jealousy and fear. They sense you are destined for greater things."

"Like real magic?" Desi felt the thrill returning.

"Exactly. Ready for the next lesson?"

"Here? Outside? Somebody might see us."

The magician scoffed. "None of the Mundane can spy without my knowing. And I would be surprised if there were any more of the Wise nearby."

"The Wise? You mean people like us, witches and warlocks?" Desi was fascinated. "Aren't we everywhere? How many of us are there?"

He shook his head. "In former times, we were legion. Now, as each generation passes, fewer and fewer are able to wield true power. There are many pretenders, of course, but very few with the talents you and I have."

"Why?"

"Better you see for yourself."

The magician opened inviting arms to the sky. Desi waited, breathless. For a long moment, the night air was still; then, gradually, all around her the sky was filled with sparkles reflected in the porch light, tiny flashes that floated down around her, as if the stars were drifting out of the sky. "It's snowing?" she wondered aloud. "It's not even September."

"Hold out your hand."

She stretched out her hand to catch a snowflake and was surprised when a tiny bubble came to rest in her palm. It did not pop but sat there, quivering with the exertion of its journey. All around her, other bubbles continued to fall. "It's snowing bubbles!" Desi felt exuberant.

"If you would see true magic," the magician said, "you will have to leave the mortal earth behind. You are going to take a trip inside the bubble."

"But it's so tiny!"

"Then make it grow," he dared.

Instantly, the kiddie spell her mother had taught her came to mind. Half-embarrassed, half-excited, she raised her palm into the air, holding out the tiny bubble. All around her, the air stirred in anticipation, as if the bubbles sensed her power. *"Hobblebobblebowlameni!"* The little bubble in her hand began to pulse. Flushed with energy, it grew, stretching its own boundaries—the size of a softball, a basketball, bigger still. It swelled to fill her vision, a transparent globe swirling with colors. The magician nodded approval and backed up to give her room.

Though the bubble weighed nothing, it grew too big to hold in her hand. She let go and it floated, swelling until it was bigger than she was, but delicate, glimmering. She reached out to touch it but drew back, hesitant. "How do I get inside?"

"Wait." The bubble kept growing. It pressed up against her nose. She was afraid it might pop or get soap all over her, but before she could blink, she was inside, looking out at a swirling, glowing world.

Weightless, she drifted inside the gossamer globe floating gently up, away from the back deck. The higher she rose, the more anxious she got. "I don't know how to fly this thing."

"Nervous?" came the magician's voice inside her head. "Don't be. You made it. You control it."

Hesitantly, Desi reached out a finger to touch the shimmering wall that enclosed her. It pulsed and swirled, twisting light into weird fractured shapes. Colors were split into a rainbow rivulet, like a prism. She was startled to see her house receding fast; far below, it waggled in a contorted dance. Uneasy at being alone, she asked, "Where are you?"

"Right beside you. First star on the right." She turned her head to see another large bubble rise alongside her, glowing with a ruby light. "That's me," he said inside her head. "Now tell me what you see."

"Everything looks funny—the colors are so bright, and everything kind of flows into everything else. The bubble changes everything." The trees were glowing, their edges dissolving into the sky. The fields pulsed with a savage life, rising and falling like waves on a stormy sea.

"You are seeing the world as it truly is," he said. "Everything has a spirit—not just people and animals but the stones, the trees, the very dirt beneath our feet pulses with energy."

Though it was all strange, it was all so familiar, too. "I've seen this before," she said, amazed. "It's just like in my dreams!"

"Only in your dreams do you live your truth. When you think you are awake, you are really sleepwalking. But it is possible to live your dream."

Desi caught sight of her own reflection in the curved wall. Instead of a fun-house-mirror version of herself, she beheld a luminous apparition of golden light, shining with an inner radiance. Quickly she glanced to either side to see if some fairy had hitched a ride with her, but she was alone in the bubble.

"If this is real, why don't I see it all the time?"

"You might, but you have been taught to close your inner eyes."

"By who? My mother?" She couldn't believe that anyone would deliberately turn away from such beauty. "Why?"

"To protect you." The thought came clear. "The Mundane fear what they cannot control—the miracle that powers the beating heart of existence. And they are jealous of the Wise, because we *can* control it. If they knew the truth, even the friendliest of neighbors would turn on you and try to destroy you."

Desi recalled her mother's repeated warnings about witch hunts and fitting in. *All those years of constantly moving and hiding out—because I could see this and they couldn't?*

Desi opened her eyes wide, taking in the splendor of the world around her. "She should have told me."

"Do not judge her too harshly." His words were kind but spiced with bitterness. "Every year, the true light of the world becomes harder to see. In time, there may be no difference between witches and ordinary mortals. Your mother has given up. Resigned to the growing darkness and with the best of intentions, your mother is teaching you to walk blindfolded, preparing you for the day the light fails."

"But why does the light have to fail? What's making it go away?"

"Mundanes again." His contempt was clear. "Unfortunately, they have an unconscious power of their own. Their collective fear pushes the world of spirit farther away with each passing day. The result is that most witches cannot perform the simplest spells and are left with a mere memory of greater days."

"But I can do magic. So can my mother." She thought of her aunt Lissa, who always asked her mother for help with her own magic. "I don't want all this to disappear." She reached out as if to clasp the beauty in her arms. "What can we do?"

His voice grew solemn. "Help me bring magic back into this world. The sacred bond between matter and spirit has been broken. The marriage of our material world and the world of pure spirit has been betrayed. The two Worlds must be reunited. As it was, it will be."

That was a lot to take in but it thrilled her to her core. "How?"

"Again, I'll have to show you. To really know the truth,

you have to experience it for yourself. Time to come down to earth. To take the next step, you must have your feet on solid ground."

Desi found that simply thinking about landing made her bubble drift gently to earth. The moment it made contact with solid ground, the fragile sphere vanished with a *pop,* and all around her the world resumed its solid, serious shape. "The magic is gone," she said with a twinge of regret.

The magician emerged from his own bubble, tall and imposing. "It's still there. But it won't be for long. This dead, dull world will become the only reality if we don't act soon."

"I'm ready. What do we do?" She looked about sadly, as if expecting to see the magic seep away behind her back. A few dry leaves drifted down from the trees; that was all.

"I warn you, it may be risky."

Desi couldn't help it—she broke out laughing. "Well, life isn't worth living if you don't take risks, right?" she quoted him.

The magician gazed at her steadfastly, his eyes shining with pride. "I swear to you, I will never let harm come to you or force you to do anything against your will."

"I know," she said. Excitement rushed through her whole body; her fingers tingled with anticipation. "So. What next?"

"Down the rabbit hole, Alice," he replied mysteriously.

33

BOBCAT WAS TRYING to bite her!

Cat couldn't think of any other reason he would wrap his arms around her and put his mouth so close. She shoved him away so hard he had to grab the edge of the tree-house wall to keep from tumbling to the ground. "Hey!" he protested. "Why'd you do that?"

"No biting. I trusted you."

·★·★·★·

When Cat had told Bobcat that they had to leave the dance early because she was concerned about Desi, he had put on the exact same expression as his old dog behind the garbage cans. But when they got home and Cat felt the crisp, calm night air and relaxed, saying she could keep watch outside for a while, he cheered up. And when she confessed that she was in the mood to cuddle up in a warm lap, he seemed to really like that idea. Then, when she suggested that they see if they could both fit into the tree house, he got all excited.

High up, Cat wriggled against him, getting comfortable. "You can see everything from here," she said, "and no one can get to you, even from above. I would be up here all the time!"

"Yeah, when I was little, I used to come here when I was mad or if I wanted to be alone."

"It's good to be alone, when you want to," Cat said, "and to have people waiting to take care of you when you return."

"I could do with less taking care of," Bob said in a rush. "My parents are always on my case about something. The way they act, you'd think I was Jarrett, running around all night getting into trouble." He paused for a breath. "Does your mom still treat you like a kid?"

"I don't remember my mother," Cat said quietly, feeling what it was like to be small again. "I was taken away from her when I was very young."

"Oh, uh, I'm sorry." Bobcat winced. "You're, uh, adopted?"

"You could say that. I am not whining like a dog. I have a good life. I do what I like most of the time, I have my food waiting, and my new family is good." Cat was lost in her own reverie. "The worst part was moving so much; every year a new home. I just got to know my territory when—*boom!*— off in the car to a new place. I didn't like that."

"Yeah, that must have been rough," Bob said. "You never told me where you live?"

"Here, now. In Desi's house," Cat said, surprised at the question.

"Really? You're going to stay here? For how long?"

"Until they move again. They always move," she said sadly.

"Maybe they won't this time," said Bob hopefully.

"Maybe. I hope so. I like it here." She rested her head on

his shoulder. When she looked up, his big round eyes were inches from hers, brighter than the moonlight. He was looking at her so intently she shivered. Slowly, he put his mouth close to hers.

And then he tried to bite her.

At least, she thought that's what he was trying to do. She shoved him away, hard.

"What's wrong?" Bobcat cried, grabbing the edge of the tree house. "Jeez, Cat, be careful. It's a fifteen-foot drop." He didn't look biting mad, just frustrated, as if he'd missed his pounce on a sparrow. "I thought you said you wanted to get closer."

Cat felt sorry, a little. "I do want to get closer; I was surprised; that is all." She pulled him back into the tree house beside her. Bobcat settled down carefully, trying not to crowd her. She snuggled down against his new shirt that she had bought him. It was silky. It reminded her of long ago, in the box where she and her sisters were born, a nest lined with soft cloth. Though she could not remember what her mother had looked like, she felt again the gentle caress of her rough tongue on her fur.

"It's all right with me if you want to do it again," she said quietly. "Just go slowly."

Bobcat's eyes grew as big as saucers of milk. He leaned toward her slowly. As he got closer, she was stirred by strange sensations, all mixed up, like feeling the thrill of the hunt and the comfort of a soft lap at the same time.

A sudden noise startled her. She froze, and Bobcat jerked back with a start.

To Cat's surprise, Jarrett's head popped up over the edge

of the platform. "Oh, it's you guys. Sorry. I thought you were gone." He looked flustered. "Did ya see it?"

Bobcat glared at him. "Can't we have any privacy anywhere?"

"Sorry." Jarrett blushed. "That strange animal's back—you know, the one I saw a few nights ago?"

"I told you before, it was just a big squirrel!" Bob said, scowling. He explained to Cat, "That was before you got here."

"Yeah, well, you didn't see it," Jarrett scoffed. "Anyway, I spotted it again just now, way back in the woods, practically flying through the treetops. It was headed this way. I was just looking to see if it was hiding in the tree house again."

Cat recovered her poise. "Is Desi with you?"

Jarrett's face scrunched up, as if he had a sour taste in his mouth. "Nah. She said she was busy—had to stay home, spend the evening with her dad."

Cat's inner alarms went off. No one would waste time with that slug in the chair. Desi was lying. Hopefully, she was lying at home.

"I must go home now."

"Now? Why?" Bobcat cried, like someone had stepped on his tail.

Surprisingly, Cat understood how he was feeling. She wasn't sure what she and Bobcat had been doing, but she had been really liking it. "I will go and come back soon, after I see that Desi is safe."

"You're coming back?" Bobcat asked, brightening. "So I should wait here?"

"Yes, wait here," Cat repeated. She swung her bare legs

over the edge of the platform to climb down, but Jarrett was in the way.

Jarrett turned bright red and quickly scrambled down. Cat reminded herself to change clothes; this shiny dress was good for dancing but not for climbing trees.

34

"DOWN THE RABBIT hole, Alice?" Desi repeated the magician's words to herself as she scanned the forest floor, thinking hard. She had certainly felt like Alice in Wonderland in the bubble, but all she could see now was ordinary shrubs and trees. "I don't see any holes."

"Then you'll have to make one," said the magician with a dramatic flourish of his hands. "Create a Portal."

"How?"

"Simple. Draw a five-pointed star on the ground. Use *Inferni*."

Desi hesitated. "Won't I set fire to the woods?"

"Not if you are Wise," he teased, arching one eyebrow.

She held out her hand and whispered, *"Inferni."* A bright flame burst from her fingertips. "Like this?" She knelt to trace a five-pointed star on the forest floor; where her fingers passed, orange fire blazed. The magician leaned toward her intently, following each wave of her hand.

Concentrating on the burning ground, she visualized the fire confined to its pattern. The star came out clumsy and lop-sided, but the magician didn't seem to care. He had said it was simple, but his eager expression told her she had done something impressive. "Perfect, and on your first try," he said. "Now, open the door that you have made."

"How?" Her whole body tingled with anticipation.

"Open your mind, as wide as you can, and feel your heart's desire. Then, speak one vital Word—*Agape*—and be prepared for anything."

Desi drew a deep breath and hesitated. "Is this what they call dark magic?"

A sneer twisted the magician's face. "Is that what your mother calls it? Desdemona, I have been places you cannot imagine; I have seen and done things beyond your nightmares, and I have come out the other side, stronger than before. There is no limit to what you can do if you are willing to risk all."

"I know," she said quickly. "What I meant was, there are four Paths to magic, right? Spells, potions—"

"Petty tricks, growing less effective every day." He dismissed them with a wave of his hand.

"And the third Path is through this Portal?" Desi asked. The magician nodded. "So, what is the fourth Path to magic?"

His expression grew veiled and mysterious. "If I told you, you wouldn't believe me. You will have to discover the ultimate Path for yourself. Now, this is important; for your protection, never open a Portal without first pronouncing the Word *Agape*!"

"Why not? What could go wrong?"

"Trust me, you never want to find out. Now say it."

Desi drew in a deep breath, held it for a moment as her heart pounded its intense longing, and let it all out. *"Agape."* As she spoke the Word of Power, her breath fanned the flames outlining the Portal, whipping them to a fury, until the fire leaped up in her face. With a start, she jumped back, arms up to ward off the intense heat.

Just as quickly, the eruption of flame shrank back, coalescing into a fiery, human-shaped figure. As the figure took form, Desi noticed with surprise it was wearing red-hot jeans. A face peeked out from the flames, like in a shimmering mirror. She knew that face; it was hers but not hers.

The Desi in the flames kept flickering in and out, one moment appearing uncomfortably real, the next moment no more than a vague outline of a girl in the column of fire. Worried, Desi recalled their first encounter—that fire-demon couldn't be happy about getting a shower from the kitchen faucet.

Flame-Desi pointed one flickering finger at her accusingly. "You don't play nice."

The magician looked from one to the other, puzzled. "You've met?"

"She summoned me," the flame-girl said, her eyes smoldering resentfully. The demon directed her fiery scowl at Desi. "You promised to let me out, but you lied."

Desi felt the magician appraising her. "So," he said. "Been summoning demons behind your mother's back?" Before she could explain, he added, "Good for you. But it does pose a problem. Once you make an agreement with an elemental spirit, however casually, you both have to keep it. One of the main differences between spirits and people, actually— demons always keep their promises."

"But all I said was 'okay,'" Desi protested.

He raised one eyebrow. Obviously, that was all it

took. Suddenly the flame-girl wasn't the only one who felt trapped.

"What exactly is it you want me to do?" Desi asked her.

"Release me!" The spirit flamed up in a roar. "I want to blaze. I want to race across the world, shining brighter than the sun. I want to *burn*." She gazed hungrily around her at all the woodsy matter waiting to be consumed.

Desi protested, "I can't let her out, can I? She'll burn up our woods."

"Wildfire is normal and natural," the fire-demon lectured primly. "Suppressing it wreaks havoc on the ecosystem."

Desi was stuck. She felt for the creature of fire, but no way could she risk letting it loose. She looked to the magician for help.

"You're quite coolheaded for a fire-elemental," he cut in smoothly. "And since so few witches can open Portals anymore, you must be a very powerful demon to get first crack at this rare opportunity."

"I am a Guiding Light that transforms matter into energy," the demon said, blazing proudly.

The magician bowed. "We're honored."

"Can you tell me your name?" Desi asked.

"I don't have one," the demon sizzled. "I'm nobody—literally. I don't have a body."

The magician continued. "As an important elemental spirit, you must know about the Plan to reunite the Two Worlds?"

The demon flounced, throwing off sparks. "I know a lot of things. I know that spirits like me smolder in chaos while the Two Worlds are pushed farther apart. I know that

Mundane humans are rushing headlong to an entirely material world, where everyone *has* everything and nothing *means* anything. I know that you, who call yourself 'the Wise,' need me as much as I need you, but you are too weak or too cowardly to act." She paused, feigning coy innocence. "Did I leave anything out?"

The magician looked shrewd. "Not all of us are afraid to act. Desdemona, take her hand."

Desi felt a jolt of fear go through her. She knew the demon's fire was real—she had almost been burned that time in the kitchen. She hesitated.

"Life isn't worth living if you don't take risks, right?" he said softly.

This was it. If this was what she wanted, she had to reach out and take it. Desi faced her flaming double. It was eerie, like looking at herself in a mirror while on fire. Maybe she *would* be on fire in a moment. Dreamily, ignoring her fear, she stepped toward the demon, holding both arms out before her.

The fire-demon's eyes blazed. Her flaming arms reached out hungrily to the edge of the Portal but no farther. When Desi's hands reached the same point, she expected a barrier, but her fingers passed through with no resistance. Just inside, their fingers touched.

A shock raced through her body, like electricity. She waited for the pain to hit her, but it never came. Instead, an energizing warmth flooded through her arms. To her surprise, the demon flared up as from her own shock.

"Now, what else do you know, O Guiding Light, Spirit of Fire?" the magician asked quietly, observing the scene with a glint in his eye.

"Such power!" the demon exclaimed, erupting in a shower of sparks. "At last! Is this the one we've been waiting for?"

"The last link in the chain," the magician declared. "Now, in the name of the Two Worlds, in the name of the Plan, I invoke the Pact. Let us pass."

"But you promised you would release me," the fire-girl hissed, gripping Desi's hands fiercely. Desi was surprised at how desperate her counterpart seemed.

"You will be released in good time," the magician said sternly. "And what is time to you? There is none where you come from. Enough. Now escort us or leave us."

The fire-girl flared up in a bright flash, startling Desi, then released her and vanished, literally in a puff of smoke. The magician waved invitingly toward the empty Portal. "Now, if there are no more interruptions, we can start our journey."

"And where exactly do you think you are going without me?" A biting voice from overhead made Desi look up. It was Cat, perched in a tree.

35

DESI TRIED HER best to conceal her surprise. "You're supposed to be at the dance!"

"I was," Cat replied. She dropped lightly to the ground, eyes fixed on the burning Portal. She had exchanged her shiny party dress for her new black tee and jeans. "I left my new friends too soon because I worried about you. Then I went home to find you, and look! I have found you here." She paced around the flaming star warily. "I thought you learned not to play with these things." She wrinkled her nose in disgust.

Desi felt her rebellious streak rising. "I am not *playing*. I am a witch. This is what witches do." She cast a quick glance at the magician, who stood silently nearby.

Cat had not looked at him, but now she snarled, "You again."

The magician bowed graciously. "Enchanted. Desi has told me absolutely nothing about you, but you are obviously as accomplished as you are beautiful."

Cat's eyes narrowed to slits, a dangerous sign. Then, pointedly ignoring him, she asked Desi with a twitch of her head toward the Portal, "Did *you* do this?" She said it as if she had caught a puppy making a mess on the floor.

"Yes," Desi said forthrightly, "I did. Things need to change, and I'm going to help change them."

"With this?" Cat said, caught by surprise. She kicked leaves at the outline of the flaming star, which burned steadily, neither spreading nor receding. "I think you do not know anything about this world."

"So it's about time that she learned," the magician interrupted. "Besides," he addressed Desi, "it's not what you know that matters—it's who you are. The ultimate power is inside you." Though his lips did not move, she heard it: *Your destiny is waiting for you.*

"I do not trust this one," Cat said, speaking to Desi without taking her eyes off the magician. "Most of him is hidden, like when I crouch in the tall grass to creep up on unsuspecting birds."

Cat was going to ruin everything. "You don't trust anybody," Desi said, exasperated.

Cat looked back over her shoulder thoughtfully. "Did you say to me that you were going to stay safe at home tonight while I went to the dance?"

"Well, yes," she admitted.

"And here you are in the woods with a strange warlock, playing with a Hole to the world of demons?"

"So?"

"So now you know why I do not trust anybody." Cat shrugged and turned her attention back to the warlock.

"We who are the Wise are subtle," the magician resumed smoothly, "with far more below the surface than meets the eye. Desi, you yourself are hidden, the tiny acorn that hides the mighty oak inside. You may see yourself as untrained, but I sense your greatness."

Cat rejected him with a toss of her head. "What about your mother? She does not know where you are going."

Desi remembered how it felt to come back to an empty house. It was scary, way worse than any demon. "You're right," she admitted. "I have to be here when my mother comes back."

The magician became grave. "I know how much it hurts to be left alone by a loved one. But what if she never lets you go? She is very powerful. She could bind you with ties you could not break."

Desi didn't want to think about that.

"And what if she never comes back?" he said quietly.

"She will," Desi insisted, but the thought shook her. "She would never leave me alone."

The magician glowered. "She already did, didn't she? Just like she abandoned your father: one day there and the next gone, without any warning."

"That was different," Desi protested, but she couldn't really be sure. "Do you know my parents?"

"Do you understand how hard that must have been for your father?" he said, his temper flaring. "Don't you think he wanted to see you? To be with you when you were growing up?"

"I know, I hoped so," Desi said, near tears. "I've wanted to see him more than anything, but he never came."

The magician clenched his fists. "He wanted to. He tried all those years. He sweated blood to find you!"

"You know where my father is? Could you take me to see him?"

The magician bolted upright, and a veil passed over his countenance. "Yes. He is waiting for you," he said solemnly, inviting her into the Portal with a wave of his hand. "Everyone and everything you ever wanted awaits you on the other side. This is your time. Take the leap. Cross the threshold and step into your power."

Her father was waiting for her? Desi felt herself drawn closer. This was what she wanted. But . . . she hesitated. She yearned for whatever lay beyond that burning line, but now that Cat was here, she felt tied to her, too, and to her mother. She couldn't make up her mind.

Sensing her turmoil, Cat turned to her. "I do not think you should do this," she said. "But if you must go, I will go, too." Her sharp face was unreadable, but Desi felt her caring and was grateful.

She checked with the magician to see if it was all right. He demurred with a tilt of his head as if he couldn't care less. "Then shall we?" he said, sweeping the doorway with a gallant wave of his arm.

"You first," Cat said in a low, suspicious tone.

"My pleasure," he said. "Watch." He stepped into the center of the blazing star, coolly, as if he did it every day. The steady flames lit his face from below, casting it in harsh shadows that made him look menacing, but his tone, though intense, was inviting. "There is nothing to fear. I'll be at your side, guiding you, guarding you. Come." He held out his arms. "This is what you've wanted all your life. It will be like going home."

The magician's open arms welcomed her. She felt herself drawn toward him. A reassuring glance told her Cat was keeping close. She took a step.

"Desi, stop!" her mother's voice commanded, a fierce, urgent plea. "Get away from him."

36

AT THE SOUND of her mother's voice, Desi wheeled to face her and explain, but at first she wasn't sure that it *was* her mother. Callida was poised at the edge of the clearing, dark against a halo of silver light that surrounded her entire body. Her thick black hair swirled around her head in slow motion, stirred by a wind that seemed to emanate from the fire in her eyes. Sparks danced at her fingertips as she extended her hand, reaching out to her daughter. In a husky voice tinged with fear and fueled by anger, she commanded, "Desi, get away from him."

"Mom, I . . ." Her mother's appearance frightened her, overwhelming her sense of relief at seeing her again. She gulped, feeling guilty and defensive. "He's my friend. He's just trying to—"

"I know what he is trying to do." Like a judge sentencing a criminal, she said grimly, "You couldn't even be honest with your own daughter."

Daughter? As her mother's words sank in, Desi turned around slowly. The magician's cool detachment had gone. He stood ramrod straight and seemed taller; in fact, he seemed to grow as she watched. Flashes of scarlet light fringed his leather jacket. His face darkened; only his eyes were visible, brilliant white surrounding coal-black pupils. Imposing as he seemed, Desi was too outraged to be scared.

"Is it true?" she demanded. "You're my father? Why didn't you tell me?"

"I knew you would not trust me, after all the lies your mother has fed you." He scowled so intensely it frightened her. But though he spoke to her, he wasn't looking at her; his eyes were drilling into her mother. That made Desi even madder.

"She never told me anything! I can't believe this," Desi cried, incensed.

"Nothing about the evil Valerian?" he sneered. "About his suicidal, insane, catastrophic schemes? His violent, uncontrollable temper? His selfish, reckless disregard for other people's safety?"

"No! She never told me about you, even when I wanted her to." Desi felt it all boiling up inside her. Furious, she let it out. "My whole life you've been gone, and now you show up and pretend to be a stranger?"

That got to him. Facing her, he paled slightly, on the defensive. "At first, I wasn't sure you were you, and then . . . I thought you would run back to your mother if I told you the truth." Around him, the Portal at his feet shrank to a faint glow.

"You were right," Callida said, her aura as terrifying and compelling as before. "Please, Desi, do what I tell you. Take my hand now." Her mother's hand reached out to her, sparkling like living fireworks.

Desi hesitated. She was literally caught in the middle, her

mother a few feet away at one side of the clearing, radiating bright silver power, and the magician—her father—on the other side, cloaked in an aura of scarlet, still with both his feet in the door to the spirit world. She could feel them tugging at her, tearing her apart. She didn't know what to do.

All this time, Cat had been poised at Desi's side, shivering with tension. Stretched as taut as a bowstring, suddenly she snapped, springing into the branches with a single leap. A wild thrashing ensued—a squeal, a scuffle—and Cat disappeared among the pine boughs.

Desi wanted her back desperately, but for some reason her best friend had deserted her, so she turned back to her father. She wanted to talk to both of her parents at the same time, but they were on opposite sides of her—and neither of them was even looking at her.

"You should have told me the truth," she said to her father. "I don't care what you thought—this is too important. I trusted you."

"I'm sorry I had to deceive you," he said stiffly. "I only wanted you to receive your birthright. Or did you want to go on, day after day, pretending to be ordinary like everybody else? Sneaking around like you were ashamed of who you are?" The wind picked up, whipping his scarlet aura higher as it would a flame.

"We wouldn't have had to hide if you hadn't been stalking us!" Callida's voice thundered with otherworldly power. Her rage fueled her silver aura until it matched his in size and intensity.

"She is my daughter," he retorted. "I want what is mine, and I want her to have what is rightfully hers." His aura expanded, reaching toward Desi. "I knew you would come with me on your own, given time."

Desi felt drawn to him despite herself. How could she feel so connected to him, after all his lies?

"You're off in your fantasy world again," Callida said scornfully. "Desi knows how much I love her. She would never willingly leave me."

"Like you left her?" Valerian's scarlet light blazed back, casting everything in a reddish glow.

"That's not fair, curse you. You forced me to leave my daughter alone."

"As I forced you to leave me years ago?"

"You gave me no choice." Callida sounded defensive.

"Just when all our dreams were in our grasp, you took our unborn child and ran as if I were some kind of monster."

"Those were your dreams, not mine," she said, but she looked uncertain. For the first time, Desi wondered what her mother had given up to keep her safe.

Valerian spread his blazing arms in triumph. "There was no limit to how far we could have gone together."

"Go where?" Callida responded bitterly. "Into the Seven Pits of Chaos? Even if I had chosen to join you, I would never have risked my child like that."

Desi felt tugged like some toy, being pulled apart by two jealous children. If only they'd stop arguing and *look* at her. That was the problem; they were so caught up in fighting about her that they couldn't even see her.

"INFERNI!" she shouted, thrusting both hands in the air. Fire boiled from her upturned palms. Her mother looked shocked. She leaped to her with her arms outstretched, casting

her silver light like a blanket to smother the flame. Valerian reacted, too, spreading his blazing red aura over her like a shield. The two energy fields struck at once. Fueled by her parents' auras, Desi's flame roared, swelling to engulf the entire clearing.

The next moment it vanished, leaving no trace but the scent of burning leaves as they wafted into the air. Desi trembled, surprised at her own power. She had to collect herself before she spoke.

"You both talk about what I want, but you never *ask* me what I want." Her parents began to protest, but she stuck her palms out to silence them. "Just listen to me." She quickly folded her arms in case any more flames leaked out. "Mom, I know you love me and I love you, but don't you see, that's not enough anymore. I have to be who I am. I'm a witch." It took all her courage to say that, especially seeing her mother's lip quiver at her words.

Quickly she turned to Valerian, who was beaming triumphantly. "You said you know how much it hurts to be left alone. Well, I do, too, and I won't do that to Mom." That was the easy part; though she felt drawn to him, she didn't fully trust him. "I want to get to know you, I want to learn magic, and I *will* live my dreams, but I won't abandon Mom. Okay?" Now came the hard part. She had to stand firm, even if it meant he would disappear from her life again. She gulped, waiting for his answer.

For a moment, his expression betrayed his inner fury, but after a deep breath, he got control of himself. "If that is what you want, I will respect your decision." He hesitated, then added, "What exactly *is* your decision?"

She glanced at her mother, who somehow managed to look loving, proud, confident, and fearful all at the same time. "Mom, can't you just, like, loosen up and let me spend time with my father? Or," she added quickly, seeing her mother's aura intensify, "he could visit us."

The air crackled with Callida's electricity, but her words were guarded. "I want you to carry on the traditions of witchcraft, and I will teach you myself, but you don't know what you are asking. It's out of the question. I don't trust him."

Desi stopped her father before he could retort. "Um, what do I call you?" Standing there, with his blazing dark eyes and long ponytail, he didn't quite fit the image of "dad."

"My name is Valerian," he answered flatly. "But I prefer Val."

"So, uh, Val, Mom's kind of got a point—you did lie to me. Do you think you could, like, chill out for a while and show Mom she can trust you? It's been tough on her."

"After almost thirteen years . . ." He clearly swallowed what he was about to say and sighed. "As you wish."

Callida shot at him, "You swear you won't interfere with Desi unless I give permission, and you won't try to take her away from me, ever?"

"Mom!" Desi protested.

But her father answered, "If that is truly what she wants, then I swear." When Callida glared at him suspiciously, he added, "I swear on the spirit of my father that I will not take her from you." Around his feet, the remains of the glowing Portal vanished. Valerian's shoulders sagged, and he looked grave. Desi checked with her mother. Callida seemed stunned by Valerian's simple oath.

At that moment, the wild wind died; all around them, frantically darting leaves dropped to the ground as if struck dead.

Callida and Valerian were just as still. Something crucial had passed between them, something Desi could only guess at. The silence went on so long she felt she couldn't stand it, but she didn't want to risk this fragile new arrangement with more talk.

Finally the suspense broke, but absurdly, when a series of high-pitched shrieks pierced the air. Startled, she heard a furious rustling in the branches, and then a comically small figure sailed through the air to land on her father's back—it was "the magician's" monkey.

Valerian cursed and scrabbled at his back to tear it away. The little creature tried to wrap its arms around his neck. Then, when it couldn't hold on any longer, it leaped for Desi, who caught it in self-defense, cradling it in her arms. The little monkey, minus its cutesy coat and cap, clutched Desi's shirt, its two big, round, almost-human eyes pleading mutely from its furry face.

With a crash, the nearby branches broke apart and Cat appeared, ninja-deadly in her black outfit. Spotting the monkey, she leaped through the foliage, hitting the ground on her toes. "Drop it," she snarled. "It's mine."

The monkey sank its claws deeper into Desi's shirt as Cat paced toward her, quivering with ferocious intensity. Desi hugged the monkey back, protecting it with her arms. "Leave it alone! What's gotten into you?" But Cat only extended her own claws—long, strong, and needle-sharp.

Freaked out by Cat's behavior, Desi turned to Valerian for

help—it was his pet, after all—but he seemed stunned, frowning. She appealed to her mother, but Callida was staring at the monkey with a look of growing horror. "Desi, let go of that thing right now," Callida whispered. "Let Devil take it!"

With no help on any side, Desi took several steps backward. Cat advanced on her. The monkey whimpered in her arms. "What's going on with you people?" she cried. "Cat, knock it off. You're scaring it."

Valerian finally broke from his daze and spoke. "Mungus, what are you up to?"

Callida gasped. "This is your doing," she accused him. "I knew it. This is exactly what I was afraid of." Desi glanced from one parent to the other, totally bewildered.

"Stay out of this." Val's tone was low but brusque. "You'll just make matters worse, both of you." He meant Cat, who was tensing herself for the pounce. Speaking calmly and deliberately, with a voice of command, he turned to Desi and said, "I have the situation under control. I don't need any interference from you. Let go and return home. Now."

Desi was hurt by his dismissive tone until it dawned on her—he was talking to the monkey.

Worse, the monkey talked back. "What are you playing at?" it shrieked in a high-pitched, grating tone. "You're letting her go?"

Desi couldn't believe her ears. What was she holding in her arms? She was too shocked to move.

"I changed my mind," said Valerian calmly, but there was an undercurrent of menace in his words.

"Changed your mind?" The monkey shook its tiny fist in

the air. "After all these years of hunting and searching, we've finally caught her and you just changed your mind?"

"My daughter needs to know she can trust me," he said, as much to Desi as to the animal.

"You're crazy!" the monkey screeched. "I've got her in my claws." Desi desperately wanted to free herself, but the creature had a death grip on her, with its long tail snaking up around her neck. "Snatch her now! Leave the old witch to me."

Desi looked to her father to see what he would do. He had his hands up as if to cast a spell, but he didn't go through with it.

Her mother did. *"Abar'ashel!"* she commanded, flinging out her hands. Wave after wave of silver light flooded over Desi, dazzling her, but it only caused the monkey to tighten its grip.

"Your spells don't work on me, witch," the monkey spat.

Callida's look sent daggers of fear and hatred toward the animal; then she turned them on Valerian. "You let that loose on the world?" she accused. "You're insane. Do something."

"Go sit on a broomstick, you old hag," the monkey screeched.

"Too much talk." Cat had been hovering inches away, poised like a trap waiting to be sprung. Now, faster than Desi's eyes could follow, her painted claws darted out, slashing the monkey. It shrieked, released its grip, and jumped straight into the air.

Callida dashed in to pull Desi to safety. So did Valerian; they collided, both wrestling her into an unintentional family hug. But they needn't have bothered. The monkey, instead of falling into Cat's waiting claws, was caught up by a sudden gust of wind. With a whirl of leaves and a scream, it flew away. Cat scowled in frustration as she watched her prey disappear.

Callida pulled Desi away from her father. "Get your hands off her!" she cried to Valerian. "You've caused enough trouble." Her mother was hugging her so tight she couldn't breathe.

"I don't get it," Desi complained, yanking free from her mother's embrace. "What's wrong with that monkey?"

"That was not a monkey," Cat said, scanning the sky in the hopes that what went up might come down. "That was a wind-demon."

Desi questioned her father with a look, but he ignored it. "The first thing," he said, "is to get you to safety."

"I'll take care of her," Callida retorted angrily. "You just call off your pit bull." She faced Desi, gravely taking her by the shoulders. "That monster in monkey's shape is an elemental spirit of the wind. There's no limit to what it might do. We have to get in the house, quickly." After a last searing glance at Valerian, she snapped, "Devalandnefariel, come," and herded Desi toward the house.

Desi balked. She desperately needed to ask more questions, and she was reluctant to leave her father so soon. But when she saw the same worry in his face as in her mother's, she let it go. Making sure that Cat was following, she ran home.

37

CAT HAD NO intention of following Callida's orders. Now that Callida was back, Desi would be safe enough, and there was a demon running around loose in her woods. She trailed her family just long enough to make sure they were not being pursued and then, when she was sure all was clear, slipped noiselessly away.

Rather than waste time trying to stalk a flying wind-demon from the ground, she decided to double back, picking up the trail of the warlock. *He* at least would stay earth-bound, and Cat had a good idea that the warlock and his flying monkey had unfinished business together.

She was right. Ahead, a violent swirl of leaves warned her to take cover to avoid stumbling upon her quarry. Slowly, patiently, placing each foot cautiously, she crept through the undergrowth.

She heard them before she saw them. "Why? Why?" the monkey screeched. Belly to the ground, Cat inched close enough to peer through the brush.

A few yards away, Valerian faced his demon, which was thrashing about in the pine branches above his head. "Quit acting like such a monkey. No one is watching," he said with icy contempt. "I changed my plans, that's all. If I had been able to take Desdemona back years ago as I wanted, I could have molded her into the proper frame of mind. But it's too late for that. Now, if she is going to be any help at all, I must gain her trust."

"*I* trusted you!" The monkey jumped up and down in frustration. "Over and over you said, 'Find her, Mungus. The Plan needs her, Mungus.' No time to sleep, never a chance to fly. All for her! Why? If she is so important, why did you let her go?"

"I did not let her go. Desdemona is tied to me, blood of my blood. She is tied to me by bonds of love."

"Love?" the demon said, confused. "What does love have to do with it?"

"Elementals do not understand love, and that is your weakness," Valerian scoffed. "Only love can truly unite the male and female energies, split so long ago. The circle must be complete, the forces balanced; only then can ultimate power be released." He scowled. "And this time without any of the romantic infatuation that weakened me with her mother. Desdemona shall love me as a daughter should, with doting admiration, and I will bear for her the proud love of a father for his dutiful offspring. Reunited ourselves, the power of our love will reunite the Two Worlds."

The monkey jittered back and forth on his branch. "You and your pretty speeches," he growled. "What about me?"

Valerian looked wary. "We have found my daughter, and I thank you for your faithful service. Now you can return to your world."

"My world?" the monkey screeched wildly. "This is the only world I know. That other place doesn't mean anything to me."

Colder and stronger than any glacier, Valerian said, "I promise you, when the Plan is fulfilled and the Two Worlds made one, you shall be free to roam with the wind. But right now you are in the way."

"In the way?" the monkey howled. "Now that you have her, you don't need me anymore—is that it? All my years of serving you, and this is how you repay me? Betray me?" A gale rose, shaking the trees. "Your Plan was just a lie. You don't want to *use* her. You want her for yourself! You want this daughter thing so she can TAKE MY PLACE!" The gale roared with such force it bent the slender pines.

"Control yourself, Mungus," Valerian shouted into the wind, struggling to stay on his feet. "I brought you into this world. You owe me obedience."

Hearing this, the demon spun like a top, whipping up a whirlwind around himself that grew in fury until it lifted him into the air, while at the same time driving Valerian backward. Cat wanted to flee, but the violent winds kept her pinned to the spot. Clawing for a hold, she watched as Desi's father raised his arms, surrounding himself with a shield of scarlet light. But his magic was useless against the demon; the cyclone blew it away like dust.

The enraged demon's tempest roared, blasting the warlock off his feet. Valerian clutched at a tree to keep from being blown away. He clung to the trunk, a human flag at half-mast, until the whole tree uprooted from the ground and went tumbling into the forest.

Cat hugged the ground. Trees and branches flew past. Senses whirling from the maelstrom, too frozen with shock to move, Cat covered her head as the world went mad.

38

AS DESI AND Callida hurried home, the wind picked up again, moaning and rattling branches as if trying to shake their nerve. When they had reached their house and were safely inside the kitchen, Callida slammed the door behind her, sealing it with a wave of her hand.

"Wait," Desi fretted. "Cat's not here."

"Devil? She can take care of herself." Letting her aura of power diminish, Callida seized Desi's arms. "Oh, my heart, you had me so worried. I could have lost you. Are you all right?"

"I'm fine." When Desi saw her mother's fear, all the anxiety of the past four days came rushing back. "Why did you leave? Do you even care about me?"

"You're the whole world to me." Callida's eyes blurred with tears. "I love you so much." She hugged Desi frantically. After a moment's hesitation, Desi gave in, hugging her back just as hard. As the pain of the last few days swept away, Callida asked, "Did you find the food in the refrigerator? How was it? Did you get any sleep while I was gone?"

"Mom, I said I was fine. Cat was here. What about you? Where *were* you? Four days without telling me?"

"I had no choice," Callida recalled, looking bitter. "The old Alarming Clock warned me that Val was almost on top of us. I had to lead him away."

"But he was here the whole time." The magician was really her phantasmal father. The idea hadn't sunk in yet—it was still buzzing about in her brain with everything else that had happened. "Why did you try to lead him away? Why wouldn't you let him see me?"

"He doesn't want to see you; he wants to take you away from me!" she said fiercely.

Though startled by her mother's outburst, Desi held her ground. "Why would he do that?"

Callida was shaking, her fists clenched at her side. "Revenge mostly, for me leaving and taking you with me. But more than that . . . Forget it; it's not important."

"It *is* important!" Desi exclaimed. "None of this makes any sense. If you were so worried about my father finding me, why did you leave me alone?"

Callida paled. "Val had never seen you in person, not once, so I thought he would never be able to find you. He shouldn't have been able to, not even with that . . . that monster to help him. My safeguards were too strong. As a result, ever since you were born, he's been chasing me around the world, just to get at you.

"For once, I decided to let him catch me. But in London, where I have friends and know my way around."

"I figured out you were in London," Desi said impatiently. "Why didn't you take me with you to Aunt Lissa's?"

Callida shook her head. "The worst thing I could do. Val would have zeroed right in on you, with poor Lissa helpless to stop him. No. I had to lure Val across the ocean alone so I could confront him without any risk to you. And I couldn't call—he might have traced it. I couldn't risk any contact with you. I'm sorry." Callida gently touched Desi's shoulder. "You've always been so responsible; I knew I could trust you to take care of yourself, especially with Devil's instincts to guide you."

"What do mean, 'confront him'?" The memory of red and silver auras colliding made her wince. If she hadn't been there to stand between them . . . "What exactly were you planning to do?"

Callida paused. "I never really thought it out. I just knew I had to stop him." She grimaced. "I left a clear-cut trail, parading around our old haunts in London. And it worked. He attack—" Seeing Desi's alarm, she caught herself. "He tried to surprise me with magic. But then, for some reason, he disappeared. He came back here and found you. I don't know how. It should have been impossible." A haunted look came over her.

Desi gulped. She knew her mother blamed herself for what could have happened. "He didn't find me. *I* found *him,*" she confessed. She had ignored Cat's warnings and walked right into her father's arms. But why was that bad? If she hadn't, she might never have met him.

She longed for more about her mother and father, but the sight of Cat tugging at the handle of the back door drove her questions away. "She's here!" Desi easily twisted the knob to let Cat in; her mother's spell had locked the door only from the outside.

Desi had never seen Cat so bedraggled. Her hair was all blown about, with bits of leaves clinging to it and her clothes. "Why didn't you keep up?" Desi asked, annoyed with herself for leaving Cat behind.

Callida interrupted. "Devalandnefariel, is Desi's father nearby? Is she in any danger?"

"I would not worry about *him* anymore," Cat said cryptically.

"What *should* I be worried about?" Callida asked, piercing Cat with a sharp look.

"Big winds," Cat said. Her eyes grew huge and round. "Very big."

"That's what I was afraid of." Opening the basement door, Callida flipped on the light, a single bare bulb hanging over a steep flight of stairs. "Thank the stars for these deep northern basements." Callida hurried over to the kitchen counter and picked up a stainless-steel carafe. "Devil, you go first, and take this down with you." She held the container out for Cat.

Cat frowned at it.

Callida grew somber. "Devalandnefariel, I'm sorry that for Desi's sake I had to put you through so much suffering and risk, but now that I'm back, I can make everything right again. This is the potion I made in London to restore you to your proper form."

"Mom, no," Desi protested.

"I like this form," Cat replied, ignoring Callida's offering. "I like being big. I can dance, and eat sushi, and talk to humans."

"Talk to—" Callida looked distressed. "What exactly did you tell people?"

"Oh, do not worry," Cat said airily. "Desi warned me to pretend to be a people. That's how I got experiences being human." She showed her teeth. "I had fun."

Callida threw up her hands. "You are not human; you are a cat and my Familiar, and it's time to change back." She thrust out the potion for Cat to take.

Cat ignored her, examining the chipped paint on her nails.

Callida demanded, "Are you listening, young lady?"

"Am I a lady?" Cat perked up her head.

Desi breathed a sigh of relief. Cat's stubbornness was better than any argument, and fortunately her mother had more important things to worry about.

The wind began to howl through the crack under the door. Exasperated, Callida slammed the potion on the counter. "We'll talk about this later. Right now we have to get down into the basement."

Desi craned her neck into the damp, cobwebby space. "Why?"

"That demon," Callida said. "Elemental spirits have almost unlimited power over their elements. That's why they should never be allowed into our world—or at the very least kept on a tight leash. If Val doesn't regain control over that thing, it may run free."

"Free to do what?"

"To play," Cat said, staring out the kitchen window at the wildly thrashing woods.

"Playing with the wind?" Desi wondered. "How bad could that be?"

In answer, a violent gust rattled the windows. "Pretty bad," Callida said grimly. "We need to seek shelter now." Waving aside their protests, Callida herded Desi and Cat down the rough wooden steps to the unfinished room below.

At the bottom, Desi hesitated; the basement felt creepy, even after what she had just been through—or maybe because of it. The room's musty odor repelled her, especially in the dark. Anything could be hiding in those shadowy corners. Brushing aside the cobwebs, she sat down on the bottom step, staying under the only light, harsh as it was. Cat slipped past her to disappear into the shadows, presumably to check for rats.

Callida took a step higher up. "You'll be safe enough from any winds down here. Safe from your father as well," she said sternly. "He won't get past my defenses."

"Mom! It's going to be all right. I heard him promise."

"It's *not* all right!" Callida stormed, lighting up the room with her blazing aura. It was worse lit up, Desi realized; now she could see dozens more spiderwebs and piles of moldy junk. "Giving that demon a body to hunt you down like some hound from hell? You don't know your father like I do."

"That's because you never told me anything about him," Desi said, exasperated.

Callida hesitated. Her aura faded, and Desi saw her lip quiver again. "I'm sorry," her mother said. "I know. I wanted to tell you, many times, but I was afraid."

"Afraid of my father?"

"Never." Her eyes flashed. "I'm his equal, and he knows it. That's why he was forced to conjure the demon to find you. No, I was afraid I . . . I might lose you," she said, her voice cracking. "I was worried that you would try to find him." Callida took Desi's hand in hers. "I'm so amazed by you; you've grown up fearless. When you get an idea in your head, you don't let anything stand in your way." Under her breath, she added, "You get that from both sides."

While Desi was letting this sink in, Callida continued. "Promise me you won't get sucked into his schemes, at least until you're older and can understand the risks. I know this is hard for you, but I'm asking you to please trust me. The way I trust you."

Desi nodded. She had to trust her mother, like she had to breathe. It hurt too much not to.

Callida called, "Devalandnefariel, come here, please," and Cat reappeared, daintily flicking cobwebs from her new clothes, hopping lightly onto the step next to Desi. Addressing them both, Callida said, "I'm going to open a Portal so Devalandnefariel can guide us to Aunt Lissa's house. Both of you stay here and please don't interrupt me. With that demon running wild, it will take all my concentration." She moved deeper into the gloom until it swallowed her up; then, with a bright flash, she reappeared in a halo of silver light.

Desi watched with excitement as her mother smoothed a patch of dirt floor and sketched out a complicated pattern with her finger, creating a Portal. But something was wrong: After waiting a few moments, Callida looked frustrated and scuffed the pattern out with her foot. Bending low, she conjured a silver beam of light from her hand and, whispering *"Agape,"* drew a star on the ground. Desi expected to see a fiery star like the one she had created earlier that evening, but no fire rose from the ground. Nothing happened at all, and after a few more passes, her mother straightened up.

"It's that demon," she said bitterly. "This is hard enough

normally, but with that thing blocking my spells . . ." She set her jaw and looked grim. "There's no help for it. We can't risk a tornado bringing the house down on our heads. I'll have to leave my body and work on the astral plane." Desi must have shown her alarm, for Callida said reassuringly, "Don't worry. I'm just going to go into a trance for a while. Devalandnefariel, stay alert, and when you sense the Portal opening up, get Desi through and then drag me along with you, understand?"

Cat tossed her head to show that she had heard, even if she didn't entirely approve.

Callida, still glowing, came over and took Desi's hands. "This may seem scary, but it's perfectly safe; it will be like I'm sleeping. Remember, I won't be able to hear you or answer if you talk to me. And don't try to wake me—let me come back to my body naturally. If you're in doubt, ask Devil."

With a final squeeze, she let go of Desi's hands and strode back to the center of the room. "I'm counting on you. I trust you, both of you."

Folding her arms across her chest, Callida leaned backward, drifting slowly into a reclining position until she lay stretched out flat, floating a few inches above the floor, resting on her shimmering energy field. As her eyes closed, her entire body went still, leaving her aura vibrating faintly around her. To Desi, it seemed as if her mother had transformed into a fairy-tale princess, encased in a magical coffin, sleeping peacefully until some handsome prince kissed her awake.

She turned to Cat, who was up on her feet, twitching nervously. "Well?"

Balanced on the tips of her toes, Cat began to circle Callida's motionless form. "I do not think it is working." She leaned down, touching her nose to the edge of the silver aura. "No Hole is opening."

"What's happening to Mom?" Desi asked, worried.

"Nothing." Cat seemed certain on this point. "She will come back into her body and wake up. I have seen this before. But we must not wake her. We must wait."

Desi trusted her mother, but just to be sure, when Cat's back was turned, she conjured flame from her hand and traced a star pattern on the floor. Though her fire burned steadily, it had no visible effect on the dirt.

She gave up and sank onto the bottom step, head in her hands, glancing up every so often to check on her mother and Cat. With so much happening recently, her mind was a jumble, so several minutes went by before a violent moaning and shaking of the house above brought her to her feet.

"Tornado?" Desi said aloud, remembering her mother's warning. "Can that monkey really make a tornado?"

Cat looked up from her vigil. "Are tornadoes natural?" she asked. "Demons are the spirits of natural forces."

"I thought demons were unnatural, evil spirits?" Desi was confused. "Before, in the kitchen with the fire-demon and now in the woods with the monkey, you acted like you hated them and were trying to kill them."

Cat looked thoughtful. "I cannot kill a demon; no one can. I fought them only to keep them from hurting you. If they do not try to hurt you, I do not hate them. Demons are just doing what they must, like anything else."

A storm shrieked over their heads. The house groaned in protest. Desi muttered, "And wind-demons make winds."

"Big winds," Cat agreed. "Very big winds, very fast."

That was the trouble—tornadoes could kill, and nobody was warning anybody. "Was Bobcat safe inside when you last saw him?" Desi asked nervously. "And Jarrett?"

Cat jerked upright as if slapped. "No. I told Bobcat to wait in the tree house." She sprang past Desi to dart up the steps. "Stay here. Your mother will wake soon. I will warn Bobcat and his Jarrett."

"Wait, I'm coming, too!" Desi shouted.

"Do not be afraid," Cat replied reassuringly. "You are safe here. While the watch-gnomes stand guard at the fences, no magic can get to you." She left, closing the basement door firmly behind her.

Desi wasn't afraid; she was torn. What if no one took Cat seriously? People could get killed! But with the watch-gnomes locked in the closet, she couldn't leave her mother unprotected, could she? Apparently the gnomes did more than just shriek a warning—once in position, they had the power to repel invading magic. Now her house was defense-less.

Desi bent over Callida's peacefully sleeping body. "Mom, listen," she said in case she could hear her. "I have to warn people that a tornado might be coming. I'll be back as soon as I can." Tearing herself away, she ran up the steps into the kitchen, banging the door open in her haste to reach the watch-gnomes in the hall closet.

All four were still there as she had left them, hands to their faces, open mouths frozen in shock. She grabbed the nearest under its chin and, puffing hard from the effort, dragged it to the basement door. Spinning the little statue around until it faced out into the kitchen, she ordered, "Stay here and guard my mother."

Once outside on the back deck, before she ran next door, she made a last check through the kitchen window. The little gnome was still at its post, but now its arms were crossed and its mouth set in grim determination.

Desi raced across her yard. Wasn't she a witch? She was the one who ought to be out there, helping to save the boys. Disaster could strike at any minute.

39

CAT CROUCHED LOW against a gale that threatened to knock her off her feet. It bothered her to be outside in this storm; the wind blew all sounds and scents away, leaving her vulnerable to surprise attack.

Oddly, once out of her yard, the wind dropped away to almost nothing—a mere brisk breeze on a summer night. She found Bobcat where she had left him, up in the tree house, his legs dangling over the edge of the little box.

From the base of the tree, she called up, "Bobcat, good, you are still here. I have something to tell you."

"Yeah, I'm still here," he grumbled. "You told me you were coming back, what, an hour ago? And like a sucker I believed you."

She began to climb the ladder. "Believe me now. A big wind is coming. You must go inside the house and be safe."

"Go away," he griped as her head reached the edge of the tree house. "I might bite you."

Cat was shocked, until she realized that he was mad about what she had said earlier. Now she said defensively, "You surprised me."

"What, you're going to tell me you don't know what kissing is?" Bob scoffed. "Do me a favor, would ya? Leave me alone."

Cat was willing, but first she had to make him understand. "Big winds are coming. Very bad. Listen to me."

Bobcat looked sullen, his head drooping between his shoulders. "Could you go play your games with somebody else?"

Cat was confused. She was not playing a game. Wasn't he listening?

Fortunately, Jarrett was. The younger boy came out the basement door. "Hiya, Cat, I thought I heard you out here." Then the welcome faded from his face, and he glared at something behind her.

Cat spun on her heels. For a moment, she was so flustered she couldn't speak: Desi had snuck out again. Cat wanted to drag her home by the scruff of her neck, but she had to warn Jarrett and Bobcat first, so she collared her instincts and controlled herself.

Desi announced quickly, "Look, I can't explain, but there's a big storm coming—maybe even a tornado—and everybody's got to get shelter. Get inside and call around, would you? Spread the word?"

To Cat's dismay, Jarrett didn't run inside. He only frowned and said, "Nothing about it on the news."

"There won't be a warning. Not this time," Desi said, breathless.

"So how do *you* know?" Jarrett asked sarcastically. "You psychic or something?"

Desi clenched her fists in frustration. "No, I'm not psychic. I . . . I'm a . . ."

Just tell him the truth, Cat thought.

But Desi wasn't listening to Cat either. Clearly struggling, all Desi said to Jarrett was "Trust me, would you?"

"Don't you have to do something with your dad?" Jarrett sneered. He turned his back on her and went into the house.

Not only was Bobcat mad at her about kissing, Cat thought, but now Jarrett was mad at Desi, and Desi seemed so upset at Jarrett she was about to burst. As the only cool, calm cat, it was up to her. She scurried up the tree-house ladder again.

"Bobcat?" she cried as the wind picked up.

"What?" he said, sulking.

The sky darkened, blocked by a curtain of clouds. "Hold on tight," she said. "Desi! Run!"

The dark curtain dropped. The whirlwind struck.

A swirling funnel of leaves swooped down, aimed straight at Desi. It enveloped her, spinning her around like a top, then sucked her off her feet. She flew into the air, struggling madly. The wind whipped her around in a tight circle, sending her crashing stomach-first into an overhanging branch of the oak. Desi clung, desperately, while the cyclone screamed. The wind beat at her with such force it could only be a few moments before she was pulled loose.

Cat leaped. Claws outstretched, she flung herself into the storm, flailing about for something solid to grab on to. As the whirlwind sucked her closer to its center, she glimpsed a spindly-limbed creature waiting like a spider in its web. Dancing crazily in the eye of the storm, Mungus the wind-demon screamed in triumph—until he saw whom he had caught.

Drawing within striking distance, Cat lashed out with her nails. Mungus screamed in pain, and the wind slacked. Free from the tug of the whirlwind, Desi hit the ground with a thud that made Cat sick. Cat tried to swipe at the monkey again, but she fell out of reach, twisting to get her feet under her as she landed.

Mungus shrieked. He shot straight into the air, borne up by a fresh gust of wind. But this time he did not fly off. Instead, he opened his mouth and sucked air. The entire whirlwind of leaves, sticks, and debris was drawn into the demon's mouth, which seemed to unhinge, his grotesque jaws open like a cavern.

Anything that came his way disappeared down that gaping hole. The little belly bulged outward as if it would burst, but the creature only grew. The more the demon swallowed, the bigger he got, and the bigger he got, the wider his jaws could open. Whole branches went in, garbage can lids, lawn furniture. He was bigger than Cat now, and heavier—too heavy to be supported by the wind. He sank slowly to the ground, sinewy arms stretching out to support his massive, rumbling belly. The rumbling sounds got louder. The demon's barrel belly heaved, bulging in and out. His jaws gaped. Mungus gagged, a retching sound, and from his throat emerged a belch. A loud, volcanic, gaseous burp.

"Aahh," Mungus growled. "I always work better on a full stomach." He straightened up, towering over Desi, who lay helpless on her back, dazed from her fall. "So, little witch," he said cruelly, "want to play?"

"Why are you doing this?" Desi asked, trying to get to her knees.

Mungus leaned over her, drooling hate. "*Why?* From the moment I opened my eyes to the light of this world, trapped in that pathetic monkey's body, I've served him. Now I find out that we were hunting you down just so *you could take my place*? All that hot air about his so-called Plan. Liar! All he ever wanted was *you*." Mungus reached out two long arms to seize her. "So I'll give you to him. Oh, yes. But after I get through with you, I don't think he'll want you anymore."

Desi scrambled to her feet defiantly. Throwing out both hands, she shouted, *"Inferni!"* Flame erupted from her fingers, forming a ball of fire. She thrust the blazing mass into the demon's face.

"Aaahh!" he roared, opening his mouth wide. He swallowed with a gulp, and the fireball disappeared down his throat. Then, with a retching noise, he opened his mouth again and belched fire. Desi threw herself to the ground to dodge the fireball. Before she could rise to her feet, the demon inhaled mightily, creating a vacuum. Desi gasped, clutched her throat, and collapsed. Mungus blew smoke from his nostrils. "Your magic cannot hurt me, witch. Weren't you listening? No one can help you. Even *he* can't save you," the demon growled. He reached out with both sets of claws.

During all the talk, Cat had been creeping closer, silently, until she got into pouncing range. Now she uncoiled, springing on the demon, raking the swollen belly with her claws. But Mungus was much stronger now—his long arms lashed out, pulling her to his chest in a crushing embrace. Squeezed within inches of the grotesque, hairy snout, she snarled defiance. Mungus snarled back with a monstrous, gaping, drooling roar. Its stench curled her nose, and the force of it flattened her ears.

She struggled to get free, but the demon was twice her size, with arms like oak branches. Her own arms were trapped at her sides, and the breath was being squeezed out of her. Then a shout came from overhead.

"Get your hands off her!" Bobcat dropped from the sky, his size-fourteen shoes smacking the demon's head with a resounding thud. Human and demon and Cat crashed to the ground. They quickly untangled—Cat rising to her feet first, then Bobcat. The demon lashed out with his claws from all fours, like a beast. Cat countered with her own razor nails while Bobcat landed a karate kick to Mungus's fat belly, forcing a whoosh of air from his lips. But this was a wind-demon; the whoosh of breath hit Bobcat with such force it sent him sailing backward to crash into the trunk of the oak tree. He sagged to the ground, unconscious.

"Bobcat!" Cat screamed, torn between helping him and defending Desi.

The demon plucked Desi from the ground, shaking her like a rag doll. Cat was horrified at the sight of Desi's limp body dangling in the air. "All that fuss for this little bag of bones," the demon grumbled. He slung Desi over his shoulder like an empty sack. Inflating his barrel chest, he huffed and puffed out a mighty breath that turned into a whirling gale-force wind. Cat began to panic. Clutching the ground to keep from being blown away, she could barely stay on her feet, much less spring at the demon.

The tempest raged, ripping branches from the trees. Protected by the cyclone, safe in the eye of the storm, the demon hauled Desi to the fence separating the yard from the woods. As he got closer, the wind shook the fence. Mungus paused, waiting for his storm to rip it down so he could pass. Cat heard the horrible splintering sound of a wooden wall shattering. Jagged shards flew through the air.

But it wasn't the fence blocking the back woods that had collapsed. Instead, the side fence to Desi's yard had burst, bulldozed to pieces by a big green mowing machine. Atop the driver's seat, resplendent in its Hawaiian shirt, the golem aimed straight at the demon, proclaiming, "Have a nice day!"

Mungus backed up, still clutching his prey. "I am not afraid of you, wizard," he snarled. "I am beyond your powers, whatever they are."

The wind screamed, whipping at the fake dad's flowered shirt, but the mower was too big and the rider too bulky to be swept away by mere air, thick or thin. They rumbled forward, engine roaring.

The demon backed up until he was against the wall and could retreat no farther. Cat was worried that he might fly away with Desi; he seemed to try, raising his arms to the wind, but his grossly swollen body proved too heavy.

Desperate, Mungus plucked Desi from his shoulder, holding her out as a shield, her limp form dangling from his paws. The golem pushed on, a lone road warrior in his chariot. Cat, still pinned, held her breath; but just before it ran into Desi, the golem stopped short. "Hi, how are you?" it asked cheerfully. Desi's eyes fluttered open.

Cat saw her chance. Crawling on all fours, she used the mower as cover to get closer. Then she jumped, gripping Desi's waist with one arm while clawing the demon with the other. Mungus howled and loosed his grip. Instantly the wind tore Cat and Desi away, sending them flying. But not far. Cat saw the earth coming to meet her and turned her body to absorb the force of the collision, grunting as Desi's body slammed into hers.

Stunned, her breath knocked out of her, she twisted desperately, ready to fight off the demon. But Mungus couldn't move. The riding mower had him trapped against the fence. The golem put its face inches from the demon's, still wearing its idiotic smile, as blithely as if it were out for a ride in the park on a sunny Sunday afternoon. "Have a nice day," it repeated, with a fearless, relentless grin.

"Not fair!" the demon screamed. He began to suck air, preparing for a blast, but before he could exhale, the golem shifted into high, ramming the mower into the demon's big, sagging belly, denting it like a balloon. The demon's eyes bugged out, his cheeks bulged—everything bulged. With a thunderclap, the elemental exploded, sending a shock wave that flattened everything in its path.

Cat ducked, covering Desi with her body. When she lifted her head to look, the demon was gone. So was the golem, blasted into a thousand pieces—twisted beer cans and crumpled newspaper covered the entire yard. The riding mower lay tipped on its side, silent. The entire back section of fence had vanished; Cat could see the forest through the gap, littered with broken boards and splinters of wood.

Cautiously she got to her feet. Desi sat up, shaking her head. "Is it gone?" she asked Cat. Bruised and filthy, she let Cat help her up but then immediately staggered over to where Bobcat lay at the base of the tree. "Is he all right?"

"Bobcat? Wake up," Cat said, worried to see him so still.

Jarrett came running out the basement door, ripping

headphones off his head. "What was that noise? What's going on?" he demanded. He pushed Cat aside to cradle his brother in his arms. Bobcat lay still, his eyes shut.

"He is hurt. Take him inside," Cat said. Her stomach lurched at the sight of Bobcat, usually so alive and strong, stretched out there like death. But she refused to feel any fear. Desi needed her.

Bobcat moaned loudly. Jarrett looked at them, confused. "Will somebody tell me what happened?"

Desi was glass-eyed, looking too stunned to speak, so Cat answered. "Big winds, like we told you." Bobcat groaned and rolled over on his hands and knees, trying to get up. Cat helped Jarrett pull him to his feet. "More winds are coming. Take him inside to be safe." She took Desi by the arm. "Come home." Gently but firmly, she walked Desi toward their own yard, stopping just long enough to see Jarrett help Bobcat stagger into his house.

"What's the hurry?" Desi protested. "Isn't the demon . . . ? I saw it blow up. It's dead."

Cat jerked defensively as heavy footsteps sounded in the scattered debris behind her. Desi's father came stumbling up, ghastly with blood running down his face from a cut on his forehead. *So he wasn't dead, either.* She was not glad to see him, but Desi clearly was, turning to him eagerly, grimacing at the sight of his bloody face.

"Are you hurt?" Valerian asked as soon as he caught up with them. "I tried to stop Mungus, but he was too strong. By the Seven Calderas, if he hurt you—"

"I'm all right," Desi said. Cat could see how distressed Desi's father was, and Desi was plainly touched by his concern, so she let them get closer. Though Desi and her father examined each other anxiously, it was clear that neither of them was badly hurt.

"It's okay," Desi reassured her father. "The demon is dead."

Valerian swallowed hard; he looked grim. For once, the debonair warlock had no easy flow of words.

It was up to Cat to explain. "Demons cannot die. It lost the body it was given; that is all. And this demon hunts like a hound. I think it will never give up. It will be back, as a wild spirit of the wind."

As if bearing out her words, the wind rose, bellowing. They hurried toward the house.

40

DESI CLIMBED UP onto the back deck, her whole body aching from the fight with the demon.

"Where's Cally?" her father demanded. "Why didn't your mother help?"

"She was in a trance." Desi rattled the kitchen door, but it was locked. "She wanted to open a way to London, to Aunt Lissa's, you know."

Valerian grimaced. "Good luck. Mungus can't open Portals, but he can block them."

"We have to get to her!" Desi peered through a window. The little watch-gnome was still at its post by the basement door. Cupping her hands on the glass, she yelled, "Mom?"

Cat said, "If your mother is out of her body, she cannot hear you."

Waving and muttering, Valerian cast several spells at the windows, but they all bounced off. Then he threw a lawn chair, which bounced off, too. "Cally continually amazes me," he said. "She's cast a protective spell on this house so strong no one can get in, by force or magic. What I don't understand is why she would lock you out."

Desi looked at Cat. "Uh, she didn't. We, uh, had to warn the neighbors, and . . ."

Valerian chuckled. "Sneaking out, eh? No doubt whose

daughter you are." Legs apart, he took a stance to scan the open sky, wiping the blood from his forehead. Cat was already standing guard on the other side of the deck. "No matter. We're no safer inside than outside. No spell can stop a demon, and no mere house can stand up to the fury of a tornado. Mungus has been taking it easy so far, not wanting to risk his precious body. Now that he's pure spirit, the gloves are off."

"That was taking it easy?" Desi gaped. "He could have killed somebody. Why did you mess with something so risky?"

Valerian looked at her seriously. "I had to see you. With his help, I thought I finally could."

"But he's a wind-demon that makes tornadoes."

He shrugged. "Fire-demons are quick but deadly; spirits of earth and stone are too slow; a water spirit would be useless on dry land. There are other spirits, countless others, but air is everywhere: invisible, silent, and as you have seen, extraordinarily powerful." He went back to searching the night sky.

Cat had been keeping one eye on him while scanning their surroundings. "Three nights ago, the big storm—your demon made it," she accused. "Desi was not just dreaming. You were trying to steal her." Her voice hissed with distrust.

"I do not need to answer to you." He appealed to Desi. "I had no choice. Mungus traced Cally to this neighborhood, but she left before we could find out which house was yours. I had almost resigned myself to starting the search all over again when Mungus sniffed out a witch in the area. It's happened once or twice before—he can sense magic. So, with

Mungus's help, I broadcast a Summons to any witch close enough to hear."

"She heard it, but I stopped her in time," Cat interjected. "Two times." She glared at him with contempt.

Valerian's lip twitched. "How fortunate she is to have such an able protector," he said dryly. "At any rate, when the Summons failed, I opened the magic shop in hopes of attracting any of our kind in the area. As luck would have it, there you were."

"You opened the whole magic shop just to find me?" Desi asked, amazed. It all fell into place. "Then later, at the zoo, it wasn't a coincidence. You were following me."

"To prove beyond a doubt that you *were* you," he said earnestly. "And you did. No other witch your age could perform such a difficult spell so quickly and with such power. There was no question in my mind whose daughter you were."

Cat sniffed in disdain. "And then, when you knew who she was, you sent the demon to attack the watch-gnomes."

"I did no such thing." Valerian's expression darkened. "Wait. Mungus came here? When? What happened?"

"It was Mungus that set off the watch-gnomes?" Desi asked, confused. "And you didn't know about it?"

"I swear," he said, shifting his gaze past her to scan the yard. "Speaking of watch-gnomes, where are they? They make a formidable defense against the dark arts."

"I sort of gave them a break," Desi said. "I was afraid they might keep you away."

"Nothing could keep me away from you," he said. At

that moment, he looked at her as if she was the most important person in the world.

Desi studied her father. He spoke calmly, but she was beginning to realize that his poise was an act. "Why did Mom have to run away?" she asked, seizing her chance. "She loved you; I know she did. If you really wanted to be with me, you could have done something to make her feel okay."

He glowered. "You are young and cannot possibly understand. Everything I did was done for your sake, out of my love for you."

"Oh, right," she said sarcastically. "You scared away Mom for my sake. You chased us so we had to move every year for my sake. You summoned that demon and almost got me killed for my sake. What screwed-up kind of love is that?"

Valerian backed away, blanching. But Desi pushed on. "You could have made peace with Mom instead of setting that demon on us."

The sky darkened. The gale strengthened. Cat raised her nose to the air and cringed. "Bad thing coming," she said. Clouds had moved in, blocking out the stars.

Desi looked to her father. "And what about him?" she said, pointing a finger at the impenetrable sky. "Mungus. Do you love him?"

Clouds moved across his face as well. "Mungus?" he scoffed. "He's not like you or me. Elementals don't need or understand love."

"But he felt something," Desi recalled. "He said he was jealous of me. That's what this is all about. He feels betrayed."

Valerian snorted. "Mungus is single-minded, I grant you. He's been at my side ever since I gave him his body, just after you were born. His life with me is all he has ever known."

Desi couldn't believe it. "He's been with you ever since I was born? Then it's like you're his father."

"I don't have to listen to this." Valerian turned his back on her, stomping to the other end of the deck.

Desi had seen enough of her father to know that he wouldn't show remorse about Mungus, even if he felt it. She left him alone and crossed the deck to join Cat. "You could have gotten killed fighting that demon," she said. "Thank you."

Cat pulled her attention away from watching the sky to confront Desi. "I do not care what *he* says." She sniffed haughtily at Valerian. "Bobcat's house is safer than here. You should hide." Cat looked nervously around her. "When the demon comes, it will come like the wind—fast."

"I have to wait for Mom," Desi replied, scanning all the windows in the back of the house for a sign. "She'll be out any second now."

Cat looked distressed, but she didn't have a chance to reply. At that moment, a howling blast from the night sky struck, knocking her off her feet. Desi clutched at Cat, who clung to her desperately as they were both blown against the wall of the house. The storm screamed, tearing at them. Desi felt herself being dragged into the air while Cat's claws scrabbled wildly at the decking.

Amazingly, Valerian stayed on his feet, his body wrapped in a blood-red aura of power, arms raised to the sky. "I'm here, Mungus." His voice boomed upward. The whirlwind tightened around him, but he held firm. He turned to face Desi, his long hair whipping madly about his face. "You're right," he declared over the howl of the storm. "It's not about you. It's me he wants."

The wind raged back, "Meeeeee!"

"Yes!" Valerian yelled. "Here, Mungus. I'm here, boy. I'm waiting for you." Shocked, Desi struggled to get to her feet, half crouching. "Stay back!" he commanded, seeing Desi try to move toward him. "Desdemona, I need your help. I can't do this alone. When Mungus comes, you must open a Portal to trap him."

"But you said Mungus could block magic!" Desi shouted back.

"Trust me." Valerian looked grim but confident. "When the time comes, you'll be able to do it, just like you did in the forest." The whirlwind centered about him, tearing at his clothes. As the storm released her, Desi was able to stand up, Cat clutching at her leg.

Valerian brought his arms together, embracing the whirlwind. "Whatever happens, you must open the Portal," he cried. "But don't get near it!" The scream of the wind tried to tear his words away before they could reach her. Only a few feet away, he seemed lost in the distance as the maelstrom engulfed him. His eyes stared straight ahead, impossibly wide.

"He's eating it," Cat snarled in her ear, sounding revolted. Her nails pierced Desi's arm. "The demon is entering his body."

"NO!" Desi screamed. "Let me go. That thing is hurting him!" She had to stop him, but Cat's grip held her back.

Breathless, tears scorching her face, she was forced to watch as the wind-demon possessed her father.

Like two monstrous headlights, Valerian's eyes burned bright red. Desi recognized the demon's mad stare in her father's face. Valerian's mouth gaped open, emitting a roar. "Mine!" cried the thing—for it was no longer her father. It groped with both arms for her, reaching for her. The whirlwind expanded, trying to suck her in.

"Leave him alone!" Desi threw out both her arms in a violent gesture. *"Inferni!"* Flames erupted around Valerian, taking the shape of a fiery star. The demon in her father's eyes looked surprised, then frightened. The madness faded from Valerian's expression, and for a moment he grinned his familiar, reckless grin. The whirlwind shrank, sucked into the flames. Master of his own fate again, Valerian laughed triumphantly.

As the flames surrounded her father, Desi felt Cat's iron grip relax slightly and she pulled free. She forgot her father's warning; all she could think about was helping him fight the thing that was possessing him. But as she rushed toward him, a silver light blazed up behind her, surrounding her and passing her on all sides. The light struck her father like a rocket, spinning him around.

"Liar!" Callida cried from the kitchen door. "You swore! You'll never take her. Do you hear me!" Before Desi could protest or explain, her mother, blazing with silver fury, swept down on her to thrust her behind her protective aura.

Valerian stopped spinning. The red eyes burned again. "Mine!" the twisted mouth growled. He reached out, lashing the whirlwind to pull Desi in.

Callida blocked the wind with her shining power. Ignoring Desi's warning shout, she kept up her charge toward the figure in the center of the storm until, driven by her fury and the wind, Callida fell upon her enemy, lashing it with her aura. In sheer self-defense, the mad demon seized her mother with her father's arms, fighting blindly as the Portal engulfed them in a wall of flames. Horrified, Desi watched as her mother and father, locked in a deadly embrace, sank into the fiery pit.

The Portal vanished, and her parents with it. Desi ran to the spot where the flaming star had been, but there was no trace left, not even burn marks on the deck. Stunned, she turned to Cat. "She didn't understand," she said in a hoarse whisper. "My father was trying to save me, not hurt me." She sank to her knees on the spot where her parents had disappeared, rocking back and forth. Cat hung back, staring mutely.

"They are coming back, right?" Desi cried. She had to believe it. "They're both powerful witches, and my father's been there before. There's no problem, right? Cat, talk to me." The bruises on her body were nothing compared to the pain she felt inside right now.

Cat ducked her head. With her face turned away, she only said, "I do not know."

Desi felt panic rising up inside her and shoved it down. "What's that supposed to mean?"

"I mean I do not know," Cat said miserably. "The winddemon was mad. Other demons will be waiting. Where your mother has gone, some witches go and do not come back. We will have to wait and see."

"Wait and see?" All she could see was the image, burned into her mind, of her parents engulfed by the flames.

Cat drooped her head, slinking inside the open kitchen door. If she had had a tail, it would have been between her legs.

41

"THERE HAS TO be something we can do," Desi insisted, but Cat had withdrawn, huddling under the kitchen table. Fearless when the wind-demon had attacked, now Cat was clearly spooked, and this scared Desi more than anything. "Well, I can't sit around doing nothing. I just got my mother back, and I just found my father. We have to do something."

Cat looked up, alarmed. "There is only one way into the world of demons, and it is too dangerous without your mother."

"I don't care." Cat had given her the clue. Quickly, before she could talk herself out of it, Desi drew a five-pointed star on the kitchen floor with a Magic Marker. She couldn't bring herself to risk *Inferni*—she had seen enough flames for one day.

She got them anyway. The moment she finished the star, a fireball erupted from its center. A stinging fear nagged her that she had forgotten to say or do something important, but when the ball of fire took on a human shape, she had a flash of hope it might be one of her parents. Hope died as the flames coalesced into her own image. Seeing this, Cat leaped up to protect Desi from her flaming double.

"I've been waiting for you," the fire-girl said hungrily as soon as she had a mouth to talk with. "Coming? Or are you going to release me, or what?"

"My mother and father just got captured by a wind-demon named Mungus," Desi said in a rush. "Do you know if they're all right?"

"Mungus?" the fire-demon replied contemptuously. "That blowhard? He couldn't capture his own gas. The witch and warlock brought him back, huffing and puffing and moaning. We never should have entrusted him to your kind in the first place."

"You know where my parents are?" Desi felt a wave of relief. "Can you let me see them?"

"No. They lied. They said they were going to free us all with that 'Plan' nonsense, but we're still stuck here. Now they are, too."

"My mother never promised," Desi objected.

"Mother, father, witch, warlock, what's the difference? You incorporates all look alike to me," the elemental said haughtily. "The point is, any witches who can trap a wind-demon in a Portal, even an airhead like Mungus, have got to be good for something. We'll keep them both until we come up with our *own* plan."

"You can't do that!" Desi was stunned. "They'll die! You have to let them go."

Cat had been shielding her from the demon; now she turned to Desi forlornly. "They cannot hurt your parents—there is no death in that world—but they can keep them forever."

Desi forced herself to be calm. At least "forever" meant she had time to think. Swallowing hard, she said to the demon, "If I go in their place, will you release them?" Hearing that, Cat scowled ferociously.

"You may come, if you dare," the demon hissed, snakelike. "But no more bargains. You never kept your promise to me." She spit fire at the floor within the Portal. "You witches are all alike. One of you swore to us that if we gave him a fresh wind-demon to raise as his own, he would bring back some other special witch, the two would join forces with us, and they would reveal some ultimate power that would set us free in your world. But he lied—the witch he brought back rages in fury against him, caring nothing about us. Plus, the little airhead Mungus has returned hopelessly twisted." The demon flared up resentfully. "No deal. We learned our lesson: never trust anything with a body, whether they're tricky witches or vile Mundanes. We will forge our own way to freedom."

"Witches may be tricky, but not all Mundane humans are vile," Cat said protectively. "Bobcat is true and good, and Jarrett is almost as honest as a cat. The more I get to know humans, the more I like them."

Fire-Desi sizzled. "At least witches can accept us. What keeps our spirits from roaming free in your world? Mundanes' fear and intolerance—nothing else. Their love is as cold as ash, and they destroy whatever they do not understand."

"Not always, and not everyone." Desi hoped it wasn't true, not completely. Thinking of Jarrett and Bob, a new plan began to form in her head. "Why do we have to do things by force, all at once? What if people played with you, instead of driving you away, at least some of them? Have you tried talking to some, um, Mundanes?"

The demon looked down her burning nose at Desi. "You must be a very new witch. Mundanes can't even see us, and if they do, they run away screaming."

"Bobcat would not. He is very brave," Cat said staunchly.

"Jarrett and Bob would be okay if we broke it to them the right way. Then they could see you and talk to you, right?" Desi insisted. The fire-demon began to smoke thoughtfully. "And if some Mundanes can accept you, then any could. You said yourself they're all the same to you."

"They *might* see me," the fire-girl admitted, "if you proved to them that magic exists. But when they find out you're a witch, they will burn you at the stake, or water-torture you, or whatever Mundanes do these days to strangers they fear."

"You can't be sure," Desi said, mentally crossing her fingers. "They might surprise you. And if you could get them to accept you, you wouldn't need my parents."

"Prove it," the elemental dared, sounding skeptical. "If you can show me any Mundane who truly accepts us as we are, we will release your parents. *If* you can."

Yes! It was a start. Now all she needed to do was tell the boys the truth. It occurred to her that Jarrett had been less than pleased with her last time they had spoken. "Cat, Bob is our best bet. He did see Mungus, after all, and he'll come here if you ask him. Jarrett might, too. Can you bring them?"

Cat confronted the fire-girl. "You promise you will not do anything to Desi while I am gone?"

The demon pointed one finger at Desi accusingly. "Why should I? She doesn't keep *her* promises."

Cat looked to Desi for help. Desperate, Desi asked, "If I

let you out someplace safe, say, the fireplace, that counts, right?"

The fire-demon looked indignant. "A cheerily burning hearth? What do I look like, Suzy Homemaker?"

Desi opened the fireplace doors. "Look: nice logs, real oak, and it's just until the boys get here."

The demon peered at it hungrily. "Seasoned oak? All right, I'll watch you make a fool of yourself in comfort."

Desi said, "I release you, but only into this fireplace and nowhere else. Agreed?"

"Deal." With a swoosh of flame, the demon left the Portal for the logs, which burst into a robust blaze.

"Cat, please," Desi begged once the fire had settled down. "Go get the boys. Hurry. They'll do it if you ask them. I'm afraid of what's happening to Mom and my father."

With a last guarded look at the fireplace, Cat slipped out the back door.

42

EVERY MINUTE SEEMED like forever until Cat brought the boys back to the kitchen. At one point, Desi checked the fireplace and was disturbed to see her own head in the flames, burning brightly, looking contented. She shuddered.

Cat had left the back door ajar. Now she burst through it with only Jarrett in tow. Seeing Desi's disappointment, she explained, "Bobcat would not come. He says his head hurts too much, but I think he is still mad at me about the kissing."

Kissing? Who was kissing who? Desi was thrown off but made herself focus. Her parents came first.

Jarrett was keeping his distance, hands in his pockets. He didn't say hi; he didn't even look at her. He said, only to the floor, "Cat said it was important, so what's up? I have to get back to check on Bob."

Nervous, Desi stammered, "W-will he be all right?"

"Oh, yeah," Jarrett said coolly. "His skull's so thick he probably hurt the oak tree more than it hurt him." He shuffled his feet impatiently. "Is that all? I'm busy."

If he said he was busy one more time, Desi swore she would figure out how to turn him into a toad. "Could you tone down the attitude for a minute?" she said. "This is no joke. My parents need help." He looked at her skeptically.

How to start? *Hey there, you'll never guess what happened.*

My parents are being held captive by demons in another world, and oh, by the way, I'm a witch.

She took a deep breath. One step at a time. "Look. I know you're mad. I'm sorry I couldn't tell you the truth before."

His eyebrows lowered. She tried to swallow, but her mouth was as dry as dust.

"The truth is, I'm a witch. I was practicing magic tonight, and I couldn't let anybody see me." Jarrett's face went blank, so she asked, "Do you understand?"

"Sure," he said, shrugging. He shifted a quick glance between Desi and Cat. "Can I go now?"

Cat cut in impatiently, "Jarrett. The truth is the truth. Desi is a witch. I am a cat."

"Cool, you're a cat?" He rolled his eyes as if appreciating her joke. "Hey, maybe some witch made Bob out of a stray dog at the pound. That would explain a lot."

"Listen," Desi said, "even if you don't ever want to be around me anymore, even if no one wants to be around me anymore, I have to tell you the truth. I'm not like everyone else. I really am a witch."

Jarrett shot her a resentful look. "You said this was no joke, but I guess the joke's on me." He turned to head out the door.

To stop him from escaping, Desi thrust her fist into the air and cried, *"Inferni!"* Desperately nervous, she could only manage a quick flame-up before it went out again, but that was enough to get Jarrett's attention.

"Pretty cool," he said, interested despite himself. "I saw that one on TV. Do it again."

Concentrating, Desi murmured the spell, igniting a bright, steady flame. Jarrett's eyebrows shot up in admiration. "Wicked!"

"That's not all." Her success building her confidence, Desi picked up the toaster. "*Tintoturner green,*" she cried. The toaster turned green before their eyes.

Jarrett took it and turned it over in his hands, enthusiastically inspecting it. "Definitely cool," he admitted, more like his usual eager self. "I didn't know you could do magic tricks. I got a bunch of them from that shop in the mall. You want to come over and try them out?"

Tricks? Was the fire-girl right? Couldn't people see magic right under their noses?

"Don't you see that?" she asked, desperately pointing at the fireplace, where a demon's head was clearly visible amid the flames.

"Sure," Jarrett said, uncertain. "Nice fire. So, you coming or not?"

From the hearth, the fire-girl was laughing at her noiselessly. The flames reminded her of her mother and father, trapped. She felt her courage melting away. "What else can I do to make you believe me?"

"I don't get it." Jarrett cocked his head to one side, puzzled.

Cat, who had been hanging back the whole time, picked up a stainless-steel carafe from the island counter. It was the potion her mother had brought to restore Cat to her original form.

"Coffee break?" Jarrett asked, brightening. "Count me in. I could use some caffeine."

"No!" Desi commanded.

"Yes," Cat said, holding out the potion to Jarrett. "This is the only way." He took it gratefully and began to twist off the cap.

Desi grew flush with alarm. "No! We don't know what it will do to him."

"Not him. Me." As soon as Jarrett got the cap off, Cat snatched the potion out of his hands. "Jarrett," she said to his bewildered expression, "I told you. Desi is a witch. I am a cat. I will prove it."

"Cat, no," Desi pleaded.

Cat looked at her with big green eyes. "If you cannot convince him, you may never see your mother again," she said. "But I trust Jarrett, and I trust you." She sniffed the contents of the carafe, scrunching her face at the smell, then addressed an increasingly baffled Jarrett. "Cats see the truth when it is in front of their noses, but sometimes that is hard for humans. If you see that I am a cat, will you believe it? And will you believe that Desi can be more than you think she is?"

He shook his head, unsure. "I don't understand. How can I see that you're a cat?"

Cat's expression grew serious. "Watch. I will show you. I do not think you have seen *this* on TV."

Desi felt a lump in her throat. She knew she ought to stop Cat, but she couldn't think of any better idea. Cat was right— the first thing was to get her parents back. Trembling, she watched Cat raise the carafe to drink. "Don't worry," she whispered, "Mom will change you back."

Cat looked at her wistfully, the potion at her lips. "Desi,

Jarrett," she said, "tell my human friends I had fun." Grimacing, she poured the concoction down her throat.

For a moment no one moved. Then, with a jerk, Cat doubled over, retching violently. Jarrett reached out to help her, but when he saw what was happening, he drew back in shock. Desi forced herself to watch, dreading what came next.

Cat fell on all fours, twitching in agony. As she sank lower, she kept going down, shrinking, her clothes sagging around her. As Desi watched, Cat's beautiful hair was sucked into her head and then grew out again, thick black fur sprouting over her face and neck. Just before her head disappeared under her shirt, two pointed ears shot out, and her hairy face grew into a muzzle.

Desi couldn't catch her breath.

The next moment it was over. There on the floor, crumpled in a heap, lay the new clothes Cat had been so proud of, the black T-shirt throbbing like it covered a beating heart. Forcing down her horror, Desi knelt to lift the shirt, afraid of what lay underneath. With a quick sob of relief, she saw her dainty black and silver cat, Devil, her small body limp but pulsating, clinging to life.

Desi knelt to take her precious friend into her arms. Tears welled up. "Cat?"

A strangled sound from Jarrett made her look up. Eyes huge, he was stumbling backward toward the kitchen door, groping behind him for the knob.

"No, wait!" Desi pleaded, cradling poor Devil. She threw out one hand to stop him. "Don't leave!" As if at her command, the dead bolt on the kitchen door slammed home, locking.

Jarrett lurched for the knob. Wild with panic, he struggled in vain to open the door. "Let me out!"

"Please," she cried, spilling tears over Devil's shining fur. "Don't go." At those words, the tiny head raised to lick at her hand. "Devil, are you all right? Why did you do it?" she asked. But she knew why.

Devil was still too weak to stand, so Desi held her as she stood up to confront Jarrett. When she got close, he backed up against the door. "Look," she said, "I know this is freaking you out, but I don't know any other way. If you don't listen, who will?"

Jarrett looked at her accusingly, but he got himself under control. "Unlock the door."

In reply, Devil leaped from Desi's arms into Jarrett's. Frightened, he made to ward her off, but when he caught her in self-defense, Devil snuggled into his embrace, looking up at him earnestly.

"I need you to help me," Desi said. "I need you to see me the way I am."

"Unlock the door," he repeated.

Desi didn't know how the door had locked itself just now, but she remembered her father's advice: It's not what you know that matters—it's who you are. She reached out her hand. Before she could touch it, the dead bolt slid open by itself.

Jarrett dropped Devil and yanked the door open to the night air. Desi wanted to stop him, but she took her cue from her cat, who waited at her feet, tense and expectant. Jarrett hesitated in the open doorway for a second, ready to dart. Then he said, "Cat was really Devil all the time? And you really are a—"

"A witch, yes. So are my mother and father, and they need your help." Desi rushed to get it all said before Jarrett changed his mind and bolted. "I can't explain everything, but if you will just talk to someone, convince them you can be friends? They will trust us enough to let my parents go."

He stared blankly in confusion. "Talk to somebody?"

"Over here." Desi led him to where she had drawn the Portal, near the fireplace. Her own face glared out from the fire with a skeptical expression. "Okay," Desi said to the demon, "he knows I'm a witch. Come on out so we can talk."

The head in the fire scoffed. "So he can run out the door screaming 'Fire! Demons!' and bring men with big water hoses? No thanks."

"We had a deal," Desi said. "He's already proved he can accept Devil and me for who we are. Now it's your turn. Or were you just blowing smoke?"

"Who are you talking to?" Jarrett asked, fidgeting nervously. Devil rubbed up against his ankles to reassure him.

"See? I told you so—Mundanes are clueless." The demon sent a shower of sparks up from the hearth. "Oh, why not. Your fireplace is boring." With a whoosh of flame, the demon flew out of the hearth back into the center of the Portal, a blazing column of fire.

Jarrett practically jumped out of his shoes. Before he could scream "Fire!" Desi cried, "That's not fair—you looked normal when I first saw you."

"This *is* normal, for me," the demon hissed, but then her flames coalesced into the form Desi had first encountered.

"She looks just like you!" Jarrett exclaimed, quivering but brave. It was true; except for the occasional spark and sizzle, the fire-girl was once again the image of Desi.

"Why *do* you look like me?" Desi asked her demon double.

"I don't have a body of my own, so I copied yours. I can copy his, if you'd prefer."

"No thanks," Desi and Jarrett hastily said in unison.

"Jarrett," Desi explained, "this is a . . . a spirit, a fire-elemental."

Jarrett looked spooked, so Devil jumped into his arms, looking pointedly at Desi as if to say, *Get on with it.*

"So," she hurried on, "the thing is, this . . . spirit . . . doesn't think Mundanes, I mean people, can be friends with dem—I mean, elementals—that they'd be scared of them or try to get rid of them or something." Jarrett didn't look too friendly right at that moment. Devil tried to lick his hand reassuringly. "So, if you could just tell the spirit you are okay with magic and everything, she will let my parents go."

Big mistake. "She kidnapped your parents?" Jarrett said, backing away.

"Told you so." The demon smirked.

"No," Desi said quickly. "It was a misunderstanding. They went to the other World on their own. I'm just trying to get them home safely."

"There's another world?" Jarrett said, looking curious.

"A whole other world, full of spirits and magical

creatures," Desi said, winging it. "And they want to share the magic with our world, only people are too afraid to accept them."

"I'm not afraid of magic," Jarrett said. In his arms, Devil purred in agreement.

"Prove it," the fire-girl taunted.

Desi wanted to slap her—she was being so rude—but kept her peace. "Isn't it enough that he's talking to you?"

"No. Mundanes say one thing and do another. You want to be friends? Let's play."

Jarrett shot a confused look at Desi. She told the demon carefully, "That wasn't our deal. Your idea of playing is setting things on fire."

Jarrett's eyes grew wide in alarm. Desi quickly reassured him, "Don't worry, she can't burn anything unless I release her."

"That's what *you* think," the demon crackled. Suddenly she erupted in flame, flaring up to the ceiling. Her fire roared past the edges of the star pattern, driving Desi and Jarrett back against the wall. Almost too late, Desi remembered her father's repeated warning about opening a Portal. *"AGAPE!"* she shouted.

At the Word of Power, the flames shrank away as suddenly as they had appeared. The demon coalesced back into her human form and threw a tantrum, hammering both fists against the invisible barrier of the Portal.

I have to be more careful, Desi thought, still feeling the heat on her skin. Apparently, *Agape* not only opened Portals but also kept demons trapped, like the elaborate signs she had drawn on the floor days ago—but better since it couldn't be accidentally erased.

Devil had jumped out of Jarrett's arms and was now at her feet, back arched, fur on end, hissing in defiance. As Desi picked up the cat to calm her, she noticed that Jarrett was halfway through the door. "Wait!" she cried, but it was too late. He escaped into the night.

"There he goes," the fire-girl taunted, scowling, "to raise an angry mob with axes and pitchforks. Sure you don't want to trade places with me?"

"It's your fault," Desi shot at the demon. "You never gave him a chance."

Boiling, the fire-girl shot back, "I told you so, witch. They'll lock you in a dungeon, and I'll never get out to play."

Desi thought of her mother and father, trapped, and panic seized her. She was about to run after Jarrett, hoping to stop him with words or spells, when a familiar voice sounded in her head. *Trust him,* Devil said, *like you want him to trust you.* The little cat snuggled tighter against her chest. *Remember, when he held me in his arms just now, I felt his heart.*

"He's not going to tell anybody," Desi said to the demon. "You scared him, that's all. Everybody's afraid of new things at first. I'll go talk with him." She hoped it would be that simple.

But as she was going out the door to look for him, Jarrett reappeared, clutching something behind his back. "It likes to set things on fire, right?" Jarrett's eyes were glowing with excitement. "Well, look what I've got!" He held out his prize— what appeared to be a tin can on a stick—to show the fuming elemental. "Why burn when you can explode?" he said. Desi and the fire-girl both stared at him, puzzled. "Can-O-Dragons," he said proudly, "my own invention. Packed with skyrockets, dazzlers, sparklers, multiple fountains, and a sunburst at the end. Nobody's ever seen fireworks like this before." Jarrett held up the giant skyrocket, showing it off.

The fire-demon sniffed hungrily. "I smell the sweet scent of explosives. Delicious!" Her form began to waver, erupting into flame. "Let me touch it!"

Desi pushed it away from her grasping arms. Even if the fire-girl couldn't get through the barrier, she was taking no chances. "If we let you out to play, will you admit I was right about people? And you'll keep your promise to release my mom and Val right away?"

"Yes, yes, you were right," the fire-demon said hastily, drooling lava. "Amazing invention! They really are clever, these Mundanes. What are we waiting for?" She was so excited she was spontaneously combusting in little bursts of flame. She hardly looked like Desi anymore.

From her arms, Devil gave a little warning cry, which Desi understood. Like Cinderella at the ball at midnight, the fire-girl had to turn back into herself when it was over. "Promise that you won't set this off until we tell you to. And you also have to promise to go back to your world as soon as it's finished."

"What a wet blanket," the fire-demon pouted. "Whatever. You'll have to open another Portal for me."

"No problem," Desi said. "I'm a witch." She glanced at Jarrett, who was gazing at her in wonder.

"What about him?" the demon said cautiously. "Does he agree, too?"

"Sure," Jarrett said. "Uh, I don't know your name?"

"I don't have one," the demon said defensively.

"Everyone has a name. What about 'Blaze'?" Jarrett asked. The elemental flared up proudly. "Okay, Blaze," Jarrett said. "I'm in. Go for it. Welcome to our world." Hearing that, Blaze sparked furiously.

Some things are worth the risks, Desi thought. "By the power that opened the Portal," she proclaimed, "I invite you to come out to play." Devil gave a piercing yowl of assent.

With a whoosh, the demon flared into a great spout of flame. Swirling into the air, she circled the room joyfully and then dove into the skyrocket. Jarrett held on, arms outstretched, his eyes shut tight against the glare. When he opened them, the room was back to normal.

Too normal. The skyrocket didn't look any different. Once again, the Portal was just some markings on the floor. Except for Devil and Jarrett, Desi was alone. Desi wondered, *Was all this for nothing?*

Jarrett admired the skyrocket in awe, turning it about in his hands. "This is too cool," he said. "What happens next?"

As if in answer, there was a burst of smoke from inside the Portal. Desi braced herself for another demon, but when the smoke cleared, she saw her mother and her father in the Portal's center, as she had last seen them, wrapped tightly in each other's arms.

43

"MOM?" FOR A long moment, Desi waited, fascinated and embarrassed by the sight of her mother clinging so tightly to this man who had so recently come back into their lives. Then Callida shook herself free and stared about the room, bewildered. When she caught sight of Desi, she ran to sweep her up in her arms.

"I thought I'd lost you again," she cried.

"I *almost* lost you," Desi whispered in her mother's ear. "Don't leave me anymore." Devil, squashed by the embrace, wriggled out of Desi's arms to escape under the table.

Valerian remained in the middle of the Portal, teetering in a daze as the burning star around him faded completely from sight. Finally he said, "Did it work? Mungus? Is he gone?"

Before her mother's temper could flare, Desi said, "Yes, he's gone. The other demon said they would take care of him."

"Other demon?" Incredulous, Callida and Valerian shouted over each other, assaulting her with questions.

"Mom, Val," Desi interrupted. "It was the only way I could think of to get you back."

"But what did you give up in return?" Valerian insisted. Callida looked terrified.

"It was no big deal," Desi said, trying to calm them. "The

demon just wanted to make some new friends." She nodded at Jarrett, who had retreated into a corner when he'd seen her parents appear in a puff of smoke. Desi saw the alarm on her parents' faces, and she joked, "They were just hanging out, you know; it wasn't like a date or anything." Something told her that this was not a good time to mention the fire-demon inside the skyrocket.

Callida threw a nervous glance at Jarrett and said, "He knows about us? Desdemona, what have I told you? He could cause so much trouble."

"I won't, I promise," Jarrett said quickly, covering his precious rocket with his arms.

Val scrutinized Jarrett like a bug under a microscope. "We'll see," he grunted. "The important thing is that Desi is out of danger."

At the word *danger,* Callida turned her ire on him. "I want you out of this house. Now."

Before Desi could protest, her father said dryly, "It's late, and we're all tired. I'll come back tomorrow—with your permission, of course, Cally."

"We'll see," she said, showing him the door with a flick of her hand. With one last curious look at Desi, her father slipped out into the night.

Jarrett sidled into the hallway leading to the front door, keeping his prize hidden behind his back. "Um, good night."

Desi wanted him to go; if her mother knew about the demon in the skyrocket, there was no way she'd let them set it off, deal or no deal. But there was another worry. "Um, Jarrett, remember, you have to wait for me before you do anything."

"No problem," he said with a nervous laugh. "You're the expert."

"And you won't tell anyone about us?" Callida insisted, pressing him.

"Nah." He studied Devil, who was still huddled under the table, and then grinned at Desi. "I don't rat on my friends," he said. Then he left.

When they were finally alone, Desi knelt under the table to retrieve her kitty. Cradling her in her arms, she stroked the velvet cheek. "Mom, Cat drank that potion. But we can change her back, right?"

Callida shook her head, looking weary. "No need. Devil's back the way she belongs. She's happier this way."

"Well, I'm not. She's like my sister now, and I want her back."

"Your sister?" Callida was taken aback. "Desi, hon, did you see what the potion did to her?" Desi gulped. She still hadn't shaken the memory of Cat's deformed body twitching in agony. Callida pushed on. "I never would have chanced it the first time if it wasn't an emergency. One more time might kill her—or worse, turn her into a twisted monstrosity. Why do you think I never transformed her into a babysitter when you were younger?"

Desi refused to accept it. There had to be a way. An idea came to her. She hesitated, knowing that it might be too soon for her mother, but she couldn't wait. "Do you think Val knows a way to turn Cat back safely?" She hugged her kitty, soft and warm in her arms.

Callida looked pained. "Honey, you can't trust him. I

didn't want to alarm you before, but you should know the truth. When I was in London, your father attacked me with a spell that almost killed me."

The image of her mother, tiny but defiant in the center of the Portal, sprang up before Desi's eyes. Feeling guilty, she said, "Mom, that wasn't my father. That was me. I was trying to summon you with a spell."

"Don't be silly," Callida said. "Sweetheart, you couldn't possibly have—"

Desi interrupted her, spilling everything: the *Book of Secrets*, opening Portals, and especially her near-disastrous attempts to summon her mother. Everything but the demon-possessed firework. She was afraid that if her mother knew, she would whisk her away to London, and she would never see Jarrett again.

It took a while to convince her, but finally Callida collapsed in a kitchen chair, looking at Desi as if she was really seeing her for the first time. Desi didn't mind. It felt good.

"So, anyway," Desi continued, pressing Devil's cheek to her own, "my father has been to the spirit world. Do you think—?"

Her mother shook her head sorrowfully. "You've done amazing things—I can hardly believe it—but you mustn't risk this. There is no power in this world or the next that can safely change Devalandnefariel back."

Seeing the disheartenment that was sweeping over Desi, Callida kissed her head in sympathy. "Honey, I'm sorry. I really am." She patted the little cat, who was already asleep in Desi's arms. "Look, we're all exhausted. I think after what you told me, we can stay here safely tonight. Things will look brighter in the morning." Despite her words, Desi noticed that Callida sealed the house up tight with her usual spell before trudging up the stairs to bed.

* * *

Out of her filthy clothes and into her sleep shirt, Desi sat on her bed with her cat in her lap, thinking furiously. "There has to be a way." Remembering the last time she had performed magic in the bedroom, she placed her hands lightly on the little cat's head. *"Restorio,"* she commanded. For a moment her hope surged; then it died as her cat remained unchanged.

Restless, she sat in the dark, fuming inside. "Did you know this would be permanent? Did you drink the potion anyway?" she whispered into the furry pointed ears. "Why did you do it? Is this really what you want? Or did you do it for me?" Desi listened for an answer in her head, but Devil had squeezed her eyes shut and closed her mind.

She had to find out. Callida had said that no power on Earth could bring Cat back, but tonight Desi had seen that there was far more to magic than this one world could hold. As soon as she was sure her mother was asleep, she made a light with *Inferni* to dig out the big *Book of Secrets* from where she had hidden it under her bed. Propped up on her pillows, her kitty curled up at her feet, she flipped through the worn pages of spells, reading by the light of her flickering thumb.

Did it all come down to making deals with demons? Her father had tried that with Mungus, and look how that had turned out. She reread the introduction: *The Four Paths to Power, Ascending in Potency.* Now she knew what the first three were: spells, potions, and demons. But even her father had refused to tell her about the fourth. "You will have to discover the ultimate Path for yourself," he had said. Why? His words taunted her. If there was a magic even more powerful than demons, why didn't her mother know about it?

As if sensing her disquiet, Devil raised her head from the bedcovers, her pointed ears twitching. "I wish you could talk," Desi said. Too tired to read anymore, she snuffed out her flame and set the book aside. Seeing this, the little cat crept daintily into her lap. Devil snuggled in close, purring to comfort her. Desi hugged her tight. "I never got to hug you when you were big," she whispered. "You wanted me to, but you were too different, and I was afraid. I'm sorry." A rough tongue licked her hand. "There's lots of things we didn't get to do," Desi sighed. "Are we still best friends?"

Devil's huge yellow cat eyes looked up into hers, luminous in the faint starlight. Round as twin moons, they grew until they filled her whole world. Desi imagined herself falling into those eyes, sinking into them until all the differences between them disappeared. For a moment they were closer than friends, or even sisters; in fact, she could not tell where she left off and Devil began. For the blink of an eye, they were one person.

The next moment she was her separate self again, holding her Cat, and this time, to her surprise, Cat was holding her, strong arms around her shoulders.

"Everything may be new and strange, but we are together," Cat said aloud as she hugged her.

"You're back!" Desi said, sitting up with a jolt. She looked up into Cat's very human green eyes. "Is this a dream?"

"Can't you see the truth when it is in front of your nose?"

the girl teased her gently, rubbing her human nose against Desi's.

"But how?" Desi checked Cat from head to toe; the girl looked like her normal human self. She was even wearing her new clothes from the mall. "How did this happen?"

"You tell me," Cat said, admiring her brightly painted nails. "You're the witch. *You* did it."

As Desi studied Cat for a clue to her transformation, she realized that she could see Cat clearly in the dark—because the darkness was shining. The very air around her shimmered with life, as it had when she flew in the bubble. In fact, just like the surface of the bubble, the persimmon bedroom walls around her glowed, translucent. So did the ceiling; she could see right through it to the night sky that surrounded her. Beyond the walls, the forest behind her house pulsated with energy, calling to the stars, which were singing the world to sleep in a radiant chorus. Desi felt that if she reached out her hand, one of the stars would come at her command, alight on her bed, and open its world to her.

"My father said that the magic is everywhere, but I couldn't see it," she mused aloud. "But now I'm seeing it, feeling it, am part of it. Could he see all this?" For the first time, she doubted it. "And what about Mom? Why didn't she tell me about this? Can't *she* see it?"

"Your mother sees magic," Cat replied confidently. "The magic of you. You are her whole world; she said so. The magic she sees in you is all that she wants to see."

"And what about you?" Desi asked, facing Cat, her feelings surging up and spilling over like a waterfall. "I'm seeing what I want. I want my best friend, my sister, back. But what do you want?" She held her breath.

"What do I want? That is easy." Cat gazed back at her with wide-open green eyes. "I want to sit in your lap. I want to go dancing. I want to catch birds and eat sushi and hot dogs or whatever I choose. I want to stay home with you and hunt through the woods at night and hunt through the mall in the daytime. I want to wear shiny dresses or shiny fur or new jeans or nothing at all if I feel like it." She paused, thinking hard. "Whatever shape I have, I will always be me, and I will always be with you." Cat wrapped her long arms around her, tender and fierce. "You are my Desi."

Desi hugged her tight. "And you're my precious Cat, forever."

Sitting there on the bed, arm in arm with her new sister, Desi felt peace spreading through her. Needing no more words to share their feelings, they sat in silence. Gradually, she noticed the lights from houses all around, sprinkled across the luminous dark. *All those people asleep, all those people with their eyes closed. I wish they could see what I am seeing right now,* she thought to herself. As if hearing her thoughts, Cat sighed in agreement. For endless moments, Desi watched the sparkling play of light and darkness until at last her eyelids grew heavy, the walls filled in, and the world of dreams held sway once more.

44

THE SUN WOKE Desi from her dreams—a heavy sun, too hot for morning. The clock on her cell showed it was late afternoon. Shaking the fuzziness out of her head, she was halfway into her clothes when she remembered: Cat was back!

Or was she? Did it really happen, or had it been a dream? She checked around for signs of Cat—or Devil—but there was nothing to prove what had happened either way. She dressed in a hurry, and on her way downstairs, she snatched up the *Book of Secrets*. No more sneaking around.

Down in the kitchen, she barely had time to ask, "Did you see Cat?" before her mother squeezed her in a hug so tight it made the book pop out onto the table. Callida wouldn't let go; she held Desi at arm's length, checking her up and down, as if making sure she was really there.

"Did you get enough sleep?" she fussed.

"Mom, I'm fine." Except that she needed coffee. Now.

"Coffee's made." Callida poured for both of them, then joined her at the kitchen table, watching her thoughtfully. Desi sipped the steaming liquid, basking in the warmth and comfort of their morning ritual.

"Mom," she said, "I'm so glad you're back."

"Me too, hon," her mother said, covering Desi's hand with her own.

Cat! "Have you seen Cat this morning?" Desi mentally crossed her fingers.

Callida frowned. "You mean Devil?" Desi's heart jumped in her throat, but her mother said, "Not today. Probably out stalking songbirds; you know how she is." Callida opened the *Book of Secrets.* To Desi's surprise, her mother's eyes were glistening with tears.

"I saw how you painted your room," Callida said, sniffling. "I like it. I . . . I just want to say how impressed I am with the way you can do things on your own, even if you don't always ask me first."

Desi glowed with pride. Her mother spun the book around so they both could read what was written inside the front cover.

"I should have done this years ago," Callida said, wiping her cheeks. "No more secrets." She pointed to the flyleaf, running her finger down a long list of names. Desi read the list of scrawled signatures, but they didn't mean anything to her, not until she came to the end. Second to the last was her grandmother's name, Calliope, written in fancy violet curlicues. Under that, in strong, plain script, brilliant silver on the yellowed parchment: *Callida.*

"Each owner has to inscribe her name in the book before using it, or the spells backfire, as you found out," Callida said wryly. "And there can only be one owner." She pointed to the space beneath her name. "Here. Go ahead."

Astonished, Desi looked at her mother to see if she was serious. Callida was still sniffling but seemed happy.

"What do I write with?" Desi asked nervously.

"Your finger. What did you think—letters of blood?"

Callida laughed through her tears. Desi cautiously touched her finger to the page, where it left a mark. Fascinated, she moved her finger across the parchment, watching it spell out in gleaming golden letters: *Desdemona*.

After long moments, her mother gently closed the cover. "It's yours now. Keep it safe in your room. Are you hungry?"

The kitchen door flew open and Cat buzzed in—on two legs. "I'm so hungry," she announced. Spotting the coffee creamer, she picked up the carton with nimble fingers and drained it in one gulp.

"Cat! You're you!" Desi jumped up to embrace her, making sure she was really real.

Cat looked startled but recovered quickly, enduring the hug with dignity. "I'm always me," she said smugly.

Callida sat up straight, goggling at the teenage girl. "How did you . . . ?"

"Last night," Desi said. "I was worried it was just a dream. Where have you been?"

Cat licked the cream from around her lips. "Talking to Bobcat."

"What did he say?" Desi wondered what Jarrett had told him.

Cat paused, recalling his exact words. "He said, 'My head hurts.'"

"What happened last night?" Callida interrupted, furrowing her brow. "This shouldn't be possible."

Before Callida could ask any more questions, Cat went very still, quivering. At the same time, Callida's hair began to crackle, giving off sparks. Desi wondered if the effects of her witchcraft the night before were coming back. But no.

Instead, in a shimmering flash, Valerian appeared, suave and dapper, dazzling against the humdrum background of the kitchen. "I hope I am not intruding." He bowed with gracious humility. "I'm here to see my daughter."

Callida burst from her chair, incensed. Desi quickly inserted herself between them. "It's good to see you," she said to her father, firmly and politely. She didn't hug him; something held her back, but just being close to him was enough.

"Desi, come over here by me," her mother ordered.

"Mom!" Desi protested, rolling her eyes to the ceiling. Pulling out a chair for her father, she said, "We're having coffee. Join us?" Valerian looked for Callida's assent with a coolly innocent let's-all-be-civilized-about-this expression.

"It's too soon," her mother said, tight-lipped. "I'm not comfortable with this."

"Please?" Desi urged. "For me?"

Looking pained, her mother spoke through clenched teeth. "As long as I'm in the room with you."

"Great," Desi said as her father took the offered chair. She noticed that her mother switched places to sit between them, and Cat was perched on the edge of her seat, tense and alert. Desi sighed. At least they were all sitting at the same table.

She poured her father a cup of coffee. "How do you take it?" she asked, upending the empty creamer carton. "Sorry, we're out of cream."

"Black is good," he replied pleasantly.

They drank in silence for a while, Desi glancing between her mother and father. Callida practically seared the tabletop with her intense glare, while her father lounged nonchalantly in his seat as if he were at a tea party. Was this what it was like having two parents? It would take some getting used to.

"So," Valerian said with a nod at Cat, "I see you have a new addition to your household."

"I still don't understand," Callida said, pulling her attention away from Valerian to examine Cat. "It's simply not possible. Tell me what happened last night."

Desi gazed at Cat fondly. "I was just feeling how much I loved her and missed her, and there she was, human again."

"Again?" Valerian studied Cat, who had never taken her eyes off him.

Desi explained, "Val, this is Cat, my best friend and new sister. She used to be our Familiar—you know, a real cat."

"Really?" Valerian said. He seemed fascinated, but not with Cat—now he was focused on Desi. "So you said you loved her and missed her, and voila, there she was?" His face gleamed. "I knew it."

"Don't even think about it, Val!" Callida looked stern.

"What's going on?" Desi asked, totally confused.

Callida explained. "You know that the world of elemental spirits once existed side by side with ours, but Mundane people's fears are driving the worlds farther and farther apart. *He* believes"—she jerked her head at Desi's father—"that if the two worlds are forcibly reunited, magic will run freely across the earth, witches and warlocks will rule the world, and everyone will live happily ever after."

"And they won't?" she asked.

"The spirit world is a place of pure energy, without form," Callida said. "Think of it like nuclear power. Forcibly uniting the two worlds is like smashing atoms. If that raw power was unleashed on our world, I don't even want to think of what might happen—total annihilation, a holocaust!"

Valerian objected. "Or unlimited free magical energy at our command, transforming the world into a virtual paradise. A paradise governed by the Wise," he added thoughtfully.

"I still don't understand what that has to do with me, or what happened with Cat," Desi said. She shared a look with Cat, feeling happy and proud. Whatever happened couldn't be bad—it had brought them together.

"The power of love," her father answered triumphantly. "The ultimate magic." She looked at him in surprise as he went on. "The songs and stories do not lie. Love conquers all. It makes the world go round." He chuckled dryly. "Love is the most powerful force in the universe, the only energy that can reunite that which was once whole and is now torn apart. It is the only element missing in the world of elemental spirits—there is no demon of love. We have retained the greatest power for ourselves."

Desi was blown away. "You mean, like, *love,* like Romeo and Juliet?" *Or her parents?*

"Yes, and love between brothers and sisters, or close friends. Like the love between father and daughter," he added.

"Just loving somebody is supposed to bring magic back into the world?"

"Exactly," Valerian said. "Look what happened between

you and your pet." With a condescending wave, he indicated Cat, who glared back at him. "Alone, without even understanding what you were doing, you performed an astounding transformation." He paused, deep in thought. "Just think of what your love could accomplish with proper training and focus."

"Haven't you learned anything?" Callida derided him. "You can't *use* love. And I refuse to let you use my daughter." She faced Desi. "Please don't ever have anything to do with the spirit world again. You don't know what could go wrong."

"But I talked with that elemental spirit," Desi said carefully, thinking about the demon-powered skyrocket Jarrett was hiding. "She didn't seem so bad."

"I still can't believe you did that," Callida said. "I mean that literally—it took me years of training to be able to open a Portal, and most witches can't do it at all."

"Our daughter," Val replied with a teasing smirk, "can do more than you think. What are you, Desdemona, almost thirteen? I was sixteen before I managed to summon my first demon. A sea-slug, I recall—a slimy, disgusting thing, but I felt like the king of the world."

Callida pointed accusingly at Val. "You're responsible for this—exposing her to such advanced magic before she was ready."

"I did it on my own," Desi protested, "before I even met him." Callida ignored her, glowering at Valerian.

He scowled back. "You know I would never hurt Desi. Or you, Cally."

Callida straightened. "You *could* never hurt me. Dark studies or no, I have always been your match."

"And I yours." He looked at her curiously. "I missed you, Cally. More than you know."

"You had a strange way of showing it," she said, shaking her head. "Admit it—you tried to take my daughter from me. You tried to trick Desi into doing what I was too smart to do."

"And you tried to deny our daughter her birthright!" Val shot back. "What did you expect from me? Give up magic? Cut my hair? Trade in my motorcycle for a sensible car?" He leaned toward her, burning. "I have a right to live the life I was born to live. So does my daughter. Someday you will see that and thank me."

Callida's eyes flashed. "*Thank* you?"

Before her parents could do anything that Desi would regret later, she jumped in: "I think we've all had enough caffeine for one day. How about breakfast?"

Callida bit her lip. Valerian leaned back, crossed his legs, and after a moment's silence asked, "So, Desdemona, any special plans for your big day?"

"You mean the first day of school?" Desi asked. "Or my birthday?"

"Your coming-of-age celebration," he said, as if she should have known. "Ought to be special, turning thirteen the day after Halloween. Any thoughts about who you will apprentice with?"

"Apprentice?" Desi looked to her mother for an explanation.

If looks could kill, Callida's would have put Valerian ten feet under. "Desi won't need to apprentice. I can instruct her myself, thank you. She'll live with me and attend an ordinary school."

"But our daughter is *not* ordinary," Valerian said coolly. "Traditionally," he lectured Desi, "on a witch's thirteenth birthday, there is a celebration to welcome her into the circle of the Wise. At that time, she leaves home to study under a great adept, making the transition to her own magical mastery. Or miss-tery." He smiled appreciatively at his own joke.

"This isn't the Dark Ages anymore," Callida retorted. "Desi can learn her craft very well from me without dancing around fires, chanting nonsense, and sacrificing goats."

"Personally, I don't recall ever sacrificing a goat, Cally," Valerian said, laughing. "That must have been some party." With a wink at Desi, he added, "Your mother was apprenticed when I met her."

"Really?" Desi asked excitedly. She wasn't sure about the leaving home part, but a real witches' celebration?

"We'll see," Callida said. Desi knew what that meant— but she also knew she wasn't going to just leave it up to her mother anymore. Deep inside, she felt the power of her birthright.

Valerian added smoothly, "I would be happy to help you learn magic, with your mother's permission, of course. You have a bright, unlimited future before you, and you ought to be properly prepared."

Desi realized that he hadn't given up on his plan for one great magical world. She studied him closely. Did he really care about her, or did he want to use her, the way he had used Mungus? He seemed earnest, but was this another pose?

It was impossible to tell. She could never follow him blindly. Her father had a lot to learn before she would trust him to teach.

Callida stood up. "Leave Desi's training to me. It's enough that you're here at all. And now I have a lot to do, so if you don't mind . . . ?"

"I am very grateful to be allowed into your home," Valerian said lightly, though Desi thought she detected bitterness underneath. "Someday, Cally, you will trust that I mean only the best for my family." He rose to his feet. "I have appointments waiting for me," he said to Desi. "Though nothing as important as seeing you. And your new sister." He bowed to Cat. "Charmed, as always." She had gotten up when he did and now frowned back at him suspiciously.

"Cally." He merely nodded, but Desi could almost see the sparks fly between them.

Turning back to her, Desi's father held out both arms. She thought he was going to hug her and wondered how she felt about that, but after a brief hesitation, he only took her hands. Feeling his strong grasp, she realized this was the first time they had touched. Quietly, he said, "Thank you for helping me find you again."

An electric tingle rushed through her fingers, sending sparks through her arms and into her heart. "You know"—the words burst out before she could prevent them—"when I got that fire-demon to let you go, I didn't try to force her or trick her or anything. I just told her the truth. And I listened to what she wanted."

His mouth twisted up. "I know." He searched her face. "After all these years imagining what you were like, I find you are so much more than I expected, in so many ways."

A little bird fluttered in her chest. "Will I see you tomorrow?" she asked.

"All the demons in the spirit world couldn't keep me away," he replied fervently. They stood there for a moment, face to face, hands clasped, until he let go and backed away. "Au revoir—until we meet again," he exclaimed. Waving his arms, he disappeared in a flash of light.

Desi gasped. Cat growled. Callida sagged, looking exhausted.

"That was my father," Desi said in wonder. Totally energized, she faced her mother. "We have to talk about this apprentice thing."

"I know," Callida said, resigned. "But not just now. So much has happened. First we have to talk about Dev—" She caught herself. "I mean, Cat."

Cat, whose bristling hair was just settling down from Val's flashy exit, went still again.

"What's to talk about?" Desi asked, though she had a pretty good idea.

"All your life you've learned how to keep people from knowing that you are different," Callida explained. "Cat's been human for four days, and what happened? The boy next door knows your secret, Cat was out dating, dancing in public—don't deny it, Cat, I saw you—leaving you alone at the mercy of your father. . . ."

Cat considered. "You saw me? Were you spying on me?"

"I wasn't spying on you; I was spying *through* you." From a kitchen cupboard, Callida retrieved a scepter with the head of a cat. "I couldn't use this with Desi, because we had never touched it together," she explained calmly. She held up the scepter, its ruby cat's eyes sparkling. "But once you'd handled it, I was able to see through your eyes." Callida shivered.

"It was difficult, chaotic. Using it for even a few seconds gave me a headache. You aren't really a cat and aren't completely human. What must it be like, being you?"

Cat looked sullen, just like she did after an appointment with the vet. Desi felt for her. Callida had trespassed inside her head? "Mom, how could you invade a person's privacy like that?"

"I would never, ever think of leaving you alone without being able to check up on you," Callida said. "It was too risky to keep in contact with you directly, so I did it through Cat. I'm sorry for not warning you, Cat, but you are my go-between. That's what being a Familiar means."

Desi put her arms around Cat. "We have to be able to trust each other," Desi insisted.

"I trust you," Callida said to Desi. "And I trusted Devil when she was a cat, but now?" She frowned at Cat, who looked insulted.

"Mom, we're family," Desi said firmly.

Callida looked overwhelmed. "Well, she has to behave like a human or it's back to being a cat again. Agreed?"

Desi beamed. Cat looked at her family, unblinking, and said, "Now that I am big, Desi and I do not fit on her bed anymore. I will sleep in that room with all the papers."

Callida put her hands on her hips. "If you're going to sleep in the office, I want you to move the office things to the front room where the golem was. And speaking of the golem, Desi, I need you to clean up the yard. It's a mess, and goodness knows what the neighbors will say."

"Mom—"

"In a family, everyone has to do their share," Callida said.

She broke into a smile. "The last thing I need is two lazy teenagers hanging around the house." Picking up the broom with a last proud, anxious look, she left.

"Family," Desi groaned, digging under the counter for the trash bags. Cat grinned back shyly and slipped out the back door.

Outside, Desi stopped Cat before she could get away. "Is this really what you want? Being a human girl?"

"I like my body," Cat said, straightening up proudly.

Desi was puzzled. "A few days ago you said you hated your body."

"It took a while to get over the shock," Cat replied. "But now I love my body because it is me and I am beautiful."

"That's easy for you to say." Desi felt a little envious. "You *are* beautiful."

Cat shrugged. "Of course—because I'm me. You are beautiful because you are you. I'm not beautiful because you think so or because Bobcat thinks so or anyone else. Humans have a lot to learn from cats about this." She twisted, looking behind her, and frowned. "But I do miss my tail."

45

THE SUN WAS sinking below the trees as Desi began collecting the trash scattered across her yard and the neighbors'. Cat had taken off to see Bobcat again, but she didn't mind. Before she could finish stuffing all that was left of the golem in her bags, Jarrett appeared, moving quickly across his lawn, darting nervous glances over his shoulder like a spy on a mission.

"Looks heavy," he said, crossing to her side. "Need help?"

Wordlessly she handed over the sack of old beer cans, careful not to let her fingers touch his. Ignoring the wondering sidelong glances he threw her way, she concentrated on bagging the old newspapers that hadn't blown away in the storm. When they had picked up both their yards, she and Jarrett lugged their bags to the recycling bins on the side of the house.

Opening the lid to the "aluminum cans only" bin, she took Jarrett's sack and silently cradled it for a moment. "Goodbye, and thanks for everything," she said to it.

"You're saying goodbye to the recycling?" Jarrett asked. "Is this some obscure witches' ritual?"

"I'm recycling my old dad," she said nervously. "He was a golem—you know, an enchanted robot made out of junk." She dumped the cans in.

"You're kidding. This was really him?" He peered into the bin suspiciously, as if the cans might magically reassemble themselves, pop up, and spout, "Have a nice day!"

"Yup, smells like him. Awesome."

"You know," Desi said, "I never thought I'd say this, but I'm sort of going to miss him."

Jarrett's face lit up. "So why not reanimate him, like Frankenstein? I'd kill to see that."

"I'm not going to miss him *that* much." She closed the lid. "Besides, I've got my real father now."

Jarrett looked at her with a funny expression. "That's cool."

The way he was staring at her was getting on her nerves. "Look, I'm not a freak, okay?" she declared. "I'm not going to start waving a wand around or go flying off on a broom. This isn't a movie. This is real."

"Sorry," he said, ducking his head. "It's just that I—"

"It's not just me," Desi said, exasperated. "Magic is all around, all the time."

"I know!" he said, excited. "I said the same thing, that time in the mall, remember? By the magic shop? Why didn't you tell me then?"

Now it was Desi's turn to duck her head.

"You thought I would make trouble for you?" he asked. When she didn't say anything, he gave her a playful jab to the shoulder.

She looked up at him, startled. For a moment, his face wore an oddly serious expression; then he blinked and was his old cocky self again. "You know," Jarrett teased, "school's starting in a couple of days. Can you make our homework do itself?" A thunderbolt seemed to hit him. "I just realized, this is going to be the best Halloween ever! You *are* going to let me spend Halloween with you, aren't you?" he pleaded.

Before Desi could think of an answer, the gate to the neighbors' yard flew open and Bob came clomping out, hugging a bundle of branches under one arm and pressing an ice pack to his head. Cat followed at his heels.

"No, I don't get it," Bob was griping. "Witches and warlocks and exploding demons? All I know is I banged my head on something, and the yard looks like a cyclone hit it." He dumped the branches next to the recycling bins by the side of his house.

Cat slipped in front of him. "I am saying thank you for trying to save me from the wind-demon."

Desi hurried over to do damage control. "Cat hasn't been speaking our language very long. You saved her from the tornado, and that's when you hit your head on the tree."

"*Wind-demon* is French for 'tornado'?" Bob peered at Cat through the fog in his head. "I still can't remember anything."

"You tried to rescue me," Cat said honestly. "You were very brave, Bobcat."

"Oh. No problem." He looked sheepish. "Uh, it's getting dark. You want to go back inside?"

Cat looked at him enticingly. "You should know by now that night is my favorite time of day. Everything exciting happens in the dark." Bob gulped. "Bobcat, I want to say a thing to you. Alone."

Desi watched the couple as they walked side by side into

Bob's yard. What was Cat going to say to him? Oh, well, that was her business. Her little cat was a big girl now. She had a right to her own life.

Together, she and Jarrett headed into Desi's backyard to give Cat and Bob some privacy. As soon as they were out of earshot, Jarrett asked, "How come you didn't tell him about last night?"

"Not everyone has to know I'm a witch," Desi said, savoring how that sounded. "Not yet. Besides, I can't make someone believe what they don't want to believe. You didn't tell?"

Jarrett leaned closer, so close that his long blond hair was touching hers. "I would never do that to you. This is our secret."

A thrill ran up Desi's spine. She searched his face. For a moment, Desi saw her reflection filling his soft blue eyes; then he backed away.

"Hey, did you get new statues?" Jarrett asked. "This is different."

They were standing near a watch-gnome at his post by the fence. Desi realized that her mother must have set them out again, taking no chances. The funny little man was not facing outward; instead, it scowled at them, arms crossed, with a look of disapproval on its cute little face.

"No," Desi sighed, "they're the same gnomes." She continued on through the yard to the one by the back fence. The gnome with the scarred nose still had its arm out, but now the broken finger pointed at Desi accusingly.

"This is definitely new," said Jarrett. "It looks ticked off."

"They're mad at me," she confessed. "I locked them in a closet. Look, I'm sorry, okay?" she pleaded to the watchgnome. "I won't do it again." The creature was unmoved.

"You're apologizing to a lawn ornament?" Jarrett joked with a gleam in his eye.

"Just because it's not human doesn't mean it doesn't have feelings," she said thoughtfully.

"Speaking of 'not human' . . . ," he said, lighting up.

"Right, we promised our new friend she could come out and play." Though the thought made her nervous, she was also getting excited. "Let's wait until it's totally dark."

⋅_⋆[⋆]⋆_⋆[⋆]

The night fell clear and soft. Warm southern breezes caressed them, as if fall was far away instead of just around the corner. Leaves swirled and crackled underfoot. Cat looked up into the branches of the old oak, saw the tree house, and remembered. "I love climbing trees," she whispered. "Coming?" A quick scramble up the ladder and she was hopping over the ledge into the tree house. Bob clambered up and squeezed in with her.

"This is purr-fect!" Cat said. She wriggled against him, getting comfortable. "Are you all right, Bobcat?" He seemed troubled.

"Yeah, I guess. It's just . . . I can't keep up with you," he confessed sadly. Bobcat wouldn't look at her; he stared past her into the night sky. "I've never met anyone like you before; that's for sure."

"No, I do not think you have."

"At least, I've never had a girl like you pay attention to me."

"Yes, they did," Cat stated firmly. "They were just too shy to say what they want, like you are."

"Sure, I guess." But it was clear he didn't mean it.

"Humans are too complicated. Someone has to make the first move or no one gets what they want."

He sighed. "What do *you* want, Cat?"

Cat stretched, arching her back. "What I have right now." She snuggled closer to him. "You can do it again," she added seriously. "I want you to."

Bob tensed up. "What?"

"What you were trying to do before. I'm ready now." She felt his body press against hers and told herself to relax. *Bobcat would never hurt me.*

Bobcat leaned closer, but with his face a few inches from hers, he stopped. "You sure?" She nodded mutely, willing herself to relax. She felt his lips touch hers.

BANG!

Lights and noise erupted in the sky. Their bodies flashed in multicolored reflections. Already on edge, Cat jumped at the sound of the fireworks, out of Bob's arms and out of the tree house. Bob gasped, reaching for her, but it was too late; he pulled back just in time to keep from falling over the edge with her.

As Cat fell away from the platform, the world spun in slow motion, picked out in different colors by the flash of fire from the sky. She tumbled head over heels until at last she righted herself, twisting in midair to get her legs and arms underneath her. Hitting the ground, her legs flexed like springs against the impact.

A quick flash showed Bob's face, peering down at her anxiously. "Cat! Are you all right?" She didn't know—she was too surprised to feel anything. In the dark, between explosions, it was hard to make him out; then a bomb burst overhead, silhouetting him in fire against the sprawling oak branches. Cat put one hand on the ladder. Should she flee or hide in his arms? What was going on?

·[*]·[*]·[*]·

The first blast from the demon-skyrocket knocked Desi and Jarrett flat in the grass, but lying on their backs just gave them a better view. Fountains of red, green, blue, and purple lights jetted up into the sky, leaping higher than the treetops to burst again in flowers of flame. Sparks drifted down like falling stars or a new snowfall of holiday lights. Small rockets burst into the shapes of faces, or birds, or mythical beasts. A brighter rocket corkscrewed into the night sky only to split and split again until it branched into a tree of light far above the forest. Jarrett had been right: nobody had ever seen fireworks like this before.

Nestled in the grass of her backyard, heart soaring, Desi spoke to the sky. "Thanks for the show, Blaze. I hope you got what you wanted. I did." Sitting up, she reached out her hand to the last drifting starburst in the sky. With one word—*Agape*—she opened it like a blossom, creating a five-pointed star hanging in the air, inviting entrance. "Our deal is done. Keep your promise—go home!" she commanded.

At those words, another bright pillar of fire rose from the

can into the sky, whirling joyfully above the yard. Desi was afraid that it might break loose and fly away, but at the last second, the fireball swooped to a halt by the starry Portal, taking Desi's form once again. Her own face appeared in the fire, wistful, as if begging for just a little longer. Desi shook her head sympathetically and waved goodbye. With a flaming hand, Blaze waved back, flew into the Portal, whirled to face Desi, and blew her a fiery kiss. Then the demon vanished, taking the Portal with her, leaving only the kiss, spilling silently in a brilliant cascade that poured bright rain onto a pool of starlight below. The rain of fire became buzzing sparks that turned and twisted together through the branches in a swarm until at last, just before they set the world ablaze, the sparks extinguished one by one, and the night air was clear.

⋅⋆⁺⋆⋅⋆

As the tumult faded, Cat bounded up the ladder to the tree house and flung herself over the threshold. Safe in Bobcat's arms once again, she snuggled closer. So did he. Just before his lips touched hers, she murmured, "Bobcat?"

"Uh-huh?"

"Do you think, this time, you could do it more quietly?"

"Uh-huh."

"Try." She pressed her mouth to his and held it there. All was still except for the soft movement of his lips and the pounding of his heart, keeping rhythm with hers.

After a long moment, Cat pulled away. "I knew you could do it," she said with a satisfied smile. "Good Bobcat."

⋅⋆⁺⋆⋅⋆

Desi hugged her knees in the grass, silence ringing in her ears, the brilliant fireworks bursting over and over in her mind. Jarrett sat next to her, his shoulder just barely touching hers, gazing around with eyes full of light and wonder. As the afterimages slowly burned away, she saw Cat glide over the edge of the tree house to join her, silently taking her place at her side to share the luminous night. Bobcat sat down a moment later, resting with his arm around Cat.

Surrounded by friends, a new and different kind of fireworks lit up in Desi's heart. *So many kinds of magic,* she thought, amazed.

She leaned back, floating in the grass under the endless sky. Which of the countless stars overhead would open up for her next? Infinite magic, endless possibilities.

Acknowledgments

I WOULD LIKE to thank:

Nick Eliopulos, my talented editor. Lee Alexander, my agent (and my sister). Patience Mason; Gay Haldeman; Meredith Ann Pierce; Bev Browning; Mary Ann Emerson; Rick Yancey; Kate Harrison; Rachel Vader; Julie Noel; Lesley Lozano; Landon Lozano; Marna, Brian, and Andrew Dahlgren; Rebecca Marten; my father "Alex"; Dave Alexander; Kate Alexander; Lynn, Harris, Sage, and Jas Max; Shravana Ogle; Cheryl Valantis; Heather Riverstone; Alan Fischer; Jazminh Lambley; Layla Smith; Bonnie Winkler; Kurt Volckmar; Pat, Fraser, and Trey for guarding Angel; and my "special editors," Anya Fairchild and Sebia Lozano-Rice.

About the Author

R. C. ALEXANDER has led numerous lives: he's been a PhD student, a theater director, a spiritual seeker, a businessman, and a stay-at-home dad. After many years in Minnesota and California, he now lives in Florida with his wife and son on twenty acres of woodlands in a house he built himself under the supervision of Angel, the family cat. *Unfamiliar Magic* is his first published novel.

THE
SEER

ALSO BY

DAVID STAHLER JR.

DOPPELGANGER

A GATHERING OF SHADES

TRUESIGHT

THE SEER

DAVID STAHLER JR.

An Imprint of HarperCollins *Publishers*

Eos is an imprint of HarperCollins Publishers.

The Seer

Copyright © 2007 by David Stahler Jr.

Library of Congress Cataloging-in-Publication Data
Stahler, David.
   The seer / by David Stahler Jr. — 1st ed.
      p.   cm.
   Sequel to : Truesight.
   ISBN-10: 0-06-052288-7 (trade bdg.)
   ISBN-13: 978-0-06-052288-9 (trade bdg.)
   ISBN-10: 0-06-052289-5 (lib. bdg.)
   ISBN-13: 978-0-06-052289-6 (lib. bdg.)
   Summary: Raised in a futuristic frontier world colony where blindness is
the genetically engineered hallmark of every citizen, thirteen-year-old Jacob
is stricken with sight and must find his way to the city of the Seers, where
he hopes to reconnect with a girl from his past.
   [1. Blind—Fiction. 2. People with disabilities—Fiction. 3. Science fic-
tion.] I. Title.
PZ7.S78246See 2007   2006020124
[Fic]—dc22   CIP
                                                                  AC

Typography by R. Hult
1 2 3 4 5 6 7 8 9 10
❖
First Edition

To my son,
Julian

CHAPTER ONE

The great ringed moon had come and gone, moving across the sky with a speed one could almost trace if the eyes were patient enough to follow. And now even its sister moon, small and pink, tagging slowly along behind, had begun its sinking, and as the morning light crept back into the world, Jacob Manford stirred within his damp pocket of grass and dreamed.

He had been following her too long—for what seemed like hours, maybe even days—along the streets of Harmony, moving from tier to tier, from north to south, east to west, cutting through the heart of the colony each time, then twisting along unfamiliar lanes before coming back around. At first he kept losing her. She kept fading around the corners and he, running to catch up, seemed to just miss her each time. Maybe he waited, maybe he turned back—it didn't matter, she always reappeared. That was at first. Now she no longer vanished and he knew that he was gaining, that it was only a matter of time. He was close now, close enough to hear her breathing, almost close enough to touch the dark strands of hair that floated behind her though there was no breeze. He was close enough that he knew he only had to whisper her name and she would hear him.

1

"Delaney," he called, "please stop. I'm tired."

He thought she might have laughed. Or maybe it was the sound of chimes, for as he looked ahead he could see the council house before them. He picked up the pace as they climbed the ramp toward the opening set into the hill, the gaping darkness of the portal framed by the great chimes that now clamored in alarm at his approach. He had been there only once before, to be judged in the shadows of the chamber, and he knew he had to stop her. He could only imagine what they would do to her.

"Stop, Delaney. You can't go in there!" he hissed.

She must not have heard him above the clanging of the chimes, for she plunged into the gloom, spreading out her arms as if to touch the edges of the doorway before being swallowed up. He raced to the opening, then paused, reaching out a hand toward the dark only to see his fingers disappear as they breached the inky surface of the entryway. He yanked his hand back and hesitated on the threshold. He had to go in after her. The chimes ceased and still he wavered. What was he waiting for?

I wouldn't go in there if I were you, he heard a voice say. He snapped his eyes up to where a striped cat reclined above the doorway, its bulk still stretched along the ledge as it had been the morning that the listeners hauled him inside before the council. Then it had greeted him with a moment of understanding, but he felt no sympathy from it now as it peered down at him through slitted, yellow eyes. *You remember what happened last time, don't you?* its voice sounded in his mind. *Maybe this time you don't come out.*

"How can I leave her in there?" he replied. "I *have* to go get her!"

2

Suit yourself. But don't say I didn't warn you. The cat yawned, its tongue curling between needle teeth, and then stretched back against the shelf to resume its endless nap.

He shook his head, angry at the creature's indifference, and reached for the darkness again. This time his hand went deeper. Something grabbed him and began drawing him in. He gasped at the fiery touch. Try as he might, he couldn't pull away. He could only feel a burning spreading through his arm as it disappeared inch by inch, as his face came closer and closer to the opaque surface. The last thing he heard before being swallowed up was the cat's voice, a distant echo of disdain:

Foolish boy, why did you return?

Then he was falling. It was only a moment, but long enough in the silent void to feel as if he were slipping away from life. He had no sensation, only an impression of absence, and in that moment he was sure that he was blind again, this time for good. *It's all been for nothing,* he thought. But soon a mild jolt of impact shook him, and he discovered he was back on his feet and running.

There was no council chamber, no council. He was in a tunnel now instead. He could see her before him once more, very close, the thin shadow of a girl, her hair flowing back, brushing the tips of his reaching fingers. There was a strange glow before her, illuminating her profile, lighting up the rough-hewn walls of the tunnel around them. He called out to her again, trying not to cough as smoke began trailing behind her.

"Stop, Delaney! Don't run! You don't need to!" he called out, trying to wipe the tears from his blinking eyes as the smoke thickened.

3

She seemed to hear his cry, for suddenly she slowed, then halted before him in the tunnel. He slowed too and came up behind her. He reached out, put his hand on her shoulder and turned her around, desperate to see her face. He had never seen her face before.

He recoiled, blinking not from smoke now but from the erupting brightness as she turned toward him. He squinted, unable to see her face, only the twin sparks of brilliance that shone from the sockets of what were once her eyes.

"What's happened to you?" he gasped, moving closer in spite of his horror.

The light dimmed slightly, but she didn't answer as a plume of smoke rose from each eye, thick black smoke that curled up and then down, winding around his legs, fixing him in place. He could barely make out any part of her face, but her mouth seemed to curl into a smile as her eyes brightened again, growing more intense every second. He peered even closer and saw how the eyes were flickering, little tendrils of light that curled out and around her face. They were flames.

A scream sounded in his ears; he couldn't tell if it was hers or his own. All he knew was that this was the end. The cat had been right—he should never have come back. . . .

Jacob bolted upright, awakened by the sound of his own scream, for a moment not sure if he was still screaming or hearing just the memory of it. But it was quiet now. He fell back into the grass with a sigh of relief and, looking straight up, wiped away the sweat that had gathered on his forehead. The blades rose above him on all sides, forming a tunnel of vegetation, a portal through which the sky looked small and contained, its emptiness marred by only a single cloud. It was a beautiful morning, clear and crisp. He told himself that the nightmare wasn't real, but it only helped a little. For the second night in a row he'd had the same dream. It was so vivid—the desperation, the fear, even the physical sensations. The sounds, the smells, the images—more real than any dream he'd ever had.

Unlike the last three days, he didn't immediately rise to his feet and continue the westward march. Instead, he lay there motionless but for his breathing, trying to let go of the memory of his dream, reluctant to shed the thin blanket that wrapped him within his nest of grass. He knew rising would reveal the stiffness he had felt yesterday when he woke soaked with dew under the same clear sky. He was tired—tired of walking, tired of thinking, his only tasks the last three days. Though he had walked late into darkness last night, before collapsing in the grass, he knew what he would see upon standing: the same uniform swell of the plains, the hills rising and falling, the grassland swaying to the currents of the breeze in waves that rippled over the terrain. He would climb to the top of one rise, only to see the same dip of little valleys that led to the next hillock, and the next.

Not that Jacob hadn't seen anything unusual. Two days ago he had seen trees for the first time—real trees, not the shrubs or small fruit trees that grew in Harmony. It was nearing sunset. Clearing a ridge, he glimpsed in a meadow a cluster of tall, dark shapes, which loomed larger as he approached, until they towered above him. With relief he discovered they surrounded a small spring-fed pool. Exhausted and thirsty, he collapsed at the edge of the spring, where the roots of the trees stretched into the water like bony fingers. Though the sun no longer blazed, it felt good to sit under the canopy of branches, to have something between himself and the sky.

There was something else he saw. As he leaned over the water to drink, a face met his, drawing nearer as he bent closer to the surface. He started at the sight before realizing it was his own face that stared back at him. It was the first time he had seen himself clearly, and he lingered over the reflection, marveling at his appearance. At the age of thirteen, his face revealed an interesting mixture of his parents' features. The overall structure—especially the cleft chin and chiseled nose—reminded him of his father, but the pale coloring of the skin and eyes was definitely his mother's. The eyes returned his stare, as if he were the reflection and the face in the pool were the real person. For a long time Jacob examined the stranger, their eyes linked until his cupped hand broke the surface, dissolving the connection into a blur of concentric circles, and he drank. He slept that night under the trees amid the roots, lulled to sleep by the rustling of the leaves.

That was the last night he'd slept with any amount of peace, free from the dream that felt like waking life. Pulling himself up now, he stretched the stiffness from his joints. He could feel hunger in his stomach, a hollow pain. For a moment, he considered looking into his canvas bag for something to eat—perhaps he'd missed some morsel of cheese, a last slice of bread. But he knew there was no point in pretending. All that remained was a single can of pears buried at the bottom of his bag. Throughout yesterday's march he told himself he wouldn't eat them, swore an oath not to. When they were gone, he'd have nothing left. It made him mad to think about how carelessly he'd packed. Why hadn't he grabbed more food? Partly it was because he hadn't been that hungry, and partly because there wasn't much left to take. Besides, he had been in a rush, so rattled by the sudden decision to leave that it never occurred to him how far he might have to go. Still, he was better off now. Wasn't he?

He turned back to the east, eyeing his dim trail running through the grass. Had it really only been four days since he had left Harmony, left his people, left the only life he'd ever known? For some reason it seemed much longer. And yet only a month ago he was still one of them. All of them were blind, content to live in the darkness, unaware of what was happening around them, oblivious to each others' actions, from minor indiscretions to the larger crimes that cut at the very heart of what Harmony was supposed to be about: purity, unity, and freedom through blindness. Oblivious, too, to the beauty and wonder of the world around them. They named their way of life Truesight, a philosophy that called for a rejection of the shallowness and deception of appearances.

Jacob glanced up at the sky where a handful of birds circled and danced in the air above him, just as they had done in Harmony. He shook his head and smiled grimly. Through some accident of fate he still didn't understand, he had discovered that Truesight itself was a deception, that it blinded his people to the realities of life, both good and bad.

They could never accept him for his difference, had tried to take his sight from him, perhaps even his life. Jacob shuddered, remembering the veiled threat Delaney's father, the high councilor, had made just before he tore himself away: *Let's just hope the surgery goes well, Jacob. The ghostbox makes mistakes from time to time.*

He didn't bother to spread his blanket out to dry in the

sun, as he had the last three mornings, but rolled the damp cloth into a bundle and shoved it into his knapsack. He needed to move; it was the only way to overcome the doubts beginning to collect in the back of his mind. He had to keep going. There was nothing else to do.

There was, however, one daily ritual Jacob kept. Pulling the finder from his pack, he extended the small device before him. Just a few weeks ago, just days before his thirteenth birthday, still blind, he'd held the cool cylinder in school for the first time and learned how to hone in on his classmate's sounder. Everyone in Harmony wore a sounder, a device that helped them navigate the settlement and identified each of them by giving off a unique pitch. Jacob had discovered his classmate in the hallway and, taking her by the hand, had brought her back to the classroom. It was barely an hour later—as he and his best friend, Egan, practiced with the finders in the schoolyard—that he experienced the first headache, the first wave of pain, the first in a series of changes that eventually brought him here to this spot in the middle of nowhere. Never would he have imagined that day that he would be using a finder in this place, for this reason.

He pressed the button and held his breath a moment before whispering her name.

"Delaney Corrow," he said.

Like always, his pulse quickened as the familiar beep began its rhythm. It only took him a moment to hone in on the direction of its greatest intensity. By now he could navigate almost completely by the location of the sun, but he loved to hear that repeating note. It was the sound of hope.

Turning the finder off, he replaced it securely in its spot. He shouldered his pack and plunged westward through the grass.

CHAPTER TWO

Wiping the sweat from the back of his neck, Jacob gazed up at the sun, now past its zenith. It was a hot day, the hottest he could remember in a long time. Though hunger still gnawed at him, satisfying it was no longer his most pressing need. All he could think about now was the thirst that had been growing in him all day. He had forgotten to bring a bottle of any kind for water, and he'd been depending on streams and springs along the way. They were few and far between. The last time he'd come across one was yesterday afternoon—a small brook, hardly more than a trickle along the bottom of a valley. Who knew when he'd find another?

He stood at the crest of a hill, gazing westward. It looked the same in all directions, just swell after swell of grass. It was about a mile to the next rise, a wide ridge taller than any he'd seen so far, so high he could see nothing behind it. He groaned at the thought of climbing it. A familiar feeling rose within him—a sickness in his stomach, a mild sensation of dizziness—but it wasn't hunger or thirst. It was fear. It was that same feeling of panic that had been rising all day, every time he thought about his situation, every time he imagined himself collapsing in the grass, swallowed up forever with no one to know where he lay. He had felt this kind of panic several times back in Harmony at the Gatherings—first as one of the crowd not long before his sight had begun to manifest itself, and then at the end when he'd stood before his people, a pariah. Now he was alone, and the feeling was more intense than ever.

As he tried swallowing, his tongue thick and swollen in his dry mouth, he wondered again if he'd made a mistake by leaving. It was his fault, after all, that they were going to blind him again and wipe his memory of sight. If he hadn't told them in the first place, he would still be living among them, living as one of them, and they would be none the wiser. They were already living a life of deception; how would his have been any worse?

None of that mattered, he realized. He couldn't change what had happened, neither would they allow him to return.

But that didn't mean he couldn't go back. He could return in secret and live among them, take food and clothing as he needed, remain in plain sight before all of them, and they would never know. He could even watch over them, like a guardian spirit, helping them when they got in trouble. He had done it before, hadn't he? Hadn't he saved that injured grower, Mitchell, from bleeding to death in the field? He had spent a whole week wandering the colony unseen. He could do it again.

Turning back, he took a couple of steps east along the slim path of trampled grass, and then stopped.

It might not be that easy. There might be one who could detect him. An image of the high councilor's face leering at him in the yellow glow of the ghostbox flashed to mind. But it wasn't just the face, it was the wink—that instant of recognition that passed between them when Jacob discovered the man could see. The whole first day after leaving Harmony, Jacob had gone over those few seconds in his mind. At first it seemed so definite, carved into a crystal moment of revulsion, but the more he recalled it from memory, the less clear it became. Now he wasn't even sure. Maybe it had been just an involuntary gesture—a twitch of the eye—or perhaps both eyes had blinked as even blind eyes do, and in the shadows he had seen only the one. In the terror of the moment, he could have imagined the whole thing.

Either way, he could risk it. Whether the man could see or not, Jacob could avoid him altogether. He never wanted to see that face again anyway.

Once more, he started numbly eastward, back the way he'd come. All he wanted was to stop the grumbling heave of his stomach, the burning in his throat. All he wanted was to live.

He had gone only a dozen steps when a sound behind him made him pause. He turned to listen.

At first it was no more than a hum, hardly distinguishable from the rustling of his legs against the grass, a single pitch like the ringing of a distant sounder. Then it grew deeper, louder, taking on an almost angry, guttural tone, a growling that peaked as a strange object flew over a ridge to Jacob's right, carried by its speed into the air, floating for a moment before dropping back down to earth, bouncing several times as it hurtled through the grass.

It was a craft of some sort. The only thing he could compare it to was the harvesters back in Harmony, the steel creatures that moved up and down rows of crops, working with the growers to process the colony's food. But this was no harvester—it moved too fast, faster than Jacob could imagine anything moving. As it came closer, he could see it was taller, too, with huge, studded tires instead of revolving tracks like the harvesters had. Bars came up over the front and rear seats like a cage, and the back half of the vehicle consisted of a boxed-in storage area. Most startling of all was the sight of a man seated within the dark frame.

For a moment Jacob watched in awe as it tore down the valley, racing in his general direction. He started to raise his hands, then hesitated. This was a Seer, his first one. All the warnings, the diatribes, the sordid stories he'd heard his entire childhood came flooding back to mind. Who knew what this person might do to him, a boy, alone on the plain with no one else around? Jacob was about to take cover in the tall grass, when it occurred to him that he too was a Seer. He was one of them. Why hide?

He stood as tall as he could, waving his arms back and forth in an effort to catch the driver's attention, but the craft continued to speed along without any change in direction. It was angled to pass about fifty yards below him. He started to run down the hill in an effort to intersect it, still waving his arms. *He has to see me now*, Jacob thought, as the vehicle came closer, but still it roared along without slowing or turning in his direction.

He was only twenty yards away when it passed him. He watched it go by with a mix of confusion and disappointment—his one chance of being saved seemed to be slipping away. Then there was a piercing squeal as the craft slammed on its brakes, skidding across the grass to a halt thirty yards ahead. Jacob began running toward it, then hesitated as it started to back up toward him, slowly at first, then faster, its engine growling in reverse. He expected it to slow down as it came closer, but it kept accelerating straight at him. He dove out of the way to avoid being run over.

Tumbling through the grass, he rolled several times before landing facedown. When he picked himself up, the craft was facing him no more than ten yards away, its engine idling. A man stared at him from the cockpit, his face blank, his eyes obscured by a pair of dark goggles. At least a minute passed while the man sat unmoving, leaving Jacob with a growing sense of uneasiness.

Finally, the engine died and there was a slight hiss as the driver's side door opened. The man emerged and jumped down to the ground, holding a dark metal stick of some kind in one hand. It was about a yard long, wide at one end, narrow at the other, with a few knobs and other strange pieces protruding from the middle section. The man closed the door and turned, making no movement toward Jacob.

They stood for a moment in silence, studying each other. The man was older, perhaps his father's age, with skin nearly as tan as the growers' back home. He had an intent, angular face, and his dark hair was cropped short. His clothes were unlike the plain, blousy smocks and tunics Jacob was used to seeing. These were more tight-fitting and of different shades, with dark pants tucked into black boots, and a light shirt and darker vest. A wide belt circled his waist, lined with tiny compartments and strange-looking tools.

The man took a few steps toward him, raised his goggles with one hand and lowered the metal stick with the other.

As he came closer, Jacob noticed his eyes. They were even paler than Jacob's, though maybe it just seemed that way in contrast to the darkness of the man's skin. Jacob tried to get a sense of who this stranger was. In Harmony he had quickly

13

learned how to read people's faces. Since they didn't know anyone was watching, his blind neighbors had made no effort to conceal their expressions. But this man could see, and his face seemed guarded, steady in its control. His eyes didn't seem unkind. On the other hand, they weren't too inviting either. That was the trouble—they didn't seem like anything, though their neutrality suggested a certain sort of wisdom. Jacob had a sudden feeling that those eyes had seen a lot.

I guess I should say something, he thought.

"You almost hit me," Jacob offered as a joke. In spite of trying to sound confident, his voice came out small and thin.

"I wouldn't have," the man replied. His voice, like his face, seemed neither hostile nor welcoming, just sure. He pushed past Jacob, donned his goggles, and scanned the southern horizon, reaching up to touch a switch along the top of the glasses from time to time.

"Looking for something?" Jacob asked.

"Gruskers," the man replied. Jacob remembered learning in school about the large herd animals that wandered the plains. "Seen any?" the man asked.

"I don't know what they look like," Jacob said. "I don't think so."

"You'd know them if you saw them," the man said, stripping off his goggles, his back still to Jacob.

"What do you want with them?" Jacob asked.

"I'm hunting them."

"What for?"

"What do you care?" the man asked, suddenly turning with a frown.

"Just curious," Jacob said, his voice shrinking almost to a whisper.

14

"For food. I like to catch my own food," the man replied, his tone softening. "A single grusker goes a long way."

"What's that?" Jacob asked, pointing to the stick now cradled in the man's arm.

"It's a rifle," he said, then added, as if anticipating Jacob's next question, "It's for the gruskers. And for anyone who decides to give me trouble." His eyes narrowed at these last words as Jacob's widened, though Jacob noticed a slight smile seemed to form along the man's mouth.

"So, what about you?" the man asked. "What are you looking for, Blinder?"

Jacob was startled at the label. "I'm not a Blinder," he said. "I'm a Seer, like you."

The man snorted. "You may be able to see, but you're not one of us. I know where you're from. It's plain enough."

Jacob wondered how much to tell him. He needed his help, but how did he know he could trust the man?

"I'm looking for the city," he said. "The big one. Where the Seers live."

The man nodded. "Well, you're headed in the right direction, then." He walked past Jacob again, heading for his craft.

Jacob followed behind, almost running to match the man's long stride.

"Wait!" he shouted.

The man halted and turned so abruptly Jacob nearly collided with him. He looked down at Jacob expectantly.

"I . . . I was hoping," Jacob stammered, "that you might be able to take me there."

The man gave a long sigh and nodded, as if he had been waiting for this all along.

"I can't. I've got things I have to do," he said, and

turned back toward the craft.

"Oh . . ." Jacob said. He didn't know what else to say.

"Don't give me that," the man replied, as if Jacob had broken into a desperate plea. "I've taken on more than my share of charity cases lately," he added.

The man reached up into the cab and pulled out a container. He tossed it over to Jacob, who caught it, almost falling over in surprise at its weight. Hearing a sloshing sound inside, Jacob unscrewed the cap with shaking fingers and immediately lifted it to his mouth, not even pausing to examine the contents. It was liquid, it was wet. It was water. Somewhat warm, a bit stale, with a slight taste of plastic, but Jacob decided it was the best water he'd ever had, as he guzzled it down.

"Slow down," the man barked. "You'll make yourself sick."

Jacob lowered the jug—already there was a clenching pain in his stomach. The stranger was right. Jacob offered the jug back.

"Keep it," the man said. He reached into one of the pouches along his belt and pulled out a small package, tossing it to Jacob. Wrapped in a shiny material, the parcel was no more than five inches long.

"Something to eat," the man explained. Jacob looked up questioningly. "Doesn't look like much," he acknowledged. "Powerful stuff, though. Enough for a whole day."

He pulled a few more out and tossed them over. "Tastes like the bark of a zephyr, but they'll hold you."

The man climbed up into the cockpit and buckled himself in. Putting his goggles back on, he looked down at Jacob.

"Listen, Blinder, don't worry. You'll be fine. Just keep

16

going in the direction you're headed. You'll get there soon enough."

"How far is it?" Jacob asked.

"Close. Closer than you think," he replied.

The door lowered with a hiss and the engine growled to life, throbbing so loudly Jacob had to cover his ears. The man gave Jacob a little wave, but before he could wave back, the craft was off, hurtling south once more. The grass swayed wildly in its wake. A moment later, it was gone.

Jacob reached down to pick up one of the foil packages lying in the grass.

So that's what Seers are like, he thought.

He had never felt so alone.

CHAPTER THREE

A day later, Jacob knew he'd been duped. At every rise, he kept expecting to see a city, but each time he was greeted with nothing but another set of swells stretching to the next distant ridge. He wasn't exactly sure what he was looking for, but at this point anything different from the plain would be a relief. What would a city of Seers look like, anyway? The people of Harmony lived underground in homes dug into the hillsides. With no need for windows, the design was simple and efficient, requiring few materials. The few standing structures in the community, mostly public buildings, were made of either steel or concrete, solid blocks, dull and colorless. He imagined the Seers' homes were above the surface, translucent and full of light, open to the world and to each other. Still, when it came to the Seers, he wasn't sure. This strange man had told him that the city was close, yet here he was, an afternoon later and nothing had changed.

If the man had lied, at least he'd given Jacob the means to go on. The stranger had been right about the food. The compact bar of dry and oddly chewy material didn't taste very good—in fact, it was like chewing on the frayed edges of his tunic—but it filled the hollow place inside his stomach. Eating just half a bar had carried him all the way through until this morning. He had finished the rest of it on waking, and only now was he starting to feel hungry again. Still, why hadn't the man been willing to give him a ride? What was so important that he couldn't help a person in need?

Jacob's disappointment made him even more determined to go on, and in this sense he was grateful to the man. With a twinge of shame he thought back to yesterday when, driven by hunger and thirst, by the weakness of his body, he'd been ready to give up, had even started to turn back for Harmony. Now more than ever he wanted to find other Seers, to make his way to the city and confirm what he felt to be true: *They can't all be like that man*, he told himself, pausing midstride. *I'll find the good ones. And Delaney will be with them.*

He set off again with new vigor, a steady march for the next rise. It was about half a mile away and loomed larger than the high ridge he had sweated up not long after his encounter with the Seer the day before.

He was halfway across a great basin set between two ridges. Places like this often held the promise of water. Having finished the last of what was in the stranger's jug a few hours ago, he kept an ear out for the sound of a trickle as he walked, casting his gaze back and forth in hopes of spotting a stray puddle of water.

A brightness in the grass to the right caught his eye. He froze, trying to figure out what it could be. It wasn't moving. Maybe it was a flower of some kind, he thought, though all the flowers he'd seen so far were the normal blossoms that seemed to cover the entire planet. It looked too big to be a flower.

Walking over to it, a prickling sensation passed through Jacob, traveling up his spine to the back of his neck where the hairs stood on end. He didn't know why, but he suddenly didn't want to get any closer to the object in the grass. From here he could see more white, mixed with something darker. Breathing quickly, he pushed aside the grass and gazed down at the pale fragments spread across the ground before him.

They were bones. Jacob had never seen bones before, but he had learned about them in school and these had to be them. For a moment he just stared, fascinated. He would never have imagined these solid pieces of legs and arms wrapped in flesh could gleam so brightly in the sun. Examining the length of the figure, he suddenly shivered. The shape they made was easy enough to recognize. The person had died lying facedown. The back of the skull was a pale globe. The arms were stretched forward and bent before the head, seeming to clutch the earth. The rotten remains of shoes obscured the feet. But what truly made him shiver were the tattered remnants of clothes still clinging to the body. They were faded by the sun, falling apart in places to expose the ribs and pelvis, but he could still recognize the familiar shape of the smock, the remains of a tunic like his own.

He had to be sure. With shaking hands he reached down and turned the body over, and then jumped back. The bones of the top half of the figure crumbled, falling softly to the grass, while the bottom half remained secure. The smock ripped as well, but there—along what was once the chest, still clinging to the rotting fabric—shone the gleaming disk of a sounder.

He turned away and closed his eyes. He could still see the skull staring up into the sky, its eye sockets deep, not quite circular, not quite square, its open jaw full of yellow teeth.

He can't hurt you, he told himself.

20

His eyes snapped open. How did he know it was a he? Could it have been a she? Could it be . . . ?

He tore his backpack off and opened the top with trembling fingers. He tipped it upside down and emptied the contents, grasping at the finder as it fell into the grass. Holding it before him, he croaked out the name.

"Delaney Corrow."

Facing the body, he felt a moment of queasiness as the pulsing started. He rotated left, away from the body in the direction he'd been traveling. A wave of relief came over him as the signal intensified. He tried again just to make sure, turning in a complete circle. It wasn't her. He didn't know what had happened to her, but this wasn't her.

Considering it further, he realized it couldn't be her. He didn't know how long it would take for a body to dissolve to bone, but he imagined it would take more than the few weeks since Delaney had left Harmony.

He went over to his pack. As he gathered up the scattered contents of the bag, he tried not to imagine Delaney stumbling through the grass blind and alone. He tried to think of something else about her instead, something happy, something he could hold onto. But it was hard. She had been so sad, so desperate the past few months. He remembered the argument he'd overheard her having with her father not long before she'd disappeared. She'd said she wanted to know what the outside world was like, had even voiced a desperate desire to see. Jacob could still hear the slap as her father reacted in rage. The next day was the last time he'd heard her voice, felt the softness of her hands. Her father had told them all that she was dead, but on his last night in Harmony, Jacob had learned the truth.

Closing up his pack, he glanced over at the remains once more. He couldn't help but wonder—if it wasn't Delaney, then who was it? Obviously, he or she had, like both him and Delaney, fled Harmony. Was it someone he had known growing up? Maybe it had been someone like him, someone who had regained his or her sight. Thinking of the difficulties his own journey had yielded, it seemed impossible that someone blind could make it so far, would even know which direction to go. Then again, in the end the person hadn't made it, had ended up here for Jacob to stumble across months or even years later.

Sitting down to rest, he stared over at the body, no longer afraid, just sad. What had this person's final moments been like? What kind of suffering had they felt? What kind of suffering had driven them to strike out blindly, to risk an ending like this? How could anyone blind think they could make it?

He had to believe they could. He had to believe Delaney could.

Jacob went back to the body and reached down, gingerly retrieving the anonymous sounder. It tore away easily from the rags. Tilting it back and forth against the sun so that it flashed a pattern against his tunic, he smiled briefly. This daring person would not be lost forever. He or she would, in some little way, be remembered.

As he placed the sounder in his pack, a thought struck him: His whole life, he had never even considered that anyone would actually leave Harmony, let alone want to. Yet now he knew of at least two people—three, including himself—who had done so. How many more were there? He thought back to his last night in Harmony. Under the light of the ringed moon he had wandered out to the burial grounds to

22

say good-bye to Delaney. He remembered the vast expanse of pathminders laid out in a grid to mark the resting places of the dead. Delaney's grave was empty. How many others were as well?

As he hoisted his pack and turned to resume his journey, an odd sensation made him raise his eyes. It felt like the pulsing of his sounder, though the throbbing was fainter and was coming up from the ground through his feet. He looked around but saw nothing. For a moment he thought of yesterday's hum that heralded the arrival of the strange craft. Maybe the man had changed his mind and was coming back for him.

There was a distant bellow in the south. He turned and saw a host of dark shapes sliding over the hill into the basin, heading in his direction. For a minute Jacob watched, puzzled. They didn't move nearly as fast as the man's vehicle had, but they were moving fast enough. And there were a lot of them—by now too many for Jacob to count as still more poured over the horizon.

Gruskers.

The stranger had said Jacob would know them when he saw them, and he was right. They were still a ways off but closing quickly, and though he didn't seem to remember learning they were dangerous, he didn't know how they might react to him. All he knew was that they were much bigger than he was.

The shaking underfoot intensified. He began jogging, then racing, up the steady incline toward the high ridge ahead as the sound of the gruskers—one long roll of thundering hooves accented by the bellowing of many voices—filled the valley. Running out of breath, he chanced a look over his shoulder. The creatures were a good fifty yards away and no longer moving in his direction. What's more, the herd had slowed, spreading out to graze as the last of them entered the basin. Stopping to catch his breath, he turned and dropped back into the grass. He gazed down across the basin, captivated by the scene.

The huge herbivores paid him no mind as he watched. He had never seen animals so big. Dark in hue with brilliant stripes and four massive tusks that emerged from the sides of their head to cover their face like a cage, they dwarfed the sheep and cattle Jacob had seen at Harmony. He had learned about the gruskers last year in school when they studied native species, and he had heard their cries on the rare occasion they passed near the perimeter of the colony, but they were far more beautiful and impressive by sight than he could have imagined in his blindness. For an hour he observed them as they headed north, intersecting his own path. Pausing individually here and there to browse, the whole herd moved with a distinct rhythm, and because their legs were almost totally obscured by the high vegetation, they appeared to float through the landscape, leaving a wake of trodden and cropped grass. Somewhere amid the mass of creatures lay the lost Blinder. Jacob hoped the bones would remain undisturbed.

Watching the gruskers, he was reminded of the starship he'd seen his last night in Harmony, floating against the star field, drifting into space. As with the ship, he wondered where the gruskers were going. Did they, too, have a destination, or were they wandering without aim? He imagined the latter. They didn't need a destination—wherever they were, that was where they were supposed to be. They were lucky.

Yes, he had a destination, a reason to move on, but with it came the burden of finding it. They, on the other hand, had no sense of urgency, no fear.

Most of all, the gruskers had their herd. They had each other. They didn't travel alone.

And what was he? He was nothing. Just a boy drifting on a sea of grass, a single speck barely visible against the indifferent plain.

He rose and continued on his way, leaving the gruskers to their grazing. But as the slope steepened, forcing him to lean in against the incline, reaching forward for tufts of grass to help pull him up the face of the ridge, his thoughts drifted back to the creatures, his envy sharpening at the sounds of their calling to one another. The calls pushed his mind back farther, all the way across five days of journeying through the plain, back to Harmony.

He tried to imagine what was happening there right now. Ever since he'd left, he'd been wondering what his people had been told about his disappearance. Did they know what he'd done? How would the knowledge affect them? Maybe they didn't know. Maybe he had received the same treatment as Delaney—another lost child to be buried and then forgotten. Most of all, he wondered about his parents. He tried to imagine his mother at this moment, sitting at the table in the darkness of the house, alone. Losing Delaney, who had been as much a daughter to her as an apprentice, had been devastating enough. Could she tolerate yet another loss? Was his father there for her right now? Did she even want him there? Jacob still remembered the sight of her secretly embracing the high councilor, and he remembered the constant fighting of his parents, the tension between them over the last year.

But he also remembered them walking together before him on the way back from the council chamber, where he'd been revealed as a Seer—they had joined hands in a moment of intimacy that seemed to carry over to the next day. How strange would it be if the event that had torn Jacob from his parents was what brought them together? All he knew was that he missed both of them now more than ever. . . .

A sudden roar shook Jacob. He looked up to see a triangular ship passing over him, its engines flaring. A second later, it disappeared over the ridge. He took a few deep breaths to try to steady his shaking body and remember where he was. Blood pounded in his ears.

To his surprise he found himself almost at the top of the hill. Over the course of his daydream he had nearly finished the ascent.

He broke into a run, hoping to catch another sight of the ship. As he rounded the ridge's summit, his eyes caught sight of the other side, its steep incline stretching below him. He froze.

At the base of the long slope the scenery shifted. Groves of dark trees—some large enough to be called forests—dotted the landscape, breaking up the uniformity of the plains. Below him lay a body of water much larger than the few tiny ponds he had encountered. The lake stretched long and thin on the floor of the depression, and he could see variations of depth in the different hues across its length. The center was dark and deep, while along its edges the shallows reflected the lighter shades of sky. From this distance he could distinguish the oval shapes of two glinting craft at the northern shore, where a grove of dark trees spread out to encircle the whole end of the lake. His breath quickened at the shapes of

26

moving figures against the sand.

The sight of people so close, however, was soon over-whelmed as his gaze continued to the horizon. There the constant edge where plain met sky was broken by another glint, this time of towers and buildings. He watched the great ship shrink as it cruised toward the city.

He had finally arrived.

CHAPTER FOUR

Creeping through the shadows, Jacob headed toward the sunlight, toward the voices just beyond the trees. Their words, while indistinct, were light and loud, punctuated with laughter. At the edge of the grove he settled behind a trunk and studied the people only a few dozen yards away. He kept his head down, remembering he was no longer invisible, the way he'd been in Harmony.

There were eight of them—four men and four women—though when he looked more closely, he noticed they appeared to be only about four or five years older than him, maybe Delaney's age. Two of the girls and a boy huddled talking on a blanket by one of the gleaming craft at the edge of the water. The other five were closer to him.

They were the opposite of the Seer he'd met yesterday, in both appearance and attitude. That man had been dark in complexion, fully dressed for the hunt. And whereas he had been somber and serious, they were anything but. They romped in the sand, laughing and shouting as they played some kind of game, batting a glowing sphere back and forth. The ball floated of its own accord; when they hit it in midair, it streaked around them, leaving a tracer of light that lasted a second before fading.

As for their appearance—Jacob blinked as he stared from one to another. They all looked the same. Both the boys and the girls had light, slicked-back hair that seemed to blend in with their tanned bodies. Their faces were round with small, symmetrical features. They wore scanty clothes, a few strips of fabric the same tone as their hair and skin, giving them the appearance of animated statues.

As he watched them play, their tall, muscular bodies kicking around the sand, Jacob suddenly felt awkward and self-conscious. *Is this what all the other Seers look like?* he wondered. He stared at his own tunic, fraying at the edges, stained by grass and sweat, and remembered his reflection in the pool, his rough features and uncombed hair. For a moment he debated whether to bypass this group and keep going, to push on to the city in the distance, but he realized that was foolish—he would have to get help from someone at some point. They seemed friendly, more so than yesterday's Seer. Besides, he could spot near the trio lying on the shore what looked like a picnic of sorts on their blanket.

He stepped from the grove, softly, quietly, and approached the group.

They failed to notice him at first. Then the players, one by one, stopped their game and turned, staring. Even the sphere, its brilliant tracer melting into air, seemed to be watching him as it hovered in place. No one said a word. The awkwardness of the moment seemed tangible, itself a sphere that hovered in the air, encompassing all of them.

"Hello," Jacob said, and tried waving like the man had done yesterday, not sure what else to do.

No one answered. He felt their eyes moving over him,

absorbing every quality. By now the group sitting off to the side had joined the others.

"Is he security?" a girl asked a boy next to her.

"Can't be. He's younger than us. And I mean—look at him," the boy responded.

"Who is he then, Garrett?" another boy asked him.

"How should I know?" Garrett retorted.

"You idiots," another girl interjected. "Why don't you ask him? Hey, you, what are you doing here?"

Jacob wasn't sure how to address the golden group. "I've been walking," he finally said, trying not to stammer. "I saw your ships." He felt foolish and awkward.

"You came all the way from Melville?" a girl asked, her voice brimming with vacuous awe. "That's a long way to come for a swim."

"Don't be silly, Raelyn," said the girl who had chastised them earlier. "He would have had to leave last night to get all the way out here, and I don't see any other skimmer around, do you? Besides, look at his clothes. Even the base workers don't dress like that."

They murmured in agreement. The girl turned her gaze to Jacob.

"So, where *are* you coming from?" she asked him, smiling.

"From Harmony," he answered. "I've been walking for a few days."

At this they began whispering to one another excitedly, glancing at him sideways, except for a boy who continued staring with a puzzled look. "Harmony? Is that a place or something?"

"Taylor," the girl informed him, "Harmony's the other

30

colony. You know—where the Blinders live?"

"Oh, yeah!" Taylor said, brightening.

"No way, Coral," Garrett said. "He can obviously see, so therefore he isn't a Blinder." He smiled at Coral, proud of his logic.

They all turned back to Jacob, silently waiting for an explanation.

"I can see," Jacob said. He didn't want to lie, but he felt hesitant, not certain how much to tell them. "Somehow I began to see. I'm not sure why. That's why I had to leave."

To his surprise, they seemed perfectly satisfied with the explanation. A few of them returned to their game, and soon they were running around in the sand once more, laughing as before, as if he hadn't appeared at all.

"Are you hungry?" Coral asked him. "Come over to the blanket and have some lunch." She motioned to Jacob to follow her to the food, and he went eagerly. Another girl tagged along. They sat together on the blanket while the others played. Jacob dove into the food, stuffing his mouth with fruit and some sort of pastry filled with cheese and a kind of spicy meat. He didn't know if it was the food's quality or the fact that he had eaten nothing the last three days except those dry bars, but it all tasted better than anything he had ever eaten before. The two girls watched in amazement as he gobbled everything down. He was so hungry he barely noticed their smiles as they struggled not to giggle. When he was finished, they asked him his name.

"Well, Jacob," Coral said, "my name's Coral and she's Raelyn. Over there are Garrett, Taylor, Marcus, Pell, Celine, and Irena." She quickly pointed at each one as she rattled off the names; Jacob had difficulty following her.

31

"So, you really were a Blinder?" Raelyn asked. "Interesting."

"I know," Coral said. "Wait till we get back to Melville and tell the others. They're going to be so jealous."

"Why?" Jacob asked. He was a little surprised. He tried to imagine how his own people would've reacted if a Seer had suddenly shown up in their midst. With a pang he realized that he had already found out.

"Because, silly," Raelyn laughed, "Blinders are so strange, and no one's allowed to go see them."

"I've asked Daddy so many times to let me go, but he says it's against the law. Some treaty or something. Anyway, meeting a Blinder is just, well, something different," Coral added.

"Yeah," Raelyn said. "If you haven't noticed, this planet's so boring."

"Oh," Jacob replied.

Soon the two girls were engaged in conversation and seemed to forget him. Between the food and the walking, he was suddenly sleepy. Letting them talk, he lay back on the warm sand. For the first time in a long time he felt his body relax. Everything was going to be okay. These strangers would help him, would take him to the city. It was a good place to start. He closed his eyes and rested, only half listening to their conversation.

Filtered through his drowsiness, the timbre of the girls' voices reminded him of Delaney. She came upon him in the darkness, a memory of her sounding in his ear. Suddenly he was back in Harmony before anything had changed, when he was still blind, and she was still happy.

They were at the piano. His mother had gone out on an errand after Delaney's lesson and the two of them had spent an hour playing guesser, taking turns molding little figures out of clay while the other deduced the shape. Jacob had been busy forming a cat, listening to Delaney tell one of her favorite stories, when she suddenly stopped and pulled him over to the piano.

"What are you doing?" he asked, the clay still in his hands.

"I almost forgot," she said. "I have something to play for you."

She began. It was a slow song, rhythmic and sweet, a waltz so pure it could have been a child's lullaby. They were both quiet for a long time after she finished.

"That was amazing," he said at last.

"You like it? I wrote it for you, Jacob."

"For me?"

"That's right. The other night I was sitting at home and I thought of you. And that's when I sat down and wrote it. It's a very special song." She put her arm around him.

"It is," he agreed.

Jacob smiled now at the memory. It wasn't long after that that Delaney's mood began to change, when she started getting sad all the time and darker in her criticisms of her father and the others. Jacob wished he had listened more.

A strange prickle suddenly burned across his forehead. His body, which just a moment ago had felt so relaxed, tensed as all the muscles in his back stiffened. For a moment he thought it was the memory of Delaney that had disturbed him, but taking a deep breath he realized it was something else, something beyond him, a darkness gnawing at the edges of the quiet.

He tuned back in to the girls' conversation and tried to

forget the sensation that had already begun to subside. For nearly half an hour they babbled nonstop. They discussed school and their parents, all of whom seemed to work together for someone or something called Mixel. They talked about parties they had recently attended, people they liked and disliked. They watched their friends, who were still running in the sun, and made funny and sarcastic observations about them. They even talked a little about him, apparently thinking he was asleep. They seemed to feel sorry for him because of his clothes and because he had been a Blinder. It felt awkward listening to their conversation. There was a strict rule against eavesdropping in Harmony. He didn't think the same rules applied here, but he couldn't shake the feeling he was doing something wrong. Maybe that was the source of the lingering uneasiness.

He was about to stir and pretend to wake when he heard Raelyn say, "I just remembered. He's like that girl. Remember, the one we heard the other night at the party?"

"That's right. I almost forgot. I wonder if he knows her?" Coral asked.

Before he could ask them what they meant, a whine sounded in the distance, and the girls stopped their conversation as the noise grew. He sat up, blinking. Shading his eyes with his hand, he looked around for the source, feeling his body stiffen once again. The prickling had returned.

"What's that sound?" Jacob asked.

"A floater, I think," Coral replied. "Someone's coming."

"Who could have followed us out here?" Raelyn asked.

The girls stood up and walked over to where the others now congregated at the water's edge. Their sudden solemnity made Jacob even more nervous. The hum intensified and a craft emerged over the far ridge from the direction of the city. It was similar in shape to the ones parked on the beach but smaller, its surface decorated with alternating stripes that angled into slim Vs along its sides. It floated over the terrain, leaving the grass swirling behind it, and skimmed over the water.

Jacob rose and joined the others, sidling up to Coral. Suddenly, he didn't want to be back there on the blanket alone.

"Oh, great," said Marcus. "Looks like Turner and those other two."

"Garrett, did you invite those creeps out here?" Celine demanded, slapping him.

"Ow!" Garrett said, rubbing his shoulder. "Of course not. You think I want those losers around?"

"Who's Turner?" Jacob asked, stepping in closer to Coral.

Coral looked down at him. "Turner's some older guy Garrett met a few months ago back when he had a taste for the black market. Works at the port. Knows all the smugglers. Now he and his friends won't leave us alone."

"They think they're tough," Pell snorted.

"They *are* tough, Pell," Irena said. "You saw what they did to that kid Zach, didn't you? I even heard they killed someone."

"That's not true," Garrett broke in, laughing. "Turner started that rumor himself. As for Zach, he had it coming, you all know that. Look, they're only a year older than us, maybe two. Forget how they seem. They're harmless. Besides, they know that if they gave any of us trouble, my father would have them all fired and deported before they could say Mixel."

The group seemed to relax at Garrett's words—everyone except Jacob.

Skirting the surface, the craft sped to the center of the lake and pulled a hard turn, circling into a tighter and tighter spin that caused a spray of water to erupt like a fountain. Coral, Garrett, and the others on the beach began cheering sarcastically and laughing, raising their hands in mock salute. The skimmer then came to a stop, turned, and moved toward them in a slow, deliberate manner.

"Garrett, I thought you told these guys to stop coming around," Taylor said.

"Well, I meant to," Garrett replied. "There was just never a good time."

The group gave a collective groan.

"Relax, people," Garrett said confidently, "I know they're trudges, but like I told you before, they're harmless. Just humor them and they'll go away."

The craft had closed most of the distance by now. From where he stood, Jacob could distinguish three young men in the floater. The driver and the kid sitting in the backseat both sported long dark hair that flapped behind them in the breeze. The one next to the driver had short, spiky hair, light in color. They looked pale in comparison to the group waiting on the beach, and all three wore dark glasses that obscured their eyes. Watching them draw near, Jacob was suddenly reminded of the skull he'd seen back on the other side of the ridge.

"Ugh," Celine groaned. "They're so creepy."

"Just smile, dammit," Garrett said, breaking into a grin himself as he waved to the approaching trio.

The craft pulled onto the sand and stopped opposite from where the group stood. The boys inside took their time getting out, laughing and talking quietly to one another as if they were having some vital conversation that had to be con-cluded.

Jacob winced, realizing he was clenching his fists so tightly that his fingernails were biting into his palms. *I should have kept going*, he thought to himself. *Being here is a mistake.* No—the others didn't seem worried. He had to trust his new friends. They wouldn't let anything happen.

Wearing jumpsuits that resembled some kind of uniform, the three climbed from the floater and jumped onto the sand, landing like cats. They sauntered over with leering grins.

"Garre. Good to see you," the man with short, spiked hair said. His voice was surprisingly gentle and smooth. His words seemed to hang in the air before melting away like smoke.

"What's up, Turner," Garrett responded with a nod.

"Nice suits, ladies," Turner said, bowing in their direction. The girls turned to each other and smirked. Coral rolled her eyes. Irena let out a snorting giggle. Turner took no notice and continued. "Nice place you picked out, kids. Peaceful. Private. Away from the city."

"We like it," Garrett said. "Just found this place a month ago."

"Who's that?" Turner suddenly demanded, pointing at Jacob. Jacob could feel himself shrinking and wished he could disappear. His pulse thudded in his ears.

"Nobody. Just some kid who showed up," Garrett said. "Hey, Turner, how'd you find us?"

"Cuts right to the chase. I like that," Turner said. He put his arm around Garrett, who seemed to shrink under its weight. "Who says we were looking for you? Got off our shift not too long ago. Decided we'd go for a nice skim out in the country. Fresh air and all that, right?"

"Right," Garrett said, sidling from under Turner's arm.

Turner laughed. "You don't mind if we join you, do you Garre? Looks like you're having fun. A real good time here."

Jacob shifted from foot to foot, listening to Turner's voice. It was so slow, laid back almost, yet with an acidic quality that dissolved whatever he said, cutting the words down to a razor tip. Jacob couldn't tell if Turner was picking up on Garrett's reticence or not. It seemed that he must. But why would he choose to ignore it? Jacob didn't understand, but it made him uneasy.

"Well, Turner," Garrett said, struggling to assume confidence, "you can do what you want, but I think we're probably leaving soon, so there's really no point in sticking around. Right, guys?" he asked, turning to the others for support.

Coral stepped forward. "I think what Garrett's trying to tell you creeps is that he wants you to leave and not bother us anymore, right *Garre*?"

"Coral!" Garrett snapped.

Jacob gasped. So did a few of the others. Turner's two friends looked over at each other, trying to decide how to react.

Turner let out a long, slow laugh and grinned, even as his face darkened to a deep shade of red.

For a moment, everyone was still, casting nervous glances all around. Coral had broken the spell and it couldn't be remade. Even Jacob felt it. Garrett appeared to be the only one who failed to understand.

"Don't listen to her, Turner. She's just running her mouth."

"Shut up," Turner snapped, his face souring. "You think I don't know? Sure, as long as I could get you the things you wanted you were happy enough to come around. Too bad you had to go slumming like that, huh?"

He advanced upon Garrett, who shrank at his approach, and pulled back his fist as if to throw a punch. Garrett winced, which drew laughter from Turner and his two friends. Jacob breathed a sigh of relief as Turner spun and walked away from Garrett. He motioned to the other two, and they headed toward their floater. But he hadn't gone far when Coral called out again.

"Next time you're lugging boxes at the port, look inside one—maybe you'll find a brain!"

Turner looked back over his shoulder as he strode away, a string of expletives spewing from his mouth, too distracted to notice the rock jutting out of the sand in front of him. His foot caught, sending him face-first into the ground. Garrett, Coral, and the others burst out laughing, not stopping even as Turner picked himself up, spitting out sand.

Stop laughing, Jacob pleaded in his mind. *Leave him alone and he'll go away.*

But it was too late. Furious, Turner whirled and once more advanced upon the group, pulling something from the pocket of his jumpsuit. The laughter died. They all stepped back with a gasp.

"He's got a gun!" Celine cried, pointing to the object in Turner's hand.

Turner menaced the pistol before them. "You like laughing? Let's hear you laugh. Come on!"

The group was silent.

"No? So what are you going to do—go crying to Mommy and Daddy? Don't even think about it. I know enough dirt to get you all in plenty of trouble, courtesy of Garrett. You think

39

you're so glamorous? You make me sick," he sneered. He surveyed the group, all of whom looked down, their faces now blank.

Jacob stood to the side, watching in shock as the spectacle unfolded. Suddenly, Turner's eyes locked with his own, narrowing to slits.

"What I don't get," Turner said, striding toward Jacob as he pocketed his pistol, "is why we're not good enough to be in your sight for two minutes, yet you let this dirty little piece of garbage hang around."

Jacob tried to back away, but Turner was too quick. His hand reached out and struck Jacob squarely on the chest, sending him sprawling backward onto the sand.

"Come on, get up," Turner snarled. When Jacob hesitated, Turner grabbed him by the front of his shirt and dragged him to his feet. Jacob looked into his eyes but couldn't tell what he saw. Was it hate? Fear? Bitterness? He wasn't sure. He wasn't even scared anymore. The whole scene was too surreal, leaving him with a strange feeling of detachment, as if none of this were really happening to him.

Turner slapped him hard across the face, knocking him to the ground once more. Pain drew Jacob back. Suddenly, the moment was all too real. Reaching up to his throbbing nose, he felt a wetness. He pulled his hand away, staring at the blood's brilliance. How did he become the target? He turned to Coral and the others for help.

They looked away in silence. A few even headed back to the blanket to begin packing up. Turner snorted.

"How do you like your new friends now?" he said, pulling Jacob back to his feet.

"Let him go," a voice called out behind Jacob. He had

heard that voice before. Turner looked up and a flicker of surprise crossed his face. Jacob peered over his shoulder and saw the man he'd met yesterday advance from the edge of the clearing.

"Who the hell are you?" Turner demanded.

"Nobody. Just like him," the man replied, pointing to Jacob as he closed in.

"He's with you?"

"That's right," the man said. He now stood before them. "So let him go."

"I don't believe this," Turner said. He shook his head and glanced around. Everyone was quiet, watching. Suddenly, he looked back, sneering. "No. I don't feel like it."

The man's arm shot out, broke Turner's grip, grabbed Jacob, and hauled him around behind him, all in one fluid motion.

Swearing, Turner yanked his pistol out and raised it. Jacob's eyes widened at the sight of it hanging, shaking, only inches from the man's face.

Jacob thought he saw a flicker of a smile, perhaps the slightest flare of the nostrils. Other than that, the man never flinched. Then there was a blur of movement. One moment Turner and the stranger stood on opposite sides of the pistol, the next Turner was writhing on the ground, unable to speak, his pistol now in the stranger's hand. As Turner twisted at his feet, the man looked down and adjusted a dial on the gun.

Turner's friends cried out and scrambled to produce their own weapons. Jacob was going to call out a warning, but before he could, the stranger pointed Turner's pistol at one and calmly pulled the trigger. A white flash erupted, striking the young man full on. Before he even hit the ground, the stranger brought the gun to bear on the other. There was another flash, and he collapsed as well. Jacob stared in horror as both of them convulsed in rhythm to the web of energy entangling them. A moment later the web faded, leaving Turner's friends still. Turner had stopped contorting and now lay facedown, groaning.

There was a humming of engines. Jacob looked over to the shore. At the first shot, the bronzed youths had scattered for their floaters with a chorus of screams. Jacob watched them finish piling in before taking off across the water. A moment later, Garrett, Coral, Taylor, Raelyn, and the rest were gone.

Looking around, the man shook his head in disgust. "Bunch of fools," he said. "All of them."

Jacob crumpled into the sand. He wanted to throw up. When he closed his eyes he could still see the two youths convulsing. The blood from his nose had seeped into his mouth. He could taste its metal saltiness on his tongue. He opened his eyes again and watched the stranger.

The man walked over to one of the motionless figures and prodded him gently with his foot. He bent down and put his fingers against the young man's throat.

"Are they dead?" Jacob managed to croak.

Rising, the man shook his head. "Though I wouldn't want to be them in a few hours," he added. He reached into the youth's pocket and pulled out the pistol, then walked over and picked up the one that had fallen at the other boy's feet. He pitched them both, along with Turner's, into the lake, where they landed one after another with a loud plunk.

"Amateurs," he muttered. He turned and marched past Jacob toward the woods.

Jacob didn't notice him as he went by. He just stared down, watching the sand absorb his drops of blood. There was a long silence.

"Hey, Blinder," the man called out.

Jacob raised his head. The stranger stood at the edge of the clearing.

"Are you coming or not?"

CHAPTER FIVE

Jacob clung to the bars surrounding him, gritting his teeth as the vibrations of the cruiser bounced him around the back-seat. The throttle roared in his ears. He looked out, watching the land slip by.

After following the stranger through the trees, weaving up the valley for nearly half a mile, they had arrived at a small clearing where the dark green craft from yesterday waited, looking beat-up in comparison with the teens' sleek floaters. Without a word, the stranger had hoisted Jacob into the seat behind the cockpit, jumped in the front, and taken off, plow-ing through the high grass, then turning onto a road of sorts where the ground had been worn flat.

At the path he veered left and accelerated. Jacob had never ridden in any kind of transport, let alone one that moved so quickly, and his stomach rose and fell with every hill. They didn't travel long, maybe ten minutes. At first, Jacob thought they were going to the city—at each rise he could see it before them. But toward the end of the trip the stranger turned off the trail and onto another that seemed equally used.

Already sick to his stomach, Jacob again began to panic. He'd had no control over anything that had happened to him today. Numb with shock by the fight at the lake, he had followed the stranger's instructions like an automaton. But now, with nothing to do except cling for dear life in the backseat, he had plenty of time to think about what was happening. He still had no idea who this man was or where he was taking him. All he knew was that the man was dangerous—more dangerous than Turner and his friends put together. Yet, he had saved him, hadn't he?

Before he had any more time to wonder, the cruiser turned between two hills. Beyond, the area opened into a meadow dotted with the same kind of trees Jacob had seen at the lake. They passed into the shade of a large copse and emerged on the other side, where a house squatted on the side of a rise. A deck encircled the front. The dwelling was different from the buildings in Harmony; the face was comprised of large panes of glass, and the structure wasn't made of metal, but a smooth material that gave the house an earthier look than the industrial buildings of Harmony. The cruiser pulled up before the house. The man exited the driver's seat and approached Jacob.

"You look a little green," the man remarked, looking him over. "I guess the ride's a bit rough when you're not used to it." As always, his face was blank, offering neither sympathy nor hostility. Jacob didn't move. The man spoke again. "Well, you can stay in there if you want, but you'd probably be more comfortable down here."

Jacob stood up, and the man helped him down onto the ground. He steadied himself against the side of the cruiser. He noticed that his hands were shaking; in fact, his whole body trembled.

"All in one piece, don't worry," the man said.

"I don't understand," Jacob said. The ground beneath him was beginning to settle, but his mind was still a whirl of confusion, anger, and fear. "Why did you save me back there?"

"You're welcome."

"Well, yesterday you didn't. You just left me to keep going."

"Guess I should have done the same today," the man snapped.

"Well, if you had picked me up yesterday, none of that would have happened. That's all I'm saying," Jacob mumbled. He figured it was foolish to challenge the stranger, but he was too tired and sore to care.

"You didn't need my help yesterday. And you wouldn't have today if that idiot Turner and his two cronies hadn't shown up. Anyway, like I told you, I had things to do." The man scowled. "Besides, why should I be responsible for every person I come across who's stupid enough to wander the plains alone?"

Jacob looked down and didn't respond. Instead, he blinked back tears, trying not to give in. The afternoon was catching up with him—the violence, the shallowness and cruelty of the teens, the indifference of this man—all of it crashing down in a wave that threatened to wash him away. *They were right*, was all he could think. *My teachers, my parents, everyone. Everything they said about the Seers was true.* He was a fool.

The man sighed and went to the back of the cruiser. He retrieved a satchel and passed Jacob, heading for the house.

"I need a drink," he called back. "And we need to take care of that nose. You look like hell."

Not knowing what else to do, Jacob followed him to the

46

house. Along the way, he reached up, felt his nose, and winced. It was swollen and tender, and his face was sticky from the dried blood.

They ascended a set of steps to the deck. Jacob paused at the top. From this height the deck looked out over the meadow, where the trees rustled in the breeze, whispering to one another. In the distance he could see the city towers.

When he glanced back over his shoulder, the man was watching him.

"Like the view?" the man asked. His voice had softened.

Jacob nodded. "I'm Jacob," he said after a minute.

"I know," the man said. "I heard you tell the girls."

"You were there the whole time?" Jacob asked.

The man shrugged. "I watch people from time to time," he said. "You probably know what that's like," he added. "Right?"

Jacob looked down. He felt himself blush but said nothing.

"I'm Xander," the man said at last. "Alexander, really. But I go by Xander." He turned and walked inside. Jacob followed.

The house was spare and neatly arranged. Most of the interior was one lofty room with a kitchen, a table with benches, and two large padded chairs facing the wall of windows. A staircase along one side ascended to a balcony where several doorways led to back rooms. The opposite wall was lined with shelves housing rows of narrow, rectangular objects. While Xander went to a cabinet in the kitchen and took out two glasses and a bottle, Jacob approached the shelves and removed one of the objects. It had a cover, which he opened. Inside was gathered a stack of thin sheets made of unfamiliar material that was flexible like the thinnest cloth

47

but much stiffer. As he flipped through them, he noticed they were filled with strangely patterned rows of markings. Xander poured a light clear liquid into each of the glasses, filling one halfway and the other less than a quarter full. He approached Jacob, carrying both glasses.

"What are these?" Jacob asked, holding up the item.

"Those are books." Xander seemed puzzled and somewhat amused by the question. "I guess Blinders wouldn't have need of them. Hell, most people probably wouldn't know what books are, anyway. They're old-fashioned. Collectibles. I've gathered most of them over the years on business. You read them—those symbols represent words."

"I've heard of reading," Jacob said. "We learned about it once in school. We don't need to read. Our recordings provide information. My teacher said it's more efficient that way."

"Right. Here, drink this," Xander said, handing Jacob the glass.

"What is it?"

"Something to help you sleep. It's medicine."

Jacob took the glass and drank it. The liquid burned in his throat and made his eyes water. "That tastes horrible," he said, choking.

"Like I said, it's medicine. Medicine always tastes bad. Now, let's get you cleaned up."

He had Jacob sit down on one of the table benches while he retrieved a small box from the bathroom just off the kitchen. Sitting down opposite from Jacob, he took a pad of soft material, soaked it in some solution from a brown bottle, and began gingerly applying it to Jacob's face. Jacob winced at the sharp pain, but soon it began to subside. He felt a mild numbness around his nose. The solution had a sharp odor that, while not unpleasant, made his nostrils prickle.

"What is that stuff?" Jacob asked.

"Cleanser," Xander said, still dabbing. Jacob could see his blood on the cloth. "It's also got a healing agent in it. The swelling should go down soon." He shook his head. "That Turner whaled you good."

"I don't understand," Jacob said. "I didn't do anything."

Xander sighed. "Doesn't matter," he said at last. "You were there. He could hit you. He couldn't hit the others."

"Why didn't they help me?"

"I don't know," Xander replied. "They're rich kids. They don't do much good or bad in the world."

He finished cleaning Jacob's face and packed everything back in the kit except for the cloth. He took it to the sink while Jacob finished what was in the glass.

"Go rest," Xander said, rinsing the cloth. "Head right up those stairs to the far room; there's a spare bed waiting for you."

"You mean I can stay?" Jacob asked.

Xander held up his hands. "Let's not get ahead of ourselves, now."

"Oh."

The man frowned. "Just go upstairs. I'll wake you for dinner."

Jacob obeyed, finding it comforting to be given orders and, most of all, to have someplace to go. By the time he reached the top of the stairs, warmth was spreading from his stomach throughout his body and lightness filled his head. He found the room and surrendered to the comfort of the bed.

• • •

A delicious aroma woke Jacob. He stretched his sore muscles before sinking back into the mattress, still drifty from sleep. Then he stiffened, seized by a moment of confusion in the darkness of the room. At last he remembered where he was, remembered everything that had happened to him since leaving Harmony—the hunger, the thirst, the fatigue, not to mention the violence and the fear—it all came rushing back. He wrapped the blanket tighter around him. It was behind him. He was safe now. He didn't really know Xander, but somehow he felt safer than he had in a long time. *Then again*, he thought, remembering the beach, *you said that before. And what happened?*

He got out of bed and went downstairs. It was dark outside; Jacob wondered how long he had slept. A few lamps cast the room in a warm glow. Going to the window, he noticed he could see his reflection in the glass. He touched his nose—it was still tender, but the swelling he'd felt earlier appeared to have gone down. When he turned around, he saw Xander watching him from the kitchen table. He seemed to have just finished eating. An empty plate lay across the table from him, with platters of food in between.

"I was about to wake you," the man said. "Food's still hot—help yourself." He rose, left the table, and stepped outside into the darkness.

Jacob sat down. He helped himself from bowls of mashed potatoes and beans and took a large piece of what tasted like beef. He wondered if it was grusker. As much as he had eaten at lunch, he felt ravenous again and stuffed himself. He couldn't remember having eaten so much food in one day. Compared with the limited portions he had been served in Harmony, this was a feast. He thought of his parents. What meager dinner were they having right now? He imagined the two of them eating silently in the total darkness of the underground house.

When he finished, he brought his plate to the sink and went out onto the deck. Where had Xander gone? With the light of the house behind him, he peered into the dark. Utter blackness lay before his eyes, pressing in on him. He had spent nearly all his life in darkness, but this momentary blindness frightened him. He could see nothing before him and felt disoriented by the vastness of the night. Slowly his eyes adjusted. In the distance he could distinguish points of light on the horizon where the city lay, casting a steady glow into the sky around it.

A breeze picked up. The smell of smoke drifted into his nostrils. His heart began to pound; growing up, he had been taught to fear fire as the ultimate danger. In school they had practiced fire drills and what to do if they detected the odor of smoke. They had learned about a devastating fire in the colony thirty years ago that had destroyed much of the eastern tier before burning itself out, and about the occasional fires that swept the prairies, consuming everything in their path. Striding to the edge of the deck, Jacob looked to the right, in the direction from which the aromatic scent wafted, and spotted a flicker of light between the trees. Taking a deep breath, he told himself that it had to be Xander's fire, that it was a controlled burn.

Should he go down there? Maybe Xander wanted to be alone, but Jacob didn't. He walked down the staircase toward the light.

He passed between the trees into a small clearing. Xander sat on the far side of a circular pit lined with stones in

51

which a fire burned. The flames illuminated the clearing from below, revealing the trunks and lower limbs of the trees around them, casting shadows that danced amid the light. In the glow, Xander's face appeared to shine. His eyes sparkled beneath the recess of his brow. He motioned Jacob to sit on a stump to the left of the pit. Jacob settled down as Xander threw a few pieces of wood on the fire, releasing a cloud of sparks.

"Not much wood on this planet, but I collect the fallen pieces," the man said.

"It smells nice," Jacob replied.

"The wood of the zephyr tree."

For a few minutes neither spoke. Jacob stared at the flames flickering about the dry limbs. They crackled as they ignited, dissolving into the white light of embers. A sense of peace seemed to radiate from the focal point of light into every part of his body. The fire, constant yet ever changing, was as beautiful as anything he had seen so far.

"Have you always lived here?" Jacob asked.

"No."

"How long?"

"A while," the man said.

"Well, where did you live before?" Jacob asked. "What did you do?" So far, the man's answers weren't very helpful. "Did you use to live in that city?" The man was quiet. "On another planet?"

The man sighed at the barrage of questions. "Five years," he said at last. "I've been here five years. I used to be a soldier, a company man. Not anymore. I fought for the Mixel Corporation—they're the jerks that basically own this planet—for twenty years all around the Rim. Can't believe I'm still alive. I shouldn't be." He shook his head.

"You fought in wars?" Jacob asked.

"I wouldn't exactly call them wars. More like two kids fighting over who gets which toy. Trade routes, resources, open planets, colonization rights, franchises—everything. Most of the battles were illegal. Some of them were secret."

"So how did you get here?"

The man paused, gazing deep into the fire before answering.

"When I retired, I put in for some land here on Nova Campi, and the bastards gave it to me along with a pension. A fair exchange for all the dirty work I did for them."

"You killed people?" Jacob whispered.

"Yeah, I killed people—people who tried to kill me," Xander snapped, glancing up. He looked back into the flames. "Can't say I enjoyed it. Can't say I hated it either."

Jacob shivered, remembering how smoothly Xander had dispatched Turner and his friends. He didn't understand everything the man was telling him, but it was enough to make him uneasy. He decided to change the subject. "You must get lonely out here by yourself."

"Never."

"What do you do?"

"Nothing. As much as possible. Other than that, I drive around, see what there is to see—which isn't much, and that's good too." He shrugged. "I read. I drive into Melville every few weeks to pick up supplies and an occasional book."

He paused, his eyes probing Jacob through the dark. "What about you? A Blinder who can see—you're a walking contradiction."

Jacob didn't know how to respond. He felt self-conscious in the firelight.

Xander sensed his discomfort. "Another time," he said. "For now, don't worry. You'll be all right."

"That's what you said yesterday."

For the first time, Xander broke a smile. "You got me."

The flames smoldered. Xander stirred the fire with a stick, collapsing the remains into dull embers. He rose and Jacob followed him through the darkness back to the house, where inside the bright light made Jacob wince. Without a word they retired to their separate rooms. Jacob undressed and crawled into bed, but try as he might, he couldn't sleep. Images of the day's events kept flashing in his mind, tiny fragments that replayed themselves over and over as he stirred within the tangle of sheets. Eventually he drifted off. As he slipped into sleep he imagined a white figure stumbling across the plains as he floated high above, helpless. Whether the figure was Delaney or himself, he wasn't sure.

CHAPTER SIX

He was in the central square. The same music still droned from the loud speakers, the same group of old men still sat hunched together on a bench along the southern wall, saying nothing, waiting for someone to come and take them home. Across the square he saw Egan wander in with several other kids. He recognized them from school, but without hearing their voices, he couldn't remember who was who. For a moment he thought about calling out to Egan, but his friend's name died in his throat. He watched as the group broke into laughter—probably at some joke of Egan's—and then separated, retiring to their respective tiers just as he and Egan had done almost every day since they'd begun school.

When they were gone he turned and headed north into his own tier, weaving around people in the street. No one paid him any mind. It was just like before. An impulse struck him, and he stopped to make faces at a group of three women walking slowly toward him, their expressions sour as they chewed over a neighborhood rumor. He struggled not to laugh as they passed by, oblivious to his teasing. Turning, he froze at the sight of two men coming in his direction, carrying another on a stretcher between them. As they passed, Jacob recognized the man being carried. It was Tobin Fletcher, the sick neighbor Jacob had witnessed stealing food a couple of weeks ago. Tobin's eyes were open as he lay on his back, his head tilted toward Jacob, unmoving. Jacob felt a chill at the unblinking eyes, and he backed up, suddenly afraid those dead orbs could see him. With a flash Tobin disappeared. In his place lay the skeleton Jacob had encountered in the basin, its tattered clothes fluttering in the breeze. Jacob blinked and Tobin was back.

He turned and ran up the street. He needed to get home. He passed the fountain and cut into his neighborhood. Soon he was on his street, and then before his door. He glanced over to the Fletchers'. Tobin's wife, Penny, was sitting in the doorway, her head buried in her hands.

He went to his door and threw it open. Light streamed in, revealing the interior of the house, and his heart raced at the sight of his mother sitting at the table. Her hair lay loose over her shoulders, not pulled back in its normal ponytail. A breeze picked up behind Jacob, sending the chimes by the door singing, lifting a tuft or two of his mother's hair. She didn't seem to notice.

He looked around as he entered. There was no sign of his father. Pulling out a chair, he sat down across from her. She was holding something in her hands. It was a small cube of metal—his music box. She wound it up, and its little song began unfurling. Jacob winced at the plinking notes. The song was in a different key than the doorway chimes, still ringing in the breeze, creating an awkward dissonance. If it grated on him this much, he could only imagine how it must sound to his mother, blessed as she was with perfect pitch. But she didn't seem to notice.

"They let you go, I guess," she said, lifting her head.

56

"They didn't keep you long. I'm glad."

"What?" Jacob said, confused. Who did she think he was? "It's me. Nobody let me go. I came back on my own. I wanted to see you."

Worry crept across her face. "I don't know who you are," she said. "But you'd better leave. My husband will be home soon."

"Ma!" he shouted, banging the table, so that she started. "It's me, Jacob. Don't you recognize my voice?" He could feel the tears gathering in his eyes.

"Jacob?" she whispered. She shook her head. "He told me you were—"

The chimes suddenly stopped. A shadow came over the room. Jacob turned toward the doorway where Delaney's father stood, one hand on the open door.

Jacob jumped up from the table and leapt for the door as it began to shut. He slammed against it just as it closed, smothering the room with darkness. He began banging on the door, crying to be let out.

Now he realized he could see his hands, ever so faintly, as the slightest glimmer from behind him grew, casting a red glow about the room, illuminating the door before him. Heat licked against the back of his neck. His nostrils flared at the scent of smoke. He whirled around—she was there.

"Delaney!" he cried out, stepping toward the figure.

Once more there was fire in her eyes, only now it began to grow, stretching out tendrils of flame that crept toward him. He withdrew, pulling away from the unbearable heat until his back was against the door, but the burning snakes whipped forward and wrapped around his wrists. They began dragging him toward her, into her outstretched arms, and he screamed for her to stop, screamed her name over and over, hoping she would hear him and have mercy, but she had none. He reached out as she drew him in, clasped his hands around her throat and squeezed, but he had no strength left in him, nothing to make the burning stop.

Jacob sat up in bed, gasping for breath. His heart was racing. He could hear it pounding in his ears, could feel the sweat along his brow. He turned to sit on the edge of the bed and looked down at the patch of sunlight shining on the floor at his feet. That dream—it just wouldn't let him go. No, it wasn't the same. It was a different dream. But the ending was nearly the same, as was the lucidity. He pushed the hair back from his eyes and sighed. He had never had dreams that felt so real before. When he closed his eyes, he could still see his mother. The memory was worth the pain.

He dressed and went downstairs. Xander wasn't there. There was fruit on the table and some rolls. *He must be outside*, Jacob thought, and sat down to eat. He finished breakfast and still the house remained silent. After putting the leftover food away in the refrigerator and clearing the table, he went out onto the deck and looked over the railing. The cruiser was gone. He hadn't heard it leave. Xander must have taken off while Jacob was dreaming.

He looked out at the view. The shadows were long—it was early. The sun was small and white behind him in the east, and the pink moon still shone on the western horizon, a fat crescent hanging above the city.

From where he was, he could see the far-off towers gleam as they caught the morning light. Hopefully Xander would be back soon. It was painful to see his goal before him in the distance, calling to him, waiting for him. He wanted to get to the city as soon as possible. He didn't even care about the Seers anymore. Who knew if he could have a life with them? After yesterday, he was starting to have his doubts. All that mattered was finding Delaney. It was the only thing left that was keeping him going.

He went back inside, settled into an armchair, and waited, watching through the windows for Xander's cruiser to come growling out of the trees and into the yard. An hour passed, then another, and Xander didn't come. Jacob rose now and then to stretch his legs. On occasion he took down a book, scanning the mysterious symbols, wondering what stories they told. He didn't dare poke around too much in case the man came home to find him snooping. Noon came. He took some leftovers from last night out of the refrigerator and ate lunch.

After he finished, he went to the window again. Still no Xander.

He fell back into the armchair and sighed. Maybe he should leave, strike out for the city now. He wouldn't reach it until at least tomorrow, but what difference did another night or two sleeping under the stars make? As for food, he figured he could take some from Xander. The man had already been generous in feeding him. Jacob couldn't imagine he'd mind him borrowing more. In fact, he still had some of those dry bars left—he could just rely on that if he had to. It seemed as if he was wasting time sitting here. Besides, how did he know Xander would even bring him to the city? In spite of yesterday, the man had been reluctant to help him before. All in all, he didn't know what to think of Xander. He couldn't even tell if the man really wanted him here or, if he did, for how long.

All he knew was that Xander lived alone in the middle of nowhere, was moody, and used to kill people. It didn't strike Jacob as a good combination.

A part of him, though, hated to go. The man *had* saved him, had shown some kindness. It was comfortable here, and it felt safe. Wouldn't it be rude to leave without at least thanking him?

Unable to make up his mind, he lingered for the remainder of the day, waiting for his host to return. Around sunset it suddenly occurred to him—he'd forgotten his morning ritual. Happy at least to have something to do, he retrieved the finder from the pack in his room and went out onto the deck. He watched the sun descend behind the city's towers. She had to be there. He knew she was—he felt it. He had followed her this far, and the finder didn't lie. On the other hand, what truth did it tell? He reached into his pocket and felt the weighty metal of the sounder he'd found yesterday clinging to the skeleton's shirt.

Pressing the button on the finder, he took a deep breath and then spoke her name. There it was, the reassuring beep. But something wasn't quite right. The tone was too low. He rotated away from the city and, to his shock, the pulse picked up. It took him all the way around in the opposite direction before it peaked. The house was before him with the hill behind it. Beyond both was where he'd come from. He must have passed her, he realized with a sinking feeling. Somewhere during the ride from the lake to this house, he went by her. He rushed off the deck and scrambled up the hillside behind the house. Reaching the crest, he took another reading.

Now he was totally confused. This time the finder pointed

west, back toward the city. So she was there after all. How could that be? *It must be broken*, he thought, heading back down the hill. The sinking feeling grew. How could he trust it from now on? Then it suddenly occurred to him—what if it had been broken to start with? What if he had been following a ghost the whole time? What if he'd left Harmony for nothing? Worst of all, what if Delaney had been dead all along?

He stumbled onto the deck. Almost completely numb now, he decided to try one last time. To his chagrin, the finder again pointed east. He closed his eyes. Then it really was broken. Unless . . . His eyes snapped open, settling on the house in front of him.

He ran inside and turned all about, his excitement growing as the finder fluctuated wildly. He raised it above him, and the pulse quickened as the finder pointed toward the upstairs. He climbed the stairs, gripping the banister tightly, listening as the tone swelled with every step. He reached the top and made his way along the balcony. The finder led him to a door. It led him to Xander's closed door.

Forgetting his earlier shyness about snooping, he opened the door and went in, his heart pounding. As he approached the bed a noise made him stop. He turned the finder off and listened. It was a note. No, it was two pitches, a chord of two sounders coming within range of each other. One pitch he hadn't heard before—it came from his pocket. He pulled the sounder he'd taken from the body out and held it in the palm of his hand. Sure enough, its tone rang strong. But that wasn't the sound that caught him, that made his hand shake as he moved closer to the nightstand. It was the other pitch, the other note—it was her sound. Tapping the sounder in his hand silent, he opened the nightstand drawer and removed the singing piece of silver. There was no mistaking the note he'd heard so many times before. It was Delaney's sounder.

He turned it off and sat down on the edge of the bed. His head was spinning. A sudden image rose within his mind's eye—the sight of Xander cutting through the tall grass, before bending down to touch the body perfect in its stillness, to tear the metal disk from its tunic, from her tattered tunic.

The image faded, replaced by another which made his heart beat harder. This time, Xander was climbing the steps to his house, escorting the figure of a girl, that same grim smile on his face that Jacob had seen yesterday at the lake, leading her into a house she would never leave.

He had to go, escape while he still could.

He jumped up and ran out into the hall, then froze at the top of the stairs. If he left now, he'd never know what happened to Delaney. Then where would he go? What purpose would he have? The man knew nothing of his discovery or of his connection with Delaney aside from their shared birthplace. He had to stay and somehow find out, play dumb and wait for the moment to strike.

The growling of an engine sounded outside. Xander had returned. Jacob dashed back into the bedroom, closed the drawer, and left, careful to shut the door behind him. He kept Delaney's sounder, though, making a vow never to lose it. He went down the hall to his own room and crawled into bed, burying himself beneath the covers.

A moment later, Jacob heard Xander come into the house. His bedroom door was closed, and for a minute, there was no sound from below. Then he heard the stairs creak, heard Xander make his way down the balcony hall to his door. He buried his face in the pillow as the door behind him creaked open, hoping the blankets were thick enough to muffle his pounding heart. To his relief the door closed again, though he didn't resume breathing until Xander had gone back down the stairs.

Jacob crept through the trees toward the light. From time to time he could catch glimpses of the flames, hear the crackle of the fire as he closed in, drawn by the smell of smoke. Gripping the long kitchen knife he'd swiped from the house, he took slow, cautious steps, careful to avoid a cracking twig or upturned root. Soon, he was close enough to see him. Xander's back was to Jacob, a dark profile silhouetted by the fire.

Jacob was at the edge of the clearing now. *Almost there*, he thought.

He had waited over an hour in bed, listening to Xander as he made supper, ate, and then cleaned up. The whole time Jacob tried to think of what to do, how to confront the man. How could a boy like him force the truth from someone like Xander? Then it was quiet below. Jacob waited a while before slinking to the door and opening it a crack. Nothing stirred. Slipping downstairs, he opened the deck door to confirm his suspicion. Sure enough, the fragrant smoke of zephyr wood lingered in the air. He grabbed the only weapon he could find from the kitchen and headed out into the dark. He didn't know if this would work, but he would do his best to make the man talk. One way or another, he would find out what had become of Delaney.

Now, as Xander pitched a small log into the fire, Jacob debated how to cross this last stretch of open terrain. Make a run for it and get the point of his knife up against the back of

Xander's neck before the man could react, or continue his silent creep? So far, Xander hadn't looked around or shown he had any idea he was being stalked. Jacob decided to opt for quiet.

Taking a deep breath, he stepped out of the shadows and started toward the figure with slow steps. The knife hovered before him, occupying the space between himself and Xander, seeming to fill it. He was close now. He reached out with the knife, readying the words of confrontation he'd been practicing over and over again for the last hour.

It was as if he were moving in slow motion, or even frozen in place, compared with the man who, without a word, turned and reached out silently with one arm, grabbing the wrist of Jacob's knife-wielding hand. He could do nothing but watch as the man pulled him in, relieved him of his knife, and flipped him over onto his back in one motion. Time resumed its normal pace as he hit the ground, grunting with impact. He was pinned, with Xander on top, looking down with what certainly wasn't surprise but perhaps the slightest bit of amusement. The flames cast shadows that danced across his face.

"Not bad, Blinder. But you're going to have to move quieter than that if you want to surprise me from behind."

Jacob cried out, struggling to free his arms, trying to get at least a kicking foot free, but Xander had him firmly restrained. *This is it*, he thought.

"I knew you weren't sleeping," the soldier said, shaking his head.

"What did you do to her?" Jacob shouted. If he was going to die, at least he'd know the truth.

"Who?" the man demanded.

"You know!"

Xander frowned. He rose, lifting Jacob with him off the ground, and placed him, panting, on his seat. He sat down across the fire on a rock.

"She's fine," he murmured. "At least she was when I left her." He looked up at Jacob. "How'd you know?" he asked. Jacob took the silver whorl from his pocket. It glinted in the firelight. Xander's eyes narrowed.

Jacob didn't feel like explaining. "Just tell me what happened to Delaney."

Xander sighed. "It was a few weeks ago. Two, three, I don't remember. I picked her up on the plains maybe ten miles east of where we met—a Blinder like you, only this girl really was blind. She was in terrible shape—dehydrated, hadn't eaten in days, cuts and bruises all over her. I noticed this flash of white clothing on top of a rise, and it turned out to be her. She didn't say much at first. She was scared of me. I figured she was lost, offered to take her back to Harmony, but she begged me not to. Kept asking that I take her to the city. Insisted on it."

"So what did you do?"

"I did what she asked," Xander said with a shrug. "I drove her to Melville. Wasn't sure what to do with her, so I brought her to Mixel. They said they'd take care of her. I haven't been back yet, so I don't know what happened."

"How'd you end up with this?" Jacob asked, holding out the sounder.

"She gave it to me as a gift when we parted. Said she wouldn't need it anymore. Said she didn't want it."

Jacob shook his head. A part of him was elated to know Delaney had survived. But the joy was tinged with dismay, even resentment, toward her rescuer. "Why didn't you tell me any of this before?"

Xander picked up a chunk of wood and flung it into the fire, sending up a shower of sparks. "Look, Jacob," he said at last, "to be honest, I didn't really want to get involved in all of this—saving her, saving you. That's not what I came out here for."

"Then why did you?" Jacob asked. Xander looked away without answering.

They were silent for a long time. The fire began to burn down.

"I heard you calling out her name last night in your sleep," Xander said, breaking the quiet.

"They told us she was dead," Jacob whispered. "But I knew it wasn't true."

"So you two were friends, huh?"

Jacob wasn't sure how to answer. All that kept flashing through his mind was the memory of the last time he had been with her, on the hill during the delivery, the sadness in her voice, the way in which she had held his hand, pleading.

"My mother's a musician and Delaney was her apprentice. She was at our house almost every day. She was practically a sister—always nice to me, but sad too, and restless. It wasn't until the end that I realized how much she was struggling, as if she was lost. I didn't know how to help her."

"Some people are just lost souls. Isn't much you can do for them—they have to figure it out for themselves. Kind of like you."

"Thanks," Jacob said.

"Well, that's how it seems. I mean, why did you leave, anyway?" Xander asked, placing another log on the fire.

66

"I told you who I am—or who I was—now it's your turn."

As the fire burned and sparks drifted up into the night, Jacob recounted the story. He told Xander about the movement into sight, about everything he had seen, and about being led to the ghostbox for correction. The man listened quietly the entire time, watching in the glow of firelight. When Jacob finished, Xander remained silent for several minutes before speaking.

"That's quite a story. I thought the army was strict, but your people have us beat by a mile, at least when it comes to discipline and loyalty."

"What do you know about Harmony?" Jacob snapped. The defensiveness in his voice surprised him. Xander nodded.

"See what I mean? After everything that happened, you're still sticking up for them. That's loyalty," he replied. He poked at the glowing embers with a stick, then continued. "Oh, I know about your home. Every once in a while I end up there while I'm driving around. I don't get too close, but I watch through the scopes from my perch on the western ridge, watch the people working in the fields and walking along the streets. Never stay long. Gets old pretty fast—like watching a colony of ants, everyone going through the motions. Place is kind of dreary, if you ask me. 'Course, I guess that doesn't matter if you're blind."

"It's not that bad, you know. I was pretty happy until . . ." He knew the words but didn't want to say them.

"Until you began to see? Until you began to see for yourself the kind of place you were living in?"

"I guess." Jacob paused. "You don't seem to like my people very much," he said in a strained voice.

"*Your* people, huh?" he snorted. "I don't dislike them, Jacob. I don't even really know them. I suppose I know you, and you're not so bad. Actually, in a way, they interest me—they're dedicated, you have to give them that. And maybe they're not even that different from everyone else. People are always searching for the perfect place away from all the garbage out there in the universe. Sometimes they'll go pretty far and do extreme things to get there." He paused, taking time to select his words before continuing. "But I don't respect the Blinders, Jacob. They're about rejection, about running away from the truth. You can't cut yourself off from the pain of the world." He paused. "It doesn't work," he finally said.

They both stared into the fire in silence for a few moments. Then Jacob said, "Those last few days were horrible, and every time I remember them, all I can picture are those strange faces in the crowd at the last Gathering. Their eyes are open, but they don't see me. I don't like the feeling that leaves me with. It's not right."

"Tell me something—is there *anything* you really miss about Harmony?" Xander asked.

"I miss knowing my place in the world, the feeling that I belonged to something, though I guess I lost that even before I left Harmony," he said, then paused. "My family—I miss my mom and dad. I never got to say good-bye. I used to think they were perfect, just like Harmony; my mother was talented, my father was strong. Near the end I got to see that they weren't so perfect, that maybe they weren't even happy. What's funny is that it makes me miss them even more."

"Family is like that," Xander said.

"What about you? Do you have a family?"

Xander stirred the fire with the blackened end of his stick, collapsing the glowing chunks of logs into embers. "It's getting late—I've got a lot to do tomorrow. I'm going to bed," he said, rising. He broke the stick across his knee and threw both pieces into the pit before disappearing into the darkness.

Jacob didn't follow him. For another hour he fed the fire twigs, watching each one ignite quickly, flare into brief and sudden light, then disappear into the bed of coals that brought the next to flames.

CHAPTER SEVEN

That night, Jacob could hardly sleep. All he could do was lie in bed and think about Delaney. The next morning, he asked Xander if they could make the journey to Melville to find her.

"Not unless you want to walk," Xander replied.

"Please, Xander," he begged. "I have to see her."

It was true. The thought of finding Delaney, of being able to actually see her face and hear her voice, was what had kept him going in his march across the plains, was what had given him the strength to leave Harmony in the first place. The idea that a person he loved, a person he had once thought dead, was out there right now, alive and waiting, was too much to bear. But there was something else that made him so eager to find her.

Lying in bed last night, in this strange house, he began to think more about his own future. Xander had said he could stay here, but the invitation wasn't open-ended. After this, where would he go? Back in Harmony, Jacob had been nervously awaiting the day when the council would assign him his role in the community. He'd been so anxious about what his place would be. Then along came his sight, driving out all thoughts of the future. Now his anxiety had returned, but with it came a hope. If he could be reunited with Delaney, he wouldn't be alone, he would have a place in the world. He could face the future with someone who shared his past.

Not only that, there was the matter of the dreams. He'd returned to the same dream last night—chasing the same fluttering white figure through the streets of Harmony, freezing in the face of her flaming eyes, screaming as the burning tendrils of fire entwined him. Somehow he felt that if he could only see the real Delaney, then maybe he could put an end to the nightly torment.

Now, seeing the hesitation on Xander's face, an idea came to mind.

"Just think," he offered, "if you bring me to Melville, then you can get rid of me. I can stay with Delaney."

Xander snorted at the proposal, but nodded at last. "I have to go to Melville next week," he murmured. "We'll be right near Mixel headquarters anyway."

"Thank you, Xander!"

"Don't get too excited, Blinder," the man hastened to add. "Who knows if she's still even there. Like I said last night—I just dropped her off. I don't know what they decided to do with her. For all we know, she might be back in Harmony."

"She isn't," Jacob said, shaking his head. "She wanted to leave so badly. She would never go back, I'm sure of it. You don't know how Delaney is when she gets something in her mind."

Xander grunted. "I'm starting to get an idea," he said.

The rest of Jacob's week was a slow torture of waiting. For the most part Xander kept to himself. He asked Jacob no more questions about his past. Some days he didn't say much at all. Jacob struggled at first to read his mood. At times the man

71

seemed friendly, easygoing. Other times he was taciturn, consumed with bitterness, then he'd climb into his cruiser and take off, only to return hours later in better spirits, sometimes with a load of wood he'd gathered. Often he'd sit in his chair and gaze out the window or read a book, and sometimes Jacob would sit beside him in the other chair and neither of them would speak. Xander seemed to appreciate Jacob's respect for silence, and in turn, Jacob enjoyed the temporary serenity that had been missing from his recent life.

Though Xander had his moments, as the week went on Jacob could feel him change. While he still remained closed about his past, he became chattier, seemed more relaxed with the idea of having Jacob around. He began taking Jacob for rides in the cruiser, showing him the countryside. They even went back to the lake where Jacob had met the other Seers. Jacob felt nervous walking onto the beach, but Xander assured him that Turner and company were long gone. So were the teens—the beach looked like no one had been back since that afternoon. While Xander waded in, Jacob sat on the sand, refusing the man's offer to teach him how to swim.

Jacob did convince Xander, though, to teach him how to identify the letters in Xander's books. He was fascinated with the concept of reading, with the ability to communicate in silence. The idea that a certain sequence of images could trigger a world of thoughts in one's head with no other voice to color the words appealed to him. Xander was reluctant at first. "It takes a while to learn to read," he said, as if unsure Jacob would be around long enough to be taught, but he agreed to at least show Jacob the sounds of letters.

He also taught Jacob the names of colors, giving him the means to understand the myriad hues that made up the world. Jacob loved learning colors even more than reading, as if being taught their names made each one more brilliant, the world somehow more vivid.

Each night as they meditated before the fire, Jacob resisted asking Xander if tomorrow was the day they would travel to Melville. But as each day came and went it got harder, so that by the night of Jacob's eighth day with Xander, it took every ounce of willpower not to put forth the question. That night, though, as Xander knocked the embers down into their glowing bed, Jacob finally heard the words he'd been waiting for.

"I've got to head into town tomorrow," Xander said. "Still want to go?"

Jacob snapped his eyes up from where they'd been watching the coals. Before he could even answer, the man began laughing. Jacob laughed too, then, riding on the wave of excitement, closed his eyes and tried imagining the moment of his reunion with Delaney. All he could see was the flow of black hair from the girl in his dream.

"What does she look like?" Jacob asked, opening his eyes.

The laughter stopped. Xander's face, red in the embers' light, grew intent.

"She's beautiful," he said.

They started out in the white light of morning. Jacob shielded his ears against the roar of the cruiser as it flew across the plains toward the city. As they traveled the worn path, taking the hills with such speed that the truck seemed to float momentarily at each rise, Xander looked back from time to time at the boy strapped into the backseat and grinned, his teeth flashing between lips curled back in amusement at his passenger's blanched complexion. Even though Jacob had ridden in the cruiser several times, he still wasn't completely used to the sensation. He tried to smile back, to show him that he wasn't afraid, and after a while he wasn't anymore, as his body relaxed to the vibrating rhythms of the machine.

The drive took longer than Jacob expected; it was nearly two hours before they reached Melville. As they crested each ridge Jacob could see the city rise, but for a long while it didn't seem to be growing any larger. Near the end, however, it began to loom before them, and he marveled at the towers rising into the sky, with one near the center of the city standing tall above the others, its black surface gleaming in the sun, bright in spite of its ebony shell. As they approached, the plains began to flatten, and near the city they passed several small neighborhoods that appeared to be mostly comprised of warehouses and repair shops. Seeing the low, square structures reminded Jacob of the storage houses in Harmony, and he wondered if the same people had built them.

Aside from these clusters Melville was remarkably contained. It seemed as if one moment they were whipping through the grass, and the next they were cruising down smooth streets, surrounded by glass buildings of countless shapes and sizes. Small craft like the ones Jacob had seen at the lake skittered above them at different heights among the towers, while at street level other vehicles meandered along the avenues between crowds of people on the sidewalks. Some of the groundcraft sported wheels, like Xander's— though none looked as battered—while others floated on an invisible cushion.

Jacob couldn't stop staring left and right as they moved deeper into the city. The buildings dazzled him. Light was everywhere. Many of the buildings' walls were moving displays of color, a multitude of people, animals, and strange landscapes mixed with writing that he could not yet read. Other glass towers reflected the light of the sky or the images displayed on the buildings across the street, creating a strange symmetry of light, a kaleidoscope of blurring shapes and tinctures. Xander had the cruiser's windows open, allowing the sounds and smells around them to drift in. Combined with colors and movement, the panorama overwhelmed Jacob, flooding his senses, leaving him dizzy from the stimulation. He asked Xander to stop for a moment, and the soldier pulled over near the sidewalk.

"You all right?" Xander asked, turning around.

"So many people. And the sounds," Jacob said. The air resonated with the buzzing of the craft above them, and loud music poured from a shopping center next to them, the thumping of its heavy bass clutching at Jacob's chest as he watched customers streaming in and out of the building's open doors. The crowd revealed a variety of different-colored clothes and complexions, from the dark tones of Xander to the paleness of his mother.

"It's beautiful," Jacob said. "So bright."

"Don't let it fool you," Xander said. "Melville looks shiny on the surface, but it's got a dirty underside like every other city. The corporation just does a better job at keeping it hidden."

Jacob barely heard him. "Why don't you live here?" he asked.

Xander shrugged his shoulders. "Doesn't do much for me," Xander said, "but I grew up in it. Not on this planet, but one city's the same as the next. Same stores, same companies, same people, just different names, that's all, and sometimes even the names are the same."

Looking around, he shook his head.

"Believe me, you'd soon get used to it until you'd almost forgotten what quiet was like. Anyway, we have business to take care of. I've got to pick up some supplies, and you've got to find your friend."

"Where do we go to do that?" Jacob asked.

"You saw that big black tower on the way in? That's Mixel's headquarters. That's where we're headed. I brought Delaney there too. But before we do any of that, we'll grab lunch. And you need new clothes."

Glancing at his frayed tunic and grass-stained trousers, Jacob's face reddened. He'd been wearing these same clothes almost every day for the last six months and was so accustomed to the coarse garments that he hadn't noticed until reaching the Seers just how ragged he was.

"We can go in there." Xander pointed, exiting the cruiser and helping Jacob onto the sidewalk.

They passed through an entrance rimmed with flashing lights into a mall. Before long, they'd entered a store that Jacob could have sworn was as big as Harmony itself and made their way to the clothing section. Xander stood by with an amused look as two young women assisted Jacob, twittering to each other when they saw him. They had him remove his old clothes, which they discarded—handling them with obvious distaste—and soon had him dressed in lightweight pants accompanied by a shirt made of a fabric that alternated between shades of blue as he moved under the bright lights in the ceiling. The close-fitting garments felt odd against his skin, but he enjoyed the freedom of movement they provided compared to his old, baggy smock. They gave him a new jacket and a pair of light boots that Xander selected for him.

"You need these where we live," he said. Jacob found it both strange and somehow comforting that Xander had used the word "we."

The girls whisked him to another section of the store, where several men and women were cutting and styling customers' hair. They had him recline in a chair so that his hair could be washed and then an older woman gave him a trim. As she snipped away, twittering to another hairdresser nearby, Jacob closed his eyes and imagined his mother's face, imagined that the stranger's fingers gently parting the strands of his hair were hers. He had always taken comfort in the closeness, the quiet, of the ritual. He could almost hear her voice, humming to the rhythm of the shears.

"Almost finished," the woman said, rousing him from memory.

When everything was completed, they hurried him back to the clothing section and stood him before a full-length mirror. He gazed at his reflection in amazement. The mirror revealed a different person from the one he had seen in the pool at the grove on the plains, though the eyes remained the same. Wide-eyed, he turned to Xander, who merely nodded.

"You clean up pretty good, Blinder."

A short while later, they were heading toward Mixel Tower. Xander drove his cruiser right up front, gunning the throttle before cutting the ignition. Its loud engine drew stares from the people passing in and out of the revolving doors at the base of the giant high-rise.

"Don't mind the suits," Xander said as they passed through the spinning glass portal. "Let 'em stare. I like to remind them that it's people like me who helped secure their brilliant futures."

Jacob followed him into the vast lobby of the tower. As they cut through the crowd toward the elevator shafts, Jacob looked around in awe. An enormous video screen, at least twenty feet wide, sat like a noble perched on a throne above them, silent, displaying a steady stream of stock prices superimposed on fragments of news stories broadcast from across space. The glowing screen cast dull and hazy beams of color that danced in the dark hall, while the footfalls and murmurs of the crowd echoed in the high, vaulted ceiling. Jacob breathed a sigh of relief when they entered the bright enclosure of the lift and the doors closed with a hiss.

They rode the elevator only a few seconds before it came to a sudden stop. The doors opened and Xander exited with his usual rapid stride, straight and determined, so that Jacob had to trot to keep up. They walked down a hallway before turning into an office that contained a waiting area with chairs and a counter up front. Behind it sat a young man with short black hair. He gazed unblinking as Xander approached. For a moment the two stared at each other.

"Hello?" Xander said, waving a hand in front of the man's face. The man started slightly, but his facial expression remained unchanged.

"Yes?" the man replied.

"I was here a few weeks ago . . . ?"

"I'm sorry, I don't remember."

Xander sighed. "Merc 32476."

Jacob watched the man punch the numbers into a machine before him.

"Yes, Mr. Payne," the man said. "What can I do for you?"

"I brought a girl in last time I was here. Remember now?"

The man's eyebrows rose, and he nodded in recognition. "That's right. Of course. The beautiful, mysterious Delaney. She's become quite popular with the board lately. A real find."

"Then she's still around? The kid here is a friend of hers and he'd like to visit her. Where is she staying?"

"Well, right upstairs, Suite 767, but I don't think—"

Xander turned and headed toward the door with Jacob trailing behind him.

"Mr. Payne, wait!" the young man cried.

"Thanks for the help!" Xander shouted as he left the office and headed to the elevator.

The elevator zipped them to the seventy-sixth floor. A few moments later they stood in the silent hallway before the door of her suite. Jacob looked nervously at Xander, who motioned toward the door with an upturned hand. Jacob knocked quietly at first, and then louder. The door opened but no one appeared. When Jacob hesitated, Xander prodded him and they entered the small hallway, the door whispering shut behind them.

They turned into a room illuminated by an enormous pane of glass along the far wall. A grand piano occupied the center of the apartment. In a chair near the window sat a young woman, her back to them. Her raven hair—the same color and sheen as the piano—cascaded down over her shoulders and over her white gown.

A prickling sensation rose along the back of Jacob's neck and his heart began to pound. For a moment, he thought he was stuck back in the nightly world of his dream. There was something eerily familiar about seeing the figure from

79

behind. The sound of her voice snapped him back.

"It's not time yet. Go away," she said. Jacob trembled at the unmistakable timbre of Delaney's voice.

The girl rose and faced them. Jacob stared in amazement at her shimmering robes and at the delicate beauty of her face. But what froze him in place, what both captivated and terrified him, were her eyes.

Her human eyes were gone. In their place sparkled almond-shaped crystal orbs. Rimmed by a thin line of gold that stretched from the corners, along the temples, and into the hairline, the unblinking eyes seemed to glow with a fire of their own.

CHAPTER EIGHT

For what seemed like a long time Jacob could only stare at those eyes, too shocked to speak. Aside from the strangeness of seeing Delaney for the first time, he was bombarded with the sensation of being back in his dream. The room was bright, but he half expected it to go black, to have the world reduced to that now familiar tunnel with just himself and Delaney, to see the fire erupt from her eyes. He had thought their reuniting would be a moment of happiness, but instead he was confused, distracted.

"Who are you?" Delaney at last demanded, brusquely trying to mask her fear.

"It's me, Jacob," he said. His voice sounded small in his ears, far away.

"Jacob?" she whispered. "Is it really you?"

She rushed over and threw her arms around him. Trembling, she sat on a couch and pulled him down next to her.

"Jacob, you have no idea how wonderful it is to hear a familiar voice. What are you doing here, anyway? And your eyes—they're following me. Can you see?"

"Yes," Jacob said. "I don't know why, but I began to see—right after you left. That's why I had to leave Harmony." He shook his head. "It's a long story."

"I'm just glad you're here," she said. Once again, she pulled him close and held him, as if she would never let him go. Jacob remembered the morning of his last birthday just weeks ago, how his mother had held him the same way before he left her to play in the sun.

She looked over at Xander. "Who's this with you? Did he bring you here?" she asked.

"This is Xander," Jacob said as the man came forward from where he lingered at the edge of the room.

"That's right," Xander said. "I brought him here, just like I brought you."

She started. "I know you. You wanted to take me back to Harmony, but I made you bring me here . . ." Her voice trailed off.

"What happened to your eyes, Delaney?" Jacob asked.

"Do you like them?" she said with a quick, high laugh. "They're beautiful, aren't they? Very expensive. You could probably buy our entire colony with them. That's what they told me anyway," she said.

"They just gave them to you?" Xander asked.

"Yes," she said. She sat back and crossed her legs. Her clasped hands balanced on top of her knees. "They've given me everything. New eyes, a new life. Anything I ask for, they'll get it. Do you like this place, Jacob? Come look out the window."

She took his hand and drew him to the expanse of glass. From the seventy-sixth floor of Mixel Tower the city of Melville appeared small and defined, stretching below like a disc with sharp edges marking where the city ended and the plains began. A few structures rose from the symmetrical grid work, but even the tallest of them was only half the height of the tower that was the hub of this colonial city.

"I could stare out this window for hours," she said. "Seeing is so incredible. Better than I ever imagined. It's like . . . well, you know what's it like, don't you, Jacob."

"Yes," he said.

It was early afternoon. Even beneath the sun, the city seemed to burn with a light of its own. From here the people in the street were specks. Even the ground cars and low-flying floaters were meager dots. From time to time a floater would buzz by, climbing to Mixel Tower's roof or dropping back into the grid below. The only nearby object of any size was a rising ship, its engine burners flaring as it drifted from the spaceport on its way to orbit or beyond.

"The world looks small from up here, doesn't it?" she said.

"It depends on where you're looking," Jacob replied.

Moving his eyes upward, he gazed at the eastern horizon. After the city dropped off, all that remained were hills of grass, low and indistinct. Row after row stretched out, punctuated here and there with the small, irregular shapes of lakes and ponds glittering in the afternoon sun. From here it seemed hard to believe he'd walked all that distance over the land. How far was it anyway? Somewhere buried in the plains beyond the horizon was Harmony, alone, cut off and oblivious to this humming island of light.

"Harmony's over there," he said, pointing.

"You can't see it," she said. "It's too far away." She turned and left the window. "That's the only thing about this suite—I wish it faced west instead of east. I'm not interested in looking east. The sea is on the western side, just beyond the city. Have you seen the ocean yet, Jacob?"

"No."

"It glimmers. It's dazzling. And there are islands. Hundreds of them. I'm going to get a west-facing room. Jack said he'd move me."

"Who's Jack?" Jacob asked.

"Jack LaPerle. He took me in and gave me my eyes. And more."

"What do you mean?"

She smiled and took his hands, glancing around as if she were about to tell him a precious secret. "I'm a star, Jacob. A celebrity."

"What does *that* mean?"

"I'm famous. Or at least I'm starting to be. Jack says soon everyone will know me. Not just here. People everywhere. People out there," she said, pointing out the window toward the sky.

Jacob tried to smile back. He was having a hard time understanding everything she was saying. He didn't know why, but the whole conversation was going just the opposite of what he'd expected. "What are you famous for?" he asked.

"Music, Jacob. That's what I do now—like in Harmony, only a hundred times as many people hear me, thousands even. Jack says I've got flair. I've got an image that people will go for."

"So what do you do all day?" Jacob asked.

"Well," she said, looking around, "I'm here a lot of the time. I practice a lot. You see the piano I've got—there's nothing like it in Harmony. The sound is amazing. Other than that, I'm pretty busy. A lot of nights, I perform. At first it was for small groups—men who work here, important men, and friends of theirs. And then they had me record. You know,

Jacob, like the recordings we listened to back in Harmony. I have my own. You can hear me singing and playing. And now they're selling them everywhere!"

"Who's selling them?" Xander asked.

"I don't know," she said. "Mixel, I guess."

"Hmph," Xander snorted.

Jacob didn't know what Xander was responding to. He only cared about one thing.

"Just tell me, Delaney—are you happy here?" he asked. "Is this what you want?"

She paused. "Of course it is," she said with a smile. "I am happy, Jacob. Very happy. I have everything I want. I have more than I could've imagined."

She moved to the piano and sat down. The opal keys spread before her, waiting. Her fingers traced along their surface, gently fell to play a single chord, her foot on the damper pedal muting the chord as it hovered before dying.

"Why shouldn't I be?" she said.

As if in answer to the chord, a light tone sounded, followed by the swish of the opening door. Delaney rose from the bench. Jacob and Xander turned as two men entered the room. The one in front was not much taller than Jacob. His slicked-back blond hair and bronzed skin reminded Jacob of the older kids at the lake. The rich fabric of his suit glistened under the light, the metallic sheen fragmenting into the suggestion of a rainbow. The man behind was huge in comparison. His suit, multihued like the other's, barely contained his thick arms and chest.

"I'm sorry," the smaller man in front cooed, his face breaking into a wide grin, "but fans are not allowed into Miss Corrow's quarters. Delaney, I'm sorry for the disturbance.

85

I simply don't know how they got in here."

"This is Jack LaPerle," Delaney said to Jacob and Xander. "It's okay, Jack. They're friends of mine."

"Friends? I didn't realize you'd made any friends, Delaney. How delightful," he said. Jacob hadn't thought it was possible, but LaPerle's grin seemed to stretch even wider.

"Well, Jacob and I go back," she said.

"That's delightful," he said again. He turned to Jacob and Xander. "We're so lucky that Delaney has decided to join us here at Mixel. I'm sure she's told you all about her success."

"It's just nice to see her," Jacob replied. "I was worried about you, Delaney."

"That's so sweet," LaPerle said before Delaney could answer. "Anyway, Delaney, I feel absolutely terrible about doing this, but, friends or fans, I'm afraid they'll both have to go for now."

"Can't Jacob stay with me?" Delaney asked, coming over behind Jacob and placing her arms around him.

"That's not for the best right now," he replied. "You've got a busy schedule and we need you to be focused."

"Come on, Jack," Delaney said. "I'm tired of spending all my time here alone. It would be good to have some company."

Jacob could hear the edge creeping into her voice. For a moment, it reminded him of how she'd spoken to her father back in Harmony.

"Listen, Jack," Xander interrupted, "this young man's a friend of Delaney's. She isn't a prisoner, is she?"

LaPerle's smile vanished. "No, Mr. Payne, she isn't," he said, seeming to enjoy the look of surprise that flashed over Xander's face at the mention of his name. "But I'm afraid that Miss Corrow is expected at an engagement shortly and must get ready. Perhaps you can visit another time. Mr. Smith will show you out. Karl?" LaPerle turned to the giant behind him. The man gestured to the door.

"Don't worry, we're leaving," Xander snapped. "Come on, Jacob." He turned back to Delaney. "Delaney, it was a pleasure seeing you again."

She managed a smile. "Bye, Jacob. Promise you'll come back soon."

"I promise," Jacob said.

He followed Xander and Karl to the door. Passing LaPerle, he glanced over. The man stared back, a thin smile on his face.

The last thing Jacob saw before leaving was Delaney. Looking behind him, he saw her standing behind LaPerle, one arm raised in farewell, her eyes gleaming points of light. For the briefest moment, Jacob could have sworn he saw those eyes flicker, flare a moment before dulling. Then he was out into the hall, halfway to the elevator before the door had even whispered shut behind them.

CHAPTER NINE

The three of them made their way to the elevator in silence. Jacob walked between the two men, trying to steal glances at both. Xander's momentary anger back in the suite had been replaced with his customary dispassionate look. The giant's face was blank, as well. They reached the elevator and still no one spoke. Jacob felt tense and oddly guilty. He'd done nothing wrong, but the huge man's presence made him feel like a criminal. An image of the two listeners escorting him from school to the council house flashed through his mind. He moved a little closer to Xander.

The door of the elevator opened and the three entered. Again, Jacob was between them, but now the two men faced each other. Jacob shrank against the wall as the pair's faces hardened into a mutual glare. *Hurry up*, Jacob thought, wishing he could boost the speed of the falling elevator. He didn't want to be in this tiny room another second with these two men.

Jacob took a sharp breath as the pair stepped toward each other, their faces now only an inch apart. Before Jacob could say anything, both men broke into a laugh and joined in a rugged, brief embrace.

"Damn, Xander, it's good to see you," Karl said, still gripping Xander's shoulder. Xander lightly slapped the giant's cheek in return.

"Good to see you too," he said.

"You two know each other?" Jacob cried.

"Karl and I," Xander said, pausing, "we worked together."

"Worked together, huh? That's a pretty way of putting it," Karl snorted. "So how are you doing anyway? Haven't seen you in ages. Since you got done, I guess."

"I'm fine, Karl. I'm here on Nova Campi now. Got a little place on the plains."

"No kidding. Doesn't surprise me."

"Yeah, question is—what're you doing here? Don't tell me you like working for that girl's handler."

Karl shrugged. "I work for Mixel, he works for Mixel— that's how that is. It pays well, and it beats risking your neck for God-knows-what."

"I suppose. But that suit. He's the kind we used to hate."

"Come on, Xander, give me a break," Karl said. "Besides, we all have our different ways of dealing, right? Look at you, after all, living in the bush."

Xander's grin faded just as the elevator door opened. Karl gestured toward the lobby. Xander took Jacob by the shoulder and the two of them walked out.

"Xander!" Karl shouted as they started walking away. They turned back to where he stood, holding open the door. "I *am* sorry," he said. "I never got a chance to tell you. I just wanted you to know."

Xander nodded and started to walk away when Karl called out a second time.

"What is it?" Xander asked.

"Better not come back here again. Okay?"

"We'll see," Xander replied.

• • •

Jacob looked back to find Melville's skyscrapers shrunken by distance. Even Mixel Tower had diminished somewhat, though the black monolith still dominated the city's skyline. Plugging his ears to block out the roar of the cruiser, he turned back around. To the left and right the grass was a blur of bluish green, consolidated into a single wave flowing away from him as they ripped across the land. Though the sun still shone behind him in the west, ahead, over Xander's shoulder, he could see the purple moon breaking the surface of the horizon. Its great rings rose at an angle, giving the swollen orb a tilted look, as if some great hand were lifting it by one end. Xander looked back as he had from time to time on the journey in, but now he wasn't smiling. Jacob was glad. He didn't feel like smiling either.

After leaving Mixel, Xander still had to pick up some supplies and Jacob tagged along, trying not to get in his way. The man had fallen into a foul mood, and by now Jacob knew not to say anything that might draw his anger to the surface. Still, he wanted to know what Karl had been talking about. What was he sorry for? And he was troubled by his warning not to come back.

But Karl's comments—and Xander's reaction to them—weren't what really ate at Jacob. He had forgotten them almost entirely by the time they started out from the city as a larger anxiety rose within, like the purple moon before him.

It was Delaney.

Ever since leaving Mixel Tower, a knot in Jacob's stomach had been growing. Nothing had turned out the way he'd hoped. First, to see Delaney so . . . different. And it wasn't just the eyes. Something about her wasn't right. It didn't feel like he was talking to the same person. But what had changed? Maybe it was just because she was happy. He'd been so used to her misery

90

back in Harmony, especially at the very end, that he must have forgotten what it was like to see her happy. Or to see her at all. Maybe that was it. Maybe the shock of seeing this person he'd known for so long in his blindness made it impossible for him not to feel strange at their meeting. He tried to think back to the first moments he saw his mother, his father, his best friend, Egan. Then it was strange too, but that wasn't quite it—there was something else. He closed his eyes, leaned his head back against the vibrating seat, and sighed. Maybe it was *him*—maybe he had changed so much that nothing would ever be the same.

All he knew was that something wasn't right. Delaney claimed she was happy, but he couldn't help wondering if she was faking it. In fact, none of it seemed real—from her eyes, to the suite, to the man she claimed had given her so much.

"I don't like that man," Jacob said later that night. He was leaning against the railing of the deck, having come out after dinner for some air. Xander had joined him and the two now looked out toward Melville. From here it was nothing more than a few meager lights, and even they were nearly drowned by the brightness of the purple moon falling fast before them, dropping toward the city.

"Karl's a good guy," Xander said. "Tough. I can't remember how many times we saved each other's skin."

"Not Karl," Jacob said. "The other one."

"LaPerle? You probably shouldn't like him. Handlers are slick. They're supposed to be."

Jacob thought back to his first encounter with the Seers at the lake. "He looked like Garrett and his friends, but somehow he reminded me of Turner."

Xander snorted. "That's not far off. But I wouldn't worry too much about Delaney. She may be miserable, but I don't think she's in any real danger."

"You don't think she's happy?"

The man shrugged. "You know her. Couldn't you tell?"

"Not really," Jacob said, then hesitated. "Maybe. All I know is that today wasn't good. I wanted it to be good, and it wasn't." He sighed. "I guess I had this idea that she needed me."

"She probably does," Xander offered.

"It didn't seem like it," Jacob murmured. *If she doesn't,* he thought, *then where does that leave me?* "Maybe I just needed her instead," he said.

"Don't worry about it."

"I can't help it. Back in Harmony, all I knew was a sad girl. She didn't fit in. She talked about leaving. I even heard her say she wanted to see. And now she's got that, just like me. Everything that's happened to me has happened to her, just in a different way."

"Do you think she's better off than you?"

"I don't know. I guess. She wanted to leave Harmony. She chose to. I didn't. And now she's a part of something. She has a new family, people who adore her."

Xander sighed. "First of all, Blinder, she may be a part of Mixel, but it isn't as cozy as you might think. They may be taking care of her, but they really only care about one thing—what they can get from her. That's how they are with everyone. I'm not saying it's bad. After all, it goes both ways. But in the end, it's just business to them. Trust me, I've been there. They're getting something from her, and I don't think she even knows it."

"Delaney's pretty smart," Jacob replied.

"Then she may have already figured it out. Or soon will.

The point is, just because she's a part of something, doesn't make her better off. Both of you were part of something back in Harmony and look how that turned out."

"But at least she has a future. I don't even know where I belong, or what's going to happen to me."

"Don't need to, Jacob. Not right now. And who knows what Delaney's future will be. She might need you someday. No one can see what lies ahead."

Jacob closed his eyes and shuddered as he recalled the sensation of déjà vu he'd felt seeing Delaney this afternoon. At least maybe now, having seen her at last and knowing she was all right, the recurring nightmare would stop.

Opening his eyes again, he looked up to see the moon now slipping into the black land, dragged down by its tilted rings. It was night, but the moonset cast a faint glow over everything, aided by the dimmer light of the cratered pink moon now at its zenith above them.

"It's bright out tonight," Jacob said.

"Once your eyes adjust, there's nothing nicer."

Jacob pointed to the horizon. "Why is that moon so much bigger than the one above us?" he asked. "And so fast—it only rose a few hours ago and it's already sinking down."

"You mean Duna?"

"That's what it's called?"

"Yeah. The other's Drake. Well," Xander said. "Duna's not a moon. It's a planet. We're the moon. Nova Campi orbits Duna, just like Drake does. People still call it a moon, though. We like to think of ourselves as the center of things, I guess."

"I didn't know," Jacob said. "They never taught us that. They said there were two moons, but they never told us their names. Maybe *they* didn't know."

"It doesn't really matter. Whatever you call them—whether you even know they're there—they still do what they do. Knowing changes nothing."

Jacob realized on one level Xander was right. But his own ignorance about this basic truth, about this fundamental part of the world in which he lived, bothered him. Still, why should he be surprised? Everything about the world was different from what he'd thought it was.

"Don't worry about Delaney," Xander said. "We'll see her again soon, and things will be better. It was your first trip into the city. You were just overwhelmed by everything today."

"But what if we don't? What if we can't? You heard what Karl said as we were leaving. He may be a friend of yours, but he sounded serious. I might never see her again."

"Don't be foolish, Blinder. Of course you will."

"How?"

"Let me take care of that," Xander replied. He turned to go inside, stopping at the door. "I spent my whole life taking orders," he called back to Jacob. "When I left the army, I promised myself I'd never let anybody tell me what I can or can't do again. Even Mixel. Especially Mixel."

"When do we go?"

"We'll wait awhile. We'll let them forget about us. It won't take long."

It took about a week. Jacob emerged from his familiar nightmare one dawn to find Xander standing over him, a dark shadow in the thin early light.

"You keep calling out her name," the man said.

"I know," Jacob said. "It always wakes me up."

"It wakes me up too. In fact, it creeps me out, the way

your voice sounds. What's wrong?"

"Nothing," Jacob murmured. His brain was a murky mix of sleep and fear, and he didn't want to talk. Seeing Delaney had not put an end to the dreams. If anything, they had grown more intense. More real. There were other changes too. Each night new details, a slight shift of when things happened, of what was said. One development in particular disturbed him. The dream had always ended with his hands around her throat, with the two of them face-to-face, though he could never see her visage through the blaze. But the last few nights the finale had altered. It still ended with him choking her, but he now found himself outside himself, standing to the side watching the struggle unfold, zooming in on the hands tightening around the white neck. And then, in this last dream just moments ago, the latest twist—feeling himself shrink the tighter he squeezed, seeing her grow larger and larger until her head loomed over him, her features cold, indifferent, in spite of the blazing from her eyes.

"Nothing's wrong, huh?" Xander said. "All right. But nothing or not, we're doing something about it."

"What do you mean?" Jacob asked.

"Time we paid Delaney another visit," he said.

"But Karl's warning—" Jacob began.

"Like I said before, no one tells me what to do," Xander snapped. He paused. When he spoke again, his voice was softer. "Besides, it seems clear enough. Until you figure this out, you'll have no peace. And neither will I," he added, looking away.

CHAPTER TEN

The city looked the same from a week ago. The same buildings, the same floaters humming between them, the same glowing pictures playing along the surface of the glass. It all became a blur. Looking out the window of the cruiser as they meandered down the avenue with the afternoon flow of traffic, Jacob thought that even the people passing on the sidewalks looked the same—a teeming mass of different colors and styles blending and flowing into a single stream. In some respects, the scene didn't seem much different from the monotony of Harmony. More people, of course, more colorful, even more dynamic, but still imbued with a sense of sameness, a feeling that life had always been this way and always would remain so, a world oblivious to its own history.

But there was one difference from Harmony that caught Jacob right away: the feel of other eyes upon him, strangers' eyes. Xander's beat-up cruiser stood out against the other groundcars around them and drew frequent stares from passersby. Every now and then one of them would look further, beyond the shell of the craft to Jacob inside. Their eyes would find his and the link would pluck them for a moment from the stream. In that brief glimpse he found a host of looks—distaste from time to time, humor, benevolence, mostly curiosity. Then their eyes would turn away and they would fall back into the flow, whisked back into their own lives.

Xander didn't pull up roaring this time before Mixel Tower. He parked a couple streets away, down a side alley.

"Best keep a low profile today," he explained, helping Jacob to the ground.

"You think they know we're coming?"

"I don't think they've thought about us at all. As far as they're concerned, they don't need to. We're nobody. But who knows."

They merged with the entering crowd, let it usher them through the revolving doors and into the lobby. Fingering the metal weight in his pocket, Jacob clung close to Xander as they made their way across the marble floor toward the elevators. He knew Delaney had given her sounder away, had said she didn't want it anymore, but he'd brought it anyway. Maybe she had changed her mind.

In the elevator, Xander leaned down and put his hand on Jacob's shoulder. His grip was tight but didn't hurt.

"You need to breathe, Blinder," he said.

Jacob managed a meager smile. "Somehow I feel more nervous than before."

"You haven't done anything wrong."

"He told us not to come back. I'm just not used to breaking the rules," Jacob replied. "Not on purpose, anyway."

Xander shrugged. "That wasn't a rule. It was a suggestion. Just think about Delaney. What would she do? If things were reversed."

"She'd be here," Jacob said, nodding.

"That's what I thought."

The door whisked open. They turned into the hallway. LaPerle was waiting, wearing the same wide grin from a week ago. Karl stood behind him, his face blank.

"Delaney's friends!" LaPerle crooned, stepping forward to block them. "Hello again."

"Jack," Xander said. He took a few steps forward toward LaPerle, prompting Karl to follow suit.

"It's so nice you came by for a visit," LaPerle said. He raised a hand and Karl froze. "But I'm afraid Delaney isn't here at the moment."

"That's all right," Xander said. "We don't mind waiting."

LaPerle shrugged his shoulders. "She'll be out for the rest of the day. Her schedule is quite packed."

"That's funny," Xander snapped. "I have a hard time imagining you'd be far away from her. After all, she seems to rely on you so much."

"I do what I can," LaPerle said. "You should call ahead next time. Let us know you're coming. I'm sure we could arrange something."

"Right," Xander snorted. He leaned in toward LaPerle and lowered his voice. "Just tell me one thing. How much have you made?"

LaPerle nodded. "Quite a bit," he said. "And it's only just the beginning. Of course, we've invested a great deal in Delaney. Her eyes are state-of-the-art. Shipped in from Earth, a pretty penny. But quite worth it, I'm sure she'd agree. And this life we've given her—it's only fair we ask a little in return, don't you think? She's a part of us, just like you are."

Xander's eyes narrowed. "Nobody owns me. I fulfilled the terms of my contract."

"You did. And quite well, at that. Numerous commendations, a distinguished record, even a tragic past—I read the file. But you're not clear of us yet. There's the matter of your pension, after all. Mixel still pays the bills, right?"

"Are you threatening me?" Xander said. He took another step forward. Jacob reached up and grabbed his arm. LaPerle waved Karl back once more.

"Of course not, Mr. Payne. I'm just trying to point out all the facts. Keep a sense of perspective. Point of view is everything, is it not?"

"Xander, maybe we should go now," Jacob pleaded. He tugged on the soldier's sleeve.

LaPerle looked down at Jacob and the grin returned. "I know you're disappointed, young man. Maybe next time you can see your friend. And then we can all sit down and have a delightful chat. I'd love to hear about how you two know each other."

Jacob took a step closer to Xander, resisting the urge to back away.

"The boy and I found her," Xander broke in. "She spent a couple days with us. Ever since I brought her here he's been bugging me to see her."

"Well, she certainly is worth seeing. Everyone wants to see her. Speaking of which," he said, reaching into his suit jacket. He pulled out a pair of thin cards and held them out. Jacob reached out, took them tentatively, and studied them. They were light and stiff, iridescent under the glow of the recessed lights.

"What are these?" Jacob asked.

LaPerle's eyes narrowed. "Why they're tickets, of course."

He took one of them from Jacob and held it out flat on his palm. A light flashed and there was Delaney, a shining figure hovering above his hand, no more than six inches tall. Jacob's eyes widened at the sight of her rotating form, her hands held forth, a smile on her face, beckoning. LaPerle flipped the card over and the image disappeared. He handed the ticket back to Jacob.

"Tonight. Eight o'clock at the Marlboro."

"Thanks," Jacob murmured.

"It's the least I can do. And like I said, we'll all get together. Soon, of course. After all, who knows how long she'll be around?"

"What do you mean?" Jacob asked, startled.

"Delaney's on the verge of a breakout. She's already doing well on the Rim. And when the Core worlds pick her up, she's going straight to Earth. Mixel's putting some serious money out there to promote her. It's only a matter of time." He chuckled and shook his head. "It's the eyes," he said. "Everyone loves them. She looks like an Egyptian princess, a goddess."

"Oh," Jacob replied. He didn't know what else to say. He looked down at the floor and tried focusing on the swirled pattern of the carpet.

"Come on, Jacob," Xander said. He turned Jacob around and led him to the elevator. "Thanks for the tickets," he called back. LaPerle and Karl remained watching in the hall, waiting until the elevator came. Jacob hardly noticed when the door opened and Xander ushered him inside.

"That was strange," Jacob said once they were out on the street. "LaPerle and Karl, it's like they were waiting for us."

"They were," Xander replied. "Building's sensors must be keyed into us. LaPerle knew we were coming the moment we walked through the front door."

"I'm just mad we missed her."

"She was there. That bastard was lying," Xander said. "But don't worry. You'll get to see Delaney again."

"So what," Jacob cried. "You heard what that man said. They're going to take her away for good. Even if I see her tomorrow, what does it matter?"

"Don't look at it that way," Xander warned. "If she leaves, she leaves. You can't control what happens to her. Just think— if you'd never gotten your sight, if you'd never left Harmony, you'd still think she was dead right now. This way, at least you know she's alive and that she's going to be fine. Hell, she'll be better off than ninety-five percent of the people out there, including us. That's got to be enough."

It wasn't. Jacob knew that Xander was right on one level, but he couldn't accept it any more than he had been able to accept her death back in Harmony.

They crossed the street and headed down the wide boulevard toward the center of Melville, leaving the cruiser parked in the alley. The Marlboro—a large concert hall—wasn't far away, and they could easily walk back after the show.

"I'm not even sure I feel like going," Jacob mumbled, giving the tickets to Xander.

"I'm not much for concerts myself," he replied, putting the tickets in his shirt pocket. "But we should go. Who knows, maybe you'll be able to see her there. In the meantime, we've got a few hours to kill. Let's walk."

They wandered into a section of the city they'd passed earlier. Jacob recognized the shopping center where last week he'd received his new clothes and haircut. He remembered the anticipation he'd felt that morning as they prepared to find Delaney. All that was gone, replaced by a fear that, once again, he'd have to resign himself to losing her.

They passed the entrance to the plaza, passed the flashing neon colors and ratcheting drumbeats raining down from the speakers above the doors, and continued on past a range of other stores. It was late in the afternoon and the earlier crowds had dwindled. Jacob was glad—even from the removed comfort of the cruiser he'd felt claustrophobic watching the mass of people flow along the street.

Gazing at all the signs, Jacob wished he could read. Though he still wasn't used to this loud alien world of people, color, and glass, he felt even more a stranger, more cut off because of his inability to understand the glowing letters above the stores and in the projected murals along the buildings. He looked across the street at one tower where the glass windows shimmered for a moment, only to be replaced by a black, star-filled sky. Through the ether came a starship, a knobby oval whose burning wake carried a line of words. Jacob was about to ask Xander what they said, when the man took his arm and turned abruptly off the boulevard into a narrow side street.

"Where are we going?" Jacob asked.

"A little place I know. You'll see."

There were no flashing displays in this alley, and the tall building rising over them on both sides cast a shadow over everything. The sky was a narrow line of light. The only other illumination came from the main street's brilliance behind them and a small lamp above the door of a shop about twenty yards away on the right. The rest of the building's face was featureless, making the storefront seem out of place, as if put there by mistake.

Jacob trailed Xander to the entrance, starting at the tinkle of bells when Xander opened the door. Xander went in and Jacob followed, closing the door behind him.

The first thing Jacob noticed was the smell. It was the tiniest bit musty, just mild enough to be pleasant, a dry smell, like withered herbs that still held the memory of sunlight. The odor was followed by the sight of books, row upon row of them stacked against walls and along the shelves that formed aisles within the confines of the tiny shop amid the dimmed lamps. It was cool inside and quiet, and Jacob took a deep breath and touched his ears for a moment in wonder at the silence.

"Xander!" a voice called out. Jacob turned to see a woman appear around an aisle. His eyes widened as she came toward them. He guessed her to be about as old as his mother but her opposite, a negative image. Instead of his mother's pale skin and hair, this woman had short jet-black hair and tight-fitting clothes covering skin that, as she strode beneath a hovering lamp, Jacob realized was a deep shade of purple. Most startling of all were her eyes. Her irises were gold, sparkling against the darkness of her face. Looking at them, Jacob couldn't help but think of Delaney. She came up to them and smiled, her teeth a flash of white.

"Hey, Kala," Xander said.

"It's been a while," Kala replied. "I was afraid I'd lost one of my best customers."

"Course not. Just didn't make it by last time I was in town."

"Who's the boy?" she asked, looking down at Jacob.

"His name's Jacob," he replied. "It's a long story."

"My favorite kind," she said. "Hello, Jacob."

"Are those real?" Jacob asked.

"He means your eyes," Xander added.

Kala laughed. "Yeah, they're real." She reached up with one hand and popped a gold concave disc from one eye revealing a hazel iris. "Fake lenses, that's all. Don't tell me you've never seen these before?"

"He doesn't get out much," Xander broke in. "So what do you got, Kala? Anything new?"

"A shipment came in last week," she said. She turned and headed for the back of the shop. Xander followed. "The usual stuff. I've got a few you might like."

"I'll be a few minutes," Xander called back. "Feel free to look around."

While Xander and the woman lingered over a crate in the back corner of the store, Jacob wandered the silent aisles. From time to time, he pulled a book off its shelf and paged through it. Like the books at Xander's house, some had hard covers, others had covers not much thicker than the pages themselves. Some looked brand-new, while others looked ancient. He especially liked the ones with pictures on the cover, each revealing strange new worlds, suggesting what wonders might be within. Despite his earlier wish to read the street signs, it suddenly didn't matter that he couldn't read these books. Just the thought that each one contained new ideas, people, and places was enough to provide him a sense of peace. It reminded him how isolated he'd been in Harmony, a place where new ideas—or any ideas at all besides those of Truesight—weren't allowed or even acknowledged.

The strange thing was, he didn't completely disagree with his people's perception of the Seers. He'd seen enough of Melville to realize it was a world in which appearances dominated, and he'd certainly seen enough shallowness these last few weeks—from the teenagers at the lake to the abrasive veneer of LaPerle's grin—to more than justify the Blinders' scorn. But that was why he loved the quiet of this store, of being here right now. These books showed him that there was more to the Seers than what he'd encountered so far. There were elements of a full life ready for the taking if one wanted to find them. At least the Seers had a chance to do whatever they wanted with their lives.

"Ready?" Xander asked.

Jacob turned to see Xander and Kala watching him.

"Sorry. I was thinking about something," Jacob said.

"That tends to happen when people come in here," Kala said. "Here," she said, handing him a book.

Jacob took it. "For me? I don't have any money."

"It's a gift," she said.

"I don't know how to read," Jacob admitted.

She nodded. "That's okay—you can use it to learn. Besides, it's got pictures, as well."

He opened the cover and flipped through the pages. Each one contained a single image that was a blend of color, words, and pictures. The letters were thin and arched, scrawling across the page in a single stream. The pictures themselves were haunting. Like the words, they too flowed, tinged with colors of the moons and grass, the brilliant hues of flowers. In some ways, the busy pages reminded him of Melville, but at the same time they lacked the polish and angular edges of the city. They had an organic feel that went against the urban grain.

105

"What is this book?" he asked.

"It's by William Blake," Kala said. "He's a writer from Earth. From a long time ago. The book is called *Songs of Innocence and Experience*. Each page is a poem. You know, like a song made up of words? He wrote the poems and drew all those pictures."

Coming across one page, he was met by a familiar scene.

"Sheep," he said. "We have those where I come from."

"That one's called 'The Lamb,'" she said, glancing down at the page. "I'm sure Xander can read it to you later."

Xander frowned. "I'm not a big one for nursery rhymes," he said. "But thanks for the book, Kala. And these too." He held up the package in his hands.

"Any time," Kala replied.

Xander nodded to Jacob and headed for the door. Jacob waved good-bye to Kala and followed.

"See you in a few weeks," Kala called after them.

"Right," said Xander.

"I liked her," Jacob said as they left the store and headed down the alley back to the main avenue.

Xander nodded. "I've bought most of my books from her," he said. "Decent woman."

"Why was her skin that color? That strange purple?"

"Some people have different skin color. Just like they do hair. Though in Kala's case, it's intentional. There's a dye you can take—changes your skin to whatever color you want. For a while, anyway."

"What for?" Jacob asked.

"Something different, I guess," Xander said, shrugging. "Because she can. I don't know, I never asked. People do all kinds of things to make themselves look different."

They reached the avenue and continued on their way. Jacob was still thinking about the bookstore when the sight of Delaney froze him in his tracks.

She rose above him, above all of them on the street, appearing from nowhere against the side of a nearby tower. She had gone from the six-inch figurine in the palm of LaPerle's hand to a sixty-foot tall giant looking down with her gold-rimmed eyes. Letters flashed around her, words scrolling by as she smiled and an invisible wind lifted her hair. There was blue sky behind her with clouds racing by as if time had speeded up. But Delaney wasn't speeding—she moved slowly, her body swaying to a nonexistent song as time took her in the opposite direction. Jacob blinked at the image. He had seen Delaney once, enough to recognize her along the building's surface, but the weaving figure seemed like a stranger.

"You see her?" he asked, wondering if she was just a dream.

"Yeah, I see her," Xander replied.

"What do those words say?" Jacob asked.

"They're selling her," Xander said. "Or a version of her, anyway. Come on, let's get out of here."

He pulled Jacob over to a kiosk on the corner and pressed a circle displayed on its blue screen. A moment later, a floater pulled over to the curb beside them. They climbed into the backseat and the craft began rising.

"Where to?" asked the driver over his shoulder.

"Anywhere," Xander replied. "We just want out of Melville for a while."

"How about the sea?" Jacob asked, remembering what Delaney had told him.

"Sure," the driver said. They were now a couple hundred feet off the ground. All the way up, Jacob's stomach fluttered as the craft buoyed lightly up and down on its gravity pad. Now he had the sensation that he'd left his stomach behind as the floater leapt forward, zipping toward a tower face before cutting sharply between another set of buildings.

Jacob closed his eyes and leaned into Xander. The cruiser, speeding and bouncing along the plains, had been bad enough, but at least it was connected to the earth. This was far worse. He was sure that any minute the slim floater would overturn or tip too far on a corner and send them hurling toward the surface.

"Don't like flying?" Xander shouted in his ear above the wind roaring through the open cockpit.

"No!" Jacob screamed back. In fact, he hated everything about the sensation, especially the howling in his ears that made thinking impossible. Xander shouted something to the driver that he couldn't make out. A moment later, the roaring stopped as the compartment went silent.

"Go ahead, open your eyes," Xander told him.

Jacob opened his eyes and looked around. The city was gone. He glanced over his shoulder and saw the towers shrinking behind him. He looked up. The sky was still there, the sun still sinking toward afternoon. Where had the wind gone? He reached up and his hand met a solid but invisible plane.

"Force field," Xander explained. "There's your ocean."

He pointed over the side and Jacob gazed down and drew a sharp breath. Delaney had been right. The waters reaching toward the western horizon were beautiful, an azure tone that made the green of the land more brilliant, particularly the archipelagoes of shining emeralds spreading out from the coast as if they'd been tossed or spilled across the surface of the sea by some giant hand.

"Do people live there?" Jacob asked, pointing to the islands.

"Some do, I suppose. Not many people live outside Melville."

"I'd like to live on an island someday," Jacob said.

"Suppose that makes sense. After all, you grew up on one."

Jacob blushed. It was true. Harmony was an island, cut off from the world in so many ways. But that wasn't the kind of island where he wanted to live. He wanted a place that was away from the world but not disconnected from it, where people could leave if they pleased, but chose to stay, a place where he belonged.

The driver reached up and touched part of the dash panel. Music filled the cabin. His fear subsiding, Jacob relaxed back into his seat and watched the sea. The song ended and another began. The sound of the piano now playing soothed him. For a moment, he felt like he was back in Harmony. Between his mother's, Delaney's, and his own playing he had listened to music every day; it had simply been a part of life's background. Hearing it now made him miss that. Maybe tonight's concert wouldn't be so bad after all.

A girl's voice came in over the piano, accompanied by drums and a host of other instruments. He sat up and leaned forward. It was Delaney. He recognized her voice immediately, in spite of the synthesized filter that altered it, giving it an otherworldly edge. His initial excitement faded as the song progressed. Musicians in Harmony as a whole frowned on synthesized music. When it was used, it was used sparingly and never on voices. Listening to the song, Jacob couldn't help but feel that the effects and accompanying drumbeats cheapened the purity of her voice. It was just like the image he'd seen displayed on the side of the building—a stranger packaged for public amusement, as artificial as her eyes.

"Can you turn it off?" Jacob asked the driver.

"Don't like this song?" the man asked, killing the sound. "My daughter loves it. Won't stop listening to the damn thing. Keeps going on about this new girl. I'm no expert, but far as I can tell, she's not much different from the rest of them. Another six months, nobody'll even remember her. Pretty girl, though. They say she used to be a Blinder. Hard to believe, isn't it?"

Jacob sank back into the seat and closed his eyes.

"I suppose it is," he whispered.

CHAPTER ELEVEN

•

By the time they reached the Marlboro later that evening, a crowd had already gathered, spilling out the doors and into the street. Jacob and Xander got in line and waited. Around them, people laughed and joked, made small talk, and even gossiped about Delaney.

"They say her eyes were designed by Charles Kivan himself," one woman said.

"I heard that they can see through walls," her friend replied.

"I had dinner with her last week," a man in front of Jacob boasted to his party.

"You did not!" someone challenged.

"I did. My brother-in-law's the assistant to the VP for marketing. He invited me."

"What was she like?" several asked.

"Boring, I thought," the man sniffed. "Didn't say much."

"She probably doesn't have a lot to say," a woman said. "You know what these starlets are like—they're all bubbleheads anyway."

"Give her a break," another woman countered. "She used to be a Blinder. You can't expect her to fit in."

Listening to them carry on about someone he'd spent a

part of almost every day with for the last three years, Jacob didn't know whether to be amused or aghast. Mostly, he felt sad. The things they were saying didn't describe the girl he knew, but he couldn't be sure he knew who she was now any more than they did.

The sound of a man sneezing broke Jacob from his thought. He glanced over his shoulder to see the man standing directly behind him cover his mouth and begin coughing. The woman with him patted him on the back.

"I told you to see the doctor this afternoon," she scolded.

"Just a touch of the flu," he replied, sneezing. "I'll be fine."

The man coughed again. The sound reminded Jacob of his former neighbor Tobin Fletcher. Shuddering, he remembered the dream he'd had soon after joining Xander, remembered the sight of Tobin being carried by on the stretcher, his eyes open in death, and later, his wife crying on the doorstep. In real life, back in Harmony, both Tobin and his wife had been sick. He wondered how they were doing now. The sense of déjà vu came upon him again and he thought of Delaney, how she had looked just like the person in his dreams. He had always thought dreams were just an echo of what a person loved or feared, an improvisation on the present or past. Now he couldn't help but wonder if they had any bearing on the future.

The line moved at a steady pace and before long they were at the doors. Xander handed a ticket to Jacob, who watched as each person stepped up to the scanner and placed their card into the slot. Each time, the tiny image of Delaney popped up, greeted the ticket holder, and thanked them. Soon it was Jacob's turn.

"Thank you," Delaney chirped. "Enjoy the show!"

I'll try, he thought, retrieving his ticket. Xander followed and the two went inside, with Delaney's voice repeating into the distance. *Thank you. Thank you. Thank you. Thank you . . .*

They entered a vast lobby and let the flow of people carry them up the curved staircase toward the hall. For a moment, the parade of concertgoers reminded him of the Gatherings back in Harmony, when everyone in the community filtered into the square for their regular sermon.

The comfort he had once felt in blindness, of being part of the group, of feeling the bodies around him, had since been replaced with unease. Now, amid the chattering, plodding crowd, he fought with the rousing urge to flee. He stared down at the patterned floor tiles and tried to push away the cacophony of voices. He tried to relax, to remember he was safe. *This gathering isn't for you,* he told himself. Reaching into his pocket and feeling the cool metal of the sounder, he remembered who the gathering was for. It didn't make him feel any better.

LaPerle had given them excellent seats. They sat down and waited. Neither spoke in the semidarkness of the vast hall. Every few moments a cool breeze washed over the crowd. It felt good to be out of the crush of people. Even the voices were subdued to a murmur now as people roamed in search of their seats. The only light in the chamber came from four spotlights shining out of each corner, converging on the center of the stage where a black grand piano rested on a glass platform.

They waited. Five minutes, ten. The lights faded and the hall went silent.

A gasp broke out from the audience as the hall filled with

113

light as beam after beam of color flashed through the air, intersecting, cutting, and twirling as the dome of the ceiling seemed to open to a blaze of infinite stars and swirling nebula. The beams widened, spread out into rainbow sheets that washed over the hall in waves, now punctured by a series of virtual fireworks that crashed and thundered over everyone.

As the fireworks subsided, a voice called out, "Ladies and gentlemen! A warm welcome for the Rim's hottest new star—the beautiful, the mysterious . . . Delaney!"

The crowd erupted in a wild cheer as a single beam flashed onto a spot on the floor below them. Jacob leaned sideways to see around the person in front of him. His eyes widened.

Delaney stood, her head down, arms at her side. Her black hair, gathered up in a series of braids, shone in the brilliant white light, matching the shimmer of her loose, almost transparent gown. She began rising through the air, raised from the floor to the stage on a nearly invisible platform of glass that made her seem to hover with a will of her own.

Reaching the level of the stage, she strode to the piano, the crowd still clapping. Jacob glanced up at Xander. He was applauding too, his eyes fixed on the glowing figure before them. Looking back to Delaney, Jacob found himself clapping as hard as any of them—it was impossible not to. She was so beautiful, so serene. And she hadn't even started to play.

She took her seat at the piano and the crowd quieted. Softly, she began. The notes rippled over the audience. There was the slightest noise in response, as if the entire crowd joined in a collective sigh. Even Jacob was taken aback by the richness of the instrument. It made the piano he'd grown up with sound like a plinky child's toy, like the music box he'd listened to growing up.

Jacob suddenly realized she was playing the song he'd heard on the radio back in the floater. Sure enough, a moment later the piano was joined by the full blast of invisible synthesizers and drum machines as she began singing. *At least they left her voice alone*, he thought as he listened to it, amplified but unprocessed.

For the second time that evening, the crowd broke into a sudden, single gasp. The lights faded to a rosy hue. But the audience wasn't responding to the change of lighting, it was reacting to the vast image of Delaney hovering over the hall, occupying the darkness above the stage.

Jacob sank back and gripped the arms of his seat at the sight of the three-dimensional image above him. Glancing down at the stage, he realized the projection was in sync with the real girl below, but the floating form was just a disembodied head. The angle of the projection was head-on, slightly elevated, as if it was the audience who was in fact hovering before her. Every part of her face was magnified—every hair along her eyebrows, every freckle across her nose and cheeks, the sheen on her lips that glistened while she sang. But it was the eyes that dominated her face, that occupied the center of the angled view, those jeweled eyes that didn't move, that showed no emotion but simply glowed. Jacob grit his teeth and looked away.

"It's okay, Jacob," Xander said in his ear. "It's just a hologram. It isn't real."

Jacob didn't respond. Yes, he knew the head was a projection. But it was real, as real as it had been in the early hours of this morning as he lay in bed dreaming. Once again, an image of his nightmare was playing itself out before his eyes.

The song ended and the crowd exploded in applause. Delaney thanked them, but Jacob barely heard. He just kept his eyes closed and hoped the show would be over soon. She started a new song. Listening in spite of himself, he wondered who wrote the songs. Clearly they weren't hers. This one was a love song of some kind, something about a girl who misses her boy. He's been out to space and won't be coming home for a long time, and she doesn't know what she's going to do, do, do . . .

Jacob opened his eyes. She was still there above him, but he found that if he kept his focus on the stage, he could pretend the head wasn't there. As the song continued, he started looking around at the crowd. They all stared with rapture on their faces, but their eyes weren't trained on Delaney. They were fixed upon the projection hanging in space, inflated and insubstantial.

The song ended. She began another, and then another. But as she continued, Jacob noticed something. At first he wasn't sure. It started with a single sour note. He cocked his head and focused. Soon came another. She had misplayed. Now her timing started to slip. She came in late on a chorus, missed the pickup after the bridge. A flash caught his eye, and he looked up at the hologram. Sure enough, her eyes had begun to sparkle. They were few and far between, but now and then he caught a flicker that flared across the surface of her eyes.

Not many seemed to notice her mistakes, though there were whispers in the hall as the last song ended. There was a long pause. The crowd silenced again.

"Is she all right?" Xander whispered.

"Something's wrong," Jacob said. He wanted to call out to her, let her know he was there. He wanted to rush up on stage and take her away, do something to help her.

She began playing again. This time there was no accompaniment, not even her voice. This time Jacob knew the song. It was his song, the one she'd written for him alone, a waltz, lulling and pure.

The crowd grew still. The piece was simple and unadorned, so different from anything she'd played so far. Listening to the song unfold, Jacob wondered if she'd planned ahead of time to play it. Did she know he was in the crowd? Was she playing this for him or for herself? He supposed it didn't matter.

His eyelids had begun to lower when once again, her fingers slipped. His eyes snapped back open. A moment later, another misplayed chord made him wince. She slowed down, then stopped altogether. An exchange of whispers, loud and hissing, ran around the hall. She started back in, picking up where she left off.

She only got a few measures. Another slip, then another, and once again she halted. The noise of the crowd now grew from a whisper to a murmur, and though the words were indistinguishable, the tone was not. A blend of curiosity and dismay with the slightest hint of amusement, it was derisive and cold. The hologram hanging above them faded quickly and the lights rose back to white. Suddenly, Delaney seemed more isolated than before. Before she'd been the hub, holding all of them in. Now she was the center of a crater from which they'd drawn back in confusion.

Delaney looked from the keyboard, first out at the crowd

and then up, tilting her head as if she were watching a butterfly flit above her or a high-soaring bird. The crowd grew quiet once again, waiting for her to make the next move. It didn't take long. Looking down, she stretched out her hands, spreading her fingers over the keys as if she was ready to resume the performance so they could all pretend the interruption had never taken place. Jacob could sense it in the crowd. She had only to start a new song and all would be forgotten.

Blam!

Her hands smashed down on the keyboard, creating a single dissonance that shattered the silence and jolted the crowd, pushing the audience back against their seats in stunned unison.

Delaney stood, shoved back the piano bench, and made a beeline for the edge of the elevated stage. The crowd gasped as she approached, striding across the glass platform with determined steps, seeming to walk on air. Jacob leaned forward, fighting the urge to leap up and make for the pit below. Stopping short at the edge, she stamped once against the glass and the section underfoot descended, carrying her to the floor.

The audience was on its feet now and the silence was shattered by a collective buzz of confusion. By the time Jacob managed to catch a glimpse down below, Delaney had disappeared. The house lights came on.

"Let's go," Xander shouted to him.

He brushed by Jacob and—to Jacob's confusion—headed down toward the stage. Though the crowd had begun to mill about, the two of them had aisle seats and it didn't take long to push through to the railing that circled the edge.

"What are you doing?" Jacob said as Xander climbed over the railing and dropped into the pit below.

"Come on. Hurry up!" Xander shouted, lifting his arms and beckoning with his hands.

A few people had come to the edge and were looking down at him, pointing. Jacob glanced around, expecting to see a group of men coming to grab him up, but all he saw was a few curious spectators and a sea of oblivious concertgoers jabbering about what had just transpired. He looked back down to where Xander waited. From here, it looked like a long drop.

"It's too high!" Jacob shouted.

"I'll catch you," Xander called back. "Trust me. Now let's go!"

Shaking his head, Jacob clambered over the railing and lowered himself until he was sitting on the edge about four feet above Xander. Closing his eyes, he pushed off. There was a second of falling before Xander caught him and lowered him to the ground.

"This way," Xander said and headed for the door from which Delaney had first appeared. Jacob followed.

The door led to a dark corridor that ran about a hundred feet before joining another. This second hallway was wider, with a series of doors along both sides. Xander immediately began making his way down the hall, opening one door after another, each revealing an empty dressing room. On the fifth try, they found her.

Like the first time they'd visited her, her back was to them. She sat before a mirror at a dressing table. Her head was down, buried in her arms, but she was quiet, not crying as Jacob first thought. They came in and closed the door.

"Don't say anything," she snapped. "I don't want you to say anything. I don't care about the stupid show."

"Are you all right, Delaney?" Jacob said.

Her head shot up. Jacob could see her face reflected in the mirror. She broke into a smile and turned.

"Jacob!" she cried. She rose and came over, embracing him. "I'm so glad you're here. I've been waiting for you to come back. I told Jack to expect you."

"Jack hasn't exactly been accommodating," Xander said.

Delaney frowned. "What do you mean?"

Jacob broke in. "Delaney, what happened out there on stage?"

She sighed and turned away. Returning to her seat, she leaned in toward the mirror and traced the gold along the edges of her eyes with her fingers before burying her face in her hands again.

"It's these eyes," she said at last. "They've ruined my music. I can't concentrate—I start watching my fingers as I'm playing and it gets me confused and then . . ." She drifted into silence.

Jacob came over and put his hands on her shoulders. She picked up her head again. He gazed down at her reflection in the mirror, uncertain if she was looking at him or at herself.

"I hate them," she blurted out. "I never thought I'd say it, but it's true. They're too much, Jacob. It's all too much." She shook her head.

"You said you liked seeing," he said.

"I did at first," she replied, "but it's exhausting. They're always on! I can't turn them off. I try to cover them up, but the light never goes away. You don't know what it's like. Nights are the worst. I haven't had a real night's sleep since the surgery."

She turned and pulled him down to her.

"Not only that, I think I'm losing them." She was whispering now, looking around as if someone else were present in the room. "They're not working right. These last few days, I have moments of static. Everything goes white, like I'm blind all over again. And after it fades, nothing looks the same. The colors are duller, the lights are dimmer. It's like everything is fading away. I feel like *I'm* fading away."

"But I thought you were happy."

"I was!" she declared. "Or at least, I think I was. I don't even know anymore. And then when you came . . . I wanted you to think I knew what I was doing, that I'd done the right thing. I wanted to make myself think that." She groaned. "Oh, Jacob, after everything that happened in Harmony, all the things I said . . ." Her voice rose, took on an edge that made Jacob's stomach sink. He'd heard that voice before, that tone of desperation those last days in Harmony. She gripped his hands so hard he winced. "What's wrong with me, Jacob?"

Before Jacob could respond, the door opened.

"What the hell was that out there?" LaPerle barked as he stormed into the room, followed by Karl. Seeing Jacob and Xander, he pulled up short and glared.

"I should have known," he said. He went over to Delaney and, brushing Jacob aside, placed his hands on her shoulder. "Poor, sweet Delaney. What happened out there?"

He didn't wait for her to answer. "Never mind about that. Everyone has a bad moment early on. You've just had yours. Good. Now it's out of the way and you can move on. I mean, it's a bit of a setback—the performance was being broadcast all over the Rim—but we'll work with it. Who knows? Maybe we can play it to our advantage—add a little mystery to your image. And there's always the sympathy vote."

He spoke quickly, his voice taking on a forced edge of cheer that couldn't quite mask his annoyance. For her part, Delaney said nothing, but Jacob could see her shoulders sag, the corners of her mouth turn down as LaPerle rambled. Suddenly, the man turned to Jacob.

"So nice of you to come by," he said. "I'm sure seeing you helped lift Delaney's spirits. Karl can show you the way out—this place is quite a maze."

"But we just got here!" Jacob exclaimed.

"Can't they stay?" Delaney said. "I want Jacob to stay with me. He can sleep over in my suite tonight. There's plenty of room. Please, Jack."

LaPerle knelt down before Delaney so that his head was level with hers. "You know I'd do anything for you," he said. "I told you so when you first came aboard, remember? Now, listen to me. You've had a difficult night. A terrible night. The thing you need most is to get some sleep without any distractions."

"But, Jack . . ." she pleaded.

"Now listen, Delaney. I told your friends earlier that we could arrange a visit. Soon. We'll make it real soon. Okay?"

She said nothing, but gave a slight nod. LaPerle rose.

"Gentlemen?" he said, gesturing toward the door.

They started to file out. On his way by Delaney, Jacob stopped and leaned down and the two of them embraced. Xander and Karl went out into the hall, while LaPerle waited in the doorway.

"I'll see you soon," he said to her.

"Right," she replied, trying to smile.

He slipped the sounder out of his pocket and placed it in her palm. "I thought you might want this back," he whispered.

Her hand closed over it. This time, she smiled for real.

Jacob rose and left, followed by LaPerle, who closed the door after them.

"It seems our little meetings have become quite a habit," he snapped, turning to face them. "And now look what you've done. See how you've upset her."

Xander snorted. "You're trying to pin what happened tonight on us?" he demanded.

"She was fine before you two showed up. Everything was on track. And now . . . well, you saw her out there tonight. There's a lot at stake here."

"For you," Xander retorted.

"For *all* of us," LaPerle said. "If this pans out, she'll never have another worry the rest of her days."

"And that's what this is all about, right?" Xander said.

"Why not?" LaPerle said. He shook his head. "I can't believe I'm wasting my time with you two. Enough. Karl, escort them out. And this time, make sure they get the message."

He turned and went back into the dressing room, slamming the door behind him. Frowning, Karl passed them and headed down the hall. "Let's go," he snapped.

They followed him down a series of corridors toward the lobby.

"Karl," Xander said after a few minutes of walking. Karl ignored him. He just kept his body plowing forward. "Karl!" Xander barked.

Karl drew up so fast they nearly collided with him. "Just shut up, Xander," he growled, his back still to them. He continued. A few moments later they came to a door and Karl turned to face them. "You wouldn't listen to me before, so listen now. Stay away from the girl. Stay away from Mixel."

"You sound like one of them," Xander said.

"Christ, Xander," Karl said, shaking his head. "Why are you doing this to me?"

"I'd ask you the same question. What's this handler got about us coming around?"

"I don't ask questions, I just do what they tell me. You remember what that was like, don't you?"

"Why do you think I left?"

Karl snorted. "We both know why you left." He opened the door. Beyond it they could see the lobby. Xander walked out with Jacob in tow, then stopped and faced Karl who stood in the doorway.

"See you later, pal," Xander scoffed.

"Look, I remember everything we went through together," Karl said, "and I know you do too. But next time I see you, there'll be trouble. I'm not risking my job over this. It's just business. That's all."

"Just business," Xander said. "That was always our line, wasn't it?"

Karl nodded and closed the door.

The sky was dark as they left the concert hall. Night had come quickly. They made their way to the cruiser in silence.

"Why *doesn't* LaPerle want us near Delaney?" Jacob asked finally as they turned into the alley.

"Control," Xander replied. It was too dark for Jacob to see Xander's face, but Jacob could hear it in his voice: that bitterness, an edge darker than the sky above them. "It's nothing personal. Just business. They want her to depend only on them. If we're around, if you're in her life, it makes it harder for that to happen. They want to keep her isolated."

"I know what that's like," Jacob replied.

They got in the cruiser and drove away, leaving the lights of the city behind. Looking back, Jacob could almost see Delaney's face still hovering, opaque above the towers, her eyes absorbing the city's glow, unable to tear themselves away.

CHAPTER TWELVE

Jacob woke up the next morning angry. He wasn't sure at first what had seeded his anger or when. He'd slept most of the return trip, dozing on and off, losing himself in the vibration of the cruiser. The entire drive back he was numb. After the long day in Melville, he had nothing left. All that remained was a hollow space inside him—everything vital had been drained by disappointment. Arriving back at the house, he'd stumbled to bed with hardly a word.

That evening the customary nightmare was gone, replaced by an entirely new one—he was no longer pacing the streets of his old home. The scene had shifted to Melville. He looked into the sky. The moon was bright and large. He looked again: it was pink and cratered; it was Drake, not Druna. Why was it so close? *It's going to hit us. We're going to collide.* He looked even closer. There were people on the moon, little dark shapes crawling like insects, kicking up puffs of pink moon powder. Someone tapped him on the shoulder, and without looking back he ran. Now he was the one being chased. He didn't try to see who it was. He didn't need to. He could hear her voice behind him, as if she were leaning forward, whispering in his ear.

"I knew you would," she said.

Over and over her words repeated as he ran an endless loop around the streets. A story that went nowhere, it was far worse than the usual nightmare, and he awoke in a dark mood.

The dream faded but his anger didn't as he remembered LaPerle in the dressing room last night, remembered Delaney sitting quiet and dejected while Jacob had walked out and left her yet again. Jacob was mad at the man, but more so at himself. He hadn't been there for Delaney back in Harmony when she floundered, and he'd sworn that, given the chance, he wouldn't let it happen again, wouldn't leave her to her misery. But here he was, making the same mistake all over again.

"We have to go get her," he told Xander at breakfast.

"Don't worry. You'll meet up with her again. After last night, I don't see her going to Earth any time soon."

"I mean we have to get her out of there. We have to bring her back here."

There was a long pause. Xander looked down at his breakfast.

"No," he said at last.

"What?" Jacob cried, jumping up from the table. It had never occurred to him that Xander would refuse. The man had been so determined about helping Jacob visit Delaney, had such clear disdain for her handler, he couldn't imagine why he'd hold back now.

"You heard me."

"But you were *there* yesterday!" Jacob exclaimed. "You heard what she said. We have to save her."

"Save her, huh? The princess in the tower?" Xander got up and went to the window. "Look, Blinder, I don't mind bringing you into Melville to see your friend, but I draw the line at kidnapping."

"It's not kidnapping if she wants to come."

"You don't know what she wants. Neither does she. She was upset when you saw her. It was a bad moment. For all we know, she might have woken up this morning and realized things were pretty good after all."

"You don't believe that. You even said before that she seemed miserable."

"Forget what I said," Xander snapped.

"But you hate that man LaPerle, you said as much to Karl. Do you want him to win?"

"Win what? It's not a game, Jacob. LaPerle's nothing to me."

"I guess Delaney's nothing to you, too."

"Well, she is *your* friend."

"Is this because of Karl? Or are you afraid?" Before Jacob could stop himself, he had blurted it out. Plopping down in his chair, he glanced nervously at Xander. There was a long silence.

"I left fear behind years ago," the man finally replied, looking out the window. His voice was icy and his fingers gripping the wood of the windowpane were white. "I just don't feel like having another Blinder around to take care of. One is bad enough." He spun and glared down at Jacob. "I didn't come out here to start a foster home. I came out to be alone. I came out here for some goddamn peace and quiet."

He turned and walked out of the house, leaving the door open behind him. Jacob didn't have to follow him to know where he was going. Sure enough, a moment later there was the growl of the cruiser's engine firing up. He listened as its roar faded into the distance.

Jacob stood up from the table and walked out onto the deck. Reaching for the railing, he could see his hands trembling. *Did that just happen?* he wondered. His recent nightmares seemed more real than this moment. The last few weeks, he'd gotten used to the man, had gotten used to this place. He hadn't thought Xander would turn on him. He had been fooled into thinking Xander didn't mind having him around, that maybe he even liked his company. And now he had pushed too far, had drawn the truth from his host. He wasn't wanted here. A sickness rose in him. This man was his only connection to the world. Where would Jacob go if Xander cut him off? How would he survive? The image of the skeleton in the grass flashed into his mind. Somewhere to the east, in the basin of a valley, the lonely bones still lay.

No, Jacob thought. *He would have asked me to leave if he'd wanted me gone. He didn't mean what he said. He's just angry, like he always gets.*

He relaxed his grip on the railing and looked out. The day was hot. The sun shone, but the sky had faded from blue to gray as a thin layer of clouds had crept in overnight, turning the sun silver. Squinting, he could just make out the black sliver of Mixel Tower through the haze. Delaney was in that tower. Maybe she was looking through her window right now, looking straight at him without even knowing it, hoping for a way out. Before he'd been to Melville, before he'd seen the world of the Seers, he thought he could find her and they'd live happily ever after. Now he knew better. Even if he could sneak in to see her, LaPerle would never let him stay, and he couldn't get her out on his own. He needed Xander to help him.

He went inside and collapsed into one of the armchairs. There had to be some way of getting Xander to change his mind.

All morning and into the afternoon he lingered in the house, trying to devise a plan. Like Delaney, Xander was stubborn. And right now, he was angry. The first thing Jacob needed to do was get back into his good graces. Then maybe he could convince Xander to help him.

Jacob suddenly realized that he'd done virtually nothing to help out since he'd gotten here. Not that he'd been asked—Xander led a spartan life, regimented and independent. Still, even in Harmony he'd had chores to do at home, whether it was washing dishes or sweeping the floor of their underground house.

He cleaned up from breakfast as well as his own lunch and then started looking around for something else to do. At first he thought about cleaning the house, but it wasn't that dirty. Even so, he could at least sweep the floor.

Looking for a broom, he tried a door that was tucked around a corner under the staircase. He'd noticed it before and assumed it was a closet. He instead found a set of stairs leading down into the darkness of a basement. His thoughts of sweeping forgotten, he turned on the light and headed down the steps.

The basement was cool and spare, even more so than the floors above. The concrete walls and earthy smell reminded him of the underground buildings in Harmony, and when he closed his eyes for a second, he could have sworn he was home. There were a few metal cylinders lined up in the corner. On the face of one was a tiny, lit screen, and all of them had several lights and dials along the front, as well as wires and tubes running from them up into the ceiling. The machines reminded Jacob of the ghostbox. He shivered and looked away to the other side of the room. A pile of boxes lay stacked against the wall, neatly ordered, aside from one crate that sat alone, separated from its companions. It looked like all the others, but just gazing at it, Jacob felt a chill run down his back. It was that same prickling sensation he'd felt the day he'd found the body in the grass. He reached down to touch it. In the back of his mind, a tiny voice told him to stop, that he wasn't meant to open this box. *You shouldn't even be down here*, it said. But before he could listen, he'd popped open the clasp and lifted the cover.

He leaped back at the sight of the yellow creature with black beady eyes that looked up at him from the crate, and then he scrambled for the foot of the stairs. Only when he paused on the third step and looked back did he realize he'd left the cover open. For several seconds he waited, expecting the furry monster to leap out and give chase, but everything was still. Heart pounding, he slunk back toward the crate and popped his head up for a quick glance. The creature hadn't moved.

Approaching tentatively, Jacob closed in on the box and inspected it once more. The creature had remained frozen, and as Jacob leaned in, he realized there was something different about it, something about the eyes—a kind of deadness. Reaching down, he felt the body and laughed with relief.

Jacob stroked the animal's synthetic fur and gazed into its plastic eyes. He turned it over and noticed its hindquarters were dirty and the fibers along one back leg were singed. Overall, the animal had a burned scent, the smell of a fire that had died long ago.

Putting the creature aside, he returned to the crate. He had expected to find something different inside. Maybe weapons, like the ones he'd already seen Xander carry, or armor, something to do with war. Instead, there were other toys inside—balls, a few other stuffed animals, toy ships and cars, small soldiers dressed in strange-looking armor—as well as clothes, none of which looked big enough to fit him. Like the first creature he'd found, the items had the same smoky odor, not nearly as pleasant as the smell of burning zephyr wood.

Rummaging through the box, he was delighted to find an instrument. No, there were two: a whistle with six finger holes and some kind of harp. He pulled the whistle out and examined it. The whistle was made of burnished wood with a marbled texture that looked like swirling water. As for the harp, it was a child's toy. Still, plying his fingers across the strings, he discovered it had a decent sound. All it needed was a little tuning. He returned the harp to the crate and went back to examining the whistle.

His fingers fitted instinctively to the holes. He'd spent so many hours holding an instrument just like this growing up. Every child in Harmony learned to play the whistle. It was one of the initial classes they took in school. He remembered playing in his first concert—five years old, twenty-seven of them packed together, puffing out the tune of some nursery rhyme, a cacophony of song that brought laughter from parents and children alike. He'd loved the sound of his whistle and had practiced every afternoon in his room before supper for the next several years, even accompanying his mother while she played the songs she'd taught him on the piano.

Putting the instrument to his lips, Jacob blew a tentative

note. At first, he recoiled from the burnt taste, but the sound drew him back. He blew another note, held it, and listened to the breathy, whispered tone so pure he wished he could hold it forever. Even as his air ran out, its quavering had a sweetness.

An idea struck him. If there was one thing Jacob could do, it was play music. He could perform for his host, put on a concert of his own. Tonight he would surprise him with the gift.

But first he had to practice. It had been a few years since he'd played the whistle with any seriousness.

He started in, first with scales, running up and down the different sets with increasing speed until he could feel the quickness in his fingers once again. Then he advanced to some simple songs, beginning with the first he'd ever learned and moving on from there. Skipping from one tune to the next, it was as if he were growing up all over again. With each song came flashes of memory—the sound of a classmate's laugh, the scent of a certain flower or food, the pang of a particular joy or fear. He lost himself in the progression. At one point he realized he'd closed his eyes, but when he opened them, he discovered he couldn't play without them closed—it just didn't feel right.

Before long he'd run through the series of his childhood songs. They were nice, but he wanted something more, something that would really impress Xander. He started in on a sequence of melodies his mother had taught him during the last year before he'd abandoned the whistle for the piano and guitar. They were fairly intricate, inspired by classical pieces from ancient Earth, melodies of Bach, but imprinted with the modern sensibility of Harmony's own musicians. It took him several tries, but before long he had a number of them down and now began running through them over and over.

With his eyes closed, the trilling notes of the familiar songs combined with the earthy scent of the basement in a wave that carried him away. He was no longer Jacob, the boy who could see. He had never left the dark comfort of his home, had never been terrified by strange dreams that spilled over into his waking life, had never been the subject of violence or scorn. Before long, he could hear the sounds of his mother's piano. She was right beside him, her fingers flying with a speed to match his own, her notes cascading out and wrapping around his own tune, merging into a single song. He could hear her breathing, uttering the little sounds that often escaped her mouth as she played, unconscious accents to her music. A longing filled him. He had never missed anyone so much as he missed her now. And now she was talking, calling out the chord changes, calling out words of praise as he kept up with her ever-increasing tempo. She was calling to him once more.

"What the hell are you doing?"

The shouting jolted him from his song. For a brief second he felt that he was falling, before he snapped his eyes open and turned.

Xander was at the bottom of the steps. A darkness had fallen over the man's face, making him look more fearsome than ever. He came toward Jacob with giant strides, though it seemed as if he were moving in slow motion. Jacob tried to move, tried to say something to ward off the man's advance, but he was frozen in place, the whistle still gripped between his fingers, suspended in air before him.

Jacob braced himself as Xander loomed over him. The man snatched the whistle from his hands, threw it back into the box, and slammed the lid so hard Jacob jumped. Without looking at Jacob, he turned and stormed back up the stairs, slamming the basement door behind him.

For a long time, Jacob remained in the basement, trying to stop shaking. Sitting on the crate, he kept seeing the fury on the man's face. Again that stunned, surreal aura swept over him. He was sure he'd discovered a way of doing something nice for Xander, but now things were worse than ever. He felt he should go up and apologize, but who knew what kind of state Xander might still be in.

There was no sound of footsteps on the floor above since the thunder of Xander's boots leaving for the second time that day. So, after Jacob's heart had returned to normal, he crept back up the stairs and opened the door a crack. He saw no sign of Xander and came out into the main room. Going to the window, his heart surged at the sight of Xander's cruiser sitting in the yard. He hadn't left. He had to be close by. Jacob slipped out onto the deck, and looked around but saw no one.

He decided not to look any further and went back inside. Pacing the room, he tried to think of the words to say to Xander when he returned, fighting off the urge to just gather his few possessions, head for Melville, and take his chances there.

The afternoon hurried away, dusk crept in the windows, and still Xander didn't come back. Going out onto the deck, Jacob paused in the twilight at the familiar scent of burning zephyr wood and saw the glint of Xander's fire through the trees. *Go now*, a voice told him. *Go talk to him.*

He headed down the stairs, and crossing the yard, entered the path through the trees. His legs felt numb, and he took slow steps toward the fire, steps that became slower the closer he got. But at last he reached the clearing, came into the circle of the fire and sat down at his usual spot, silent. Xander never raised his eyes from the flames. It was as if Jacob were invisible, coming upon this man for the first time, unnoticed. It reminded him of his last days in Harmony when he had moved unseen among the people, watching them go about their lives, his neighbors never knowing he was at hand.

One minute passed into the next, piling up, weighting down the silence until Xander's voice broke the stillness.

"It was my last campaign," he said. "Fighting had broken out in a Mixel system. We'd been stationed there for a couple years—most of us had families there. My wife, my two boys—Mixel had set us up in some nice quarters. We'd fought some skirmishes in different parts of the sector, but business was slow and we all had lots of time at home. We were uneasy about the fighting once it got close, of course, but nearly all of it had been confined to orbit; things were peaceful on the ground."

He paused. Jacob could feel him struggle to continue.

"My platoon was topside, packed in shuttles on our way to raid a freighter, when we heard the news. By the time we got back, our settlement had disappeared. Barracks, residentials, everything bombed. Where our families had been was nothing but a pile of rubble."

Jacob gasped. It was as if, for the slightest moment, he could see the wreckage—the broken stone, the twisted metal. Then the image faded, leaving him with nothing but the memory of the singed bear in the basement and the odor of acrid smoke that lingered over all the toys, just the faintest echo of destruction.

"I'm sorry," Jacob whispered. He didn't know what else to say. But now he knew what Karl's cryptic words of consolation had meant, not to mention Xander's stormy reaction that first night at the fire when he'd asked him about his family.

Xander snorted in disgust. "It was Mixel that did the bombing. They'd gotten word that the enemy had established a base on the surface and were determined to get rid of it. But it turned out to be a setup. The other corporation had sent a false report, disguised of course, and at the last minute hacked in and changed the bombing coordinates."

"They'd really do that?"

"Well, that was Mixel's story. Whatever really happened, Mixel screwed up—even if their story's true, they could've reconned the base to see if the report was accurate, or sent in a company for a ground assault, or had better ship security when they launched the attack, or a million other things. But they were in a rush and wanted a clean sweep."

"So what did you do?"

"What could I do? Mixel came to all of us who had lost our homes and families and offered us a deal—land rights in any Mixel colony, along with immediate retirement and full pensions if we didn't push for an investigation. They'd do anything to avoid the bad press and even more to prevent the trade sanctions that would follow. The writing was on the wall, so we took the deal. We'd all seen enough in our careers to know that when Mixel wants something, they get it, one way or another. That's why I'm here on Nova Campi. After all that, the only thing I wanted was to get away from the world, and this was the farthest I could go."

"And those things in the crate?"

"I spent two days picking through the wreckage. That was

about all I could find that was worth keeping."

"You didn't find them?"

"No, I found them," Xander murmured. He cleared his voice and for the first time looked up at Jacob. "Sorry if I scared you before," he said.

"I shouldn't have opened that box."

Xander shook his head. "It was just hard seeing you with that whistle. That was Marty's—my older boy. He'd be nearly your age now. I told my wife he was too young to learn to play an instrument, but she wouldn't listen. Said he'd grow into it."

"It's a nice whistle," Jacob offered.

"It sounded nice. You can keep it if you want. You play pretty well." He threw another log into the fire.

"I play okay, but not as good as Delaney. Almost every day when she'd come over for lessons, I'd just lie on the couch and listen to her and my mother play. Usually piano, some-times harp or violin. It didn't matter. It was enough just to be around her."

Xander looked down at the dwindling flames. "You wouldn't think so, listening to you talk in your sleep."

"What do you mean?"

"You always sound terrified of her."

Jacob hesitated. A part of him didn't want to even think about his recurring dreams, let alone talk about them. But there was another part of him that did, that hoped that in the telling, the mysteries behind the dreams might be brought to light.

And so before he knew it, he began describing the dreams to Xander. He told him about being back in Harmony, about the habitual chase, the strange images and variations, and worst of all, the final confrontation at the end.

138

"Seeing those hands reaching out around her throat, the fire everywhere, it makes me sick. Why would I want to hurt her? Or her me? It doesn't make any sense."

"Dreams never do," Xander assured him.

"But these are so real—the fire in her eyes, the expanding head just like that projection at the concert, the fact that she looked the same in my dream before I ever saw her in real life. It's as if my dreams have come true. Not exactly, but close enough. Too close. It scares me."

"It's just a coincidence, Jacob. Reality and fantasy mix in nightmares. I know. I have them too."

Maybe Xander was right. After all, last night's dream had been different. It was still a nightmare, but there was no doubt in Jacob's mind that Delaney's accusatory voice chasing him through the streets of Melville was a product of his guilty conscience and his imagination working against him.

"Forget about your dreams," Xander said. "No point worrying about things you can't control."

"Maybe if we can be together, the nightmares will stop."

Xander didn't respond. Taking a stick, he stirred the collapsing remains of the fire, darkening the clearing.

Looking up through the opening in the trees, Jacob could see the outline of a ship passing low overhead, dragging a trail of light across the stars.

"What kind of ship is that?" Jacob asked, pointing at the sky.

"That's a trader's craft, a smaller one," Xander said. "Lots of them make their way to Nova Campi. Mixel has their own fleet of cargo liners, but they've got plenty of freelancers working on the side."

"What's it like?" Jacob asked.

"What, riding in a ship?"

"Being in space."

"It depends. It can be beautiful. It can be boring. And sometimes, it can make you feel lonelier than you'd ever thought you could feel."

"I remember the first time I saw a ship, the night before I ran away from Harmony. It looked so peaceful up there in the sky, so far away from anyone's problems. I just wished I could be on that ship. It didn't matter where it was going, I just wanted to be up there. "

"Maybe you will one day. Some people are drawn to space. They wouldn't want to be any place else."

"I wish I had a place like that, where I fit in, and things made sense."

"You and me both," Xander said.

He got up and headed for the house. Jacob watched him disappear and thought once more about the story Xander had told him. He took one last look at the fallen embers, their red glow already starting to fade, and then followed Xander from a distance.

They hardly spoke at dinner and went to bed soon after. It took Jacob a long time to doze off. He kept seeing Xander picking through a pile of smoldering rubble. Finally, he gave in to sleep, and then to his recurring nightmare. It had a new intensity. Never before had the tunnel seemed so dark, never before had the fire from Delaney's eyes burned so hot. As the fire overwhelmed him, Jacob awoke to find himself soaked in sweat, the sheets drenched. Taking the blanket folded at his feet, he slipped out of bed and curled up on the floor, wrapping the blanket around himself. For the remaining hours of the night, the burning sensation lingered. He slept fitfully and was grateful when morning finally came.

Hearing Xander get up and go downstairs, Jacob rose and got dressed. He felt woozy at first, but by the time breakfast was ready he was better, last night just a memory.

Breakfast was as quiet as dinner had been, and Jacob had started to worry that Xander had fallen back into anger. All morning the man was withdrawn. When Jacob spoke to him, he acted as if he'd barely heard him, taking his time to respond and, even then, saying little. When he left the house after lunch, Jacob debated whether to follow, but Xander returned a few minutes later.

"We leave in five minutes. You'd better get ready," he said.

Jacob froze. "For what?"

"We're going to Melville."

He gave Jacob a smile, then turned and went back outside.

All the darkness Jacob had felt the last two days—the anger, the fear, the homesickness, the regret—all of it washed away in an instant. He grabbed his jacket, and was headed for the door, when he suddenly stopped. He was sure he knew where Delaney was, but he didn't want to take any chances. He turned and went up the stairs, down the hall, and into his room, where he slid open the top drawer of his bureau. The drawer was empty but for one item, the only thing of value he possessed. He grabbed the finder, put it in his pocket, and left.

CHAPTER THIRTEEN

"So what made you change your mind?" Jacob shouted over the throb of the cruiser as Melville's towers rose before them.

Xander shrugged. "Got tired of listening to you scream at night," he shouted back.

Jacob knew he was only half-serious but decided not to press the matter, afraid the man might change his mind. Besides, what difference did it really make? What mattered was that soon Delaney would be with them. Hopefully.

"How are we going to do this, anyway?" Jacob asked an hour later as they pulled over and parked the cruiser several blocks away from Mixel Tower. "LaPerle isn't going to let us take her."

"You're right. We can't just walk in as we are—they're ready for us now. We'll have to sneak in. And that's going to take some thought, not to mention some special toys."

"Like what?"

"You'll see."

Jacob started to get out. He paused to watch Xander open the dashboard compartment and retrieve a small pistol. After checking a few switches, the man slipped it into his shirt pocket.

"What?" he demanded, looking at Jacob's widening eyes.

"Nothing," Jacob said. "I just didn't think about having a gun."

"Relax. It's just a stunner. We may need it."

"Okay," he whispered.

Xander gave a brief smile. He got out of the cruiser and helped Jacob down onto the street. They went in the opposite direction of Mixel headquarters, toward the center of the city. As they walked, Jacob kept thinking about the gun in Xander's pocket and of Karl's warning the last time they met.

Soon, they were on the main avenue. It was noon, and the streets were packed with people heading out for lunch and midday shopping. Jacob still wasn't used to the sound of voices, music, and vehicles converging around him, or to the barrage of colors, lights, and movement. He found himself, as before, clinging tightly to Xander.

"When do we go back to Mixel?" Jacob asked.

"Tonight. We'll try to hit it at the end of the day. The lobby will be swarming with people headed home. That's when we'll have the best chance of blending in."

A few minutes later, they turned off the main avenue and onto a familiar narrow street. As before, the lamp marking Kala's bookstore glowed in the deep shadow of the buildings.

"We're going to get some books?" Jacob asked. "How does that help?"

"We're not going for books, Blinder. The things we need you can't buy in any store. Kala may sell books now, but she didn't use to. She knows the right people in Melville, the ones we need to see."

"What did she do before?" Jacob asked.

"Most everyone in Melville either works for Mixel or used to. We're all one big happy family," he quipped. "Kala's

143

no exception. After Mixel she moved into, well, other areas. Once she'd made enough money, she decided to get out and spend her time with something she really loved."

"Books?"

"That's right."

The bell over the door rang as they entered. As before, the store was empty.

"Twice in three days. To what do I owe the honor?" Kala said, coming around the corner of a bookcase, her gold eyes flashing. "Or have you come to make a return?"

"Hey, Kala," Xander said. "Nothing like that."

"Then what can Kala do for you?" she said.

"We're looking for a few items. Hard-to-get items. You used to be in the business. Thought you might be able to help."

"*Used* to be in the business," she said. "I don't play those games anymore, Xander. You know that."

"I know, Kala. Just a name, a place, somebody we might go to."

She looked down at Jacob. "What's he getting you into?" she asked him.

"It was my idea," Jacob said, trying to hide the tremor in his voice.

"So *you're* the mastermind here," she said, smiling.

"Come on, Kala, go easy," Xander broke in. "It's nothing major. Not even illegal—at least, I don't think so. We just need to be someplace without anyone knowing we're there. That kind of thing."

"That kind of thing, huh?" she said. "All right, I'll help. You are my best customer after all. But you're going to need plenty of cash. He doesn't give the stuff away. Stay here."

She went to the back of the store. Jacob turned to Xander.

"What's cash?" Jacob whispered.

"Cash is money. You know, what you use to buy things with."

"But I don't have any money," Jacob hissed.

"I've got some," Xander replied.

"But she said we'd need a lot. I don't want you to use all of yours for me."

"Look, if we can't afford what I'd like to get, we'll just make do. It'll add to the challenge."

Kala returned and handed Xander a slip of paper. Xander opened it, read it, and laughed.

"Raker?" he said. "You got to be kidding me."

"Know him, huh? Figures. You were both mercs. Well, he's the man now."

Xander laughed again. "Thanks, Kala. I owe you," he said, slipping the paper into his pocket.

"Don't worry about it. Just don't get yourselves hurt, okay? Especially this one," she said, giving Jacob's shoulder a squeeze. "He's too cute."

Jacob's eyes widened at her words. Seeing the look on his face, she broke out laughing.

"Stop scaring the kid," Xander said. "Come on, Jacob. Let's go."

"Give Raker my best," Kala called out as they left the store.

Back on the main street, Xander broke into such a quick stride, Jacob practically had to trot to keep up.

"We might have struck a little bit of luck for once, if Raker's who I think he is," Xander said.

"Is he like Karl?"

"No. Karl's a buddy. Or was, anyway. Raker and I weren't that close. Didn't know each other long."

"So how is that good? Is he going to help us?"

Xander shrugged. "Maybe not. But I think he will. We worked together a few times early in my career. I saved his sorry butt the last time we went out. Carried him the better part of a mile out of the middle of a firefight. Don't even know why I did it—never really liked him. Not a bad guy, just kind of a baby. Anyway, looks like there was a reason for it after all."

"Let's hope," Jacob said.

They walked for about twenty minutes toward the edge of the city, putting downtown between themselves and Mixel Tower. From time to time, Jacob stole glances at the black structure dwarfing every other building in the city. Jacob wondered what they would find there, wondered what kind of shape Delaney would be in. What if Xander had been right yesterday? What if she didn't want to leave? All of this would be for nothing. Then another question came to mind.

"What if she isn't there?"

"Then we wait, I guess."

Glancing around, Jacob noticed that most of the stores and shopping centers had disappeared. In their place squatted enormous buildings that looked like much larger versions of the storage houses in Harmony: plain, boxlike, with few doors or windows. The crowd had likewise dwindled, trickling to an occasional passerby, and the floater and groundcar traffic had been replaced with large haulers scuttling between the buildings and a collection of concrete structures visible at the far end of the street. He guessed that the buildings were warehouses and factories of different kinds, but what were those strange bunkers ahead of them?

"We're heading toward the port," Xander said, as if anticipating Jacob's question.

No sooner had Xander spoken than the ground beneath Jacob's feet began to vibrate slightly, accompanied by a distant rumble that reminded him of the great storms that swept the plains from time to time. Jacob looked ahead in the direction of the noise and gasped. Not far away, a starship was lifting off from its bunker, rising above the concrete walls, drifting upward and rotating as it climbed. It was oblong, painted white with blue circles along its sides. He had a hard time figuring out how big it was. It didn't appear to be a huge ship from here, but he couldn't tell how far away it really was. They stopped walking and watched as it climbed into the sky like a feather riding a current of warm air before bursting forward with a flash of its engines. A moment later it had disappeared from sight.

Xander pointed ahead. "I think that's it."

They stopped at a corner. Across the street stood a steel warehouse, indistinguishable from all the others around it but for a set of numbers painted across the front. A single row of windows stretched the entire length of the building just below the roof several stories up. After waiting for a hauler to go by, they crossed the street and stood before the building.

"I don't see any door," Jacob said.

"Neither do I."

They walked down the street and around the corner to the other side. Still there was no door. They continued walking. Turning another corner they saw several large bays big enough for the haulers and, along the edge of the building, a side entrance. They went to the door and tried it. It was unlocked.

"We're in luck," Xander said.

"This is a weird place," Jacob said, looking around at the empty street. "Where is everybody?"

"Working, I guess. Let's go."

Coming in from the street, their eyes took a moment to adjust to the darkness. The windows along the top cast a dim light into the warehouse, enough to reveal its vast size but little else. Jacob was used to being inside dark spaces, but always tight, cozy ones like his house or his room, nothing this immense. It was like a huge cavern. To their left by the bay doors was a platform, but everything else around them was empty space, a black void. The floor underfoot was metal grating. It extended ten feet before them and ended in a staircase that descended into the dark.

The windows rattled as a nearby ship took off, its sound a muffled throb.

"I guess there's nowhere else to go but down," Xander said, his voice echoing in the dark. Though he stood right next to Jacob, he sounded far away. This place, this trip, it didn't feel right. Nothing felt right, Jacob realized. Over the last hour, he'd begun noticing the slightest feeling of wooziness coupled with a warmth gathering in his forehead, an echo of this morning that now simmered at the edges of his awareness.

They started down the stairs, their boots clanging against the metal steps, sounding all the louder against the hollow silence. The staircase turned back and forth, zigzagging every twenty steps.

"Back in the store with Kala, both of you kept saying 'the business.' What business were you talking about?" Jacob asked.

"Smuggling. Certain things are illegal, but people still want them. So other people like Raker provide them."

"Don't they get caught?"

"Now and then, I guess. But hardly ever, unless it's something really bad. The corporations that run these planets mostly turn a blind eye. Hell, some of them probably get a take of the action."

It reminded Jacob of all the bad things his people had told him about the Seers back in Harmony. But the people of Harmony also turned a *blind* eye to the corruption in their midst. The only difference was the Seers did it by choice. Which was worse?

A minute later, they reached the bottom of the stairs. The light from above was almost nonexistent here, barely enough to illuminate the cargo crates and containers rising above them, stacked into piles that loomed like buildings, creating narrow streets between them. Down at the end of one of these corridors, Jacob could see a light.

"Is that where we're supposed to go?" he asked Xander.

"We're about to find out," the man replied.

They started toward the light. As they got closer, a dull throb began to emerge. At first, Jacob thought it was the sound of his pulse—his heart was pounding harder with every step as a growing nervousness spread out from his stomach. But as they continued the sound grew louder and took on a rhythm different from his heart. For a moment, he thought it must be another ship taking off, but it wasn't the slow, steady roar he'd heard up on the street. It was too frenetic, rising and falling in a wave of sound.

It's music, Jacob realized as they approached.

Now he could make out the source of the light, could see

the blue lamp over a door. Then he stopped. A man was sitting beside the door.

"Come on, Blinder. Don't worry," Xander said, looking back.

As they walked up to the doorway, the man rose from his chair. Jacob edged closer to Xander and looked up at the man with wide eyes. In the glow of the lamp, the man's face was rough, the shadows exaggerating his craggy features. His hair was long and unkempt, not pulled back but hanging around his face like tendrils of prairie grass grown wild. He was shorter than Xander, but seemed bulkier, though it was hard to tell under his baggy clothes. As the muffled pulse of bass and drums shuddered behind the door, like a beast struggling to get out, he looked the two of them over.

"Haven't seen you before," he said.

"We're here for Raker," Xander replied.

"Of course you are," the man replied. "Everyone is. But not this time of day. It's early. And you've got a kid. What's the idea of that?"

"Can't be helped," Xander snapped. "I'll have him keep his eyes closed if it makes you feel better. Is Raker here or not?"

"Maybe. What do you need?"

"Nothing major. Kala told us to come here."

"Kala, huh? All right. Hang on."

The man turned around and murmured something. There was a pause. The man nodded and turned back. Without another word, he opened the door, releasing the noise. Jacob watched Xander wade into the sound. He took one last glance at the man looking down at him.

"Have fun, kid," the man said with a grin.

Jacob hurried after Xander.

Covering his ears against the frenzied mix of drumbeats, bass, and electronic pulses blasting from a bank of speakers over by the bar, Jacob glanced around. The whole place was like some low-ceilinged cave, bulging out in different directions. It was hard to tell how far it extended. It wasn't any brighter than the corridor outside. There were a few lamps glowing at the tables, some purple, some red, some green, but most of the light came from the tiny screens planted before the dozen or so people scattered among the tables, bathing their smiling faces in a blue glow. The men and women sat transfixed before the screens, eyes open wide, faces leaning down and in.

"What are those people doing?" Jacob asked Xander, practically screaming to even hear himself above the music.

"They're loaders," Xander shouted back. "Mostly spacers here on shore leave, looking for a little diversion. Those screens they're watching aren't normal—they grab your brain waves and pull you in. Show you whatever you want to see, or think you do anyways. I tried it once."

"What did you see?"

In the dim light, Jacob could see Xander frown. "I won't do it again," was all he said.

Jacob watched as Xander approached a man in a black robe. The man gestured to the both of them and they followed him through another door in the back of the room. Jacob breathed a sigh of relief as the door closed behind them, cutting off the sound.

His relief didn't last long. As they proceeded down a hallway toward yet another door, Jacob fell behind, his steps slowing as a wave of dizziness overcame him. It was more intense than the sensation he'd felt upon waking this morning, and he had to concentrate to keep his balance, his fingers tracing along the wall as he drifted sideways. The image of Xander and the strange man in front of him blurred, shimmered, the hallway seemed to stretch out into the distance, and the sounds of their footsteps echoed in his brain. It felt as though he'd been walking forever. He paused to lean against the wall and close his eyes. *Relax*, he told himself. *You're just nervous. Everything will be fine. You're with Xander.*

He opened his eyes to discover the wave had passed and hurried to rejoin the two at the entry. The man in the black robe knocked and the door whisked open. He ushered Jacob and Xander inside.

The room was small, dark but for a small lamp on a desk across from them. Jacob froze at the sight of the man seated behind the desk. He was massive, with huge jowls that hung down the sides of his face, and his torso was so swollen that his arms, folded on the desk before him, seemed to have shrunk into his body. Strangest of all was his baby face, framed by curly red hair and sideburns.

"Good lord, Raker," Xander said, "look at you." He plopped down in one of the two chairs facing the desk. Jacob sat in the other. The man who had brought them remained by the door.

"Xander Payne," Raker said, breaking into a smile. "I knew it was you the second you walked through the door."

"So you're in the business now, huh?"

"Well, yeah. I've been at it for quite a while. Started after I left the unit. Wasn't any good as a soldier. You probably know that."

"It's been a long time."

"Too long. I still think about you, Xander, even now. I remember what you did."

"That's good, Raker. I was hoping you would. I remember you saying you owed me when I left you with the medics. I'd like to call that favor in."

"Of course, Xander. You need a job? I can always use a guy like you."

Xander shook his head. "Nothing like that. The boy and I need to visit someone. But security's likely to be tight, and I wouldn't mind having some help avoiding interruptions."

"What do you need?"

"A few cloakers would be nice. And a skeleton key if you got one."

Raker whistled and settled back in his chair. Jacob held his breath, afraid for a moment that the enormous man's mass would propel him backward onto the floor.

"I don't know, Xander. Cloakers are pretty valuable. Hard to get, you see. Worth a lot of money. A lot."

"Maybe we could work something out," Xander said, shrugging.

"Where you going that you need a cloaker, anyway?" Raker asked.

Jacob looked over at Xander, who shifted uncomfortably in his seat for a moment. "Mixel," Xander said at last. "We need to get into the tower."

Raker threw his hands up into the air. "Then there's no question," he said. "I can't let you have them, even if you could afford to pay. If you got caught, and they traced them back to me, I'd be shut down for sure."

"We won't get caught," Xander assured him.

"They all say that."

"Come on, Raker," Xander pushed. "You remember, don't you? Bullets, plasma bolts flying everywhere. You on the ground, bleeding, crying for help as everyone took off. And who picked you up? Who carried you all the way back?"

"You did," Raker said, looking down at his desk.

Jacob tried to imagine Xander carrying Raker's rolling mass even ten feet. It seemed impossible.

"Damn right I did," Xander said, "And let me tell you, you weren't light, even back then."

Raker looked back up. "Who is it you need to see at Mixel?"

"A friend," was all Xander said.

"That's it? A friend? What's so special about that?"

Jacob could see Xander hesitate. All along he'd been watching the exchange with a sinking feeling. He'd held off saying anything, letting Xander work it out, but he couldn't hold back anymore.

He pulled the concert ticket from the night before out of his pocket and held it flat in his palm the way he'd seen LaPerle do. Up sprang the small, glowing figure of Delaney. Raker's eyes widened at the sight of the rotating image.

"Her? I can see why you're so determined, Xander," he said, nodding. "Wait a minute," he said, looking more closely, "she's that singer, right? What are you, a fan or something?"

"Not exactly," Xander retorted. "She's an old friend of the kid's," he said, gesturing toward Jacob.

"We're like family," Jacob said. "And Mixel won't let her go. Please help us."

The image disappeared as Jacob lifted the card. "You can have this, if you want," he offered, holding the ticket out. When Raker didn't take it, Jacob put it on the desk and pushed it forward.

"Like family, huh?" Raker replied, reaching out and taking the ticket. He pulled Delaney's image back up for a moment, then put the card in his shirt pocket.

Shaking his head, Raker removed a metal tag from a chain around his neck and inserted it into a slot on his desk. A large panel in the wall behind slid open, revealing a compartment. Raker struggled from his chair, shambled over to the compartment, and removed a box. He came back to the desk and plopped down into his chair with a groan.

"Don't have a skeleton key," he said, setting the chest gingerly before him on the desk. "Not one that would work where you're going, anyway. But I know *these* beauties will."

He opened the small chest. Jacob leaned over and looked in. Embedded in a soft fabric lay six silver capsules no bigger than his thumb, a glass ring wrapped around the center of each one. Xander pulled one out and gave a low whistle.

"Pretty things, aren't they," Xander said. "Haven't seen one of these in a few years. Don't think I've ever come across ones so nicely made."

Raker nodded. "Girl on Botana makes these. A real artist." He pulled another out and handed it to Xander. "You can *borrow* these," Raker said.

"That's fine, Raker," Xander replied, taking the second capsule. "They work like any other cloaker?"

"Yeah. Just give it a twist to activate it. Should block even Mixel's sensors. As far as they're concerned, you'll be invisible. Only one catch," Raker warned. "Cloakers soak up a ton of power. Can't say how long the batteries'll last. You'll want to move quickly."

"Don't worry about that," Xander said. He stood up. Jacob did the same. "Thanks Raker," he said. "I guess we're even now."

"I'm glad I could help," Raker said. "Just don't get caught, for chrissake."

Xander looked down at Jacob. "You ready?"

"I hope so," Jacob replied.

CHAPTER FOURTEEN

Twilight was falling across the city by the time they reached Mixel Tower. The revolving door was jammed with a steady stream of workers pouring onto the sidewalk as others passed in. For a few moments they stood outside and watched. Jacob wished Xander would just hurry up and plunge in. Every second that ticked by, every second he craned back his neck and stared up at the black, glass tower stretching before him into the clouds, the more nervous he became, the more he began to believe that the venture was bound to fail. Another wave of dizziness swept over him. *Not now*, he thought. He took a few deep breaths, and the wave passed once again. It seemed like his fever was getting worse. He glanced over at Xander, who just looked down at him and winked.

"Just remember," Xander said, "this is your adventure. No matter what happens, you've brought us to this point. You're a brave one, Jacob."

Jacob nodded. As the crowd flowed around them, Xander took one of the capsules from his pocket and twisted it. Jacob heard a click and saw the glass ring light up. Xander handed the cloaker to Jacob. It was heavier than he thought it would be and warm to the touch.

"Keep it in your pocket and you'll be fine. Their sensors

won't be able to pick you out," Xander said, activating his own cloaker.

"What if Karl or somebody else sees us?"

Xander shrugged. "Not much we can do about that. Hopefully the crowd will be enough cover," he said. "Let's go."

They merged with the swarming bodies and were swept into the lobby. Jacob followed Xander as he wove his way across the marbled flooring. Instead of heading for the elevators, however, they turned toward a corridor at the far end of the main floor.

"Where are we going?" Jacob whispered.

Xander pointed to a sign above the entrance to the corridor. "Service elevator is back here. It'll be quieter."

"Won't it be more suspicious?"

"Only if somebody notices us. Anyway, look at us. We don't exactly fit in with the suits—might as well go where there are fewer people. Besides, the only ones using this elevator are the drones, and they rarely ask questions. Go ahead, press it," Xander ordered as they came to the elevator. Jacob reached with trembling fingers and pressed the up arrow, jerking his hand back as the button lit up.

"Relax," Xander assured. "You're doing fine. I told you before—this isn't life or death. It's kind of fun, actually. I always liked covert operations. Clean and quick. Mounting an assault on an orbital platform, now that's messy."

While Jacob wondered what an orbital platform was, the elevator doors whisked open and they ducked inside. Xander pressed for the seventy-sixth floor, and the elevator began its ascent with a jolt. The compartment was dimly lit; the illuminated digits above the doorway, which flashed in succession

158

with the increasing pace of the elevator, cast as much light as the bulb in the ceiling. After a moment, Jacob could feel the compartment slow and then come to an abrupt stop.

"We're here already?" he asked Xander.

"No. We're only at twenty-five—someone else is getting on."

Jacob held his breath as the doors opened. A young man in some kind of white-and-green uniform entered the elevator pushing a cart loaded with covered dishes. A delicious aroma wafted from the tray, and a green bottle stood amid the platters. Jacob and Xander moved back to accommodate the passenger. He pressed for the sixty-ninth floor and the compartment resumed its ascent.

"Didn't expect any company," the man said. His hair was brushed low, almost covering his eyes, and he leaned forward, peering through blond strands and dim lighting to inspect the two passengers.

"Pardon?" Xander asked, as if he hadn't been paying any attention.

"This is the service elevator, that's all. The main elevators are more comfortable."

Xander ignored the statement. "Making a delivery?" he asked, lifting one of the platter covers.

"Dinner party in Suite 696. The usual. You work here too?"

"Something like that. Mixel pays the bills."

"Right. Barely, though. So what do you do?"

"You ask a lot of questions for a drone with a cart," Xander said, frowning. Jacob watched Xander step toward the man, reaching for his breast pocket where the pistol was hidden. An image of one of Turner's friends dropping on the sand at the lake flashed through Jacob's mind, followed by another of the young waiter writhing in pain on the elevator floor.

"Take it easy on him, Marshall," he said, reaching over to stay Xander's arm. "Forgive my bodyguard—he's protective. Sometimes too protective. Right, Marshall?"

Xander, looking at Jacob, smiled briefly, then turned back to the young man. "That's right—I am. It's my job, just like delivering food is yours. And when you've got the CEO's nephew to guard, you take no chances, including the main elevators. Up against the wall, please, with your arms spread wide."

The young man looked at Jacob and his jaw dropped. Then, looking at Xander, who now stood over him, he smiled and faced the wall.

"Sorry, I had no idea. Do whatever you have to do. I wasn't trying to make trouble."

"Don't worry about it," Xander reassured, patting him down. "We won't mention it if you won't."

Jacob noticed Xander slip something into his back pocket as he stepped away from the worker. A second later the elevator came to a stop and the doors opened. The young man whisked the cart into the hallway, eager to escape. When the doors had closed again, Jacob breathed a sigh of relief and Xander chuckled.

"Not bad, Blinder. You're a good little liar."

"I guess I am," Jacob said, trying to laugh.

"It occurred to me that he'd have a room service key. It'd come in handy on our trip upstairs. I was going to stun the kid, but your idea accomplished the same thing." He held up a silver card and grinned. Then his smile faded. "Jacob, are you okay?"

Jacob barely heard Xander as his image wavered, doubled, rejoined, and then stretched into the distance. Suddenly, he couldn't tell if Xander was dropping away or if he was the one falling.

A moment later, he came to. Xander had him propped up against the elevator wall. He could hear the man calling his name, could feel him shaking him.

"What happened?" Jacob asked.

"You tell me. You just passed out."

"I'm all right," Jacob said, struggling to his feet.

"Like hell you are. You're burning up with fever. How long have you been sick?"

"Since morning," he whispered.

Xander shook his head. "We should get out of here."

"No!" Jacob cried. He gripped Xander's arm. "We're so close. We're practically there. Trust me, I'm all right. I'm feeling better." It was partly true. The wave had passed. The ground felt solid once more. But Jacob still felt as if he were burning up. Most of all, he just wanted to lie down, curl up in a ball, and go to sleep.

A tone rang out. Xander glanced up at the lit number above the door and shook his head. The door opened and they entered the hall. It was empty. Everything was quiet.

"Guess the cloakers work," Xander said. "No welcoming committee. I'm almost disappointed."

"I'm not," Jacob said. "Come on, her room's this way."

They hurried down the hall and found her suite. Xander inserted the service key into the slot and the door whisked open. Jacob staggered by him.

"Delaney!" he cried as he rounded the corner into the suite.

The room was empty. At first, Jacob thought Delaney was just out. He'd almost expected it. But looking around the suite, he realized something was wrong.

"Her piano's gone," Jacob said, as Xander made a quick sweep of the rooms.

"The closets are empty," Xander said, returning from the bedroom. "Looks like she's been moved." He sighed and looked grimly at Jacob. "I don't know what to tell you," he said flopping onto the couch. "We could try searching some other rooms, but she could be anywhere in this place, if she's still here at all. We may be invisible to the sensors, but not to people. It'd only be a matter of time before we were caught. I'm sorry, Jacob."

In spite of how he felt, Jacob managed to smile.

"Don't be," he said. He pulled the finder from his jacket pocket, pressed the button, and spoke into it.

"Delaney Corrow."

Immediately, a beep sounded, a quick, steady pulse. He turned toward the hall outside and the sound rose in tempo and pitch.

"It's homing in on her sounder," Jacob explained. "You know, her silver pin?"

"But she doesn't have it anymore. She gave it to me, remember?"

"I returned it to her," Jacob explained. "After the concert. I thought she might want it back."

"Smart, Blinder. Very smart." Xander laughed. "After you, then." He gestured toward the door and Jacob took the lead.

They followed the finder's pulse down the corridor. A minute later it brought them to another suite on the other side of the hall. Once again, Xander inserted the service key, and the door hushed open. This time, though, Jacob didn't rush in. He paused before the door and hesitated. *Please be there*, he thought. He took a deep breath and entered.

Once again, the suite was empty. The piano was there—occupying the same spot as in the other apartment—as were her clothes in the bedroom. But Delaney was gone. The finder's pulse was almost a steady stream now. Jacob turned it off, noticing her sounder gleaming on the edge of the piano.

"She'll be back soon," Jacob said. "I know it."

"Let's hope so," Xander said. He pulled his cloaker out and examined it. The glowing ring that circled the capsule was partially dark now. "This thing's running out. Won't be long before it's drained and their sensors pick us up."

Jacob nodded and went to the window. He leaned against the sill and pressed his forehead to the pane. The glass was cool, a welcome relief against his skin. He tried to fight back the fatigue, the aching now settling into his bones, the feeling that his whole body was shutting down.

He gazed out the window to where the dying glow of sunset brooded on the horizon, enough to illuminate the sea stretching toward it. The water sparkled, just like Delaney had said.

"She wanted to be on this side," he murmured. "She wanted to be able to look out at the sea."

"Guess she got her wish," Xander said, coming to the window as the last light faded.

"I just can't believe it," the handler's voice barked as the door opened an hour later. Peering through the screen of the closet door behind which he and Xander were hiding, Jacob watched as Delaney marched into the room with LaPerle at her heels. "I mean, twice in three days? I thought we worked this out yesterday."

"I told you, I'm not feeling well. I have a terrible headache."

"I hope that's true for your sake. The whole episode was a total embarrassment; even worse than last time. You were absolutely terrible."

"Thanks," she said, throwing her sequined purse aside, groping for the couch. Finding the edge of it, she turned and collapsed into the cushions. "I'm not a machine, Jack. You can't expect me to be on at every show."

"I realize that," he replied through clenched teeth, standing over her with folded arms. "But to stop in mid-performance, right in the middle of a bloody song, and walk out like the night before? Very unprofessional. I can only do so much damage control. Your sales actually got a boost after the first fiasco, but keep this up and before long it'll be over. You'll be finished."

"I don't care," she shouted.

LaPerle crouched down in front her and placed his hands on her knees. "Don't talk that way. Does this have to do with your little friend's visit? Are you punishing me for not letting him stay the other night?"

"No, I've had a headache all day," she said, pushing his hands aside. "I haven't felt right for a few days now."

"Is it your eyes?" he demanded. She remained silent. "Well, we've scheduled an examination for tomorrow. In the meantime, think about your responsibility to us. Think carefully."

"You sound like my father," she snapped.

"I'm not your father, Delaney, but I do care about you."

164

He donned his smoothest tone of voice and caressed her cheek; she brushed his hand away. Listening to LaPerle's voice, Jacob shivered. Delaney was right. He *did* sound like the high councilor.

"Go away, Jack," she said. "I want to be alone."

He rose slowly and stared down at her bowed head. "Fine," he said after a moment. "I have to go back upstairs and smooth things over anyway."

Jacob watched LaPerle turn and storm out. A moment later the door hissed shut. Through the screen, he could see Delaney fall back against the sofa and press her hands to her eyes. He looked up at Xander, who only nodded in Delaney's direction and nudged him. He opened the door and stepped toward her, uncertain of his words, reluctant to disturb her. Before he could speak, she heard his footfalls and jerked her head in his direction. She gave a startled gasp and recoiled to the far end of the couch.

"Who are you?" she cried.

"Delaney, it's me," Jacob said, freezing in his tracks. "Can't you see me?"

He held up his hands as she craned forward, as if probing a distant speck. Her face relaxed at the sound of his voice, though not completely. Something was different about her from the other night, and as he returned her gaze, he suddenly realized what it was. Her eyes—they glowed, but less intensely than before.

"Jacob! Yes, I can see you now. So you decided to come back?" She smiled and beckoned him to sit beside her. "Is Xander with you?"

"Right here," Xander said, stepping out of the closet. While Jacob sat down, Xander crossed the room, going to the

165

door to listen before settling into a chair next to them.

Jacob was about to ask her about the dimming in her eyes when she took his hand.

"I'm glad you came back, Jacob," she said. "You'll stay with me now, won't you."

"I didn't come here to stay, Delaney." He glanced over at Xander and paused. "We've come to get you out of here," he said, turning back.

She didn't reply at first. Her eyes, unchanging, unexpressive, conveyed nothing; they merely smoldered. But her smile faded. For the second time, she buried her face in her hands. Xander shook his head and, rising from his chair, went to check the door again.

"Leave?" she said, raising her head, "And go where? What good would it do? First Harmony, now Melville."

"It doesn't matter. We can worry about it later. You just seem so unhappy here."

"Why is that?" she asked. He couldn't tell if she was asking him or asking herself. Her eyes suddenly crackled, blazed bright, and then dimmed lower than before. The corners of her mouth tightened as the flickering pattern repeated itself several times.

"Delaney, your eyes!" Jacob cried, grabbing her arm. She rose from the couch and walked to the mirror with slow, deliberate steps. Jacob followed. Standing behind her, he saw her reflection in the mirror. With a dark frown, she leaned in closer until her quick breaths left moments of vapor on the surface of the glass, and her fingers probed around the metallic edges of the orbs. There was no mistaking it—the earlier glow had withdrawn, replaced by a dimness that reminded him of the dying embers of Xander's fire, their light barely discernible beyond a thin layer of ash.

"It's failing," she whispered. "The vision, all of it. I'm supposed to see the surgeon in the morning, the man who planted them in my sockets when I first arrived. He removed my dead eyes and replaced them with these, but I don't know if I want him to see me." She turned from the mirror and faced both of them. "I loved them at first. They were beautiful. But now . . ."

Before she could say more, the brightness flared again, this time with a greater intensity. She screamed and covered her eyes. Tiny shafts of light shot from between her splayed fingers.

"Delaney!" Jacob shouted and reached out as she started to pitch forward. He caught her arms, made the mistake of looking up just as a voice inside told him not to, told him to let go and look away. But it was too late.

Time stopped. The room went dark, and all Jacob could see was the light shooting out of her eyes. A burning sensation ripped through him. In the distance he could hear himself wondering if it was the fever or the blue streaks of energy rolling off her and licking against his skin that made him feel like he was on fire. Most immediate, though, was the horror of recognition as his nightmare was once again made real.

No, he thought. *I'm dreaming. This isn't real. It's just the dream. I'll wake up and be back at Xander's.* But deep down, as the pain overwhelmed him, he knew it wasn't true.

Still, the last thing he heard before being swallowed up was what he always heard in his dream. A cat's voice, a distant echo of disdain:

Foolish boy, why did you return?

Through the pain, through the light, he could see its

167

golden eyes blinking in indifference.

A sudden blow struck him. He felt a moment of falling and then a thud as he hit the floor. He opened his eyes to see Xander standing over him.

"Sorry about that, Blinder," Xander said, helping Jacob to his feet. "But you were having trouble letting go. Hope I didn't hurt you."

Jacob shuddered, still foggy. "Thanks," he managed to say.

The sight of Delaney moaning on the carpet brought him to his senses. He knelt down beside her, wanting to help but hesitant to touch her again, and looked up at Xander.

"Should we call for help?" he asked.

"We have to do something," Xander replied, pulling his cloaker out. He held it up and shook it a few times. The ring was almost entirely dark. "We've only got a few minutes."

"Don't call the doctor," Delaney broke in, managing to sit up. The burning had faded and she seemed to relax slightly.

"What do you want to do?" Jacob asked, taking her hand.

"I can't stay here," she said. Her voice sounded weak but calm now.

"Fine, then let's go," Xander snapped. "Grab some clothes. I'll check the door. By the way, should we be expecting anyone?"

"I don't know," Delaney said, struggling to sit up. "The last few nights Jack's been sending Karl to check on me. They must be worried about me running away or something."

"Look's like they were right," Xander said.

"All clear." Jacob stepped into the hallway, carrying a small suitcase, and Xander followed with Delaney, who clung to him, taking meager steps. They were heading down the long, curved hallway toward the main elevators when a tone chimed around the corner.

"The elevator," Delaney whispered in a frightened voice. Xander swung her around and headed in the opposite direction toward the service elevator he and Jacob had taken earlier. A moment later, rounding a corner, they reached it. Xander leaned Delaney against the wall.

"Call the elevator, Jacob. I'm going to check things out," Xander ordered. Before Jacob could beg him not to leave, the man had disappeared. Jacob pressed the button and held Delaney's hand, trying to steady himself. He felt worse than ever. He still had a fever, and having been thrust back into his dream hadn't helped. Letting go of her hand, he leaned against the wall.

"Thanks for saving me, Jacob," Delaney said, standing behind him, placing a hand on his shoulder.

"I couldn't leave you here," he said. "I had to do something."

"*I knew you would,*" she whispered in his ear.

Jacob shivered at the words, the ones he'd heard her whisper over and over in his dream the night before last. Now he knew—he had been hearing the future. He gripped the frame of the elevator doors and closed his eyes.

The doors opened as Xander reappeared, and he hurried them into the compartment.

"It was Karl, all right," Xander said as the doors closed, "and he wasn't alone. They might know something's amiss." He paused before pressing the button for the roof.

"What are you doing?" Jacob asked in alarm as the elevator began rising.

"We can't go down. In about three seconds they'll discover

169

she's gone and cordon off the lobby. If we can't go down, we'll go up."

"Won't we be trapped up there?" Jacob asked.

"There are floaters on the roof. I rode in one last week," Delaney offered.

"I was hoping you'd say that," Xander said as the elevator continued to rise.

A moment later it stopped. The doors opened and they stepped onto the roof. A stiff breeze pushed back Jacob's hair and made his eyes tear.

The elevator doors closed, darkening the roof. The air around the edges of the tower was sharply illuminated by the streets below. Aside from that, there was little light. Everything had shut down for the evening. No one was around.

In spite of the haziness riding in on the wave of his fever, Jacob could see a number of floaters parked across the way. They headed toward them, Jacob stumbling ahead as Xander helped Delaney along. After a dozen yards Xander simply swept her into his arms and began running as if she weighed nothing.

It seemed to take forever to cross the roof. Jacob felt as if all the energy was draining out of him with every step, and the wind did nothing to soothe the burning sensation spreading across his skin.

Don't quit, he told himself. *He has Delaney. He can't take care of you.*

Closing his eyes, Jacob forgot the pain, forgot Xander and Delaney, forgot everything and just ran.

He reached the floaters first and jumped into the backseat of the closest one. As Xander came up and placed

Delaney in the passenger seat, a flash of light caught Jacob's eye—the elevator doors were opening.

"Someone's coming!" Jacob cried as Xander jumped into the driver's seat.

"Give me ten seconds," Xander replied, ripping out a panel at his feet. Jacob watched as three men burst from the elevator and spread out, their silhouettes fading as the doors closed. Jacob hunched down in his seat, peering over the edge of the craft, searching for the men.

"What's taking so long?" Delaney cried.

"Have to jump-start it," Xander answered. He sounded relaxed, as if all this were routine. "Don't worry, I know what I'm doing. It's just been a while."

The roof flooded with light. Jacob saw the men as they scanned the area, quickly settling their gaze in his direction.

"They see us! They're coming!" Jacob screamed as the men, banding together, stormed across the roof. He could hear them yelling orders to stop.

The men were thirty yards away when lights began blinking all across the dashboard and along the edges of the doors. A flash shot toward them from one of the men, crackling over Jacob's head; another flash struck the side of the craft, dissipating energy across its frame.

"Hang on!" Xander shouted.

The floater shuddered before jerking forward and rising into the air. Jacob watched the three figures shrink below him as they shot into the sky. Xander banked the floater hard, throwing Jacob against the side of the craft. Both Jacob and Delaney screamed and clung to their seats as the floater plunged over the edge of the roof. *This is it*, Jacob thought as Xander dove the craft down along the side of the tower before jerking it back into the normal flow of hover traffic not far above the streets.

"Sorry," Xander apologized over his shoulder. "It's been a while since I've steered a floater. They're too delicate. I'm used to the cruiser."

Both of them were too terrified to respond as Xander circled around the tower and landed the floater on the street, across from the cruiser. Crowds of people were passing by. Many of them stopped to stare, pointing to Delaney and whispering as the three of them abandoned the floater and crossed the avenue to the waiting cruiser.

They sped through the darkness without speaking, Xander pushing the cruiser nearly full throttle across the plains. Rattling in the backseat, Jacob sat next to Delaney, looking over from time to time at the dim twin sparks glowing in the darkness beside him. He asked her how she was feeling, only to realize she'd fallen asleep. He wanted to sleep too. He wanted to drift off beside her, to give in to the fever that had worked itself into a fury, but a part of him resisted. Through the burning haze, a voice told him that if he gave in, he might never wake again. So instead he stared ahead, leaning forward against the front seat behind Xander, eyes glued to the perimeter of the headlights, the tall grass a blur along the edges of their sphere of driving light. They were moving so quickly it seemed as if they would outrace the sphere of light itself and plunge into darkness.

Sleep won over near the end of their flight. One moment he was watching the path ahead cut through the sea of grass toward a point in the center of the dark and the next he was being wakened by Xander. The vibration had disappeared and the cruiser was parked in the driveway. There were no moons in the sky. The night was peaceful and full of stars.

Xander lifted Delaney from the cruiser, and Jacob followed after. He dropped to the ground and walked toward the house. After a few steps, though, his legs began to wobble. He was sure they were melting, dissolving into the ground, pulling him down in the process. Before he knew it he was on the ground looking up at the stars.

The cold points of light began to spin, to twirl in circles, trace lines across the sky. The stars danced before him, and he knew that all he had to do was reach out his hand and he could touch them. But his hand was lead. It had melded with the earth that now suddenly opened beneath him, falling away and pulling him down with it. The last thing he remembered before slipping into the black was the dancing of the stars. He'd never seen anything more beautiful.

CHAPTER FIFTEEN

The chimes woke him. Jacob could hear them from outside, muffled and distant. He stretched and opened his eyes.

He saw nothing.

He bolted up in bed, gasping, gripping the blankets and pulling them up around him. He waved a hand before his face, but there was no change to the blackness around him. *I'm blind*, he thought. *It's all gone.*

Leaning toward the edge of the bed, he reached out with a fumbling hand. His fingers brushed against a wood surface. He ran his hand up its side, reached a corner, and was struck by a sudden familiarity. Lowering his head, he inhaled deeply. Yes. It was the same old smell, the same earthy dampness. He reached a little farther along the top of the bureau until his hand closed on the textured metal cube. He didn't need to open the music box to know what song it would play, to know he was back in his old room in the underground house.

He swung his legs around and got out of bed, made his way to the door, and headed down the hall, just as he had done countless times.

What am I doing here? I shouldn't be here. The words echoed in his head over and over as he made his way down the hall. Suddenly, he stopped. *But where am I supposed to be?* He couldn't remember.

He went to the front door and threw it open. The brightness of morning hurt his eyes, but a wave of relief washed over him in spite of the pain. He could see. Squinting, he gazed out into the yard and smiled. The flowers were blooming, busy with hummingbirds and insects, and the grass was green and lush. Neighbors drifted by, engaged in conversation. It was like any other morning in Harmony. He closed his eyes and drank in the sounds and smells of home.

This is real. This is my life. He had never left. He had never revealed his secret to anyone. He had considered telling his best friend Egan, but thought better of it. Why spoil a good thing?

As for last night, it was just a dream, one long dream he couldn't remember and didn't want to. He lingered in the doorway, feeling the heat of the sun on his face, sensing its brightness through the red glow of his closed lids.

A pain flashed along his temples. The glow faded, and as he opened his eyes, his smile faded too.

The bright sky had darkened. There were no clouds. Instead, a uniform gray coated the sky. He watched in dismay as the flowers in the dooryard drained of all their color, drooped, then withered into ash. Looking up, he saw the grass shriveling as well. The chimes hanging beside the door began to ring as a breeze picked up, a wind that carried the ashes of petals in a dusty cloud down the street, leaving a stubble of stalks.

Suddenly, it all came back to him—Xander, Delaney, Melville, everything that had happened since escaping Harmony, he could remember it all. He knew where he was supposed to be. But how did he get here? And how would he get back?

He left the house and ran down his street, the echo of chimes fading into the distance. Rushing into the North Tier Square, he made his way toward the fountain at its center. He felt scorched, desiccated. He needed to cleanse himself in the water, cool his body, and drink.

He had nearly reached the fountain when an odor of smoke froze him. It wasn't the smoke of a zephyr tree. It smelled more like the scent that had lingered over the toys he'd found in the basement of Xander's house. He raised his head and sniffed the breeze, trying to make sense of where the smell was coming from.

A flash in the sky caught his attention. He looked up to see a streak of red light hurtle toward earth, slanting in an arc toward the west. A moment later, there was an even brighter flash on the horizon followed by silence. The breeze died.

The quiet was short-lived. A distant boom rolled over the colony. Jacob could feel it in his chest, a wave of pressure to match the sound. Looking up into the western sky that was approaching the color of night, he saw another streak of light and then another. It was as if stars were raining from the sky.

We must be under attack, he thought. *But from whom?*

Another thought struck him as he followed the tracers of light down to the horizon. *That's where Delaney and Xander are.* How will they ever survive this? Suddenly, he was glad he was in Harmony—at least he'd have a chance.

He raced up to the fountain, noticing as he approached that its usual array of sprinklers and streams had ceased. *The power must have died again*, he thought. It had happened many times before. Gazing in, he saw the surface of the water.

Usually an impenetrable ripple of spray, it was now placid and clear.

Jacob reached down to scoop some water, when an image flashed across its surface, staying his hand. He saw Xander and Delaney huddling alone in the house with the bombs falling all around them. He could see his reflection, the shadow of his face, superimposed over their figures.

I should be there, he thought. *I belong with them.* It didn't matter if they all died. He wanted to share a final moment of life with them. How could he have been glad to be in Harmony? He was selfish. He was a Seer.

Jacob reached down and broke the surface with his hand to scatter the image. It shattered like glass, shards falling down into the basin, revealing an empty fountain. He wondered if it had always been that way.

Lifting his head he noticed the smell of smoke was stronger now. He looked around. The air had grown hazy as the sky continued to blacken. He ran to the nearest row of hillhouses, scrambled up the steep side to the top, and gasped.

A wall of flame stretched all the way across the horizon, sending thick, black smoke into the air. And it wasn't staying still. It was closing in, eating up the plain, and he knew it wouldn't be long before it would engulf Harmony, swallow everyone whole.

His heart began pounding. He felt his legs weaken. *You've got to do something,* he told himself. *You've got to warn them.* Taking a deep breath, he stumbled down off the hill and ran toward the central square.

As he ran, he kept a lookout for someone, for anyone, who could help him get the word out. But the streets were empty.

177

They've all left, he thought. *Maybe they found out.* But somehow he didn't think so.

Gasping for air, he hurtled down the last street toward the center of the colony. Already the acrid smoke hanging in the air had set his throat aflame. Through the haze he could make out the shapes of people as he neared the entrance. He dashed through the opening and into the square, pulling back in surprise.

A thousand faces greeted him, blank and indifferent. He had stumbled onto a Gathering. It seemed as if everyone in Harmony had collected in the square and now stood mute, waiting.

He scanned the stage. It was empty. The high councilor was nowhere in sight. He dashed over to the steps and ran up onto the platform. Recalling the last time he'd stood on this spot, it took him a moment to find his voice.

"Everybody," he called out, "you have to leave! There's a fire out there. It's coming straight for Harmony!"

No one replied. The crowd remained still. It was as if they hadn't even heard him.

"You have to believe me!" he shouted, his voice cracking. He could feel the frustration mounting within. "You're all in terrible danger!"

"Blindness is purity. Blindness is unity. Blindness is freedom," the crowd chanted in reply.

"No!" Jacob shouted back. "You're not listening. You have to get out!"

Still, no one moved. Jacob looked around, desperate for something that could make them understand.

"Where's the high councilor?" he asked the crowd. "Shouldn't he be here?" No one replied. The sky grew even darker now as the breeze continued to blow smoke closer. Jacob coughed. He had to find Delaney's father. As much as he feared and despised the man, he at least would know what to do, know how to get the people to move.

He left the stage and raced toward the high councilor's house, an aboveground concrete bunker not far away. He bounded up the steps and began banging on the door, not stopping until it finally opened and Martin Corrow stood before him.

"Fire's coming," he gasped. "Got to get everyone out."

"Jacob?" the high councilor replied. "What are you doing here? I told you when you left that you could never return."

"Who cares about that now?" Jacob cried. "Didn't you hear me? You've got to do something. Everything's going to burn!"

"I don't detect any fire." Delaney's father sniffed the air. "This is just another lie of a Seer."

"What? You can smell the smoke, can't you?" Jacob shouted. He turned and looked west. The wall of fire was closer now, casting a glow under the black sky. "And you can see it," he said, turning back. "Don't lie to me. You can see it! I know you can."

The councilor's face darkened. At last, he nodded. "You're right, Jacob. There is a fire. But it's not coming for us. It's coming for you. You're the one in danger. You came here to hide, but it found you."

"How can that be?" Jacob replied. He was so confused. It didn't make any sense, but somehow he felt that the man was right. He glanced back at the flames. "So what do I do?" he asked.

"We'll ask the ghostbox," Martin Corrow intoned. "It

knows everything. It will tell us what you need to do."

He strode past Jacob down the steps. Jacob followed. They hurried through the streets toward the bunker that housed the ghostbox. Before long, they'd reached the edge of the colony. From here, a stone path stretched toward the squat structure, a dark island amid the grass. Delaney's father started down the path and the two of them made their way toward the building, with Jacob stealing glances back from time to time. The fire had grown very close—it had to have reached the edge of Harmony by now. The fields must be burned, the harvest lost, and now what would the people eat? Still, looking ahead, Jacob was equally frightened. He remembered the last time he'd journeyed to the ghostbox and had faced that cold machine. Yet here he was, going back, led by the very man who'd brought him before to the room of threats and revelations.

Reaching the bunker, Jacob paused beneath the door as the high councilor waited on the other side of the threshold. Even before he looked up, he knew that he would see it. Sure enough, there the cat lay, stretched across the sill.

"You're always around," Jacob whispered. "Why don't you ever help me?"

I'm just a watcher, it replied. *You know what that's like, don't you?*

"I'm not just a watcher anymore," Jacob said.

That's true. You're changing. And you're about to change even more. Just go inside.

"I'm afraid."

Of course you are, it said. *You should be.*

"How do I know I'll come out?"

You may not. Nothing's been decided yet. It all depends.

180

"On what?"

On how strong you are.

"I don't know if I can fight."

You shouldn't. That's not how you'll get through this.

"What do you mean?"

You'll find out.

With that the cat rolled over on its back and went to sleep. Jacob started as if waking from a trance and looked around. The door before him was open. The high councilor was gone. Glancing up, he noticed the cat was gone too—he was alone. He turned back for a moment, squinting at the flames' brilliance. The fire had made its way through Harmony. He could feel its heat from here, could hear its roar as the flames twisted up into the sky, spewing pillars of smoke. Obscuring the entire colony now, it lingered at the end of the path, as if waiting for him to make the next move. He grappled with the urge to run, to tear off into the plains. But deep down he knew it would do no good. The wall of fire would follow, and he wouldn't be able to run forever. His best chance was to hole up inside and hope to make it through.

He ducked into the bunker. The doors hissed shut behind him, cutting off the roar of the fire. The room was dark except for the ambient glow of computer screens and the constellation of lights shining against the walls. In the center, rising monolithic from the floor was the ghostbox, just as he had last seen it. The yellow monocle centered near the top of the obelisk glowed brighter than the other lights, seeming to shine down on him like a spotlight, intensifying as he approached so that he nearly had to look away.

"Ghostbox," he said, hesitating. He wasn't sure what to say to it. He wasn't even sure it heard him or would answer.

"Speak," a voice said, androgynous in its reverberations.

Jacob gasped. "There is a fire coming," he said at last. "The high councilor said it was coming for me."

"He is correct."

Jacob's heart sank. Through the walls of the bunker he could hear the roar of the fire—it had reached him at last. The room was now growing warmer. He wondered how hot it would get. He gazed up at the eye.

"What can I do?" he asked.

"You can do nothing. You can only give in to it and wait. Let it do its work."

Jacob nodded. Hearing the words, he felt oddly at peace. His eyes remained fixed on the ghostbox's monocle. He couldn't have torn his gaze away if he wanted to. But he didn't want to. He wanted only to stare into the yellow light and forget all else as the walls grew hotter and the heat crept closer, licking against his skin, which now began to drip as sweat trickled down his body.

The roar now faded to a distant echo, and the eye hovering in space began to stretch out and morph. It became Delaney's eye, then his mother's. Now it was the slitted eye of the cat, now the high councilor's eye, winking its knowing wink before changing back once again to the eye of the all-knowing mainframe.

The eye was fading now as the heat reached an unbearable level. As it winked out, plunging the bunker into total darkness, Jacob knew what he had to do. He turned and walked up to the door, feeling the heat radiating from its steel. Sensing his presence, the portal slid open to reveal a world on fire, the flames now at Jacob's feet. The warmth was so intense Jacob could almost feel his body wither and burn. But he didn't wince. Instead he took a deep breath, closed his eyes, and walked into the light. Opening his eyes for a moment he could see the flames dance all around, flicker across his arms and legs, could see himself on fire. In spite of the heat, he felt no pain. He smiled and surrendered to the flames, to the fire that would somehow make him new.

Jacob!

He heard the voice. It was calling from far away, a stranger's voice, rousing him.

It was dark, just like when he'd awoken before. But this time there was no smell of earth, no sheets around him, no mattress underneath. He was floating in a void.

Jacob, look behind you, the voice called again. Like the voice of the ghostbox, it was difficult to pin down. It was a male voice, but was it young or old?

He glanced over his shoulder to see a distant pinpoint of light growing larger by the second. He had nothing to push off from, but somehow he willed himself around, hovering in place as the glowing sphere approached. Soon it loomed before him, and he basked in its light. It drew him in, enveloped him in its warmth. There was a flash as he breached the surface of the sphere and discovered ground beneath his feet. He was standing once more.

This new place was as white as the previous void had been black, with nothing around to give him any sense of perspective. He could be in a small room; he could be surrounded by infinite space. It was impossible to tell. All it was was bright.

He sensed a presence behind him and turned to see a boy standing not five feet away. He was about Jacob's age, perhaps a bit older, with a simple robe like the ones worn in Harmony only made of a rich purple cloth with gold embroidery running down the center. He smiled at Jacob and reached out a hand in greeting. Jacob tried to take it, but his own hand passed through it. He looked closer and realized the figure was shifting in and out, fading slightly then darkening, like the blades of prairie grass tossing in the wind.

"You're not really here," Jacob said.

"No," the boy replied. It was the same voice as before, modulating in pitch, giving the boy an unearthly quality. "Then again," he said, "neither are you. This place isn't real."

"Then where am I?"

"The same place I am—inside of you, inside your mind."

"Are you a part of my mind?" Jacob asked.

"Oh, no," the boy replied. "I'm merely visiting. We just found you. We sensed you were out there, but we didn't know for sure until now. And so they sent me to greet you. And to congratulate you."

"For what?"

"For surviving. You were very sick. That fever almost got you."

"The fire," Jacob said, nodding.

"Yes, the fire. You let it burn you. You stopped fighting it. And so it didn't kill you. Though it did change you."

"I don't feel any different," Jacob replied. "But it's hard to tell. There have been so many changes lately."

"Yes. But they are all tied together. The change I'm referring to started weeks ago, the fever merely accelerated it. In fact, it started the moment you began to see."

"How did you know I was blind?" Jacob asked, startled. He felt powerless. This person seemed to know all about him, but he knew nothing in return.

"Because I was too. All of us were Blinders. We are all children of the Foundation. And like you, we too began to see."

"Then I'm not alone," Jacob murmured, more to himself than to the boy.

"You've never been alone, Jacob. Even now you've got people who love you, who are taking care of you. I can sense them."

"I know," Jacob agreed, thinking about Xander and Delaney. "But I guess I meant alone in the sense of what's happened to me." He paused, gazing more intently at the boy. It seemed as if the stranger's image had blurred ever so slightly. "Did I know you back home?" he asked.

"No. I'm from a different colony. But there are a few from Harmony."

Jacob strained to hear the boy's voice, which was beginning to modulate more severely. His form began to flicker, lose its definition.

"I don't have much time left," the boy said. "I'm talking to you from very far away. From another world."

"There's so much I want to ask you," Jacob whispered.

"There's so much to tell. Gaining your vision, Jacob, was just the first step, the first change of many. Your sense of sight goes beyond what your eyes can tell you of the moment. You've had glimpses of the future already."

"The vivid dreams I've been having since I left Harmony," Jacob said. "Parts of them have come true."

"Yes," the boy said, his face now a blur. "Your first taste of what's to come. Primitive steps, but steps nonetheless."

"What comes next?" Jacob asked, the hairs rising on the back of his neck.

"It depends. It's different for all of us. But I can tell you that you'll find your powers wonderful. And terrible. And strange."

Jacob could barely hear him now. "How will I recognize them?" he shouted at the flickering shadow.

"You'll know," the voice said amid the static. The modulation had grown so severe, the voice no longer seemed human. "But . . . need to learn to . . . them. . . . Want you to come to us. . . . Can show you."

"Where? Tell me where to go!" he demanded, reaching out toward what remained of the visitor.

There was a muffled ripple of sound, but Jacob could no longer make out the words as the last particles of color and shadow dissipated. He looked all around him, bewildered, hoping for a sight of the boy, but the figure was gone for good.

His disappointment was short-lived as the floor beneath him vanished. Once more he was falling, leaving the sphere of light behind, falling back into the black, suddenly too shocked and tired to care where he'd end up.

CHAPTER SIXTEEN

Jacob woke to her singing. At first he thought it was his mother, singing to him the way she always had when he was sick. A moment of panic struck him—he was back, still trapped in the dream. But then he recognized the voice. It was the voice he'd been longing to hear, low and calm, as soothing as the cool, damp cloth that lay across his forehead. For a while he said nothing. He just kept his eyes closed and listened to the song, wishing it didn't have to end.

"Delaney," he said when she finished. His own voice sounded far away and weak.

He opened his eyes and realized he was in his bed, the one Xander had given him. It was morning. The light in the window was dim, but he could see Delaney sitting beside him, could see the smile on her face, and even now her body seemed to sink slightly, relaxing in relief at his awakening.

"What happened?" Jacob asked, removing the cloth from his forehead. He remembered the ride back from Melville, remembered collapsing on the way into the house. He even had the faintest recollection of a long, strange dream— retained whiffs of it like the scent of flowers on a shifting breeze.

"Aurelian Flu. That's what Xander called it. It can be

pretty dangerous, I guess. There isn't any way to treat it. You just have to let it run its course."

"Well, how did I get it?"

"He said you could have gotten it anywhere—it's pretty common in Melville. The spacers bring it in. Most everyone has immunities against it already, so even if they come down with it, it hardly affects them."

"So why did I get it so badly?" he asked.

"I don't think they vaccinated us for it in Harmony. Since we didn't have any contact with the outside world, they probably figured there was no point. When I first came to Mixel, they gave me quite a few shots." She reached out and found his hand, squeezing it so hard he winced. He could hear the tremor in her voice. "For a while there, we didn't think you'd make it."

She leaned forward and kissed his forehead before pressing her cheek against it for a moment. "Fever's gone," she said.

"I feel okay," he replied, sitting up. His head was a little woozy, and he could hear his stomach rumble with hunger, but it felt good to be awake.

Delaney handed him a glass of amber-colored liquid. He took it, sniffed, and recoiled at the odor. It smelled worse than the medicine Xander had given him the day he'd arrived here.

"Xander wanted me to have you drink this when you awoke. It's a restorative. He mixed it himself. He said it would give you back your strength."

"I do feel a little weak," Jacob acknowledged. "Where is Xander, anyway?"

"He's sleeping. I made him go take a nap. He was up all last night."

"So I was sick all night, huh?"

"Actually, Jacob," Delaney said, "you've been unconscious for the last two days."

"What?" Jacob cried, almost spilling the drink.

"Oh, Jacob, I was so scared." Once again, her voice trembled for a moment. Then she collected herself. "Anyway, I'm glad you're back. I missed you."

"I missed you, too," he said. He downed the mixture, shuddering at the taste. Still, almost immediately, a warmth began spreading through his torso and out into his limbs. His head cleared. It was as if his whole body had been disassembled before and was now being drawn back together, stitched whole.

He turned to tell her how he felt when something caught his eye.

"You're blind, aren't you," he said, looking at her eyes. The light in them had died completely, leaving two burned-out stones, dim amid the gold rims.

She lowered her head and nodded, a thin smile crossing her lips.

"Yes," she said. "The last of it faded yesterday. It's all gone now."

The casual air in her voice surprised him—she didn't seem upset. If anything, she seemed relieved. It bothered him. On more than one occasion he had thought about how it would feel to lose his sight, to return to darkness. The thought terrified him.

"We'll take you to a doctor. We'll get them fixed," he said. "Right?"

"I like this place," she said, settling back in her chair. "It feels good to be away from Melville. All those lights. And the

189

noise. It's quiet here, a good place to think. That's what I've been doing, Jacob. Ever since I left that tower I've been sleeping and dreaming, then waking, sitting here with you and thinking. When I dream, all I see are the lights of the city and the faces of the crowds at dinners and parties, and the keys I played on every night. It's all I ever saw. My view of the world was confined to one place and one time, and now it fills my dreams. When I woke up this morning, I heard the birds outside, the day birds. They're the same ones we have in Harmony. I woke and it was dark, but I wasn't scared. I simply rested and thought and then decided."

"What did you decide?" he asked. But he didn't want her to answer. A dark feeling swept over him. Somehow he knew he wasn't going to like what she was about to say.

"I'm going back to Harmony."

"*What?*" he cried, bolting forward. He had been half expecting her to say she was returning to Mixel. Why would anyone ever want to go back to Harmony, Delaney especially? And after everything that happened . . . what made her think she even *could* go back?

"Just hear me out, Jacob," she said. She paused for a moment before speaking. "I thought that once I left Harmony and joined the world of the Seers, life would be different. Everything would be better. I'd be free to start over. But it wasn't any better; maybe it was worse. I was just as much a prisoner, in spite of what they gave me. These eyes showed me pretty things, but they weren't enough to overpower all the other things I saw: greed, shallowness, envy, human beings clawing one another in pursuit of power, huge towers built by a company that couldn't care less about anyone, certainly not me. I got to see for myself that everything they told us about the Seers back in Harmony was true."

Jacob sighed. In some ways, she was right. Closing his eyes, he again saw Turner's anger and cruelty, remembered the blows he'd received. He thought back to Coral and her friends on the beach, remembering their boredom, the jaded way they referred to their lives. But he also remembered the kindness they had shown him when, dirty and hungry, he had appeared in their midst. And then there was everything Xander had done for both of them.

"I know you haven't had an easy time, Delaney," Jacob replied, "but that's how the world is. If there's anything I've learned from seeing, that's it. Things were bad for you in Melville, but they're no better in Harmony. Our teachers always told us that Truesight allowed people to avoid the evils of the world, but you can't escape them. They're everywhere; our people just don't want to see them.

"I remember when I was brought before the council and they told me that Truesight was about embracing hardship, about being strengthened by adversity—but that's not life in Harmony. If anything, it's easier to hide behind blindness and simply pretend that because you can't see something, it doesn't exist. It just seems childish, and I don't want to be a child anymore."

"What's wrong with being childish?" she retorted. "After LaPerle and all those other creeps, I wouldn't mind being a child again. I feel so soiled. Look at my eyes, Jacob. I don't care how beautiful they are—they're not real. I feel like a monster with these circuits and wires and pieces of metal grafted into my head. In Harmony, people won't be able to see what I've become. Besides, even if you're right and Harmony is just as bad, then what does it matter whether I'm

191

here or there? At least there I'll be like everyone else. I won't be alone." She spoke with the familiar bitterness Jacob had heard so many times before, but it was strange to hear it emerge in defense of the place that had once been the object of her scorn.

"You're not alone, Delaney," he said. "I'm here, and so is Xander."

"I know," she said, softening. She reached out and touched her fingers to his cheek. "But if I stay here, I'll just be a burden to both of you. Listen, I've been thinking about this for a while, but until you showed up, I never imagined I'd have a chance to go back. I belong there, Jacob. They need me—or maybe I need them. After everything that's happened, I know I can be useful there, serve a purpose."

"But your father told everyone you were dead," Jacob said. "You can't just show up. Not without everyone knowing he lied, and he's never going to let that happen."

"I can't worry about that right now, Jacob. Father can be a harsh man," she admitted, "but I have to believe he loves me enough to find a way to set everything right." She paused. "Don't you ever think about going back?"

Jacob didn't answer. He envisioned his mother's face, smiling on the hill as the breeze swept through her hair, and his father, joking with friends on his way home from the fields.

"I'm not asking you to return with me, Jacob," she said finally when he failed to respond, "but I do need your help. Talk to Xander—he's already helped us. I'm sure he'll do it again. Talk to him. Please?"

"Why don't you ask him? You're the one who wants to go back."

"You know him better. You know the right way to ask him. I can tell how much he cares about you. He'll listen to you."

"No, I can't do it. It's crazy." He had to talk her out of it, but he needed time to think of the right words to say. For now he had to stall. "You just got out of Melville, Delaney," he said. "Give yourself some time before you make up your mind for sure, a few days at least. If you still want to go, then I'll talk to Xander. I promise."

She hesitated. "All right," she said finally.

Jacob breathed a sigh of relief and settled back into his bed. They were quiet for a moment.

"I'm hungry," he said at last.

"Xander will be up soon—he never seems to sleep long. He'll make us breakfast."

"Hope he wasn't too hard on you," Jacob joked. "He can be a bit gruff at first."

"No one's been as kind to me since I left Harmony as he has these last few days. He's a good man, Jacob. We're lucky."

"We are," he agreed.

"Grab that piece over there, will you Jacob?" Xander said, pointing.

Jacob walked over to the massive branch and grabbed on, grateful for the gloves Xander had given him to protect his hands from the sharp, rough bark. The wood was heavy, but he was still able to drag it over to the edge of the trees and lay it on the pile.

"Don't push yourself too hard, Blinder. It's only been a couple days since you came back to life. Take a break if you're tired."

"I'm feeling okay," Jacob replied, but he took his gloves

193

off anyway and sat down on the dry leaves for a rest. "That horrible drink you made me did the trick."

"Old family recipe," Xander said, laughing. "I know—it tastes bad, doesn't it?"

The shadows darkened slightly in the zephyr grove. Looking up through the branches, Jacob could see the purple clouds that had moved in over the last half hour, ushered in by a rising wind.

Earlier in the afternoon, Jacob had pestered Xander to take him for a ride. He needed to get out of that bed, that room, that house where he'd been sequestered for the last several days. As happy as he was to see Delaney again, to finally be with her at last, the awful request she'd made on his awakening—and the strange calm that had followed her ever since—had put a cloud over their time together. He had hoped that a ride on the plains might clear his head, give him a sense of how to deal with Delaney's new yearning.

Then there was the matter of the dream. The recurring nightmare that had plagued him ever since leaving Harmony finally seemed to have gone away, but there was the echo of another dream still with him, the fever-induced vision he'd experienced while unconscious in his sickbed. It lingered at the edges of his memory, palpable yet just out of reach. He wished he could recollect it—a voice inside told him it had been important, vital even.

Too many worries, too many cares, he thought. Delaney was back—wasn't it supposed to be easy now?

"How's your friend?" Xander asked, leaning against a tree across from Jacob and also taking off his gloves. They had enough wood now to fill the bed of the cruiser parked just at the edge of the grove.

"She still seems pretty tired," Jacob replied, looking away through the trees.

"She's been through a lot," Xander offered, "but she'll feel better when she's rested. You were the same way when you first got here."

"I was?" Jacob asked. He had trouble remembering. It seemed so long ago, though in reality it had been only a few weeks. "I guess I was."

"Damn straight. You've come a long way, Blinder. And I've been meaning to tell you—you did a good job back there in Melville. You kept your cool and helped your friend. Not everyone holds up under that kind of pressure."

"It wasn't that hard," Jacob said.

"No, but it wasn't that easy, either. You've got guts. Crossing the plain alone—that was hard. Hell, leaving Harmony in the first place, breaking free and leaving behind the only life you'd ever known, that was the hardest part of all."

"I don't know if I had much choice," Jacob countered.

"Sure you did. You could have submitted to the surgery and gone back to what you'd always known. Or you could have kept quiet about your sight in the first place. You could have spent the rest of your life in Harmony, living with an advantage over everyone."

"But keeping the secret, staying, even with an advantage—or maybe because of it—would have been much harder than leaving. When I told them, I took the easy way out."

"Seems like a difficult choice to me."

"It didn't *feel* difficult."

"Maybe that's because you knew you had more to lose by staying. Either way you would have lost something. Listen,

195

Blinder, it's not what you choose, it's *that* you choose. Choice is difficult, Jacob. What if you make the wrong one? What if you make a mistake? Not having choice, letting other people choose for you, is easy. That's why places like Harmony exist."

So what do you do if you think someone you love is making the wrong choice? "I just hope Delaney will be okay," Jacob said.

"Me too," Xander replied. "They'll figure out pretty soon what happened to her, if they haven't guessed already."

"What do you mean?"

"Mixel. They may come after us. I'd be surprised if they didn't."

Jacob's heart sank. The possibility that Mixel might come looking for Delaney hadn't even occurred to him, but now it seemed so obvious. In fact, thinking of the power contained in that black tower rushing down upon them made all of his other concerns seem suddenly trivial.

"What'll we do if they come?" Jacob asked.

"Don't worry about it. After twenty years in the muck, I know how to handle a few suits."

Jacob nodded. That was the thing he loved most about Xander—he could say things like that, and Jacob believed him.

Jacob was about to tell him so when he stiffened. A web of lightning rose within his skull, firing along the surface of his brain and down into his eyes. It was a familiar sensation— the same one he'd felt at the first awakenings of his sight well over a month ago.

The realization was short-lived as his vision blurred, then went dark. But before he even had time to be afraid, the light returned. Once again, Xander was sitting before him talking, but Jacob couldn't hear what he was saying; all he could do was marvel at how different the world around him suddenly appeared. It was as if all the colors had been drained from everything around him but for one: a monochromatic blue tinge. He tried asking Xander if he saw the same thing, but a sudden blast of wind drowned out his voice. There was a loud crack. Jacob started as an enormous limb fell from above, catching Xander across the head, knocking him to the ground and covering him with leaves. Jacob sprang forward screaming, trying to pull the limb off, but it was too late. He knew it was too late. . . .

"Sounds like a storm is coming in."

Xander's voice snapped Jacob back to the moment. He gasped and looked around. The world looked normal once again. There was a distant rumble of thunder. The sound made him shiver. He closed his eyes and tried to drive the strange, sudden image from his head.

"Suppose we could stay here," Xander said, glancing around the grove. "Enough leaves overhead to keep us dry. Probably only a passing shower anyway."

"No," Jacob said, trying to hide the urgency in his voice. A sudden impulse to get out of the grove seized him. He jumped up. "Let's load up the cruiser," he said. "I want to get back to Delaney. Come on, let's go!"

"All right. Take it easy, Jacob," Xander said, getting up. "We're not in that big of a hurry."

"Yes we are," Jacob said, grabbing Xander's arm and pulling. He didn't know what to make of the strange image that had gripped him, or the dread that had followed it. It was like his dreams, only this time he'd been awake. It didn't make sense.

"What the hell's gotten into you?" Xander snapped, breaking Jacob's grasp.

"I saw something," Jacob said. "A moment ago. There was wind and a branch fell and you got hurt. Really hurt."

Xander smiled and shook his head. "Oh, come on, Jacob. You need to relax. First with the dreams and now this?"

"Can we just go? Please, Xander," Jacob pleaded.

Xander sighed. "Fine. We've got enough wood anyway."

They walked out from under the trees and began pitching dead wood into the cruiser's bed.

They'd only been loading for five minutes, the thunder rolling louder from the darkening sky, when a burst of wind swept over them from the plain, followed by a crash so loud they both jumped. A moment later, the gust had faded. Jacob didn't need to look back to know what he would see. He'd already seen it.

From the edge of the grove, Xander gave a low whistle. Jacob walked over and stood beside him. Sure enough, the ground where they'd been sitting was littered with branches and leaves from the fallen limbs. It looked as if half the tree had snapped off.

Jacob glanced up to see Xander watching him with a strange, intense look. Jacob could tell he wanted to ask him about what had just happened, but the man said nothing. Perhaps he could see the look of confusion on Jacob's face, or maybe he was too shocked to speak. Either way, Jacob was glad Xander didn't ask—he didn't know what to tell him. Even now something was rising, an image in the back of his mind of a boy, someone he'd never seen before, but someone who seemed to understand him better than anybody.

They finished filling up the truck just as the rain started.

Riding back, staring out at the blurred world through the rain-coated windows, Jacob sank further and further into his seat as the fever-dream came back to him, piece by piece. Soon, he could remember it all. The strange boy's words were still echoing in his mind as they pulled into the driveway. Now, everything made sense.

CHAPTER SEVENTEEN

Two days passed. Both Jacob and Delaney continued to recover their strength, going for short walks in the fields near Xander's house or resting in the shade of the zephyr trees that filled their small valley. This evening was no exception as they climbed the hill behind the house after dinner to catch the evening breeze and listen to the birds. Reaching the top, Jacob turned to watch Xander and Delaney follow behind. Delaney was laughing—probably at some joke of Xander's, who walked beside her, guiding her by the arm. Jacob suddenly realized how good it was to hear her laugh—it was a sound he hadn't heard in a long time, even before she'd left Harmony.

Jacob dropped the rolled-up blanket he carried in the grass and plopped down on it to rest. More than anything, he wished things could stay just the way they were. Delaney had made no more mention of her desire to return to Harmony. For his part, Jacob didn't mention it either. *Maybe she's changed her mind*, he kept telling himself. Deep down, though, he knew it was only a matter of time before she would ask him again.

He was conflicted about the whole matter. He knew that it was a mistake for her to go back, but after what Xander had said about the importance of choice, he was no longer sure it would be right for him to try to stop her. A part of him wondered if any attempt to keep her here would simply be selfish on his part. After everything that had happened, he didn't want to lose her again. But, if you really loved someone, didn't you have a responsibility to keep them from making a bad decision?

The decision was made more complicated by another matter: Delaney's father. Ever since she'd expressed a yearning to go home, Jacob had been struggling over whether to tell her what he suspected about the man. The image of the high councilor winking at him in the murky light of the ghost-box chamber in those last few seconds before he'd fled kept rising before him. Shouldn't she know the truth about her father? But what was the truth? He still wasn't entirely sure. The whole thing might have been the mistake of his frightened mind. Telling her he suspected that her father could see, whether it was true or not, would change everything for her if she went back. It could even put her in danger.

Something else had begun to gnaw at the edges of his mind. He had been so intent on getting Delaney back, and had settled so quickly afterward into life with the three of them together, he'd forgotten for the moment about his own future. Even if it was, in Jacob's mind, backward, Delaney at least had an idea of where her life should go. And what about him? With Delaney gone, would he stay here with Xander forever? Even if she didn't go back, would the three of them always be together? He kept going back to the dream, to the words of that strange boy that had seemed to promise so much. He just didn't know what to make of it all.

Jacob had had no more visions since the grove and was

wondering when the next would come or if any would come at all. He'd related the vision in greater detail—along with the dream of the boy in the purple robe—to Xander and Delaney, hoping they could provide some degree of insight. Both listened with care and amazement but had little to offer in the way of understanding. The whole experience brought him back to the time when his sight had first begun to emerge: the confusion, the uncertainty, the excitement—it was all too familiar.

But all of these concerns paled against his fear of Mixel's arrival. A knot formed in his stomach every time he imagined the face of LaPerle with that plastered-on grin. It had been five days since he and Xander had infiltrated the tower and taken her away. At first, Jacob thought he would be relieved as more time went by and no one showed, but it only made him more anxious as the inevitable moment drew closer.

Xander and Delaney had now reached the top of the hill. Xander helped Jacob spread out the blanket and the three of them sat down. To the west, Jacob could make out the Melville skyline on the horizon. It looked small and contained, and all of a sudden, Mixel seemed far away. To the east, Duna—the colossal moon that wasn't really a moon—was rising visibly, its rings glittering as they caught the light of the setting sun. The breeze was cool and carried the mild scent of the prairie flowers that had recently had their second bloom. Jacob had a sudden flashback to his last birthday, when he'd shared a picnic with his parents on the grassy roof of their home. It was the first day he'd seen clearly and had been amazed watching the faces of his mother and father, seeing how their expressions had corresponded with the tone of their voices to enhance, or in some cases belie, the meaning of their words. It was then he had realized how seeing made the world a more complicated place.

"It's nice here," Xander said. "I've never really bothered to come up before."

"I missed this smell—and the song of those birds—back in the city," Delaney said.

"Let's just stay up here forever," Jacob murmured. "Keep things just the way they are." He said it as a joke, but all of them felt the truth in it.

"Everything changes, Jacob," Xander replied. "Nothing stays the same."

Jacob looked over at Delaney, who bowed her head slightly. Her smile faded.

He reached out to take her hand when the sky seemed to darken for a moment and the grass drained of all its color. This time he was more prepared as once again a flash of painful light ripped through his head and into his eyes. His surroundings disappeared and now he saw a silver craft settling down into the yard before the house. There was another flash, and suddenly he saw LaPerle taking Delaney by the arm. She was calling to Jacob, trying to pull away as Karl, his face bloody, stood over Xander, who lay in the dust nearby beside another man.

An instant later, it was over and Jacob was back with Delaney and Xander on the hilltop. They were talking and hadn't seemed to notice him. Gasping, Jacob wondered how long he had been gone. There was one thing, though, he didn't wonder about.

"They're coming," he said.

Xander and Delaney paused and looked over at him.

"What do you mean?" Delaney asked.

Before he could reply, a hum crept over the whisper of grass and evening bird songs. They all turned in the direction of the noise and saw the speck on the horizon grow larger as it approached from the direction of the city.

"Good ears, Blinder," Xander said, both of them shading their eyes to see the silhouette that had grown from a black speck to the gleaming oval of a floater. "Just when I thought they might have let it go."

"I didn't just hear it," Jacob said.

"Another vision?"

Jacob nodded. "We can't go down there."

"What do you suggest we do?"

Jacob looked around. "Can't we run away?" he asked.

"And go where? You can't always run, Jacob."

"I don't want you to get hurt," Jacob said.

Xander smiled. "I refuse to worry about what might happen. I'll leave that to you. Besides, they can't hurt me anymore."

He went to Delaney and helped her to her feet, keeping hold of her hand. Jacob joined them and took her other hand. She was trembling slightly as the hum grew louder. Jacob squeezed her hand reassuringly, and a brief smile flickered across her face. Comforting her was the only thing that alleviated his own fear.

The floater glided down and landed in the driveway near Xander's cruiser. From the hilltop Jacob could see that Karl steered the craft, his massive bulk filling the driver's seat. LaPerle and another man even larger than Karl were seated in the back. The three got out and lingered in the yard, waiting.

"Guess we better go see what they want," Xander joked. Delaney gave a nervous laugh. Jacob wished he could laugh also, but his stomach was too tied up in knots.

The three of them took their time going down the hill, catching the last rays of the sun before it slipped down over the horizon as they came from behind the house and into the yard.

"Nice little place you have here," LaPerle called out as the three approached, coming up to stand beside the cruiser. Xander said nothing. He simply leaned against the cruiser with his arms folded.

"I get it—the strong-silent-type routine. Is that what she's looking for?" LaPerle sneered.

Xander ignored the question. "What took you so long?" he asked instead.

"Business, the usual. Besides, I figured she'd return on her own. After all, look around—not quite the luxury we've provided. Look, I don't want to spend any more time out here in the bush than I have to, so let her go and we'll be on our way."

"Unlike you, I'm not keeping her here. She just doesn't want to go back."

"Doesn't she? That's for her to say."

"He's right, Jack," Delaney said, stepping forward. "I'm not going back."

"It's not that simple, Delaney," LaPerle stated. "We've invested a considerable sum in you. You owe us."

"I'm not an investment. Besides, the eyes don't even work. They've caused me more pain than they're worth."

"Blind again? I told you before—implants can be tricky. If you'd allowed the surgeon to make the right adjustments, you'd be fine right now. Delaney, we can make this work. Stop being ungrateful."

"Don't worry, I'm plenty grateful for everything these eyes have shown me," she said.

LaPerle either didn't understand the sarcasm or chose to ignore it. "Then start acting like it. Besides, think of all your fans. Think of what you're doing to them. They miss you, Delaney. Your last couple screwups haven't hurt you. Believe it or not, it's made you more popular than ever. We're getting inquiries from all over the Rim. People want to know the truth behind the mystery."

"Well, I'm going to have to disappoint them," she replied. "I don't care about any of that. I thought I would at first, but I don't. All I can think about is what I've done to myself. And I don't like it. I don't want that life. I'm sorry."

"What's this guy filled your head with, anyway? Whatever he's offering you, I can offer you far more. You know that."

"You just don't get it. It isn't what's offered, Jack, it's what's demanded, and he hasn't demanded anything. He's the *only* one who hasn't."

"All right, enough of this banter," LaPerle said in a bored tone. He turned back and nodded to the giant beside Karl, who stepped up. LaPerle snapped his fingers and gestured toward Delaney.

Jacob darted forward to stand in front of her. Xander continued to lean against the cruiser but stared intently at the man. As he approached, the man fixed his gaze on Xander in return, puzzled at the other's passivity. Xander never wavered as the man drew near, but it didn't matter—one second Xander was leaning, the next he was a blur, springing before anyone could react.

He caught the giant with a chop to the throat, and the

man fell to his knees, gasping with one hand on the ground, the other at his neck. In spite of his terror, Jacob felt an instant of relief to see the man go down. But as Xander closed in to finish him off, the man lashed out, swinging his massive arm in an arc that caught Xander in the face, knocking him backward onto the ground. Jacob watched in horror as Xander struggled to pick himself up. The man loomed over him, as if daring him to rise, too distracted to notice Jacob, who, bending down, scooped a handful of sand from the driveway and threw it in the giant's face. Blinded, the man cried out and retreated, bringing both hands to his face. His stumbling gave Xander enough time to recover and lunge forward. He drove his fist into the man's stomach, following it with a series of blows. With a grunt, the man dropped into the dirt as if he had been struck with a stunner.

Breathing hard, Xander pulled himself erect and straightened his shirt. Blood ran out of the corner of his mouth. LaPerle, not moving from his original position, just sighed and, looking down at the man, shook his head in disgust.

"Very nice, Mr. Payne," he said to Xander, "but like I told you once before—don't think you can bite the hand that feeds you any more than our young lady friend here can. I don't care what you've done for us or what you've gone through in the process; if you don't step aside, we'll cut you off completely. No more pension, your land rights will be revoked, and you'll be shipped out to space. How's that for a deal?"

Xander had now caught his breath and was smiling, as if he had been waiting for this threat all along. "You want a deal? Fine, I've got one for you. For over ten years I fought for MixelCorp. That's a long time to do someone's dirty work, and believe me, I did enough of it and saw even more. A long time ago, I realized that it might be smart to keep records of everything I'd done and seen—call them memoirs, if you like. I finished them just last year and sent them somewhere special, somewhere secret, where even Mixel can't find them. So here's my deal: you back off and maybe I won't publish those memoirs after all."

"You're lying," LaPerle said, his eyes narrowing.

"I might be. Investigations, inquiries, fines and bad publicity—those are all ugly words to have to hear just to find out if I'm telling the truth. Look, *Jack*, I may be a mere soldier, but I've spent enough time in the company of suits to know that it all comes down to the bottom line. I don't care how much you've put into this young lady—you and I both know it isn't worth it. Especially to you."

LaPerle didn't respond for a minute. He only stared at Xander, trying to glean any hint of the truth from the man's blank face.

"A ridiculous bluff," he said at last. He turned back to Karl. "Karl, I guess it's up to you to do the honors," he said.

Jacob watched as Karl stepped forward, a dark look on his face. The memory of his vision flashed through his mind. He knew he had to do something fast. He ran forward and stepped in front of Xander.

"Don't, Karl! Please," he shouted. Karl pulled up in surprise and stared down at Jacob, frowning. Everyone was quiet. Jacob realized all eyes were on him.

"You don't want to do this," he continued. "I know you don't. Xander's told me what the two of you went through. Back in Melville you said that it was just business, but you know that's not true. This isn't just business."

Karl's frown deepened as he looked over at Xander, who simply looked back and shrugged. Finally, he shook his head and turned back. While Jacob breathed a sigh of relief, LaPerle gave the passing man a dark look.

"What're you doing?" he snarled.

Karl shrugged his shoulders. "Can't do it," he said. "Kid's right."

"You want to keep your job?"

"Yeah, I do. But not this way. Besides, you should believe Xander about those memoirs—I used to see him writing all the time. We all did."

LaPerle stared at both men for a moment in disbelief. "Isn't anybody loyal these days?" he shouted at last. He turned and kicked the ground, sending up a small dust cloud along with a string of obscenities. By the time he turned back, he had regained his composure.

"Get up, you idiot," he said to the giant, who only now was beginning to pick himself up off the ground. "We're leaving. I have a meeting in an hour."

With another groan, the man rose and, brushing the sand off his suit, limped back to the floater with Karl and LaPerle. The three of them got in. LaPerle never looked at Xander or Jacob as he settled into the floater that had already begun rising off the ground. A minute later it disappeared from view.

Jacob ran over to Xander, who now leaned back against the cruiser, rubbing his jaw and spitting out saliva mixed with blood.

"Are you okay?" he asked.

"I'm fine. Good move back there. You really covered me," Xander said, reaching out and squeezing Jacob's shoulder. Delaney joined them, her hands groping until she found Xander. She felt along his shoulders to his face, drawing her hand away when he winced as she brushed his cheek.

"You're hurt," she observed.

"Just like old times," he joked. "Nothing like a good blow to the head to make you feel alive."

"Xander—" she began before he interrupted.

"Don't thank me. It was worth it just to ruffle his feathers a bit."

"Did you really mean it?" Jacob asked. "Do you really have all that stuff written down?"

Xander shrugged his shoulders and smiled. "Why spoil the surprise?" he quipped.

This time all three of them laughed.

"You'd better get some ice for your face," Delaney said.

"Right," Xander grunted.

He turned and went inside. Jacob turned to follow when Delaney stopped him.

"Jacob," she whispered.

His heart sank hearing the quiet sound of his name, but he turned back to her. She reached for him, and pulled him in close.

"Is he gone?" she asked.

"Yes."

She leaned in, her voice soft but intent. "You have to ask him. Tonight. You promised me you would."

"But it's only been a few days. Can't you wait a couple more before you decide?" he pleaded.

"I'm not going to change my mind, Jacob. You know I won't. And what just happened has given me an even bigger reason to leave. I need to get away from Mixel for good, for your sakes as well as mine. If there's one place they can never touch me, it's Harmony."

"But you don't need to worry about them anymore. You heard what everyone said. You heard what happened. It's over."

"I didn't hear that, Jacob. LaPerle never said it was over, did he?"

Jacob couldn't remember hearing the words. Still, he didn't want to give in.

Delaney sighed. "Maybe it is, maybe it isn't. I don't want to take that chance, Jacob. Trust me, I know what I'm doing."

"No, you don't," he replied, his voice rising. Before he could stop himself, the words rushed out. "You're just doing this because you're desperate, because you don't think you have any other choice. This is just like you, Delaney. Everything has to be taken to the extreme. Back in Harmony it was the same way. I don't think you'll be satisfied no matter what you do. At least if you stay here, you'll make me happy. You'll make Xander happy. Doesn't that matter?"

For a moment, they were both silent. Jacob searched Delaney's face, afraid of what her reaction might be. But to his surprise, she seemed to give no reaction at all.

"I'm sorry, Delaney," he whispered. "I just don't want to lose you again. After everything that's happened."

"You don't want me, Jacob," she said. "I'm broken. An outcast."

"We all are, Delaney. Xander, me, you. None of us fit. That's why we belong together. Why can't you see that?" He winced as soon as he finished saying the words. She reached up to touch her jeweled eyes and gave a flicker of a smile.

"Listen to you," she said. "You sound so grown up. Thinking back to all those afternoons we spent together in Harmony makes me realize how much you've changed. I wish I were as strong as you."

"You are, Delaney."

She shook her head and sighed.

"You might be right, Jacob. All those things you said about me before—they're probably true. But I still feel like I have to try this. It's my decision, after all. Isn't it?"

"Yes," Jacob said. He thought about going home, what it would be like. In some ways, it felt like he already had. An image of his mother, seated at the table with his music box, mourning, rose before his eyes, a memory from one of his earlier dreams.

"I'll talk to Xander," he said at last.

CHAPTER EIGHTEEN

Jacob stepped into the firelight and occupied his customary spot across from Xander, who looked up before returning his gaze to the flames. The man threw a log into the pit and followed the flaring sparks until, having exhausted their own energy, they disappeared.

"How's Delaney holding up?" Xander asked.

"She's all right."

"Hope that scene didn't rattle her too much," the man said, bringing a hand up to touch the swollen side of his face.

"She's scared they'll come back."

Xander shook his head. "I don't think they will. It's over."

"That's what I told her," Jacob said.

For a few minutes, they were silent as Jacob worked up the courage to speak. He'd spent the last hour pondering how to convey Delaney's wish to Xander. And in that time, thinking about his own future, another idea had gathered in his mind. Now, he had his own request to make. He looked up at Xander.

"I had an interesting talk with Delaney earlier," he said, trying to keep his voice from shaking. "She wants to return to Harmony. She wants you to take us back."

Jacob held his breath, wondering how Xander would

respond. The man didn't speak for a moment, but in the dim light Jacob could see his eyes narrow and the creases of his face deepen as he frowned.

"You can't be serious," he said at last. "I know she had a bad experience in Melville, but what makes you think she'll be any better off in Harmony?"

"I don't understand it either, but she's made up her mind."

"Besides, didn't she run away? Why would they take her back?"

"No one knew she left. Her father told people she was dead."

"All the more reason. And you said 'us'—'take *us* back.' Don't tell me you're going with her?"

"I am," Jacob said. "But not to stay," he added as Xander's scowl deepened. "Ever since I began to see, I've been trying to understand my place in the world, who I am. And my dreams and visions have only made the feeling grow stronger. I want to know why all this has happened to me. I want to know what I'm supposed to do. The only place I can think of to start looking is back where it all began. I don't know what my future's going to be, but maybe going back is a good place to find out."

"Oh, really? And what are you going to do? Walk up to Delaney's father and ask him to tell you what he knows?"

"Maybe," Jacob retorted. "I don't know right now, but I'll think of something. Someone there must know the truth. After all, the boy in my dream said there had been others like me from Harmony."

"Go back to move forward?" Xander said, shaking his head. "I don't buy it, Blinder. You have to accept the truth—

they're not going to help you. They don't want anything to do with you, at least not the way you are. You're a Seer to them now and always will be. Even if they had blinded you again, they would've always thought of you that way. And what if they keep you there, throw you to the ghost machine, or whatever you called it? It's dangerous, Jacob."

"I have to try," Jacob replied. "Otherwise I'm just running away, like I did before, only this time for good." He suddenly realized how much he sounded like Delaney. For the first time he felt like he understood her. "Besides, didn't you say back when I first arrived that the problem with Harmony is that they're running away, rejecting the truth of life's pain?"

"That's different," Xander growled.

"I don't know, maybe it is. All I know is that there are others out there like me, and I'm going to find out about them if I can. As for Delaney, she'll never change her mind—she's too strong-willed."

"Maybe that's why she escaped in the first place, or has she forgotten that? Besides, don't forget that you're depending on me to get the two of you there. She sure as hell can't make it herself on foot in her shape, even with your help. Suppose I refuse to take you back? In fact, why should I?"

"Because it's her decision and mine. Remember what you said before about choices—even bad ones."

The fire had burned down and darkness was encroaching. All Jacob could see of Xander now was his glittering eyes. He tried to imagine what those eyes had seen.

"Maybe I'll help you and maybe I won't. We'll have to wait and see. If I do, it won't be for a while."

"That's fine, Xander."

"Don't get too excited. A lot can happen. Despite what

215

you said, she might change her mind. Remember, she's come from a tough place and anything looks good right now, even Harmony. Now that she's blind again, maybe for good, her old life probably looks even better. But in a few days, after things settle down and she becomes stronger, she'll remember her reason for escaping in the first place."

He stood up and kicked some sand onto the coals, darkening the circle.

"Maybe you're right," Jacob said, standing up to join him. But he knew he wasn't.

The next morning, Jacob found himself being shaken awake. He sat up from the sleeping pad and blankets he'd used since giving Delaney his bed and looked out the window of the room they shared. The sky was early gray.

"So did you ask him?" Delaney said, kneeling on the floor beside Jacob.

"What time is it?" Jacob asked, yawning.

"I don't know, but the birds started calling at least a half hour ago. I hardly slept last night. So did you ask him or not?"

"Yes," Jacob replied. "He said he'd think about it."

"But he didn't say no?"

"No." Jacob didn't add what Xander had said about the idea.

She smiled. "Good. That's good. He'll do it, Jacob. I know he will."

"He said that even if he did, it wouldn't be for a while," Jacob warned.

"That's okay. We'll give him time. That's all he needs."

Jacob lay back on the pad and listened to the morning birds outside. "Delaney," he said at last, "have you ever visited the ghostbox?"

After talking to Xander, he'd spent the rest of the night trying to think of who might know about the changes that were happening to him. The only person he could think of to ask was the high councilor, but Jacob didn't see how the man would be willing to tell him anything, nor did Jacob feel like ever facing him again. Maybe one of the other councilors would know something. He thought of tracking down his friend Egan's father, Mr. Spencer, or perhaps Sonya Donato, the councilor from his own neighborhood, but it all seemed too risky. How could he trust any of them?

Then he suddenly remembered a moment from his dream when—with the flames encroaching—he'd hurried to the high councilor's door and asked him for help.

We'll ask the ghostbox, the man had said. *It knows everything. It will tell us what you need to do.*

"Sure," Delaney said. "I used to sneak over there from time to time. It was a nice cool, quiet spot to hide from Father and everyone else."

Jacob was relieved. The bunker that contained the ghostbox was strictly off limits to the citizens of Harmony, but Jacob figured if anyone had broken that rule, it would have been Delaney. "Did you actually talk to it?" he asked.

Delaney nodded. "It was a good listener. It didn't scold or judge. Of course it didn't have too much to offer in the way of advice, but now and then it would surprise me."

"Weren't you worried it would tell your father?" he asked.

"It never seemed to have told him I was even there," she said, shaking her head. "I don't think it really cared. It just did its job and minded its own business."

"Then maybe it doesn't know anything after all," Jacob murmured. He told Delaney about his plan, his hope that

217

maybe he could find out more about what the boy from his dream had told him.

"My father told me once that it was linked to the Foundation's mainframe back on Earth. If there are secrets in Harmony or the Foundation, the ghostbox probably knows them," she said.

"I wonder if it would tell me anything. It must be protected."

"The building is locked. But I know where Father keeps his key. When we go back, I'll get it for you. Once you're inside, you should be okay. I think you just need to know the right questions to ask."

Though her eyes remained two dead stones, Delaney's spirit grew brighter by the day as her strength returned. To Jacob, her decision to go back seemed to be the source of this lightening, which fed his own desire to return, his hope of finding a clue to the nature of his visions.

A week went by. Then another. Another followed that, and still none of them spoke of the return. But it was there, hanging over every meal, over every walk they took together with Jacob and Xander guiding the young woman on either side, over every evening when Xander would read to them from one of his books. It didn't seem to dampen the time they spent in each other's company, at least in Jacob's mind. If anything, it made him cherish it more. Jacob thought the feeling was true for all of them, including Xander, maybe Xander most of all.

He'd told Jacob how much Jacob had changed since first coming to live at the house, but if anyone had changed it was Xander, especially since Delaney's arrival. Jacob noticed how much lighter he seemed in the mornings, how he spoke more often and with less bitterness in his voice. At first, Jacob had been nervous of the man's volatility, the sudden and unpredictable mood swings that would drive Xander out into the plains for long rides in his cruiser. The solitary excursions were rare now. Jacob wondered if all that would change with Delaney's departure. So far, Xander had given no indication of his intent, but Jacob felt it was only a matter of time before he acquiesced to Delaney's request.

Maybe today will be the day, Jacob thought as he floated on his back in the water, staring up at the afternoon sky.

As he had every day for the last several weeks, Jacob had spent the morning learning to read. With Xander's help he'd made quick progress. Already he knew the alphabet and the different sounds its letters made. He could read many basic words. He'd even managed to read by himself most of the first poem Kala had given him at their first meeting—a simple song about a lamb.

To celebrate, after lunch they'd driven out to the same lake where Xander had rescued Jacob weeks ago. It was strange for Jacob to return to the place he'd first made contact with the world beyond his old life. He half expected to see himself still there, a little boy ghost, hungry and ragged, but all signs of his earlier visit had been erased; it was as if no one had ever been there at all. The sands had been blown clean, and the water was clear and striking beneath the sun.

For the first time in his life, Jacob swam. Waist-deep in the warm water, Xander showed him how to float and how to hold his breath, and he taught him a few basic strokes. Delaney waded in too, her blindness causing her to step with slow grace to midthigh. Her dress floated out on all sides as she dipped her fingers in the water.

Though Xander and Delaney soon tired of the water and left to sit on the hillside overlooking the lake, Jacob remained. Again and again he pushed himself over the surface, gliding with his head down, relishing the sensation. After a half dozen times, he dared to open his eyes under water as he floated and marveled at the hazy blue that deepened on the horizon until it was nearly black against the plain of sand below him. The water stung his eyes at first, but he became accustomed to it, and soon the pain was obscured by a wonder of the underwater world in which the pale skin of his hands seemed to acquire a transfigured glow. Bubbles plucked from the surface curled around his fingers, tickling his skin on their return trip.

But he loved floating on his back most of all. It took Xander a good hour to teach him how to spread his arms and legs out, tilt back his head, relax his whole body, and let go. That was the best part. The sensation of floating was wonderful, but forcing himself to calm down, to unclench his whole body, was an even more welcome experience. He hadn't been this at ease since before he'd recovered his sight, maybe never.

Now he closed his eyes, felt the water close over his face until only his nose remained above the surface. The world was quiet underneath. All he could hear was his breathing and—when he went totally still—his heartbeat. He felt his mind spin, roll up into itself, and it seemed as if his body was following along, turning somersaults in the water. It felt like he was drifting away. . . .

Jacob opened his drowsy eyes and gazed in wonder. He was up on the hill overlooking the lake. Before him Delaney and Xander were sitting in the grass. He turned his head slowly, confused by his surroundings.

How did I get here? he wondered. He couldn't remember leaving the lake. He had been in the water. He had been floating. He shielded his eyes and stared down at the lake, down to where he still floated.

There I am, he thought. *How strange.* Somehow he thought that this new aspect of his emerging sense of sight should bother him—to be detached, to be two places at once—but it didn't. Perhaps it was due to the drowsy lull that hung about his head, the feeling of relaxation that seemed so alien in its comfort. Or perhaps it was because it just felt right being here, together with the two people who accepted him for who he was. He flopped down in the grass behind the couple. They didn't turn to say hello or even seem to notice him—he was invisible. They just continued their conversation. He lay back in the sun on his side, watched, and listened.

"I don't think he'll ever stop," Xander said to Delaney.

"What's he doing now?" she asked, and Xander shaded his eyes, looking below at the boy in the water.

"Oh, he's just playing around, floating on his back."

"I'm glad he's having fun," she said. "He is still a boy, after all, despite what's happened."

Delaney lay back against the hillside. Like her dress in the water earlier, her long black hair fanned out on all sides, and for a moment it looked as if she, too, were floating.

"I can feel the sun on my face," she said, "and the wind bringing the scent of those trees up the hill from along the water's edge. What did you call them?"

"Zephyr trees."

"Right. We don't have them in Harmony. We should." She smiled. "Tell me what you see," she said.

"I don't need to. You've already described it. Besides, that's what poets do. I'm no poet."

A hawk flew over them from the ridge, its shadow flickering across Jacob's eyes for a brief second as it soared away from them, maintaining an almost even plane with their position on the hill before diving and gliding across the water and into the darkness of the trees on the opposite side.

"Jacob told me what happened to your family," she said after a moment. "I'm sorry. Our suffering is nothing next to yours."

"Everyone's suffering is different, but pain is pain," Xander said. "We all deal with it in our own way, don't we? Even if it doesn't always make sense."

"Yes," Delaney said, pausing. "I want to thank you for everything you've done for Jacob and me. With the others, there was always an expectation, a price. You've asked for nothing in return."

Jacob watched Xander gaze down at her for a moment, at the lines of gold that rimmed the pale crystals, at the blades of grass that sprouted between her hair, before turning away.

"I don't feel the need," the man replied.

"You've done so much, and that's why I know you'll help us again. You'll bring me back," she said.

He was quiet a long time. "After tomorrow," he said at last, and then lay back in the grass.

One more day, Jacob thought.

"I still think it's a bad idea," Xander continued. "In fact, I don't understand it at all."

"I'm a Blinder. I was before and now I am again. Where else would I go?"

"But you ran away. You've been declared dead by your own father, all because he couldn't tell them the truth. Why? Because he was ashamed? Because if you left openly, others might want to leave also? Even if he does take you back, returning will just reinforce everything they already believe about the world and play right into his hands."

"I'm aware of the problems involved here. I remember what it was like, what it has always been like. But things change. Maybe if I return and he's forced to explain what happened, things *will* change. A good dose of truth never hurt anyone."

Xander laughed. "You're too innocent for your own good. People don't change easily, if ever. Asking your father to admit a lie and expecting everyone else to suddenly understand that it's just the first of many lies and half truths is as cruel as . . ." He stumbled for an analogy. Delaney stepped in.

"As cruel as a Blinder suddenly being able to see?" she asked.

He remained silent, turning away to look down at Jacob still floating in the water.

"You don't have to go," he said after a moment, and this time she was silent.

The next day flew by. Jacob tried to make it pass slowly, taking notice of each moment, and at times it worked. Then something would happen and he'd lose his concentration and before he knew it an hour had passed or maybe two. Now it was evening and they were gathered around the fire. Delaney had joined them tonight, one of the few occasions she'd made it down. As before, Xander had given her his seat—a smooth, flat stone—to sit on.

They were quiet. The stream of conversation, which usually flowed so quickly, had slowed to a trickle at dinner as they shared their last meal together. Now, each seemed content to listen to the cracking of the wood as the fire took each piece and to smell the fragrant scent of the zephyr's smoke.

"When do we leave?" Jacob asked.

"Early," Xander said. "If we head out in a few hours, we can be there by dawn."

"It'll be quiet then," Delaney said.

"That's what I'm hoping," Xander replied.

The silence resumed. Finally, Delaney spoke up.

"What do you think, Jacob? Shall we do it now?"

"Okay," Jacob said. As Xander looked on in confusion, Jacob got up and went behind a tree, returning with a bag. He pulled out the small harp and the whistle. Xander started at the sight of the instruments. Jacob walked over to Delaney, put the harp into her hands and, still standing beside her, turned to face Xander.

"Jacob took these from the trunk in the basement," Delaney said. "He told me where they came from. I hope you don't mind."

"No," Xander rasped.

"I'm glad. We wanted to do something to thank you for saving both of us on the plains, for rescuing me from Mixel, for giving us a place to stay. For everything you've done for us. We'd like to play you an old song from Harmony, something Jacob and I can both play. It's one of our favorites."

Xander shifted in his seat. Jacob could tell he seemed uncomfortable, but he nodded his thanks.

Delaney started first, plucking each of the little strings in succession before settling into the melody. A minute later

224

Jacob joined in, adding the breathy notes of the whistle to her strings. The song began slow, almost mournful, and Jacob watched as Xander looked away from them and down into the fire, his hands clasped before his mouth. Delaney's fingers danced along the strings, moving effortlessly as she wove the intricate layer of tones into a steady and seamless pattern.

As he played along, Jacob realized he'd never felt so close to her. It was as if the sound each of them created stretched toward the other, wound together into a single cord that could never be broken, and for the first time he felt at peace with the idea of her leaving—at least this moment, this song, would be with him always. It was then he realized that this performance was as much for his sake as it was for Xander's, maybe even more for him, though Delaney had never said so.

The song shifted now, picked up in tempo, grew lighter as it pushed toward the finale. This was Jacob's favorite part. He stopped watching Xander, forgot about Delaney and her leaving, and focused solely on the rapid fingering of the tune. The mourning had left the song and become joy. He could feel it wash over him like the warm water of the lake. He had practiced the song many times before, both in Harmony and with Delaney over the last couple of days, but he had never played it this fast before, or with such precision.

The song ended with a succession of quick strums against the strings and a final trill of the whistle. Jacob, realizing he had closed his eyes somewhere along the way, opened them to see Xander smiling broader than he'd ever seen. The man clapped and laughed, as if in spite of himself.

"Amazing," he cried. "I liked that last part especially. You can't help but feel good listening to it."

"That's the idea, I think," Delaney said.

"Who would've imagined that little harp could sound so good. It's just a child's toy, really," Xander said.

"I spent some time this week tuning it. It's a nice little piece."

"It is," Xander said. Jacob saw his face fall for a moment. "That first part," he said, "the slow one. It was so sad. What's it supposed to be about?"

"Whatever you want it to be," she said.

Xander nodded. For several minutes the song's presence remained with them, hovering about their ears and over the fire between them.

"You two had better turn in," he said at last. "Be good for you to get at least a little sleep before we take off."

Jacob helped Delaney up and the two of them started out. Reaching the mouth of the path, Jacob looked back. Xander was still seated by the flames. Jacob watched as he pitched another log onto the fire. Then he turned and led Delaney onto the path toward the distant lights of the house.

It was dark when Xander woke them. They rose, silent in the cool night, gathered Delaney's few belongings, and headed out to the cruiser. Jacob looked up at the pink moon as they crossed the yard, a slim crescent in the eastern sky, hovering over their destination.

Jacob helped Delaney into the backseat while Xander fired up the engine. A minute later they'd left the valley, climbed the nearest hill, and were heading east where there were no roads.

CHAPTER NINETEEN

Jacob watched the pink moon slip through the crack of sky that shone between cloud and horizon, surrendering to the half light that had begun to gather over everything. In the predawn no color appeared, merely textures of light and dark. Xander and Delaney were forms of gray, almost indistinguishable from the cruiser behind them. It should have been brighter, but a blanket of clouds muted the sky, and a sudden stir of breezes, unusual for the morning, hinted that a storm was rolling in.

From their spot on the ridge, Jacob could barely distinguish the emerging shape of the colony below. When he was blind, it had seemed so large, stretching among the rises in the darkness of his perception. It had grown smaller as his sight defined its borders. Now, after having crossed the plains and navigated the streets of Melville, it seemed smaller still.

"We'd better go," he said, as much to himself as to Delaney. All night, plunging through the darkness, Jacob had been stirred by that same mix of apprehension and excitement he'd felt on the approach to Melville to rescue Delaney. And now here they were, preparing to deliver her back to the one place he'd never thought he'd return.

They had arrived less than an hour ago, stopping only

once to eat and to stretch their legs. Then they had waited; they would enter the colony when Jacob could see enough to lead Delaney, but before the day had begun in earnest and people had left for their duties. In another hour, the workers in the fields would be relieved by the next shift. Jacob wondered if his father was there right now, busy with the labor of preparing the land for the next planting.

"Jacob's right. You'd best be going," Xander said, handing over her bag. Delaney embraced him quickly and whispered her thanks in his ear.

"I know," he said. "I just hope it turns out the way you've imagined."

She left Xander and reached for Jacob's hand. He took it, and they walked down the hill.

"I'll see you soon," Jacob called back.

"I'll be waiting," Xander replied, adding, "you've got an hour, Blinder. Then I come looking."

It seemed to take forever to make their way into Harmony. The entire time he kept imagining standing before the ghostbox, kept seeing that glowing eye.

In the dim light the colony seemed alien and unfamiliar. Though he had walked these streets his entire life, he felt disoriented. He knew where Delaney lived, but it took him several attempts to find the correct path to the high councilor's quarters. On the way they passed several citizens out early in preparation for the day. Each time, Jacob squeezed Delaney's hand and they froze, afraid that the slightest footstep might reveal their presence, but each time, the person simply walked past them, unaware. Finally, they arrived at the house—a concrete block close to the council chamber in the heart of the community.

Jacob opened the front door and they entered, closing it silently behind them. Delaney disappeared before his eyes as the darkness swallowed them. He felt her take his hands and draw him near her. Jacob realized that he had to say good-bye.

"Where is he?" Jacob whispered.

"He's probably still sleeping. The bedroom's just down this hall," she said, sounding far away in the dark. Her hands were steady in his grip, but her voice trembled, and he could hear her breath quicken. "Stay here," she whispered. "I'll be right back."

Before he could say anything, she let go of him and was gone. A minute later she returned and pressed a small card into his hand. "Here's the key."

"Thanks," he said, and then paused. "Well, this is it, I guess."

"Yeah, I guess it is," she said. "Good luck with the ghost-box, Jacob. I hope you find what you're looking for."

"I just hope you'll be okay," Jacob replied.

"I'll be fine. I really will. He'll be glad to have me back— I'm his daughter. Right?"

"Right," he said. "I'll miss you, Delaney."

She drew him into her arms and kissed him on the fore-head. "You'll see me again someday. I feel it. Who knows, maybe you'll come back too. Everything could change," she said.

It already has, he thought.

"Wish me luck," she whispered and released him to the dark.

He heard her walk away, her steps fading as she turned a corner. It was her house. She knew where she was going. He

229

reached out before him, turning in the pitch-black, taking slow steps until he reached the wall, tracing his hand along it to the door. His fingers were on the latch when he stopped, gasping as a new light absorbed the darkness.

It started with a flash in his eyes. And then the familiar scene.

At first, he thought he was back in his dream. There was Delaney, her mouth open in a silent scream. Everything was just like it was in the last transmutation of his nightmare: him standing to the side, watching in the blue light as his disembodied arms extended to her throat. He was puzzled by the moment. Why was he reliving the dream now after it had been dormant for so long? And why in his waking life?

He looked closer and realized something else was different. Her eyes were no longer aflame the way they'd always been before. They were simply the adorned, prosthetic eyes she wore now. He looked closer still at the neck and saw something even stranger.

His hands were old.

It didn't make sense. He looked down at his own hands. In the dim light of his vision he could see they were the same as always—slender and smooth, not the thicker, wrinkled hands that encircled Delaney's throat. He looked back and suddenly he knew.

Those aren't my hands.

He realized now that in every dream he had never looked at the source of those arms, those hands, too terrified of seeing himself in the act of killing the very person he'd wanted all along to save. He forced himself now to look.

Delaney's father—his face twisted by a horror that matched her own as she sank down at his feet—stood over her, his arms reaching out, his hands gripping her neck.

The image disappeared with another flash, and the darkness returned. Jacob realized he was gasping on the floor. He picked himself up and leaned against the wall, still reeling from the image.

It wasn't a dream. It was a vision like before.

He turned back and made his way down the hall, moving as silently as he could, hoping for any sound that might reveal where Delaney was. He had to warn her. He had to stop her and save her.

If only there were some light in here, he thought. He hated this darkness, hated trying to navigate without sight. He couldn't remember ever feeling so helpless back when he was blind. He thought of calling out to her but held back. He didn't want to wake the high councilor. If he was still asleep and Jacob could find Delaney, then maybe they could both get away before her father ever knew they were there. If her father was awake, Jacob didn't want to reveal himself until absolutely necessary.

Groping along, his hands came across an open doorway. He froze, leaning against the wall, and listened. Sure enough, he could hear the faint sound of snoring coming from the room. Delaney must be in there. What was she waiting for? *She must be nervous*, he thought. He didn't blame her—he was nervous too. He was about to leave the comfort of the doorway, strike out across the room to find her and get her out, when there was the rustling of sheets.

"Father?"

"Who is it?" the high councilor cried. Jacob started at the

voice. The man sounded feeble in his terror, so different from the man Jacob knew.

"It's me, Father. It's Delaney," she murmured.

The man didn't respond at first, but Jacob could hear his breathing, different now, fast and drawn.

"Delaney? Is it really you? How can this be?"

"I've come back."

"Back from where?" he asked. The fear disappeared from his voice, replaced with a familiar coldness. "From the Seers? You've been with them, haven't you. Did you bring them here? Does anyone else know you've returned?"

"No," she said. "I came to you first."

A long silence followed. Jacob could almost hear the high councilor thinking, processing the moment.

"Why have you come back?"

"I didn't like it out there," she said. "I knew I belonged here, with my own people."

There was a pause before the high councilor spoke. "You should have listened to me, Delaney. I warned you that the Seers would hurt you, that you would meet pain. Goodness knows how they've corrupted you."

"I'm glad I left Harmony, Father, even if it was just for a while," she said. Jacob could hear her own voice harden against the force of his, could hear her slipping into the rhythm of her old antagonism. But when she spoke again, her tone had softened. "You're right. There was pain, a lot of it. It was intense. But I've come back now, to stay. I want to be a part of the community again."

A minute passed. Jacob's heart began to pound as he waited for the man to reply. Why wasn't he responding?

"You can never come back to Harmony, Delaney," he said

at last, pausing to let the words sink in.

Jacob could feel her absorbing them, could feel them hanging in the darkness.

"For so many reasons you cannot come back. It would violate every principle of the Foundation. Who knows how many people you would infect, the kind of damage you would do. Harmony has already said good-bye to you. I've already said good-bye to you. It was a beautiful farewell, far greater than you deserved after your betrayal." He sounded weary. Weary and sad. Jacob heard him rise from the bed.

"Please, Father. You have to let me," she begged. "I'll tell people whatever you want me to about the Seers. And we can be a family again."

Jacob winced at her words. Suddenly, she was the Delaney he remembered from the very end of her days in Harmony—depressed, broken, and desperate.

"How?" her father exclaimed. "You're not the same anymore. You've been out there. You're not the daughter I once had. She's dead. In my mind, in everyone's mind, she no longer exists."

"Why did you have to tell them that?"

"I did it for their good, Delaney, and for yours."

The doorway suddenly filled with a light that spilled out into the hall. Jacob ducked back against the corridor wall. The blue light wasn't bright, but in the pitch-blackness of the house, it had its own intensity.

There could be only one reason for the light.

I was right all along, Jacob thought, seeing the high councilor wink all over again in his mind, the memory made more vivid by its confirmation. Delaney's father continued.

"A clean break is always—" His voice froze. The only

sound was the faintest hum of the light, like the quietest of sounders. "Your eyes!" he cried. "Look at what they did to you. What have you become?"

Jacob chanced a peek around the corner in time to see the man reaching, grabbing Delaney's arm so roughly that she cried out. She pulled away from him and collapsed on the bed, scuttling back until she cringed against the wall. Her eyes glittered in the light of the small lamp humming on a nearby table. The lamp, a cylinder of cold blue cased in steel, bathed the room more in shadows than in light. The gleam of her gold rims and diamond eyes disappeared as her father came forward to stand between her and the lamp, his back to Jacob.

Delaney couldn't see his shadow loom before her or the light that glowed behind him, but Jacob knew she didn't have to.

"The eyes don't work, not anymore. Not like yours, Father."

He sighed. "So now you know," he said. "The only one to ever find out."

A pang struck Jacob. *She's not the only one*, he thought. *I should have told her.*

"How long?" she asked.

"A long time. Since I was young. But not completely—it only came to one eye. But one was enough."

"Enough for what?"

"To have experienced all the sins of the Seers," he cried. The pain in his voice surprised Jacob. For a moment, he softened. He knew what that pain was like. "I succumbed to the same temptations, allowed myself to be tainted. I am a corruption, Delaney. Just like you, but in a different way." He

234

paused. "So many times, I wanted to submit myself to the ghostbox, have my vision stripped away. More than once, I came close to cutting the eye out myself, like a secret Oedipus."

Jacob shuddered at the suggestion. The Oedipi—like his best friend Egan's father—were born as Seers but joined the Foundation and became Blinders by choice.

"But there's no grace in that sort of tragedy," the man continued. His voice began to shake as he sat down on the bed, took his daughter by the hand, and drew her to him. Jacob could see her tremble beneath her father's fingers that now traced the line of gold around her eyes, following the paths that receded across the temples and into her hair. "And I realized that my corruption had a purpose. It is the source of my moral authority. It allows me to realize daily why we need Harmony, why the Foundation is the truth. The people need me. I have tarnished myself for their sake—yet they must never know what I've done for them. That's the true tragedy, isn't it?"

He was now inches from her face and trembling as much as she. His fingers tightened along the sides of her head. Jacob watched in horror as she gripped the man's forearms, his dream unfolding as the man's hands moved down to her throat.

"What are you doing?" Jacob heard her gasp before the sound was squeezed off completely.

"I told you before that you were dead to me, Delaney," he said. "I have to do this, for all of us. I'm sorry."

He began repeating these last words, a consolation for them both as he wept and she gaped with open mouth.

Suddenly, he cried out, then stiffened, releasing his grip

235

as both of them collapsed onto the floor.

Jacob stood frozen over the two figures at his feet. The steel lamp in his hands, now filtered red with blood on one side, still glowed, unfazed by the blow. It was only Delaney's sudden gasp for air that stirred Jacob to movement. He dropped the light, which clattered and rolled, sending shadows dancing about the room, and rushed to her side. She continued gasping as he helped her sit up and cradled her in his arms.

"Are you okay?" he asked. She nodded, her mouth tightening in fear and sorrow, before breaking out into sobs. Her body shook as she cried, her hands instinctively raised to her eyes, though no tears could be shed.

"I think I killed him," Jacob whispered, looking at the red shadow against the floor.

A moment later there was a moan. The high councilor stirred beside them. Jacob forced himself to reach over and feel the man's head. A large welt had surfaced and blood matted the hair, but it wasn't as bad as Jacob had feared.

"Let's go," Delaney said. Jacob rose and helped her to her feet.

Though it had grown brighter outside, it was still early and the streets were quiet. They moved as quickly as possible, Delaney struggling to keep up with Jacob as he pulled her along behind him. Soon they worked out a rhythm and picked up the pace, disregarding the echo of their steps against the path. When they encountered people on the street, Jacob ignored the looks of confusion and fear that met the sound of their passing.

They approached the edge of town. Jacob felt a surge of relief at the sight of the cruiser parked on top of the ridge and

Xander in the distance, now running down the slope to meet them. Holding Delaney's hand, Jacob leaped into the tall grass. Xander, traveling much faster than the two of them could, caught up with them. Jacob could see the concern on his face as he noticed the bruises on Delaney's throat.

"We're all right," he reassured Xander in a loud whisper. They were all panting from the run.

"You have blood on you," Xander said, seeing Jacob's hands. Jacob looked down in surprise.

"I had to, Xander," he said in a choked voice. Now that he'd stopped moving, it had all begun to catch up with him. "Her father—he was hurting Delaney. He was trying to kill her."

"You did the right thing, Jacob. Now let's get out of here."

As he had the night of her rescue, Xander swept Delaney into his arms and headed across the meadow toward the hill where the cruiser waited. Jacob followed him at first, bounding to keep up with the man's long strides, before lagging behind. The adrenaline was fading and he felt tired, but he knew that wasn't the reason he was slowing down.

"Wait!" he shouted. Xander stopped and turned. "I have to go back."

"No. They might have found him by now. It isn't safe."

"I need to do what I came here to do. Please, Xander."

Xander sighed and put Delaney down. Pulling out his stunner, he walked to Jacob. He adjusted a few settings and tried handing the pistol to the boy, but Jacob refused it.

"I won't need it," he said. "Just go to the northern edge of the colony and wait."

"We'll be there," Delaney said, coming forward and taking Xander's hand.

Xander frowned briefly and shook his head. "Don't be long," he said, leading Delaney to the cruiser.

Jacob watched them as they climbed the hill together. "See you soon," he whispered back.

CHAPTER TWENTY

Jacob paused at the edge of the stone path leading to the distant bunker. Here the pathminders ended, and the squat shape rising out of the grass seemed detached, as if a piece of Harmony had broken off and was floating away. He looked around and, seeing no one nearby, headed out.

The last time he'd been here, in his dream, he'd been slow, fearful, following the high councilor's ghostly drift as the fire closed in behind them. Now he sped down the path, eager, light under the morning sky, until he reached the bunker.

Looking up as he approached, he half expected to see the enormous striped cat reclining across the top of the doorway as it had been in his dreams, but the spot was empty. To his surprise, Jacob felt a moment of disappointment—he wouldn't have minded the comfort of a familiar face right now, even that of an animal's.

A small panel to the right of the door contained a narrow slot. He walked over to the panel, reached up, and inserted the card Delaney had given him into the slot. There was a loud, metallic click and the great door slid open with a hiss.

Jacob took a deep breath and stepped into the darkness.

As before, both in real life and in his dream, the ghostbox

chamber was cool and quiet, a murky room of ambient light. As he entered, the monolith at the center of the room waited, its one dark eye glowing suddenly to life.

Jacob hesitated. What was one supposed to say to a machine?

"Good morning," he said, at last, deciding at least to be polite.

"Good morning," the voice said, startling Jacob. It spoke in the same timbre from his dream: an androgynous voice, calm, knowing, servile.

"You *do* speak," Jacob whispered.

A beam from the solitary yellow eye shot forth and washed over him, scanning every inch of his body.

"You are not High Councilor Martin Corrow," the ghostbox said.

"No, I'm not," Jacob replied. "Do you know who I am?"

"You are Jacob Manford."

"Do you know why I'm here?"

"I do not know," the ghostbox replied in a matter-of-fact tone. "You were scheduled for termination, but it did not occur."

Jacob shivered, remembering once again the high councilor's final words before Jacob had torn himself away. *Let's just hope the surgery goes well, Jacob. The ghostbox makes mistakes from time to time.*

"By whose order?"

"High Councilor Martin Corrow, under instruction from the Foundation. By the Foundation's order, all abominations are to be terminated."

Jacob had done his final report for civics class on the Foundation. He knew that even the high councilor had to

240

answer to the orders it gave from its headquarters on Earth. But abomination? Jacob wondered what that meant.

"What's an abomination?"

"According to Foundation policy, all those who have acquired the sight mutation are to be treated as abominations."

"Mutation," Jacob said, repeating the word to himself. Was that a good or bad thing? It didn't sound good. "Is that what I have?" he asked the ghostbox.

"Yes."

"Are there others who have it too?"

"Yes."

Jacob paused and took a deep breath. *Now for the most important question.*

"Where are they? What happened to all of them?"

There was a momentary silence. "Please wait while I search my files," the ghostbox replied. The sound of distant voices came in through the open door. Jacob ran to the entrance and peeked out. A group of men had just entered the path leading to the ghostbox. They were Listeners, men who policed the colony, making sure everyone followed the rules.

How did they know to come here? he wondered. Had he been discovered?

As they drew closer, Jacob noticed some of them carried finders. He glanced down at the high councilor's key still in his hand. Could they be programmed to zero in on it? He shook his head and pulled back inside.

"Well?" he cried, staring up at the glowing monocle.

"One moment," it purred.

Hurry up! Jacob wanted to scream. The men were getting closer. He wasn't worried about confronting the Listeners outside, but he didn't want to be stuck in a room with them or, worse, be sealed inside and at their mercy.

"There are no known locations for those you have requested," the ghostbox intoned. Jacob felt his stomach sink. "However," it added, "Foundation records show a suspected group of abominations are believed to have gathered on Teiresias, though confirmation is pending. I shall now produce the reports in full."

"That's okay," Jacob replied. "But thanks anyway."

He placed the high councilor's key on the floor and dashed for the exit as the ghostbox began reciting.

Plunging through the doorway, Jacob pulled up at the sight of the Listeners only ten yards away. Hearing him, they started as well, slipping into a crouch as they raised what Jacob suddenly realized were pistols. They were different than the stunner Xander had offered him, larger, with barrels that widened into cones. He dodged sideways, running as fast as he could. From the corner of his eye he could see a wave of distortion roll toward the bunker doorway, as if the air between them was melting, and he leaped, feeling the wall of energy roll past him, brushing his back, its force propelling him forward into the grass.

Recovering, he tore off through the field, turning in a wide arc back toward the colony, where he could weave his way north through the maze of streets in safety. He took one last look behind him at the bunker before disappearing around the corner. The Listeners were following, but they were no longer a threat. He turned and headed for the northern edge of the colony where Xander and Delaney waited.

Coming into the North Tier Square, Jacob stopped for a moment to rest. He splashed his hands into the fountain, washing off the dried blood. The water felt cool, and when his hands were clean, he took a long drink.

Several people walked in the square. He watched as they passed in and out. No matter how many times he had witnessed this scene, it still made him anxious to be unknown in the midst of other people. His entire trip through the colony had only intensified this feeling. Watching the figures drift along the streets among the dirty concrete buildings and pitted walkways made him feel like a ghost come back to haunt the scene of his crime. Sometimes it seemed as if they were ghosts and that he was the only person alive. Either way, Harmony was different now because he had changed, and it satisfied him to realize that nothing here would be missed. Except for one thing.

He glanced back from where he'd come. There was no sign he'd been followed.

There's enough time, he thought. He could spare a moment to say good-bye.

The street was empty as he made his way to his former home, pausing as he neared the steps. The door was open to let in the morning air. He slipped silently to the threshold and looked in.

His mother sat quietly before an empty place at the table. There was no sign of his father. It was so much like his dreams, for a moment he looked back, half expecting to see the color drain from the street, smell the burning in the air as the flowers withered to ash.

His mother sat motionless but for the movement of her hands, which turned a small silver cube over and over, stopping occasionally to caress its textured sides. It was Jacob's music box, the one she'd given him weeks ago for his birthday. She opened the lid and the familiar tune began to issue forth, the tiny notes evenly plinking their simple song. He continued to watch her as the tune ended and after the briefest pause repeated itself again. She was singing with it now, first humming the melody then mouthing the words in a husky whisper, her tender voice sounding more fragile than the tiny machine.

Finally she closed the lid and set the box on the table at the place where he used to sit. He opened his mouth to greet her, but she suddenly rose from the table. She went over to the piano, sat down, and began playing. It was a new song, one Jacob had never heard her play before. As the song grew louder, the notes pounding around the house, another noise from behind him made him turn. Again, as at the ghostbox, he could hear the distant shouts of men. *They must be searching the whole community*, he thought. Or maybe they had discovered the intruder's identity and guessed where he would most likely have gone. He couldn't stay.

He turned back to where his mother still played, lost in the tune. He couldn't interrupt her now—there would be no time to say the things he wanted to say. Worse, if he was discovered, it could mean trouble for her.

Glancing down, he caught sight of a nearby flowerbed. He spotted some yellow flowers, ones with a black center, and plucked five from their bed, ducking inside and laying them on the table by his music box as the voices outside grew closer.

Leaving the house, he crossed the street and climbed up the grassy slope of the other side, peering down from the neighbor's roof as the Listeners entered the lane. As they rushed toward his house, he remembered the last time he'd escaped Harmony. *It's just like before*, he thought, turning away. But as he came back into the square, he realized it wasn't. Before he was running away, frightened and alone. Now there were people who waited, eager for his return. He took one last look at the fountain and left the square.

After that, he didn't stop. He only ran, back to the edge of the northern tier, over the top, and down the hill into the fields where he and Egan had often raced, where he had run that day he first left Harmony in fear. He was breathing hard, but he didn't care. He didn't stop running. He didn't even hear the wail of the pathminders when he burst across the colony perimeter. He just focused his sight on the distant point where Xander's cruiser waited on the horizon.

EPILOGUE

There we are, he thought.

Jacob was flying, soaring over the plain like one of the falcons that inhabited the open skies. Spotting the figures on the crest, walking together through the grass, he began dropping toward the land, swooping in for a better look.

As he drew closer something puzzled him. Usually in this particular dream it was the three of them, with Delaney in the center, her white gown flowing, escorted by Xander and himself. But as he swept overhead, he saw that there were only two. He was missing.

Sailing by, he chalked it up to the distortion of his dreams. Though he had grown used to the lucid visions that marked most nights' passage, he was always startled by the little ways the details changed, how the permutations of his mind gave reality its subtle twists.

Gliding to a landing, he turned toward the pair in the distance and waited eagerly for them to approach, his shadow stretched before him, long against the setting sun that had painted the sky gold. He gasped in wonder as Duna, swiftly cresting the horizon behind them, silhouetted the approaching figures. They continued to draw nearer and still Jacob wondered why he wasn't with the pair. Then they were running and laughing, bounding toward him through the grass, Xander leading Delaney by the hand and waving, as if in greeting.

How do they see me? Jacob wondered. In his dreams, he was always invisible, a watcher without form.

Jacob heard a rustle in the grass behind him and turned in time to see himself hurrying to meet them, dropping a worn pack and breaking into a run. *So I am here, after all*, he thought. But something was different. He drew a sharp breath at the sight of the older features on his young man's face and at the taller body, broad shouldered, sure of himself. There was something in the run, in its urgency and its confidence, that told him he'd been gone, had traveled great distances only to come back once again.

He drew up and watched, unable to contain his own smile, as the young man met the pair, joining them in a group embrace before turning back to the moonrise, the three of them arm in arm.

A moment later he was back in the air, watching the linked figures shrink against the plain below as he raced toward the glittering rings of Duna.

Jacob was still soaring when he woke. The feeling of lightness followed him as he dressed and descended the stairs for breakfast. Xander and Delaney were at the table, talking, laughing. Nine months had passed since their trip to Harmony, and the bruises on Delaney's neck had long since healed. Watching the two of them, Jacob wondered if Delaney could sense the smile on Xander's face as he gazed at her.

"Morning," Jacob said, coming to the table.

"Good morning, sleepy," Delaney said. "I was wondering if you were ever going to wake up."

"He must have been having a good dream," Xander joked.

"You could say that," Jacob said.

"I'm heading out for a drive," Xander told him. "Hurry up and eat some breakfast if you want to come."

"Just make sure you're back by lunchtime," Delaney broke in. "You promised to read to me this afternoon, didn't you, Jacob?"

"I did," Jacob replied. Xander was still teaching him every day, using the first book Kala had given him, though she'd given him others since.

"Don't worry, we'll be back in time. Won't we, Jacob?"

Jacob looked at the two of them at the table and smiled. "Everything'll be fine," he said. He sat down at the table between them and closed his eyelids, the dream still heavy upon him. He was still flying in his mind's eye, but by now he'd left the atmosphere, had passed Duna and the sun and had headed out for deeper space, drawn by a force he couldn't resist and didn't want to. And suddenly he knew. The months of waiting were over. Now was the time.

"Xander," he said, opening his eyes. "Tell me about Teiresias."